A DEADLY ACT

AN ADAM LAPID MYSTERY

JONATHAN DUNSKY

A Deadly Act

Jonathan Dunsky

Copyright © 2020 by Jonathan Dunsky

Cover by DerangedDoctorDesign.com

Cover Photographs © ProStockStudio/Shutterstock (man); Protasov AN/Shutterstock (street); Max play/Shutterstock (sky); Neo-stock (man)

All rights reserved.

ISBN: 978-965-7795-04-0

Visit JonathanDunsky.com for news and information.

BOOKS BY JONATHAN DUNSKY

The Adam Lapid Series

Ten Years Gone

The Dead Sister

The Auschwitz Violinist

A Debt of Death

A Deadly Act

The Auschwitz Detective

The Unlucky Woman (short story)

Standalone Novels

The Payback Girl

For Aharon Pollack

1

The old man howled as he carried his dead daughter in his arms.

He bellowed his grief, staggering forward, one plodding step after another, burdened by her weight and her death.

His daughter was young and slim and beautiful. She had on a long midnight-blue dress that accentuated the paleness of her skin. One of the old man's arms clasped her beneath her knees; the other cradled the back of her neck. Her head lolled a little backward, her tawny hair hanging straight down in a single intricate braid.

She had been an impressive woman not too long ago. Honest, valiant, noble. But now she was no more.

The old man had been impressive as well. Other men had looked up to him, respected him, did his bidding. He had emanated generosity and wisdom and kindness. Now he was but a shadow of his former self. His fall had been long and swift and hard. I could relate, for though I had never been as high as he, I too had suffered a fall into near nothingness. And I, too, had lost daughters.

His appearance matched his current circumstances. He wore a

dirty white shirt and even dirtier loose black pants. His beard was scraggly, his fringe of white hair long and matted. His suffering had chiseled deep new lines on his aged face. His expression was twisted in torment. He shook his head as he stared down at his lifeless daughter, as though struggling to deny what could not be denied.

To my left, a young curly-haired woman gasped. Her eyes were riveted to the old man and his anguish, and even in the relative darkness that enshrouded us, I could see the glitter of tears on her cheek. To my right, a portly middle-aged man was puffing on a cigarette, his gaze equally welded to the old man and his daughter, the air between us filled with acrid smoke.

Emitting a low groan, the old man sank to his knees and gently laid down his burden of love and loss. With a trembling hand, he caressed his daughter's cheek. He shook his head once more, swelled his torso with air, and let out his deepest howl yet. It echoed around me like a hundred tolling bells proclaiming a funeral.

The sound he emitted was familiar to me. Or at least I knew what it was supposed to be. The cry of a man who had lost everything—all that he had, all that he loved, all that he had taken for granted, all that had defined him.

It was a worthy approximation, but no more than that. I could appreciate the similarity and the talent that had produced it, but I had heard the real thing too many times to be fooled. The harrowing wail of a man who had truly been stripped of everything had a distinct, soul-rattling edge to it. I doubted it could be reproduced by anyone, no matter how gifted.

The old man, seized by a glimmer of hope, begged for a hand mirror with which to test if his daughter still breathed. She did not. His hope was now dead as well.

A younger guy, one of a handful who stood in the vicinity of the old man, had given the mirror to him. Now he knelt at his side and attempted to console him. The old man did not recognize him; his mind had room only for his daughter. He cursed those around him. "A plague upon you, murderers, traitors all! I might have saved her; now she's gone forever! Cordelia, Cordelia! Stay a little."

But Cordelia was already gone, as were the old man's two other daughters—neither of whom had been as noble as Cordelia. And now all that remained of this man who had once been a king was his raw pain, his crushed spirit.

A hand suddenly gripped my left forearm, just about where a number was tattooed to my skin. It was the curly-haired woman in the seat beside mine. Her fingers grasped my flesh with a hard, steady power. I did not know her, had never seen her before that night. Looking at her now, I could see only her profile. She was leaning a bit forward in her seat, her body as rigid as a rifle barrel. Her lips were parted in anticipation. Her eyes stared intently, barely blinking, at the unfolding scene before us, and I realized she was not aware of where her fingers were placed, that her hold on my arm was merely an instinctive extension of her emotional state.

And she was not the only one held captive by the drama we were watching. A deep hush had settled upon the audience that surrounded me. Absent were the whispered murmurings and the awkward clearings of the throat that had sounded during the previous acts. Now it felt as though all of the spectators were holding a collective breath, waiting for the end that was drawing near.

A minute later, it was upon us. The play was over. The old man was dead, completing his crashing fall. His story was done. His body lay motionless next to his daughter's, his face turned away from us, as though to spare us a final stab of pain. Slowly, a red curtain descended upon the stage. It swallowed the dead and the living that remained to mourn them in an undulating wave of cloth that made me think of a spreading pool of blood. The woman to my left had relinquished her grip on my arm and was now wiping her cheeks with her hands.

A few spectators began clapping. Others quickly followed suit. Soon a steady rhythm was established. The curtain did not remain lowered for more than a minute. Then it was rising again, revealing an empty stage. Onto it, one by one, walked the cast. Each of them lavished the audience with a smile and a theatrical bow before stepping aside to make room for the next cast member. First were those who had played minor roles in the play, and then came those who had acted the major characters—Kent, Regan, Gloucester, Edgar.

When the actress who'd played Cordelia stepped on the stage, the clapping intensified. The actress, her face flushed with plea-sure, smiled a dazzling smile and pressed her hands to her bosom as if overwhelmed by the applause. In her joy, she looked even more beautiful than during the play.

Cordelia—which was the only name I had for her—stepped aside, still beaming. The center of the stage, brightly illuminated by overhead lights, stood empty for a moment. Then came the star of the show.

He was still dressed in his dirty clothes, still wearing the makeup and beard of the fallen old monarch, but he no longer acted the part. Gone were the stooped posture, the shuffling step, the tormented expression. The man who now swaggered into the light did so with an easy stride, a straight back, and a face that seemed on the verge of splitting open due to the width of his grin. He stood with his hands at his sides, surveying the audience, basking in its adoration, glowing as men do at moments of personal achievement. It was a strange sight—the ancient, frail man with the grin, stance, and evident vigor of a much younger fellow.

The applause grew louder still. Someone shouted, "Bravo!"

People began to rise from their seats. The woman to my left and the man to my right also stood clapping, and I did the same, though not for the same reason. I did so partly so that I would not stand out, and mainly so the people in front of me would not obscure my view.

For I was not there to see a play. I was there to see just one man. The actor who had played the English king who had sought to divide his kingdom between his three daughters and had ended up losing all three and his kingdom as well. The man who now stood at center stage, beaming in triumph.

Isser Rotner was his name.

He had a right to be satisfied with himself. It was a good performance. He had acted well. He had been a convincing king and a persuasive dispossessed old man. His talent and skill were undeniable.

As I stood there with the thunder of applause in my ears, I scrutinized him, attempting to see past the beard, past the makeup, past the smug grin and the blazing dark eyes, and straight into the depths of Isser Rotner's very soul.

I was trying to determine whether this man, this actor, had a few years ago played a different role, one for which he had never taken nor was given any credit.

I was trying to see whether Isser Rotner was a murderer.

2

Slowly, the audience filed out of the theater hall. With my fellow spectators pressing me on all sides, I wedged myself through the door that opened onto the second-floor landing and descended the stairs to the lobby. Once there, people began to disperse, and I no longer had the unpleasant sensation of warm bodies crowding me. Some people went straight to the exit, while others clustered about the lobby, chatting. I rummaged in my pocket for my cigarettes and had gotten them out when a voice called my name.

The voice was familiar. I recognized it even before I turned and saw its owner's face.

The face was freckled, round, and soft. Topping it was a bald scalp fringed with light-brown hair. A pair of discerning eyes, also light brown, gazed at me from behind horn-rimmed glasses.

"Good evening, Adam," Shmuel Birnbaum said. "Were you watching the play?"

"Yes, Shmuel. I was."

We shook hands. He smiled a small smile. I did not reciprocate. Despite the fact that over two and a half years had passed, I still had not forgiven him for the story he'd written about me in his column in *Davar*. The story recounted my final battle during the War of Independence, specifically how I had eliminated an Egyptian machine-gun position and nearly gotten killed in the process.

The story made me out to be a hero, but I did not enjoy the attention it got me. I resented even more the invasion of my privacy, which included Birnbaum sneaking into my hospital room and snapping a picture of me unconscious in my bed.

In truth, much of my negative opinion of Birnbaum had dissipated with time. He was a fine journalist and a good writer, and when he gave you his word, you could count on it. The problem was that he was always sniffing for a story, and I did not want him to point his nose in my direction. Especially not on this particular evening.

"I never knew you were a theater aficionado," he said.

"There's a great deal you don't know about me, Shmuel."

"A most lamentable fact, one which I aspire to change. You could help me. I still want to know more about what happened to you in Europe and what you did there, both during and after the war."

"You're very certain I have an interesting story to tell. You may be wrong."

"I'm never wrong about a story, Adam. I can always tell if there's one lurking about. And I've heard rumors about you. Very intriguing rumors."

"From whom?"

"I never reveal my sources, Adam."

"Why don't you just print these rumors, they being so intriguing and all?"

"I'm not the sort of journalist who would do such a thing. You should know that about me."

"I know you'll do anything for a story, even take a picture of a man in his hospital bed."

"Will that one transgression hang over my head forever?" Birnbaum smiled. "You misunderstand me, Adam. I don't have many qualms about how I get my stories, but they need to be real stories. Factual, not based solely on rumor, innuendo, or hearsay."

"I'm glad to know you have a high ethical standard."

"Joke all you want, but you know for a fact that I do."

Which was true. Birnbaum did not print lies if he could help it, nor did he derive pleasure from destroying people on the pages of his newspaper, which other reporters seemed to do for sport. He had also, on one occasion, upon my request, kept my name out of his column. So he was conscientious, as far as his job would allow. I had to give them that.

He said, "What did you think of the play?"

"It was good. The actors did a fine job, especially the lead."

"Yes. King Lear is tailor made for Isser Rotner. He does tragedies very well."

Maybe he does, I thought. *But did he also create one in real life?*

"You've seen him perform before?" I asked.

"Several times. This theater has been around for a while, you know."

I did know, but there was no benefit to him knowing that. "Oh?"

"Almost twenty years. I think they opened in 1933, or was it '34? I forget which."

"They must be doing well to last that long."

"You would think so, wouldn't you? But if they were, they would have their own exclusive venue and wouldn't have to share this one with the Philharmonic Orchestra. Even tonight there were more than a few empty seats. Truth is, they've had their share of bad luck over the years, and rumor has it that they're in dire financial straits."

"More rumors, Shmuel?"

"Yes, Adam. More rumors. But it's impossible to know for sure, especially since these rumors have been circulating for years."

"You never tried to find out for sure?"

"No. There's nothing interesting about theaters losing money. It's so common, it's boring." He looked around him at the lobby and the people milling about in it. He shook his head in wonderment. "Shakespeare in Hebrew. Who would have thought such a thing would ever come about, eh? This is certainly a glorious time we Jews are living in."

"What about Isser Rotner? What do you know about him?" I asked, and immediately regretted it when Birnbaum turned his eyes back on me, and I saw an inquisitive glint in them.

"Why do you ask?"

I feigned indifference. "Just wondering, that's all. I'm curious after having seen him perform."

Birnbaum's eyes stayed on my face, trying to divine whatever secrets I might be keeping. *If only you knew, Shmuel, you'd be salivating all over the floor.*

He licked his lips, and I could read the uncertainty on his face. He couldn't tell whether I was being truthful or not. This pleased me no end. Perhaps some acting skills had rubbed off on me during the play.

"Anything in particular you wish to know?" he asked.

I shook my head, knowing that any show of interest on my part would only inflame his suspicion. "Nothing, really. I was just making conversation."

"Hmmm. You're here by yourself, Adam?"

"Yes."

"Just felt like catching a play?"

"Something like that."

"You a fan of Shakespeare?"

I could have said yes, but then I might have been called upon to prove it. This I could not do since I knew next to nothing about

9

the man or his work. So I said, "You're barking up the wrong tree, Shmuel. There's no story hiding among the branches."

"If you say so, Adam," he said, clearly unconvinced. "If you say so."

I lit a cigarette and offered him one. He took one whiff and shook his head.

"My wife wouldn't like that stench on my breath."

"She's here?"

"Yes. And her sister is, too. Which is why I'm here. She's decided to drop by for a visit. A ten-day-long visit."

"You don't sound too thrilled about it."

"Perhaps I would be if I enjoyed listening to two women gossip and chatter about the most inane topics imaginable well into the wee hours of the morning. I swear to God, until a week ago I never would have believed that two people could talk for an hour about nothing but different styles of dresses, but now I do."

I laughed. "Maybe you should write a column about it."

"Maybe I will. Who knows, it might prove very popular with my female readership." He sighed. "Anyway, living in a moshav in the Negev, my wife's sister doesn't get much of a chance to visit the theater. So every evening over the past week we've gone out to one show or another. I like the theater, always have. Early in my career, I even wrote theater reviews. But these days, seeing a play every night just wears me out. Not to mention the cost of the tickets."

I gave him a long look, thinking that he might possess information that would aid in my investigation. Birnbaum had lived his whole life in Tel Aviv, he knew a lot of people, and inside that bald head of his was a veritable reservoir of facts and details. And since he had actually written about the theater, he would likely know something about the crime I was investigating.

The problem was that were I to ask him about it, even circuitously, his curiosity would be piqued. Birnbaum was no fool. He would know my interest was professional, and while he might be persuaded to share information, he would want something in return. A story. He would want to know why I was investigating this crime and who had hired me to do so. I couldn't tell him. Certainly not now.

I decided not to risk it. There was no need to involve him at this time. I had barely begun working on this case, which I had been hired to undertake just a few hours ago. I might be able to learn all I needed without his assistance.

I said, "If you're so fed up, why don't you stay home and let your wife and sister-in-law go by themselves?"

"My wife wouldn't like that, Adam. I have to be a good host, you see. Give her sister all the respect and attention a visiting dignitary might expect. So I *schlep* myself along to whatever show they choose. And pay for it, of course."

At that moment, a pair of women appeared at Birnbaum's side. You didn't need to be a detective to know who they were. His lips, which had been pulled down in dejection, reversed direction abruptly, tilting upward into a wide, warm smile. He made the introductions. I shook hands with both women. Birnbaum's wife said they were going to have a late dinner at a nearby restaurant and asked me to come along. I knew the place by reputation only. It was on the expensive side. I saw Birnbaum wince at the prospect of even more expenditure and barely managed to refrain from smiling.

I begged off, saying I was tired and would be heading home. Outside, they went one way and I the other.

But I did not go home. My work for the night was not yet done.

3

_____

I needed to be at one of two places, and I did not know which. Luckily, both were located on the same street, a handful of buildings apart.

The street was Dizengoff, and the two establishments were Café Kassit and Café Roval. The first was at number 117, the latter at 111. Both were known as regular haunts of the city's artists and Bohemian crowd, a fact that contributed to them becoming among the most popular cafés in Tel Aviv. If you wanted to rub shoulders with actors, poets, and authors, you went to Kassit or Roval.

If what I'd been told a few hours ago was true, Isser Rotner would be coming to one of these two cafés to celebrate his performance.

I took my time getting there, ambling north from the Ohel Shem building on Balfour Street where the play had been performed, thinking about King Lear and the man who had portrayed him.

Isser Rotner.

I wanted to see him again, this time without the makeup and

beard. I wanted to see him in regular clothes. I wanted to see him off stage, in a normal environment.

What I hoped to accomplish by this was unclear to me. It wouldn't provide me with any evidence of his guilt or innocence. But the urge to see him was there all the same, and I did not resist it.

Once on Dizengoff, I headed first to Café Roval. Scores of patrons sat at square tables scattered around the outdoor seating area, enjoying the cool evening breeze. Inside were at least two hundred people more. Waiters in pressed white shirts and black trousers meandered between tables—pouring drinks, taking orders, igniting cigarettes with swiftly drawn lighters.

The place was busy but far from full. It could easily have seated a hundred more inside and even more outside. Those who were there all looked to be having a splendid time.

Isser Rotner was not among them.

I went out to the street and walked the short distance to Café Kassit. On the sidewalk in front, a man and a woman were dancing awkwardly, in rhythm to some melody that only they could hear. They laughed, both clearly tipsy, their bodies breaking contact to allow the man to twirl the woman about. She giggled, almost tripped, but he kept her on her feet, pulling her back to him. Both their faces were flushed with excitement and alcohol. A small band of onlookers stood watching, laughing and goading the couple to more extravagant dance moves. Someone shouted for the man to kiss his partner, which he did, rather sloppily, to the cheers of the crowd. I skirted the happy assemblage and entered the café.

Kassit was smaller than Roval and far less pretentious, with tables placed close together, giving it a somewhat cramped feel. Pictures thronged the walls, and if anyone had given any thought to their order or grouping, they had done a poor job. Smoke from numerous cigarettes, each with its own unique scent, swirled a foot and a half below the ceiling—a grayish, winding cloud cover that would never bestow rain.

Below that were dozens of people, some at tables and others at the bar. I recognized a few of the patrons. Over by the window, Nathan Alterman, poet and playwright, confabbed with a pair of women, one of whom looked vaguely familiar. At another table, Ezriel Carlebach, founder and editor of *Ma'ariv* and probably the most powerful newspaperman in Israel, was having drinks with a trio of young men who appeared to be hanging on his every word. Seated at the bar was General Moshe Dayan, in his crisp uniform, an eye patch covering what remained of his left eye, his right fixed on the curvy brunette on the stool next to his. She looked much too young to be his wife.

And off to the side, seated in the middle of four tables that had been pushed together, was the man I was seeking. Isser Rotner.

He wore a dark-blue jacket over a white, open-necked shirt. His hair was black and full and combed back from a widow's peak over a high forehead. His face was clean-shaven. A straight sharp nose, a tapering chin, and prominent cheekbones gave his features a vulpine cast. His eyes, dark and large and deep set, added to the effect. The mouth contributed too. It was thin-lipped, straight when closed, but capable of stretching very wide in a grin that would be charming if you didn't suspect the man who was giving it of murder. It showed a lot of teeth, that grin, all straight and white. All in all, it was a handsome face, in a lean, untamed sort of way.

Seated with him were ten men and women, mostly in their twenties. It took me a minute, but I recognized most of them. They were the actors and actresses from the play I had seen. There was the man who had played Edgar, and to his right sat the actress who had been Goneril, one of King Lear's disloyal daughters. Across the table from her was the actor who had portrayed Kent, a glass of beer in one hand, a cigarette in the other.

It seemed like a good combination to me, so I found an empty stool at the bar, ordered a beer from the thick-bellied bartender, and lit a cigarette of my own. It was good beer, unwatered and cold, neither of which could be taken for granted in Israel's troubled economy. It went well with the smoky warmth of each drag I took off my cigarette.

I sat at an angle that allowed me to watch Rotner and his party without being too obvious about it. They were having a grand time, he especially. No trace remained of King Lear, but he still maintained an air of royalty. Part of it was how he was clearly the big man in the group. Another was how people kept coming up to the table, and the manner in which he received them, like he was holding court. From my position at the bar, I couldn't hear the conversations, but by the way the actors reacted, I guessed they were receiving praise for their performance, or perhaps just the usual ingratiating adulation some people have for those in the arts.

Rotner reveled in all the attention. He shook each hand that was offered to him, exchanged words with every admirer, and flashed each of them a gracious smile. But he did so with a certain aloofness, like a benevolent monarch accepting flattery from his subjects and deigning to confer on them a morsel of his rarefied wisdom.

And he did not treat his admirers equally. He appeared to be warmest toward young and attractive females, and his smile, when he held their hands and spoke to them, had a distinct predatory edge.

Twenty minutes or so after I'd settled at the bar, another member of the theater troupe entered Kassit. It was Cordelia, only now she wore a simple white dress cinched at the waist by a black belt, and her hair flowed unbraided and free. A delicate necklace twinkled at her throat, and a small handbag hung from her arm. She threaded her way between the tables with a straight back and a dancer's gait, snaring the eye of more than a few men.

I watched her too, appreciating her lithe body, lustrous hair, and beautiful face. A mischievous smile played across her red lips. She was aware of the stares aimed at her, but she acknowledged none of them. She kept her eyes forward and made straight for the quartet of tables at which the rest of her party sat.

Her arrival instigated one instant development. Rotner broke off the conversation he was having, shot to his feet, circled the table, and grabbed both of her hands in his, giving her his most wolfish smile yet. He led her to the chair he had vacated and got another for himself from a nearby table. He sat next to her and ordered her a drink from the waiter who hovered nearby. He lit her cigarette. For the first time that evening, his eyes did not roam about; his focus was solely on her.

"Gorgeous, isn't she?" came a deep voice from behind me.

Swiveling my head, I found the bartender, a good-natured smile on his face.

"She is quite beautiful," I agreed. "What's her name?"

"Pnina Zelensky. An actress like the rest of them."

Pnina. Not as exotic or alluring as Cordelia, but the familiarity of the name did not detract one iota from the effect of her beauty.

I turned back to gaze at my quarry and the lovely Pnina. For a few minutes, the two of them talked, heads close together, in a bubble of their own. A couple of times he must have said something funny, because she threw her head back and laughed, the firm skin under her chin quivering. She was young, early twenties, and he was in his forties, yet they appeared to be completely comfortable with one another.

But apart from that initial contact when she'd arrived, they did not touch, at least not with their hands. What their legs did under the table, I could not see.

Gradually, their isolation faded and they joined the larger

conversation. There was plenty of talk and laughter, lots of drinks and food. I watched it all from the bar, nursing one beer and then another, taking my time with them, burning through four or five cigarettes. I began to wonder how long they would stay there. I asked myself why I was wasting my time. Why did I continue to sit there? Why did I not go home and call it a night? Perhaps if the new Western I had started that morning had been more captivating, or if I had more to look forward to in my apartment than another lonely night with only bad dreams for company, I would have done so.

But then again, perhaps I wouldn't.

Truth was, I was intrigued by this new case. I'd never had one like it, at least not one that began like this case did. And since I was already there, and so was Rotner, I decided to stick around for a while longer. Maybe I would learn something after all.

Another hour passed. Ezriel Carlebach left. So did Moshe Dayan and the curvy brunette. I switched from beers to coffee. My head had begun to throb. My stomach rumbled. I'd had nothing to eat in the past five hours. I was about to order a sandwich when something happened.

It was Rotner. He had risen from his chair and was counting out money from his wallet. He slipped on the jacket he had taken off a while back and was shaking hands with some of his party, waving goodbye to others. He was leaving. It was time for me to go. I fished a few coins from my pocket and put them on the bar. Nodding goodnight to the bartender, I slid off my stool and hurried for the door.

Out on the street, I took a lungful of clean night air, rubbing my eyes. I crossed the street, paused at a bus stop, and pretended to tie my shoe. I was there less than a minute before Rotner came out. He walked north. I followed, giving him plenty of space, keeping my eye on him from the opposite sidewalk.

When he stopped beside a black Ford and started fumbling in

his pocket for the keys, I figured my night was coming to an end. Soon he would drive off and I would go home.

But he got in the car and did not start the engine. He just sat there, a black blob in the darkened automobile. I kept on walking for another block before coming across a narrow gap between two buildings. I squeezed myself into it and waited to see what he was up to.

He didn't do anything for ten minutes, not until a svelte figure in white approached the car from the south. It was Pnina Zelensky, her heels clicking a jaunty rhythm on the sidewalk. Rotner must have seen her coming, because he leaned over and opened the passenger's door from the inside. She coiled herself into the car, pulling her long legs after her, and shut the door. The dark interior of the vehicle did not prevent me from seeing what they did next. The way their shadows melded together could not be mistaken for anything but a kiss.

And not just one, but a whole slew of them, seamlessly flowing from one to the next. When they finally came up for air, Rotner turned the ignition and flicked on the headlights. The Ford rolled forward, engine purring. The vehicle picked up speed, sweeping by my position, and I caught a final fleeting glimpse of them through the side window.

And then they were gone, the Ford vanishing around the next corner.

I did not know where they were going, but it wasn't to a spacious second-floor apartment on Chen Boulevard.

Because that was where Isser Rotner's wife lived.

4

I'd first met Mrs. Rotner earlier that afternoon. She'd telephoned Greta's Café, where I was alternating between playing solitary chess games and reading a Western I had picked up that morning.

I was in the middle of a game when the phone rang. I heard it ringing as though from far away, so focused was I on the board before me. I moved a white rook three squares forward, and the next instant responded by taking a white pawn with a black bishop. A score of pieces lay scattered around the board like battle casualties. Approximately three-fifths of them were white. Black had the advantage. But in the sort of game I played—lightning fast, with me playing both colors—I could never know how things would develop. Not having time to think between moves often led to stupid mistakes, which kept things interesting.

I'd closed my fingers around the white queen when I heard my name being called. It was Greta, and she was holding the receiver up, gesturing me toward her with her other hand.

"Hello? This is Adam Lapid."

The voice on the other end was female, rich, and resonant. The sort of voice that fills your ears to the brim, commanding your fullest attention. The sort of voice that leaves an indelible impression on your mind.

"Adam Lapid the private investigator?"

"That's right. Who's this?"

"My name is Dahlia Rotner." And after a brief pause, "You may have heard of me."

"No, I don't think so. Have we ever met?"

There was another pause, a longer one, and then came an almost inaudible exhalation of air, and in it I sensed—what was it? Disappointment? Resignation? Or perhaps it was nothing at all, just my imagination playing tricks on me. Then Dahlia Rotner spoke again, her intonation crisp and dry. "No, we haven't. I would like to hire you to do a job for me. Can you come over to my apartment? I live on Chen Boulevard."

"What time?"

"How about right now? I'm not going anywhere."

I glanced toward my chessboard. The game was not yet over, but it had served its purpose. It had given me something to do for a spell while taking my mind off everything. But now I had something else with which to occupy my time and thoughts. A job. Or at least the prospect of one.

"I can be there in thirty minutes," I said.

"Good. I'll be expecting you."

After she gave me the exact address, I hung up and asked Greta, "Ever heard the name Dahlia Rotner?"

"Why, yes. She was an actress. A theater actress."

"Was? Why was?"

"I'm not sure. She stopped acting, but I don't know the reason. Was that her on the phone?"

"Yes. Ever seen her perform?"

"A couple of times, but the last must have been at least four, five years ago. She was very good. Very talented. What does she want with you?"

"I don't know. I'm going to find out. See you later."

Out on Allenby Street, a boy was peddling that day's edition of *Haboker*. He tried to sell me one, but I waved him off. I had gotten my fill of news by being an unwilling audience to the heated discussions of other patrons at Greta's.

Most of the news was dismal, the world near and far in turmoil and instability. Wars and myriad other calamities raged as if to remind us that, though the biggest war in history had ended but six years ago, disasters, man-made and not, were to be our lot in life.

At least the weather was good. It was a sunny June day—warm, but not hot and humid as Israeli summers could be. Birds could be heard chirping and trilling, and on a day such as that, no one begrudged them the occasional bodily discharge they deposited on benches or windshields or the shirt of an unfortunate pedestrian.

People walked with a buoyant step and said "hello" and "good morning" to each other with greater frequency and feeling than usual. They smiled more often, too. It was a day that made it easier to forget about your troubles. Like the bad economy, or the rationing of basic food products, or even the recent tensions along Israel's borders. It was a day that invited optimism, even the sort one suspected was unfounded—and isn't that the most prevalent kind?

I could have taken a bus, but I opted to walk. The sun felt good on my face, warm and tender, and there was just the faintest whisper of breeze to ruffle my hair and keep myself from heating up.

As I walked, Dahlia Rotner's rich voice kept sounding in my ears. I tried to imagine the face that would go along with that voice. I wondered what sort of job she needed done. It was pointless; I would learn the answers soon enough. Yet I did not attempt to expel these frivolous thoughts, nor did I belittle them. They served a noble purpose. They kept my mind free of darker, weightier thoughts and memories, and for that I was grateful.

Chen Boulevard stretched north to south between Malkhei Yisrael Square and Dizengoff Street. Dahlia Rotner's building was a three-story structure close to the corner of Frishman Street. I ascended the stairs to the second floor and knocked on the door to apartment 3.

"The door is unlocked, Mr. Lapid. Come in."

The voice sounded a bit far off and muffled by the door, even though it had clearly been raised. I pushed down the handle and found myself at one end of a hallway.

"Last door on your left," the voice came again, from deeper in the apartment.

I hesitated, suddenly feeling like prey being lured to its death by some enticement. I shook off the notion and strode forward.

Framed photographs bedecked both walls of the hallway. They all shared a theme. The theater. Some pictures showed actors engaged in their craft. Others were solitary shots, taken either during a performance or recording the application of makeup. The pictures on the left wall had one element in common: all featured the same woman, whether alone or in the company of her colleagues. Those on the right shared a different subject, a man. I recognized neither of them.

I couldn't say why, but as I walked down that hallway, I felt as though these two picture-laden walls were in competition and that I, or perhaps merely my attention, was the prize.

I passed a kitchen to my left and two closed doors to my right. The next door was on the left and it was open.

Beyond it was a living room. Spacious in comparison to most Tel Aviv apartments. Better appointed, too. Large framed landscapes. A grandfather clock ticking away in one corner. An ornate writing desk. A radio and gramophone, and next to them a few dozen music records standing in a serried line.

A plush armchair stood before a glass-topped coffee table, on the opposite side of which sprawled a brocade sofa big enough to sit three people without them having to touch.

Currently, it was occupied by just one.

She ran her eyes over me, sweeping the length of my body before scrutinizing my face. Whatever her impression of me was, I couldn't say. Her face showed nothing.

"Adam Lapid?"

I nodded.

"You're punctual. I like that."

I didn't need to verify her identity. It was her apartment, after all, and she was expecting me. Besides, it was the same voice I'd heard over the telephone at Greta's. The same unforgettable, unmistakable voice.

The woman it belonged to was in her forties, long-limbed and fair-skinned. Her wavy shoulder-length black hair, infiltrated slightly with gray, framed an oval face with powerful angular features—an aquiline nose, a large mouth, big brown eyes, and a jaw that was wide but still feminine. It wasn't a beautiful face, but it was certainly an arresting one. It was a face that snared your attention and would likely be able to hold it for as long as its owner wished. It was a face that hinted at resolve, determination, pride, and inner strength. It was the face of the woman in the hallway pictures, though this one had more years on it.

It was a face that went well with that voice.

She had on a long turquoise dress that fitted her so well it had to have been made to measure. Her only jewelry was her rings. A gold wedding band and a diamond ring with a quartet of elegant stones that sparkled in different shades of yellow, blue, and green.

"Please sit down, Mr. Lapid," she said. "You're tall enough as it is, and it hurts my neck to look up at you."

The neck in question was ensconced in a white brace that went all the way from the base of her throat to just below her chin.

It looked rigid and tight and unpleasant to wear. It made her head look like a marble bust supported by a plinth. I wondered why she had to wear it. Whatever the cause, it must have been serious, as her neck was not the only part of her that was injured.

I took the armchair. It was as comfortable as it looked. Seated though I was, she still had to raise her gaze to meet mine, but not by all that much. I estimated her height at five seven or maybe five eight. Her posture was very good, straight and firm. Just like her braced neck. Combined, her bearing, face, and voice gave her a regal aura. She reminded me of a story I'd read many years before of a medieval queen who had been banished by her husband, the king, to a monastery. I couldn't remember the name of that queen, nor the country in which she had reigned, but if anyone ever wrote a play about her, Dahlia Rotner would be the obvious choice for the part. She exuded a restrained sort of dignity. The kind that was inherent and could not be ripped from her. I supposed that she had played a queen more than once in her career, and I had no doubt that she had done so with excellence.

"There's coffee in that pot over there," she said. "Real coffee. It should still be hot. Help yourself."

The pot was made of silver, as was the tray on which it stood. I poured myself a cup. The aroma wafting from it was wonderful. She had been truthful. This was genuine coffee. The sort that many Israelis were understandably stingy with, having mostly to settle for the rationed chicory alternative that left much to be desired. Judging by this, her diamond ring, and the furniture around me, I deduced that Dahlia Rotner had money. The fact that she had a telephone in her apartment, when the great majority of Israelis did not, was further proof of this.

I took a sip. The coffee was rich and smooth. A pleasant warmth spread throughout my body.

"This is good," I said, taking another sip. "Thank you."

She smiled without parting her lips. A smile of simple satisfaction rather than one of true joy. Something in her face, something almost as rigid as her neck brace, gave the impression that the latter sort did not happen very often. At least not recently.

She said, "I appreciate you coming over on such short notice, Mr. Lapid. Unfortunately, venturing out is not something I do often."

She indicated the walking stick that was propped against the sofa by her right leg. Made of wood and as thick as a shepherd's staff, its handle had been intricately carved into the shape of a galloping horse—mane flaring, mouth gaped, legs stretched with muscles in action. It seemed an odd choice for an implement built to aid a person who had trouble walking—a true work of art, but one with a cruel, mocking edge to it. Most invalids would be repelled by such a constant reminder of their handicap. Evidently, Dahlia Rotner was made of different stock.

"A pretty thing, isn't it?" she said, hoisting the stick and holding it horizontally before her.

"I've never seen one quite like it," I said.

Her mouth twitched as she ran her hand along the shaft. There was a strange look in her eyes. Small part affection, big part something much less positive.

"The most dependable friend I've ever had," she said, "and I hate it with all my heart. I've had it for five years now. Well, five years, two months, and eleven days, to be precise." She returned the walking stick to its former position and raised her eyes to mine. "Car accident. Left me with permanent damage to my neck, hip, and right leg. I can walk, but not very far and only very slowly. And it hurts like hell. The doctors at the time said I should count myself fortunate to be alive."

"But you don't feel that way, do you?"

"No," she said flatly. "I don't. That accident may not have killed me, but it deprived me of what I loved most dearly."

"You mean acting?"

She looked surprised. "I thought you said you didn't know who I was."

"I asked around after you called."

"And what did you learn?"

"That you were an actress, and that you stopped performing about five years ago. But the woman who told me this did not know the reason."

She looked at me, as if waiting for me to say something more. When I didn't, she said, "Most people at this point in the conversation would tell me how sorry they are for my condition, or something to that effect. But you're not going to, are you?"

I gave a half smile. "I have a feeling you wouldn't like that."

She smiled back, and this time I caught a glimpse of her teeth. "You're right. I wouldn't. I've heard it too many times. If it ever helped, it ceased doing so a long time ago." She paused. There was appreciation in her eyes. "You're perceptive. It appears that I've picked the right man for the job."

"What job is that, Mrs. Rotner?"

She opened her mouth to answer, but what emerged instead was a cough, rattling and moist. It sounded like someone was churning a pot of liquid deep inside her chest. She grabbed a handkerchief that had been lying on the sofa next to her and pressed it to her mouth, muffling the coughs that were making her shoulders shake and her face contort in agony.

"Hold on. I'll get you some water," I said, rising from my chair, feeling alarmed. She shook her head, gesturing for me to sit down with quick motions of her free hand.

A few seconds later, her coughing died down. She wiped her lips with her handkerchief and set it aside. She sat still for a moment, catching her breath, eyes shut, head turned to one side.

"You all right?" I asked.

She nodded. A short up-and-down movement of her head, as much as her neck brace allowed. "It's not as bad as it looks."

"Glad to hear it, because it looked pretty bad. Sounded bad, too."

She opened her eyes and stared right at me, composed once more. If I hadn't seen it with my own eyes, I would not have believed the woman in front of me had been gasping for breath less than a minute ago. "I appreciate your concern, Mr. Lapid, but I assure you that I'm quite fine. I had pneumonia a while back. A rather severe case of it. But I'm better now. This cough is all that remains of the illness. It's persistent and has the annoying habit of popping up at the wrong moment, but, all in all, it's nothing to worry about."

"Sure I can't get you some water? How about a cup of your excellent coffee?"

"No to both. Really, I'm fine. I'd rather we get down to business, if you don't mind."

I signaled my agreement with a shrug, drank what remained of my coffee, returned the cup to the tray, and sat back, waiting for her to begin.

"I understand you were a policeman," she said, "that you have experience in investigating serious crimes."

"Where did you hear that?"

"An acquaintance. Does it matter who?"

"Not really. The answer to your question is yes. I was a police detective in Hungary before the world war. I investigated all sorts of crimes—from the petty to the horrific."

"And since then you've worked as a private investigator?"

Not exactly. There was the time I'd spent in a Hungarian forced-labor battalion, made up entirely of Jews. After that came my imprisonment in Auschwitz, where my mother, sisters, wife, and daughters were murdered. Then I hunted Nazis for a while, trying in vain to quench my thirst for vengeance. And finally, in 1947, I immigrated to Mandatory Palestine, joined the nascent Jewish forces battling for independence, and took two bullets fighting the Egyptian army in the south of Israel. It was only when I was discharged from the hospital that I became a private investigator in earnest. But I saw no reason for her to know all that.

"Just about," I said. "What is it you want me to do?"

"I want you to help me bring a criminal to justice."

"For what crime?"

"Murder."

I raised an eyebrow. "Murder?"

"The murder of a young woman. Right here in Tel Aviv. Her killer was never punished. I want that to change."

"The police investigate murders in Israel, Mrs. Rotner."

"The police tried to solve this case and failed."

"What makes you think I'll succeed where they didn't?"

"Because I can supply you with a crucial piece of information the police never possessed."

"What piece of information?"

"The identity of the murderer."

She said this in a tone almost devoid of inflection, as though she were remarking upon the weather on a dull day. But a slight shift in the lines of her mouth, an almost imperceptible curling of her lips, belied the blandness of her delivery. She was enjoying this, piecing out details, building anticipation—like in a play. She the performer, and I the audience.

Frowning, I took a long breath and let it out very slowly. The distinct impression that I was wasting my time came over me. Had she invited me here just to play a part? Was she making this all up as a form of amusement? Or did her injuries extend beyond the physical and into the mental? Had being exiled from the stage driven her mad? Or was she simply lonely, desperate for any sort of audience to act before?

Yet, eying her, it seemed that she was utterly serious and honest and sane. So in spite of myself, I found myself asking, "Who is it?"

She waited a beat before answering, milking the moment, ratcheting up the tension. Her eyes gleamed with a distant light, like a bonfire on a barren mountaintop. Her lips curled a bit further before she uttered two simple words.

"My husband."

5

I stared at her. "Your husband?"

"Yes," said Dahlia Rotner.

Anger flared like a lit fuse. "You think this is funny? You enjoy dragging strangers into your home for this sort of nonsense?"

"Mr. Lapid, I—"

"Because I don't enjoy being played with. Not even by an obvious master of the trade such as you." I got to my feet, not caring one bit if looking up at me made her neck hurt. "And I don't appreciate having my time wasted."

I turned to leave, but her voice stopped me dead in my tracks.

"Mr. Lapid! Wait!"

It was the same voice, but she had made it deeper and thicker and impossible to ignore. Some ingrained part of me—maybe the soldier I'd once been, or perhaps it was the Auschwitz inmate—responded to that voice instinctively. My back went ramrod straight and a prickle of fear scratched at the nape of my neck. Still, her command would have held me for no more than a second or two if she hadn't reached into the pocket of her dress and brought out a triplet of ten-lira bills.

"For you," she said, holding them up. Her voice had returned to normal. "Just to sit back down in that chair and listen."

I switched my gaze from the money to her. All trace of the amusement I had spied on her face a moment ago was gone. She looked dead serious.

"Please," she said, extending the money toward me, her tone free of the beseeching that single word implied. "This is no game, I promise you."

I took the money and made a home for it in my pocket. It was a tidy sum. More than enough just to listen for a while. Even if all I ended up hearing were lies.

I sat down. I didn't say anything, just waited for her to proceed.

She let out a low breath and attempted a smile. It didn't go very far or last very long. She plucked at some invisible wrinkle on her dress and brushed it smooth over her knees. I realized that I was witnessing something she had not planned on showing me—her in a perturbed state of mind. My reaction had surprised her. She was not used to people walking out on her, or even threatening to do so.

Finally, she ceased her tinkering, locked her eyes on mine, and said, "I feel I owe you an apology, Mr. Lapid. It's just that old habits die hard. Especially the ones you loved. I couldn't help being just a touch theatrical. But I assure you that what I'm about to tell you is the truth. Some of it, you'll be able to verify easily enough. The rest—well, you are a detective, after all. You'll need to do that part yourself."

"All right," I said. "You're forgiven. Now what's this about a murder?"

Folding her hands in her lap, she said, "It happened five years ago. May 28, 1946. I was already back here from the hospital. Here in my home, my jail cell. I was still growing accustomed to the new reality of my life. And the pain...well, it had sharper fangs back then.

"It was a Tuesday, and the street outside my window was lively with people out and about—being industrious, or just strolling aimlessly, making the most of the spring sun. I remember envying them quite powerfully.

"My husband, Isser, had gone out earlier, before I finally pulled myself out of bed. I slept fitfully in those days. The pain kept jolting me awake. The medication failed to suppress it for very long. And pain, I discovered, never ever sleeps.

"When Isser returned, a little before one in the afternoon, I could tell immediately that something was wrong. There was an odd look in his eyes, and it was only much later that I interpreted it as fear. I asked him what was the matter, and he told me that Anna Hartman was dead. And not just dead, but murdered.

"I asked him how he knew, and he told me the police had come by the theater earlier. They had asked him some questions. In particular, they wanted to know where he'd been the night before. I don't know if they suspected him or merely wished to rule him out. He told them he had been here, at home with me, the entire night."

"And this wasn't the case?"

"No, it wasn't. While I slept very poorly back then, I did spend a good deal of time in bed. The night before, I turned in at approximately eight o'clock. I was alone when I did so. Isser was out. I awoke at ten and again at a quarter to midnight. Isser was not here. When I awoke again at one thirty, I could hear the shower running. I fell back asleep, and the next time the pain hit, Isser was sleeping beside me."

"And this was when?"

"Four twenty-five. I could tell because I have a small table clock on my nightstand."

I nodded, still wary. But in spite of myself, I found that I was sitting forward in my chair, listening intently as she told her tale.

She said, "It's strange what one notices and remembers, even things that seemed unimportant at the time. I remember his face was all scrunched up, his eyebrows knitted, his jaw clenched. And it wasn't merely his face; his entire body was wound up tight. He lay on his side, facing me, and I could tell he was dreaming. Whatever the dream was, it must have been bad, because he kept muttering to himself, and his breath would catch, his mouth open, as some picture playing in his head put an intense fear into him. I had never seen him like that. Not once in all the thousands of nights I had shared a bed with him."

"What was he saying?"

"I couldn't tell. As I said, he was muttering. His voice was so low it was impossible to make out his words. And I was so exhausted that I didn't stay awake for long. I closed my eyes and this time slept for a few hours straight. And, like I said, he was gone in the morning. The next time I saw him was when he came home and told me about the murder."

"Of Anna Hartman."

"Yes."

"Who was she?"

"An actress in our theater."

I waited, but she didn't elaborate. Those five words were it.

"How did she die? And where?"

"She was stabbed. Her body was found in Trumpeldor Cemetery."

"Really? Inside the cemetery itself?"

"That's what I was told. But I don't know the details of the case."

I frowned. "Surely you know more than what you told me, her being your friend."

Her eyes blazed with a sudden flame. "What makes you think she was my friend? When did I say that?"

Her tone was sharp and snappish. It sliced the air like an

artillery shell. I leaned back, looking at her. The only sound in the room was the rhythmic ticking of the grandfather clock.

Dahlia pointed her eyes at her knees, looking abashed. It was not a natural look for her. Laying a hand on the top of her walking stick, she caressed the galloping horse as though seeking comfort or reassurance from it. For the second time, she had shown me a part of herself she preferred remain hidden. It was plain to see how much she disliked having done so.

It took her less than five seconds to compose herself. Then she said, "Anna Hartman was a colleague. We worked together. Nothing more."

But there was something more. Otherwise, I wouldn't be here. I decided to put the matter aside for the moment and changed the subject.

"So your husband came home and asked you to lie for him."

"That's right."

"Which you did."

"Yes. When the police came to see me later that day, I told them that Isser had been here the whole night."

"They believed you?"

This time her smile was unconstrained. Unconstrained and proud. The smile of the actress who had played a part and had done so with perfect authenticity.

"Beyond a shadow of a doubt," she said.

"The police are usually skeptical of alibis provided by spouses."

Her smile widened. "This time they weren't. If they ever suspected Isser, they no longer did once they stepped out of this apartment."

"If you're that good an actress, how do I know you're not lying to me right now?"

"Why would I lie?"

"I don't know. For fun, maybe. Or just to prove to yourself that you still have what it takes. A woman like you, unable to act on stage, would probably derive great pleasure out of putting one over on someone. Someone like me."

"I'm not lying to you. You have my solemn word on that."

I nodded noncommittally, knowing from experience how little some people's word was worth. I had no way of knowing whether Dahlia was such a person. But as she said, I should be able to confirm or refute at least part of her story without difficulty.

I said, "Why did you lie for your husband?"

"For the most stupid and juvenile reason: I loved him and he asked me to."

"No hesitation?"

"None whatsoever."

"You must have wondered where he'd been that night. Did you ask him?"

"He told me he was at the theater. Isser is a perfectionist, very dedicated to his craft. The theater was about to put on a new production. Whenever Isser is preparing for a new part, he spends hours upon hours at the theater, rehearsing his lines over and over, working out exactly where to stand on stage as each word leaves his lips."

"He does this alone?"

"There are general rehearsals in which the entire cast takes part, but Isser often stays late and continues working well into the evening and night." She paused. "We used to do this together, many years ago." Her tone had turned wistful, and for a moment I could imagine how she'd been when she was young and whole and deeply in love with her husband.

She still felt a measure of admiration for him—the way she'd told me about how he prepared for a role made that quite clear. But did she still love him? Surveying her now, with her expression distant and almost dreamy, I couldn't say one way or the other. But if she did, it was a love that had lost much of its sweetness and had filled the ensuing void with a rancid stew of bitterness and resentment.

"So you believed him?" I said, breaking the spell, bringing her back into the moment.

She blinked and cleared her throat. "Again, without hesitation."

"Did you ask him why he'd lied to the police?"

"No. I assumed it was so they wouldn't bother him with their pesky questions, and also to preclude any malicious tongues from wagging. People in our line of work are often targets of nasty gossip."

Scratching my forehead, I took a moment to process all that she'd told me. I had not written anything down, believing initially that all I was about to hear were the carefully woven lies of a lonely, possibly deranged woman. But the more I heard, the more I began to question this assumption.

She might have been toying with me, but if so, this was an expensive game she was playing. Even affluent people did not go around throwing thirty liras on trifling amusements, and I did not see how I could possibly provide her with more than just that.

Similarly, I did not believe that she was anything less than sane. And that left me with but one conclusion. She was telling me the truth.

Still, it was a bizarre beginning to a case, as bizarre as I'd ever experienced, one that gave birth to a host of questions. The first of which was: "What's changed?"

She quirked an eyebrow. "What do you mean?"

"Why do you not believe your husband anymore?"

"Because I know things about him now that I did not know then."

"Such as?"

"That he's a liar. A liar, a deceiver, and a cheater."

Which did not surprise me. I had suspected this was what lay behind her reversal of trust. "Your husband cheated on you?"

"Cheated, cheats. His unfaithfulness is nothing new."

"But your discovery of it is?"

"More or less. I've known for a few months."

She said this without a sliver of hurt showing, without the slightest chink in her armor of steely dignity. Yet I could tell that she was deeply wounded by her husband's betrayal. And her being here, cooped up in this apartment, had allowed this injury to simmer and fester inside her, augmenting her pain, stoking her anger.

Gently, I said, "Cheating on one's wife does not make a man a murderer, Mrs. Rotner."

Her mouth tightened. "I'm well aware of it, Mr. Lapid. I am neither a fool nor a child."

"I assure you I did not mean to imply either of those things."

Her expression relaxed, but not all the way. She was still angry, either with me or with her husband. Or perhaps it was with another person, as her next words suggested.

"He cheated with Anna Hartman," she said.

Which explained her harsh reaction when I'd said that she and Anna Hartman had been friends. It also told me that this was not about finding justice for a murdered woman. This was about revenge. Dahlia wanted to avenge a betrayal. A betrayal by her husband.

This was not the first time I'd encountered a love that had soured. When I was younger, before the war, before Auschwitz, this sort of thing would just slide off me. Now, after losing my wife in the gas chambers, I could not help but marvel at the fathomless depths to which love could plummet. And this gave me a sharp pang of sadness and loss and longing for my dead wife.

I swallowed the lump that had formed in my throat and said, "Why would he kill her? What would be his motive?"

"I don't know. Perhaps they quarreled. This is what I'm hiring you to find out."

"Did the police know they were lovers?"

"If they did, wouldn't they have asked me about it?"

Not necessarily, I thought. Not if they believed the alibi Dahlia had given her husband as unquestioningly as she thought they did.

In that case, they might have stayed quiet about it, judging this to be a private matter between a man and his wife, unrelated to their case. Given that they were men themselves, the officers might have felt a kinship to Isser Rotner and chosen to keep his infidelity hidden from his wife. Ironically, Dahlia's acting talent might have worked against her in this instance, as it could be the reason why she had remained ignorant of her husband's philandering for so long.

Another question came to me. "How did you suddenly discover your husband is unfaithful?"

"Someone told me."

"Someone? Who?"

"It doesn't matter. It has nothing to do with this case. I was simply informed that my husband is currently sleeping with another woman, and once I was, it was as though blinders had been removed from my eyes. I have a lot of time to think these days, a lot of empty hours to fill with reliving the past. I realized this has been going on for years, with various women. In retro-spect, I should have known. There were signs, plenty of them. I suppose I did not want to see them for what they were." It was plain by her tone how much she detested herself for this unawareness.

"So you have no actual proof that they were lovers?"

She gave me a cool stare. "Mr. Lapid, I may have been blind before, but I see clearly now. Trust me, they were lovers. I remember how they looked at each other, the smiles they exchanged, like they had a secret only the two of them knew. Oh, they were lovers, all right, and they were laughing at me and my obliviousness the whole time."

This time, her loathing was not aimed at herself but squarely at her living husband and the dead Anna Hartman.

It felt strange hearing this murdered woman talked about with such venom, when just about all I knew about her were her name and profession, when she was but a faceless victim to me. Did she deserve all this rancor? I had no problem speaking ill of the dead, but only if they'd lived a life that justified it. At the moment, I knew practically nothing of the life Anna Hartman had lived.

I considered what I did know so far. I had a victim, the day on which she died, the location, and, perhaps, the cause of her death. All this, and much more presumably, had been known to the police investigators at the time, and they had failed to apprehend the culprit. The only thing I knew that they didn't was that Isser Rotner's alibi was bogus. And, perhaps, that he and the victim had been engaged in an illicit affair.

I said, "You realize that there's no direct proof connecting your husband to this murder. For all you know, he might indeed have been in the theater that night, and the only reason he asked you to lie for him was to avoid being questioned by the police. Or he might have been with another woman and did not wish for this to be exposed."

For the first time, she seemed disappointed with me. "You forget something, Mr. Lapid. You forget how Isser was that night, when he slept beside me after returning late. His nightmare, the tension in his body, the fear that gripped him. This was before the police came to see him in the morning, before he even knew about the murder. Unless he had committed it."

Heat rose to my cheeks. She was right. If her description of her husband on that night was accurate, it was indeed suspicious. I attempted to hide my embarrassment by scratching a nonexistent itch on my nose and said, "Do you really think your husband is capable of something like that? Of murdering a woman?"

"Yes," she said, and her tone was of such utter conviction that for a moment I was struck dumb.

I looked at her cane, at the way her right leg was bent awkwardly before her, at her braced neck. The way she held herself, the self-assurance she projected, contrasted sharply with her physical condition. "In that case, do you feel safe being here alone with him?"

Her lips bent into something approximating a sneer. "Don't worry about me, Mr. Lapid. I'll be fine. All I need from you is to know whether you're my man or not."

The way she said this brooked no argument. She wanted my protection just as much as she wanted me to commiserate with her on her injuries. Which was to say, not at all.

I said, "Why do you need me? Why not just call the police and tell them you lied?"

"And what if they do nothing? What if they decide I'm lying right now as opposed to then? Or maybe they'll think I'm crazy. You did, didn't you? I don't blame you. Being stuck in this damn apartment, deprived of what you love most, can do that—though I don't suppose you would know anything about that, would you?"

But I did. I knew exactly what she meant. And it was the absolute truth. Madness always lurked at the edges of profound loss.

She did not wait for me to answer. "Even if the police did reopen the investigation, there's no guarantee they'll lock Isser up. Those incompetent fools, in all likelihood, they'll fail to find the evidence necessary to convict him. If that happens, I'll be condemned as a liar or a madwoman. I'll have ruined my reputation for nothing. And my reputation is very dear to me, Mr. Lapid. It is practically the only thing of worth I have left."

She started coughing again, her body shaking, but this time

the fit lasted but a few seconds. She wiped the spittle off her lips and regarded me with her large expressive eyes.

"I'll sacrifice my reputation if it leads to Isser being branded a murderer and thrown in prison. Not for anything less. That's why I need you."

So I was right. This was about revenge, not justice. I asked myself whether this was a battle I wished to take part in. For a moment I was about to reach into my pocket, retrieve the thirty liras nestled within, give them back to her, and tell her I did not wish to be a pawn in some covert war she was waging on her husband. But something stayed my hand.

Part of it was base greed. A thirty-lira retainer did not land in my lap every day. And if she was willing to pay me this much just to listen to her, she would probably be willing to cough up more if I actually took the job.

The other part had nothing to do with either Dahlia or her husband. It had everything to do with Anna Hartman.

I did not know her, but if what Dahlia had told me was indeed true, she was a victim of murder. An unsolved murder.

Her killer roamed free, unpunished. And she was dead, without justice.

This was not about to change on its own. Dahlia would not officially retract her earlier statement. I had no illusions that I would be able to change her mind on that score.

I could go to the police myself and tell them what she told me, but I doubted it would do any good. She would simply deny it, and if she was as good an actress as she claimed, they would likely believe her. My word alone would not suffice to compel them to reopen an old case.

No. The only way Anna Hartman's killer would ever be brought to justice was if I went after him myself.

Dahlia's voice severed my contemplation. "What will it be, Mr. Lapid? Will you help me make sure my husband is punished?"

"No," I said.

She frowned, obviously surprised by the bluntness of my refusal. "I'll be happy to pay you an additional sum for your services. Thirty more liras? Forty?"

"Forty," I said. "If the case drags on for some reason, I may come back to you for more, and you'll decide whether you want me to carry on or not. For now, forty will do, but not to prove your husband is a murderer."

Her frown deepened, and I saw anger glint like lightning in her eyes. "Who the hell do you—"

"Your husband may be a liar, a cheater, and the biggest son of a bitch in Israel," I said. "He hurt you like no man should ever hurt his wife. I understand why you want to see him suffer, but I won't be your instrument of vengeance. Deciding in advance who is guilty of a crime and then trying to find evidence to convict him is not the way I do things, Mrs. Rotner. I'm willing to look into this case, but my goal will be to catch the murderer, whoever he might be. You want to hire me? That's what you'll be paying for. Justice for Anna Hartman, no matter who killed her."

She gave me a look that should have resulted in an attempted murder conviction. Her right hand, perhaps unconsciously, had closed around her walking stick. I could tell by the taut tendons in her hand that her grip was a tight one, as though she were clutching a weapon.

I attempted to placate her. "If you're correct, it won't make a difference, right?"

She considered me for a moment longer, unmoving, again reminding me of a piece of statuary. Then she drew in a long breath through her nose, and the tension in her face slackened. "You're right, it won't. All right, Mr. Lapid. Consider yourself hired."

6

When I left her apartment, it was just past four in the afternoon. The wind had picked up. Leaves swirled along the sidewalk, pirouetting around my shoes before skittering away. I crossed the street and stared up at her window. Was she standing there, leaning on her cane, watching me watching her? The way the sun glared off the windowpane made it impossible to see inside.

We had talked some more once the deal was struck, but I'd gotten almost nothing useful from her. Just some background information on the theater and on her husband, including his habit of frequenting Café Kassit or Café Roval after a successful performance. Superficial stuff. She did not wish to open her life before me; that was not what she'd hired me for. And as for Anna Hartman, it was plain as day how little Dahlia thought of her by how little she knew about her, despite them having been colleagues for over six years. She summed up her opinion of the dead woman in one short, skewering sentence: "Her ambition far outweighed her talent."

I started walking south, then cut west on Dizengoff Street. An ice vendor stood at the rear of his wagon near the corner of

43

Shmaryahu Levin Street, chopping up ice blocks for a line of waiting customers. A gaggle of boys had gathered, too. They were hungrily sucking on ice splinters—the byproduct of the chopping —and grinning as though what they held in their hands was a piece of three-layer cake and not frozen water.

A little further on, I came upon a bulletin board plastered with election posters. Israel's second general election was to take place the following month, on July 30, 1951, and the various parties were engaged in vigorous campaigning. At least seven different parties were represented on this single bulletin board. David Ben-Gurion's ruling party, Mapai, had a poster listing its plans for the next four years—security and prosperity and increased immigration. The poster appeared in Hebrew, of course, but also in Yiddish and Russian, to appeal to those new citizens who still hadn't mastered the national tongue. Elsewhere, I'd seen it in Spanish and French.

Another poster, this one by Maki, the Israeli Communist Party, demanded in hysterical blood-red ink that Ben-Gurion reject President Truman's request to send Israeli troops to fight in Korea. The poster called American troops murderers, invaders, and aggressors. A vote for Maki, the poster assured, was a vote for peace.

But the most creative poster of the lot belonged to the General Zionists, a center-right party that was shaping up to be Mapai's main challenger. The poster mocked Mapai's idea of democracy. It depicted the ruling party as a bald, obese man, whose prodigious rear end occupied just about every seat in the Knesset, while on the parliament's wall hung a picture of David Ben-Gurion dressed in an ornate uniform like a fascist dictator, tasseled epaulettes on his shoulders and oversized medals pinned to his chest.

A handful of people were arguing over the merit of the various posters and of the parties they extolled or lambasted. I hurried on before someone could pull me into the discussion.

A minute later, I found a café with a telephone and placed a call to the police station where Reuben Tzanani worked.

Three rings later, his soft voice with his subtle Yemenite accent came over the line.

"Hello, Reuben, it's me, Adam."

"Adam, it's good to hear your voice. How've you been?"

We exchanged pleasantries for a while. Reuben and I had known each other for almost four years. We'd fought side by side during Israel's War of Independence and had forged a bond in the process, though our lives and history and circumstances could not have been more different. He had been born in Mandatory Palestine, a descendant of Yemenite Jews who, in 1882, had made the arduous journey across the Red Sea and Egypt and into the Holy Land. I had been born in Hungary. He had lived his whole life in the Land of Israel. I had arrived in 1947. My parents, sisters, wife, and daughters were all dead. All but my father, who had died naturally before the war, had been killed by the Germans. Reuben had parents and siblings and, together with his wife, Gila, had produced five children. He also had numerous cousins and nephews and nieces, a veritable tribe of relatives, while I had none.

I was happy for him, but also envious. It hurt to hear him speak of his children, their triumphs and achievements, the immense joy they brought him and Gila. I had experienced some of the same milestones with my own two daughters. All that had come to an abrupt end in the spring of 1944, when, at the behest of the Nazis, Hungarian policemen had crammed us and other Jews into stifling cattle cars and sent us to the death camp of Auschwitz-Birkenau. My wife and daughters perished the day we arrived. I was sent to the men's camp and managed to survive.

And now I was alone.

So when Reuben spoke of his family, especially his children, my gut would clench and a sharp, prodding pain would stab the inside of my chest. It even happened when he griped about the mundane hardships of parenthood—the childhood fevers, the broken nights, the teething, the incessant wailing of their new baby. I would have given everything I had to experience those moments again with my daughters.

"I need a favor," I said, once he had filled me in on his life and I had mumbled something about my own. "I've been hired to look into an unsolved case and—"

"And you need to look at our files," Reuben said. "What sort of case? What crime?"

"A murder."

"Murder? How'd you get involved in that?"

"An acquaintance of the victim hired me."

"I see." There was a short pause. "The case is unsolved, you say?"

I knew what he was thinking. If the case was still ongoing and I started poking my nose into it, trouble might ensue. Trouble for me and for him as well. And he had five children to feed.

"Unsolved and old," I said. "Five years. It's a cold case, Reuben. I won't be stepping on anyone's toes. I doubt anyone is still working on it after all this time."

Still he hesitated, so I added, "Reuben, the killer has never been caught. And he won't be unless someone takes another crack at this case."

After a moment I heard him sigh. Reuben took great pride in his work, in being a policeman, even though he had been assigned an unglamorous office job. The idea that a murderer had evaded justice did not sit well with him. Different in nearly everything, this was one trait the two of us shared.

"What's the name of the victim?"

"Anna Hartman."

"A woman," Reuben murmured in a loaded undertone.

Another thing we shared. For the both of us, the murder of a woman was a more grievous offense than that of a man. Only the murder of a child was worse.

"Yes. And she was young. In her twenties."

"You know the date the murder took place?"

I gave it to him. I could hear the faint scratching of his pencil leaving its mark on paper in between his intake and outtake of air.

"I'll get on it straightaway. With luck, I'll have it by tomorrow afternoon. Call or come by then?"

I said I would, thanked him, and hung up. I stayed seated by the phone, wondering what to do next. There was nothing I could do, that was the problem, not until I read the police report.

I got up, paid the proprietor of the café for the use of his phone, and was heading out when I spotted a carelessly folded copy of *Ma'ariv* on a table by the door.

An idea came to me. A way to pass some time and maybe advance the case as well. I spread out the newspaper and flicked to the back pages where there were listings of various cultural events taking place across Israel that week. I ran my forefinger down the page until I located the small box where that week's program of Shoresh Theater was printed. They were playing that night at Ohel Shem. King Lear.

7

At nine in the morning after the play, I arrived at Greta's Café. Greta wasn't in her usual spot by the window that afforded a wide view of Allenby Street. Instead, she stood at the center of the café, large hands planted on wide hips, gazing upward with a disapproving frown on her fleshy face.

The cause of her displeasure was busy doing the only thing it knew how and rattling as it did so. I stopped beside her and added my gaze to hers. The offending party ignored both of us. It would not be shamed into silence.

"I had it fixed four weeks ago," Greta said without shifting her eyes to me. "And again last Tuesday. And here it is making that grating noise again." She sounded defeated and disappointed rather than angry.

"It's been rattling for a while," I said. "It did last summer and the one before that."

"Not like this," she replied. "Not even close."

She was right. The noise had gotten much worse. A year ago, it was like a background hum you could easily ignore. Now it was like a heckler, intruding on your thoughts or conversation, disturbing the tranquility of your meal. I could handle noise better than most, but even I could see that something had to be done.

"You can always replace it."

She looked at me, horrified. "But I've had it for six years now."

I waited, but that was the extent of her argument. Above us, the ceiling fan rattled its way through a few more revolutions, its four blades whirling about like airplanes in an interminable dogfight.

Greta noted my bewilderment. "It's been here for so long. I can't just chuck it out."

I smiled. Greta was a woman for whom loyalty was second nature. It wasn't a loyalty of grand gestures or flamboyant promises, but a sturdy, steady foundation of support and assistance to those who were dear to her. I was lucky to count myself a member of this privileged group. As, apparently, was the ceiling fan.

To the rest of the world Greta was kind, generous, and unfailingly cordial. To her customers she offered a sympathetic ear, a nonjudgmental spirit, good inexpensive food, and the best coffee you could find in Tel Aviv.

Her café was a simple establishment, cozy and unpretentious. It would never attract the sophisticated clientele of Kassit or Roval, nor did Greta want it to. She seemed happy with the way things were—with the old chairs and tables, the handful of cheaply framed pictures hanging on the walls, the serving counter with its accumulation of scratches. And with her small but ardent band of customers who frequented her café with unflagging regularity. None more so than me.

Greta's Café was a place in which you could be alone or with company, to read a newspaper in peace or engage in a heated political discussion over a sandwich or a bowl of soup. It was a place you could sit in for hours without getting the evil eye from the staff. It was a place to relax, to unwind, to think deep thoughts or none at all. If you were into loud music or bright lights, you would need to look elsewhere. But if, like me, you wanted a place that felt like home minus the loneliness, you would be hard pressed to find its equal.

"What are you going to do about the fan?" I asked.

Greta gave the rebellious appliance a long reproachful look and then sighed. "I'll get Mr. Lebenberg to come over and fix it again. In the meantime, I'll turn it off. It won't get too hot until noon." She turned to me. "What can I get you?"

"Coffee would be nice. And a little breakfast."

I went to my table at the rear. A few minutes later she came over with a tray bearing utensils; a steaming cup of coffee; and a plate holding three pieces of toast, a few strips of vegetables, and a small cube of margarine. She set it all down on the table and said, "You saw Dahlia Rotner yesterday?"

"I did," I said, smearing a thin layer of margarine on a piece of toast. I took a bite. The toast was perfect, crunchy but not dry. "An impressive woman. I wish I had seen her on stage. I went to see her old theater perform last night. Shakespeare. King Lear."

"Really? I didn't know you were a theatergoer."

"I'm not. But she hired me to look into something concerning her theater, so I thought I'd go and get an impression."

"And did you?"

I thought about the play and the emotions it had evoked in the audience. I thought about Isser Rotner, eying each attractive female who came into his orbit with a wolfish hunger. I thought about him and Pnina Zelensky kissing in his car, driving off somewhere to do much more than that.

"Yes, I most certainly did." I took a sip of coffee. "Greta, does the name Anna Hartman mean anything to you?"

Greta furrowed her brow, deepening the wrinkles carved across it. "It's familiar, but only barely. Who is she?"

"Was," I said. "I'm told she was a theater actress who was murdered five years ago."

"Murdered?" Greta's eyes widened.

"Her body was discovered in Trumpeldor Cemetery."

"Oh, now I remember. I read about it in the newspaper at the time. Ghastly. They didn't report the details of the crime, but the place..." A shudder went through her big shoulders. "A murder in a cemetery. There's something uniquely scary about that. Is this what you're looking into? This murder?"

"Yes," I said, not mentioning the fact that my client suspected her husband was the killer, even though I knew Greta would not breathe a word of what I told her to anyone. I trusted her implicitly, but I doubted Dahlia would approve of my sharing her suspicions. For the time being, at least. In fact, apart from Greta, who already knew of our meeting, I did not plan on telling anyone the identity of my client. "What else do you remember from the newspaper reports?"

"Hardly anything, I'm afraid. Just where she was found and her profession. I don't even remember how she was killed. I may have seen her perform, but if I did, she did not leave a lasting impression on me."

Dahlia's voice echoed in my head. *Her ambition far outweighed her talent.*

Just then, another regular stepped into the café, and Greta went to see to his needs. I steered my mind away from the case and concentrated on my breakfast. I took my time, chewing slowly, remembering days in which this meager meal would have seemed like a banquet fit for royalty. It was strange, and disheartening, how these dismal memories could pop up at any time, without warning, like a body rising to disturb the placid surface of a lake in which it had long been submerged.

I gritted my teeth and gave a violent shake of my head. The memories dispersed like shadows before light. But they weren't really gone. I knew that from experience. They had simply scuttled away to some dark corner of my mind, one which I could never reach and cleanse. They would bide their time. They would be back to torment me.

But for now I was free to enjoy what remained of my breakfast. I focused on the taste of each bite—the subtle saltiness of the margarine, the juicy tang of the tomatoes, the earthy freshness of the cucumbers and carrots. It was a simple pleasure but one that I did not take for granted. There was scarcely anything I took for granted anymore. That blissful ignorance was one of the things I'd lost in the camps.

On the other side of the front window, Allenby Street bustled with activity. Pedestrians marched purposefully in both directions. The occasional truck, bus, car, or wagon—drawn by either horse or mule—rolled up or down the wide road. Traffic was light as usual, since most Israelis, myself included, did not own a vehicle.

Once I finished my breakfast, I cleared my dishes to the service counter. Greta took them from me with a smile. I shook my head when she asked if I wanted anything else, then reached over the counter to where she kept my chessboard and pieces and took them to my table. I played chess for a while, read through that day's newspapers, and hoped that Reuben would have the investigation file for me that afternoon.

A little before noon, I went up to King George Street to buy food. At the grocery store, I presented my ration card to the grizzled vendor, and he wordlessly tore off the appropriate strips and gave me the products that I had been allotted. Nearly all food was rationed in Israel. Each citizen was allotted a monthly ration of corn, rice, sugar, legumes, cheese, onion, flour, eggs, meat, and a host of other staples. If you had money, you could dine at cafés like Greta's, but if you expected the menu to include anything but the basics, you were courting disappointment.

To truly eat well, you needed to forsake lawfulness and supplement your rations by procuring contraband food on the black market. This was illegal, of course, but also widespread and, for the most part, socially acceptable. People who had never committed a crime in their life routinely violated the law by buying a little extra meat for their children or selling illicitly obtained sugar to their neighbors.

The government propagandized against it on the radio and in lurid posters that depicted the black market as a snake that needed to be strangled, or an inky hand that was raised against the unfortunate onlooker. It also employed inspectors who searched cars, rifled through bags, and sometimes even raided homes and businesses in search of contraband. People settled old scores by snitching on each other to the authorities. Quite often, this did not keep the snitches from dabbling in the black market themselves.

All this did little to deter the local citizenry from patronizing the black market in droves. Israeli mothers were particularly fervent in their quest to provide their children with the best nourishment their pockets would allow, and against this maternal instinct the government was impotent.

Once I had acquired my rations, I crossed the street and hiked north a few blocks until I arrived at a hardware store. The inside was a touch gloomy, and the air smelled faintly of old dust. Hammers and pliers and screwdrivers, not to mention nails and screws and bolts of all sizes, crowded the shelves. But I was in the market for none of these.

The owner, a man by the name of Dostrovsky, ran a lucrative sideline. An unknown source supplied him with hard cheeses from the Netherlands. Dostrovsky kept them in the back room of his store. The price was high, but so was the quality. Without hesitation, I parted with a small portion of the money Dahlia had given me the day before, and emerged from Dostrovsky's store hefting a small bag, which emitted a pungent yet mouthwatering scent.

At my apartment on Hamaccabi Street, I stashed my purchases in the icebox and kitchen cupboards. I sliced an apple into a bowl and peeled off a few strips of Gouda to go along with it. I carried the bowl into my apartment's single room, the one that served a triple role as my bedroom, dining room, and living room.

I sat on the bed and gazed at the opposite wall. Two pictures hung on it, the only ornamentation in the entire apartment. They hung on nails that had been hammered in by a previous tenant. Those nails had stood barren for a long time, the majority of my residency. Both pictures were recent acquisitions.

The first was a landscape that had been painted by a man named Tadeusz, whom I had met on a case a few months ago. The painting was rich and elaborate and intricate. The sort of painting that reveals something new every time you stare at it, that stirs something deep inside you.

The other painting had been in my possession for only a month. I'd bought it on impulse from an old man who had been hawking his art on the street. His talent did not come close to that of Tadeusz, and, objectively, the painting I'd bought from him was not very good. But when my eye had alighted on it, I had stopped mid-stride, entranced.

The painting showed three figures, all with their backs to the viewer, walking down an old European street. The figure in the middle was the only adult, and by her dress and hair, it was clear she was a female. On either side of her were two smaller figures, both girls, their dark hair plaited and hanging down their small backs.

By their clothes, it was winter. By the violet sky above them, it was dusk. By the way the woman held each girl by the hand, they were a mother and her two daughters. The girls were both very young—the oldest about six, the youngest no more than four.

Their mood could not be discerned. Neither could their destination. Nor did I know the name of the street in which they walked, or what city it was in.

I might have learned all this from the old man who had sold me the painting, but I decided not to ask. By his accent, I could tell he was Polish. In all likelihood, he had painted a city he himself had trod, somewhere in Poland. But as long as I didn't ask, I could pretend it was a street in another country.

Hungary.

For something in the stance and posture of these three figures —the mother and her two daughters—brought to my mind another mother and her two daughters. My wife, Deborah, and the two girls we had birthed together.

All three were dead now. Not a stitch of their clothing remained for me to hold. Not a single photograph of them survived for me to gaze at. All that was left were my memories, and these were dangerous things. They were often trailed by dark imaginings. Whenever I called forth a happy moment of our life together, it was usually followed by an image of horror and death. I couldn't help but picture their last moments, the terror they must have felt, the despair, the convulsions of their bodies as the gas invaded their lungs. I imagined my girls had cried out for me, and I had failed to save them. Little in this world could hurt more than that.

So even the good memories were tainted. Even they caused immeasurable pain. For a long time, I did my best to avoid them entirely. Which was why I did not fully comprehend why I had bought that picture, why I'd hung it where I could not avoid seeing it every day.

But once I did, I never felt inclined to remove it from its nail.

For a very long time, the bare walls of my room had suited me just fine, as had my spare, utilitarian furniture. My apartment was a place to lay my head, to store my food, to take shelter. Nothing more. Now, as I gazed at these two paintings, I realized that their addition had made the place feel a little bit like a home. The first I'd had in some years.

I ate my apple and cheese, then lay down in bed and read a Western called The Feud at Single Shot by Luke Short. I read for the next two hours, then left my apartment and headed downtown to see if Reuben Tzanani had come through for me.

8

I found him in his office on the second floor of the police station on Yehuda Halevi Street. On his desk was a mountain range of papers, some in brown folders, others in uneven piles. He lifted his head when I knocked on the doorjamb and gave me a smile so wide and innocent that it made him look more like a teenager than a father of five.

"Adam, come in, come in."

I stepped inside and took up the chair before his desk.

"Give me a minute, okay? I have to put this file in order."

I watched him as his nimble fingers ordered a stack of papers. His skin was very dark and smooth, his hair black and short and tightly curled. His features were delicate, giving the impression of a weak, flimsy man. This was as wrong as one could get. Reuben Tzanani was one of the toughest men I had ever met. He did not pack as powerful a punch as some, but when it came to stamina, resilience, and perseverance, you'd be hard pressed to find his equal. He was also brave and loyal as few men were. I had seen it firsthand in numerous battles during the War of Independence and was alive that day because of it. On that fateful day when I was shot twice, it was Reuben who had carried me on his back to the rear lines, where I got the medical treatment that saved my life.

Finished with his stack of papers, Reuben set it aside, leaned back in his chair, and sighed. "The powers that be have decided that the petty crime files could do with some tidying up. Guess who they chose for the task."

He did not sound bitter. Most cops would grumble at such an assignment, but not Reuben. He was proud of his job, of being a police officer, and he always seemed content. I often wondered how he would fare in an investigative role, but he had never been given the opportunity.

"It's quite incredible, the range and type of crimes people commit in this city," he said. "They steal bicycles, snatch clothing off lines, sneak into cinemas. Yesterday, I read a report about a teenager who raided his neighbor's flowerpots, making off with a dozen of her best roses. When asked about his motive, he said the flowers were a gift for a girl in his class. He didn't have the money to buy a proper bouquet. Now, he could have gone to a field somewhere, picked wildflowers, but no. Nothing less than roses would do for the girl of this young man's dreams." He smiled. "The neighbor, upon hearing this, withdrew the complaint. It's nice that people believe in love, isn't it?"

I grunted something that could be interpreted as agreement.

"But you're not interested in this petty stuff, are you, Adam? I got the file you wanted right here." He pulled open a squeaking drawer and brought out a folder about two inches thick. He rose from his chair, rounded his desk, and made for the door, motioning me to follow him.

Across the hall was a closed door. It was unlocked. Reuben ushered me into the office beyond it. It was even smaller than his. On the metal desk stood a picture of a brawny cop with sergeant stripes, a woman at his side, his arm on the shoulder of a boy of nine.

Gesturing at the photo, Reuben said, "Sergeant Binnenfeld is on vacation, so you can use his office. When you're done with the file, bring it back to me, okay?"

I thanked him, and he handed me the file. I sat down in the absent sergeant's chair, flipped open the folder, and then realized Reuben was still standing there.

"What is it?" I asked.

"I was just wondering why you think you'll be able to solve this case when the detectives at the time couldn't."

"I didn't choose this, Reuben. I was hired to do it. I have no idea what will come out of it."

"So you don't have any leads?"

I hesitated. I hated lying to him, but all I had so far was what Dahlia had told me—and if I shared it with the police, she would simply deny it. "Nothing yet, no. But I have solved a cold case before, remember?"

"I remember," said Reuben. "I hope you'll solve this one, too. I had a look at the file. No woman should die this way. Well, I'll leave you to it. I've got plenty of files to go through myself before I call it a day."

He went out, closing the door behind him. I lit a cigarette and started reading.

9

The body of Anna Hartman had been discovered by Pinchas Sheftel, a fifty-eight-year-old resident of Tel Aviv who had gone to Trumpeldor Cemetery that day to visit his mother's grave. He did this twice a year—on her birthday and on the anniversary of her death. This occasion was the latter.

An early riser due to both age and inclination, Sheftel entered the cemetery by the main gate shortly after six in the morning. As he expected, the cemetery was empty of mourners. This suited him fine. He tended to cry openly whenever he stood over his mother's headstone—despite the fact that thirty-two years had elapsed since her passing—and, like most men, preferred his weeping to go unwitnessed.

He was engrossed in memories of the times he had spent with his mother. Because of this, he only noticed the body when he was almost upon it.

Sheftel did not need to check her pulse to tell that she was dead. The knife jutting out of her chest and her open, glassy, lifeless eyes were clear evidence of that.

He had the presence of mind to not disturb the scene. Or

maybe it was simple fear that restrained him. As he explained to the detective a little later, the moment his mind fully grasped what his eyes were showing it, he was gripped by a powerful dread that the killer was still lurking among the headstones, and that at any second he would pounce on him.

Terrified, Sheftel bolted for the nearest exit as fast as his old legs could carry him, one hand clamped to his yarmulke to keep it from flying off his bald head. As he ran, he found himself unable to stop from repeatedly mumbling the *kaddish*, the traditional Jewish prayer that is said at funerals and memorials. He had planned on reciting it over his mother's grave, but at that moment he wasn't certain who he was saying it for—his mother or the dead woman.

After alerting the police that a murder had taken place, Sheftel waited for them by the main gate. He did not dare to venture inside by himself.

So the body remained unattended in the time it took the police to arrive. This had unfortunate consequences for poor Mr. Sheftel. Deeply distraught by the sight of the body, he did not wish to lay his eyes on it ever again, but he was made to do so by the police. They needed him to affirm that the body remained exactly as he had found it. Only when he did so was he allowed to stagger away, accompanied by the detective who took his full, somewhat rambling statement in a section of the cemetery from which one could not see the victim.

Sheftel contributed little to the investigation. He was a suspect of course—almost anyone who finds a body is—but only for a brief time. His story checked out. His clothes displayed not a speck of blood. And, most important, a neighbor walking his dog recalled seeing Sheftel leaving his building approximately twenty-five minutes before the time Sheftel claimed to have arrived at the cemetery.

It wasn't much of an alibi, as the murder was later determined to have transpired several hours earlier. But, combined with Sheftel's obvious distress, it was enough to convince the police that his only crime was his plan to say the *kaddish* for his mother without the required *minyan*—ten Jewish men present—which was unorthodox but not illegal.

The detective who got the case, Sergeant Hillel Meltzer, thanked Sheftel for calling the police and admonished him to not share the details of the crime scene with anyone. Sheftel left the cemetery as soon as he was allowed to, failing, for the first time in over three decades, to visit his mother's grave on the date of her passing.

Sergeant Meltzer's initial notes of the crime scene were included in the file. He had used a pencil and had clear, somewhat slanting handwriting. He had arrived at the scene at six fifty-five sharp, and his first action was to dispatch a patrolman to each of the cemetery's three gates. No one was to be allowed onto the premises until further notice.

He then ordered a search of the cemetery. He doubted the killer was still around, but, as every policeman soon learned, one must never underestimate the propensity of criminals to act stupidly. Besides, even if the killer had gone, he might have left evidence behind. So a group of six officers were charged with scouring the grounds for anything that might point to the killer's identity.

Once the search was underway, Sergeant Meltzer turned his attention to the body. It lay atop a wide flat tombstone. The name of the couple interred beneath it made me pause and sit back in my chair. It was the grave of Meir Dizengoff, the first mayor of Tel Aviv, and his wife, Zina, after whom Dizengoff Square was named.

Was there any significance to this? Had the killer deliberately chosen this grave as the spot in which to carry out his crime?

Numerous photographs were snapped of the victim. I spread them out on the table and pored over them. In conjunction with

Meltzer's written report, they gave me a pretty comprehensive picture of the death scene.

The dead woman lay sprawled on her back, one foot dangling over the edge of the tombstone. Her arms were stretched to either side, as though she had attempted to break a fall. With the knife sticking out of her chest, she looked like a human sacrifice offered on the altar of some vengeful, primitive god.

She wore a dark-red dress and one black shoe. The other shoe lay on its side at the foot of the tombstone. The photographer had snapped a picture of the forlorn shoe. There was something eerily desolate about it.

The victim had honey-blond hair, a north-European complexion, blue eyes, and a lean, feminine figure. Her hair was spread unevenly beneath her head. The fingers of one hand were slightly bent.

Her mouth gaped open in a silent scream, her eyes in a blind stare. Blood stained her dress, a dark circle around the knife lodged in her body.

No bag was found near the body. Meltzer assumed it had been taken by the killer. The victim's dress had no pockets. Therefore, the police found no identification papers, nothing that could give Meltzer the victim's name.

Fortunately, the medical examiner who was called to the scene was a theater fanatic. He recognized the woman almost instantly. Her name was Anna Hartman. She'd been an actress at Shoresh Theater.

More pictures were taken, and then the body was carted off to the morgue. The search of the cemetery yielded plenty of cigarette butts, a couple of empty bottles of soda, and assorted other debris. Nothing that made Meltzer's job easier. Nothing that could be attributed to the murderer.

I gathered the crime scene photographs into a small pile and set it aside. Then I read the medical report.

The cause of death was a single stab wound to the chest. The knife had pierced the victim's heart, nearly severing it in two. That explained the relative scarcity of blood at the scene. With the heart stopped, there was nothing to pump blood out of the wound.

The murder weapon was a generic kitchen knife, with an eight-inch blade and a wooden handle. Judging by the fact that the knife had breached the victim's ribcage and had sunk nearly to its hilt, the medical examiner believed that the killer had struck with considerable force.

The victim's hands were free of scratches and other marks consistent with a struggle. There were some minor abrasions on her calves and ankles and elbows. The medical examiner theorized that these might have been caused when the victim fell across the tombstone after being struck.

One startling discovery was made when the victim's dress was removed at the morgue. Anna Hartman was naked beneath. Her underwear was missing. An examination of her vagina and genitals revealed no trace of semen or bleeding. The hymen, the medical examiner noted, was no longer intact, but this had happened some time prior to the night of the murder. If Anna Hartman was raped, her assailant had not been overly brutal or forceful, and he had likely used a prophylactic.

Other than her dress, the victim had been wearing a thin necklace and a stud in each ear. All three were made of silver. The killer, for some reason, had opted not to take them. Her wristwatch—a simple, inexpensive model—had also not been stolen.

I studied the pictures taken at the morgue. The harsh, unforgiving light, coupled with the oddly impersonal nature of these very intimate photos, added a further insult to that of Anna Hartman's death. They stripped her of her dignity just as thoroughly as the killer had stripped her of her life. The dead should not be probed, scrutinized, touched. But this is what happens to murder victims. Before they are allowed to rest, their bodies undergo a further, involuntary intrusion.

Sadness welled up inside me as I stared at the lifeless figure of this young woman, at her waxen face, at her broken chest. I had no notion of who she'd been. I knew nothing of her character. I did not know if she had been kind or cruel, loving or hateful. I only knew that she had been robbed of her life, that she had known fear in her last moments. And I felt a burning desire to see to it that her killer faced justice.

"I'm coming for you," I muttered, the sadness inside me morphing to anger. "You don't know it yet, but I'm coming."

I went on reading. Judging by the report, Sergeant Meltzer had proceeded in a methodical, meticulous manner. Officers were sent to canvass the streets surrounding the cemetery for anyone who might have seen or heard something strange during the night of the murder. Dozens of residents were interviewed by the end of that first day. No one had seen anything amiss. No one had heard cries of pain or fear, or the sounds of a struggle. All had been dismayed that such a murder could take place so close to their homes.

That same day, and over part of the next two, Meltzer interviewed Anna Hartman's neighbors and colleagues. The goal was to get the lay of the land, to gather some basic facts about the victim, to determine whether anyone had reason to want her dead, and to establish who among her acquaintances had an alibi.

Summaries of the interviews were included in the file. I read them all, taking notes. The picture painted by her colleagues was of a hardworking woman, driven and determined, dedicated to her career, sociable and yet distant. It appeared that none of the other actors in the theater had been her friend, and that none of them had truly known her.

Meltzer was the sort of detective who did not put his intuitions and impressions and thoughts in writing. He stuck to the dry facts.

The only place in which he had deviated from this was in the summary of his conversation with Dahlia. At the end, Meltzer had scribbled: "Mrs. Rotner says husband was home all night. Seems truthful."

I shook my head, partly in disgust at Meltzer's gullibility and partly in grudging admiration for Dahlia. She had not overstated the persuasiveness of her performance that night. Sergeant Meltzer had fallen hook, line, and sinker for the false alibi she had provided her husband. From that moment on, it seemed, Meltzer had not considered Isser Rotner a suspect.

Nor did he seem to have known that Rotner and Anna Hartman had been lovers. There was no mention of it in the file, not even as a rumor or possibility. Which was all it was, I reminded myself. At the moment, I had no proof that they'd been lovers, only Dahlia's assertion that this was the case—though after seeing her husband's behavior the other night, I tended to believe it was true. Especially after a batch of photographs of Anna Hartman, taken when she was alive, fell out from between two reports I'd been holding, a few of the photos landing near the edge of the table, a couple ending up in my lap.

She had been a dazzling woman, a true beauty. Even in death, her image recorded in cold police photographs, it was clear she'd been attractive. But in life, with her face animated by thoughts, emotions, and desires, she was much more than merely pretty.

Her beauty was a union of contradictions. The contours of her face, the angles of her jaw and cheeks, the lines of her nose—all these combined to give her a classical allure, aloof and distant and conservative. As though she were a strictly raised lady, accustomed to sitting in well-appointed European parlors, her life regulated by rules and rituals and expectations.

But the spunky spark in her eyes, and the message that her full-lipped mouth appeared to impart—a mischievous delight in her smile, an invitation to share in some secret bliss in her pout or parted lips—suggested that Anna Hartman had lived life according to her will and was not constrained by custom. This dichotomy was so appealing in the pictures, I could only imagine how powerful it had been in real life.

A man like Isser Rotner would have found her irresistible. Indeed, he might have made it his mission in life to pursue and conquer her.

But if he had, if they had indeed been involved, none of the people Meltzer had interviewed was aware of it. Or if they were, they'd chosen to not share this fact with the police.

I leaned back in my chair and rotated my head around slowly, working the kinks out of my neck. I'd been reading for almost two hours. My eyes were tired and the muscles in my neck, shoulders, and upper back were sore and stiff. I rose from my chair, stretched my arms high above my head, and sighed with relief as the stiffness subsided. I lit a cigarette, smoking it slowly as I paced back and forth across the tiny office.

I wanted to get out of there. I wanted a cup of strong coffee and a bite to eat. But I'd told Reuben I'd give the file back to him when I left, and I knew he'd prefer it if I did not come back for it tomorrow. I had to finish reading it today.

While Meltzer had eliminated Rotner as a suspect, he had given no such exemption to the other people he interviewed. A minority of murders are committed by strangers. The culprit and the victim are usually acquainted. So anyone who knew Anna Hartman was a potential suspect.

Not that this helped Meltzer any. Because none of the victim's acquaintances stood out as suspicious. And the late-night hour of the murder—determined by the medical examiner to have been between midnight and four in the morning—made it difficult to refute or confirm alibis. The only reason Rotner's alibi was considered ironclad was because his wife had convinced Meltzer that she had woken up several times during the night, due to her injuries, and that at each of those times, her husband was by her side.

As the third day of the investigation was drawing to a close, Meltzer found himself in the unenviable position of having many potential suspects, but no solid evidence and no leads. No workable fingerprints had been found at the scene or on the murder weapon. No one had seen or heard anything that might lead to the culprit. It was a situation that was liable to drive a police detective mad.

Even the unexpected appearance of a new witness three days after the body was discovered, a witness who might have seen the murderer leaving the scene of the crime, did not aid Meltzer in his investigation.

Anna Hartman's bag was never recovered, nor her missing underwear. No new evidence presented itself, and no main suspect emerged. The possibility that this had been a random killing, the hardest kind to solve, loomed ever larger.

Meltzer, like all police detectives, had other cases to work. Slowly, gradually, Anna Hartman's case shifted in status from active to inactive. And like more murder victims than the general public would be comfortable knowing about, she joined the sad ranks of the dead and unavenged, a victim awaiting justice in the cold embrace of death.

10

I gathered the reports and pictures and stuck them back in the folder. They were probably out of order, but I didn't care. I doubted anyone would be looking at this file anytime soon.

Unless I managed to catch the murderer.

I crossed the hall to Reuben's office. He was still there, working. He'd made some headway. The mountain range of papers on his desk was not as tall as it had been.

"I'm done," I said, crossing over to his desk and handing him the folder.

He put it back in his desk drawer. "Got everything you need?"

"Just about," I said. "I would like to talk to the lead detective. Hillel Meltzer. You know him?"

"Sure. But he doesn't live in Tel Aviv anymore. He moved to Netanya a few years back." He glanced at his watch. "He probably went home for the day. I can call him tomorrow morning."

Through Reuben's window I saw the sky was a dark purple. It was a quarter to seven. I felt a twinge of guilt.

"You waited here for me?" I asked.

Reuben shrugged. "It's all right. As you can see, I got plenty to do."

"But nothing that couldn't wait till tomorrow, right?"

He got up from his chair and smoothed his uniform shirt. He had always been a tidy man, almost fastidious, even during the war. "We can talk about it, or we can get out of here. I know what I prefer."

We walked out of the station together. The evening air was cool and smelled fresh and clean. Reuben stuck his cap atop his head. He glanced again at his watch.

"You want to come over, Adam? Gila will be happy to see you."

I shook my head. "Thank you, Reuben, but I got to be someplace. We'll do it soon, I promise. And I'm sorry that you stayed here so late because of me."

He waved a hand. "Forget about it. I just hope you catch this murderer."

We shook hands and he turned and walked away. I watched him for a moment. I almost ran after him and told him I'd changed my mind, that I would be glad to come over. Instead, I remained rooted to the sidewalk until he rounded a corner and was gone. Only then did I head off myself.

I had lied to him. A half lie, because I *was* meeting someone that night, but not until much later. Maybe I'd done it to spare his feelings. Or to spare myself the need to explain my reluctance to visit him and his family.

Either way, I felt bad about it. I also felt lonely. But it was that strange sort of loneliness in which you feel the pressing weight of your isolation, but also don't want to talk to anyone who knows you.

So I did not go to Greta's Café. Instead, I wandered around a bit, bought a soda at a kiosk, found myself near Gruzenberg Street, and went to see a movie at Ophir Cinema. I sat on a hard wooden chair surrounded by strangers and watched the drama unfold on the screen. It was sort of like the previous night when I'd gone to see King Lear.

Only no one wept. No one clapped. My fellow spectators did not refrain from whispering among themselves—which they did in Yiddish, Bulgarian, Romanian, Hebrew, and a slew of other languages. And I wasn't there to see a potential murderer.

It was midnight when I arrived at the cluster of shabby warehouses on the outskirts of Tel Aviv Harbor. On either side of a lane of pocked asphalt stood lines of blocky structures, several rows deep.

A minority of the warehouses boasted a single desultory light bulb, which shone above their door and did little to illuminate the lane I was treading on. Others hulked like giant black rocks, shrouded by darkness. In the narrow spaces between warehouses, shadows converged, thick and sinister. Anything could have hidden there. Man or beast.

The place was deserted, all the workers safely in their beds. There was a night watchman, but I'd been assured he would not be around.

The blast of crashing waves carried on the light breeze, sounding strangely closer than it should have. In between one crash to the next, I could hear the pitter-patter of tiny feet—scurrying rats, probably—and twice the woeful howl of a night creature, though in both cases it was impossible to tell from where. My nose filled with the smell of rust, rotting wood, and the sea.

I counted off warehouses as I walked. After eight, I stopped before a wooden door above which no light shone. I had my instructions. Three rapid knocks, a pause, and then two more.

Half a minute later, a key turned in the lock, the door creaked open, and I found myself standing before a man I did not know.

"You Lapid?" he asked, his accent local.

I could hardly make out his face in the gloom of the doorway, and I doubted he could see mine, but it was clear he wasn't the man I was there to see. I could tell that by his voice—low and raspy.

"Who are you?" I asked, tensing, my hands bunching into fists.

He grinned, a slash of white teeth opening in the shadows crowding his face. "Relax, it's okay. I'm Meir's cousin. He's out back, taking a leak. Come in."

He moved aside to allow me to enter. He locked the door and then led the way through a narrow aisle lined with wooden crates heaped ten feet high. At the far end, a pool of light beckoned, painting an empty patch of floor a tarnished yellow. It was only when we got there that I got a proper look at him.

And he at me.

It all happened fast then. Much too fast for me. His face twisted in surprise, rage, and blazing hatred. His hand flashed lightning quick under his jacket, and before I had time to draw in a breath, he had pulled out a gun and had it aimed straight at my face.

11

I stood there like a pillar of ice, stock-still and freezing cold, as I stared at the gun and the man holding it.

The gun was a Browning Hi Power pistol, with a thirteen-round magazine. Not that he would need thirteen bullets to kill me. Not when he was standing just five feet away. Not with his hand as steady as it was and his finger curled around the trigger, when all it would take was a tiny squeeze to blow my brains out.

Wondering what had led to this abrupt shift in his attitude toward me, I said, "Listen, I don't know—"

"Shut up." His finger tensed just a bit more on the trigger. "You just shut your mouth." His teeth were bared, but his voice, firm and flat, betrayed not a hint of nervousness. This wasn't the first time he'd pointed a gun at a man, and would not be the first time he shot one either. My heart was hammering so hard my chest ached. My blood rushed through my arteries, as though eager to convey life throughout my body while it still could. I became acutely aware of every inch of my skin. It vibrated with fear.

We were standing near the center of the warehouse, in a wide empty space framed by towers of crates and boxes. Dust motes floated through the air like a cloud of insects angry at our disruptive presence.

The man who could kill me with a jerk of his forefinger was lean and wiry, early thirties, five nine or ten. Full black hair that had been smeared backward with brilliantine. It glinted in the light cast down by the naked bulb that burned above him. He had a narrow, feral face, with high cheekbones, a curving jaw, and a tight, mean-looking mouth with thin, pallid lips. But his eyes were what grabbed my attention, and what made me even more terrified than the gun in his hand.

Deeply set and utterly black, those eyes caught the light and smothered it, creating the illusion of great, impenetrable depth, with something baleful lurking just under the surface. A maniac's eyes. The eyes of a man who would not think twice before hurting another person. I'd seen such eyes before, as a policeman and in Auschwitz.

I'd have to fight him. I wasn't about to let him shoot me where I stood. But I did not like my odds. I'd seen how fast he was. The instant I moved, he would fire. Judging by those eyes and the hatred on his face, it was a wonder he hadn't shot me already.

Just then, a familiar, agitated voice sounded, "Amiram, Amiram, what the hell? What are you doing?"

Meir Gadot, his shirttail only half tucked in his trousers, hurried into the light with short, snappy steps. A chubby, moon-faced man with blubbery lips and blotchy cheeks, he looked from me to his cousin with wide, darting eyes.

"What are you doing?" he said again. "What's with the gun?"

"It's some kind of trick," Amiram said, not taking his eyes off me. "This man said he was Lapid."

"He *is* Lapid," Meir said.

Amiram flicked an angry glance at his cousin. "Then you're a goddamn fool for bringing him here, Meir. He's a cop."

"He's not a cop," Meir said, waving his hands side to side for emphasis.

"He is. I knew it the minute I looked at his face. I can always tell. Hell, I can smell their putrid stench too." And as if to prove it, he sniffed loudly and made a disgusted face. "I'm not going to prison again, Meir. I told you that already."

"Put the gun away, Amiram. I tell you, he's not a cop. He was one, but not anymore."

Amiram narrowed his eyes. "What do you mean, was?"

"He was a cop once, but he hasn't been one for a while. Ask him; he'll tell you."

Amiram snorted at this, but then he said to me, "All right, what's your story?"

So I told him about my being a policeman in Hungary before the war, and that I'd stopped being one over ten years ago.

"You've never worked for the police here in Israel?"

I shook my head.

"Not even when the British were in charge?"

"No."

Another glance at Meir. "How do we know he's telling the truth?"

"He was vouched for, Amiram. And he's worked for me before. He's okay. Trust me."

Still Amiram hesitated, slowly running a thin tongue over his bloodless lips, like he was sampling the taste of imminent violence and was reluctant to let this opportunity for bloodshed pass. Then, with a look of childish disappointment, he lowered the gun and gave me a grin that was all teeth and no warmth.

"No hard feelings, right?"

It took a couple of breaths before my chest no longer felt constricted, before my skin regained some heat, before my heart stopped pounding. I shook my head slowly, a rush of relief making me slightly dizzy.

I looked a question at Meir, hoping my face showed none of

the rage that was quickly replacing my subsiding fear.

"Amiram's my cousin," Meir said. "We're working together now."

"You never told me about this," I said.

Meir shrugged. "It's a new development."

I turned to Amiram. "How long have you been out?"

A raised eyebrow. "Six days. How could you tell?"

"What Meir just said. And what you said before about not going back to prison. And you're pale, like you didn't get enough sun for a long while."

"Two and a half years," he said. "Two and a half goddamn years."

"Adam's a private investigator," Meir said, the blotches on his cheeks fading now that the tense moment had passed. "That's why I hired him."

Amiram flashed me a crooked smile. "So now you work for criminals like us?"

"Like Meir," I said, letting my anger get the better of me. "You, I haven't decided yet."

His smile vanished. His jaw clenched so hard I would not have been surprised to hear it crack. The fingers holding the gun flexed around the grip.

Meir's blotches were flaring again. "Come on now, you two. Let's all be friends here, all right?"

"I don't think he wants that," Amiram said.

"You're the one with a gun in your hand," I said.

He glanced down at it, then back up at me, smirking. "Yeah, and don't you forget it."

For ten seconds, no one spoke. The only sound was Meir's heavy breathing. The air smelled of dust and old wood, but mostly of the rage-and-fear-induced sweat of all three of us. Meir was sweating the most, his forehead dripping. He mopped a hand across his brow, but that didn't seem to help much.

"Put the gun away, will you, Amiram?" he said.

"No. I think I'll keep holding it for now. Just in case I need it."

But I didn't think he was going to use it. Not anymore. He might have wanted to, but being out for only six days meant that Meir was the guy in charge, not him. For now, at least.

"All right. All right. Just keep calm. You got something for me, Adam?"

"Yes," I said. "Why don't we talk in private?"

"We're partners," Amiram told me. "Or haven't you figured that out by now?"

"Meir is the one who hired me, so I'll talk to him and no one else." I gave Meir a look. "Your call."

Meir bit his fat lower lip. His cheeks were blazing red now. He looked pleadingly at me, but when he saw I wasn't about to budge, he let out a deep sigh and addressed his cousin. "Let me talk to Adam alone, all right?"

Amiram glared at him. "What the hell, Meir?"

"Just for a few minutes. I'll tell you everything afterward."

Amiram's features knotted in fury, but then he shrugged as if it didn't matter to him one bit. "Fine by me. I can use some fresh air anyway. It stinks in here. Smells of cop." Then he stuck his gun under his jacket, smoothed the lapels, and began sauntering to the door, draping himself in a thick pretense of indifference. I noticed he moved lighter than a cat, sort of gliding along, almost as if his feet weren't really touching the ground. His footfalls were no louder than whispers. Neither Meir nor I spoke until we heard the door bang shut after him.

Meir wiped his brow again, this time with a hairy forearm. "You didn't need to do that, Adam."

"He shouldn't have pulled a gun on me."

"Amiram's a bit itchy now. Just getting out and all."

"That kind of itchiness could get him in serious trouble. Along with anyone who's working with him. What are you doing partnering with someone like that?"

"Not partnering. It's my operation, same as always. He's working for me."

"Uh-huh. You didn't answer my question. Why are you involved with a man like that?"

"He's my cousin," Meir said. "I owe him. He watched over me a lot when we were kids. Saved my hide a couple of times. He's not so bad, Adam. That bit with the gun, just a misunderstanding. Don't judge him by that."

"That's the kind of misunderstanding that leaves people dead. What did he do time for?"

"Burglary."

"Hurt anyone in the process?"

"No. No one."

"What about when he was locked up before?"

Meir stared at me. "What makes you think he was?"

"A guy like that, with his attitude, at his age, it's a safe bet."

"Nothing big. Robbed a few more apartments, caught fencing what he stole. The man can pop just about any lock in twenty seconds flat and not leave a mark."

"That's nice. Anything violent?"

Meir shook his head, but the way his blotches darkened made me think that while Amiram might not have been convicted of a violent crime, Meir had seen him hurt others before. Perhaps as part of watching over Meir in his childhood.

And now I had a decision to make. Whether to tell Meir what I'd uncovered in my investigation. If I kept it to myself, I'd have to return the money he'd already paid me, and forfeit the remainder I still had coming. But if that meant not giving his gun-wielding cousin a target to lash at, it was a price I was willing to pay.

On the other hand, I liked Meir. He was a smuggler, but a harmless one at that. The sort of man who would not be a criminal if rationing didn't exist. The sort of man who would one day, when rationing finally ended, revert to a legitimate life. If he didn't first end up in jail or dead.

He specialized in jams and canned goods, though he sometimes brought in chocolate and cigarettes as well. His goods weren't of the highest quality, but scarcity adds varnish and luster to even purely mediocre products.

He made good money. Enough to buy nice clothes and shoes and rent a large apartment on a quiet street in Tel Aviv. Still, he would never be really big; he didn't have the required ferociousness. Which was fine by him. He wasn't doing this to get rich, just to make a good living. And since I frequently patronized the black market myself, who was I to judge him?

I had done a job for him a year earlier, when one of his employees began helping himself to a quarter of every jar of strawberry jam Meir smuggled in, making up the deficit with water. The employee kept the rest for himself or sold it. It didn't take long to find out who he was.

Before I took the job, Meir assured me that his only form of retribution would be to cut off ties with the yet-unidentified thief. When I suggested that a little roughing-up was to be expected in such matters, he shook his head and said, "I hate violence," and he looked so earnest that I couldn't help but believe him. And it turned out that I was right. Meir was as good as his word.

A few weeks ago, he had come to me with a new problem. Over the past six months, he'd noticed that a larger-than-usual share of his shipments was seized by customs. A ship would dock at port and a cursory inspection would commence. Same as always. What changed was that the customs inspectors seemed to know exactly which container to check for Belgian chocolate, which crate held jars of English marmalade, under which sack of potatoes Meir's associates had stashed packs of French cigarettes.

"Those bastards used to rummage around like blind beetles,"

he'd told me. "All of a sudden, they're bloodhounds."

Usually, a call to the police would follow the discovery of illicit goods, but Meir had a senior customs official on the payroll, and he hushed things up. Still, the uncovered merchandise was confiscated, dealing a painful blow to Meir's finances.

What aroused his suspicion even more than the frequency of the discoveries was the fact that all of them were made by one of two inspectors. The rest remained their usual ineffectual selves.

"Someone's tipping them off, Adam," he'd told me, "and I want you to find out who it is."

And I did. It took a bit of legwork and an excruciating bus ride to Haifa, but I learned where Meir's confiscated goods ended up, and who was involved in the racket.

I had come to the warehouse that night to tell Meir what I'd discovered. But now I wasn't sure I should.

I said, "I know who's responsible, Meir. And where your goods go."

His eyes lit up. "You do? That's great. Who is it?"

"I'm not sure I feel comfortable telling you."

"What? Why?"

"Because I don't want anyone to get killed for mere stealing."

"Well, that's no problem. You know me, Adam. I'm not the type."

"It's not you I'm worried about. It's him." I jerked a thumb over my shoulder, in the direction his cousin had gone.

"Amiram?"

"Yes. Something tells me he's not as averse to violence as you."

Meir didn't bother to deny it. He just said, "Amiram works for me, Adam. He'll do what I say."

"You're sure about that?"

He nodded. The sweat had cooled on his face, giving it a bright sheen. The blotches on his cheeks looked wet. "You can count on it."

I studied his face. He looked serious and certain, which made me feel slightly better about my options. Still, I wanted to make sure we understood each other.

"All right, Meir. I'll tell you who's robbing you. But if anything bad happens to him, I'll hold you responsible. Are we clear?"

Meir gulped, taking a tiny step back. Good. I wanted him to be a little frightened of me.

"I understand," he said.

So I proceeded to tell him the name of the sailor who was tipping off the customs officials and explained how the confiscated merchandise made its way to a black-market vendor in Haifa, who then sold it to the general public. When I was done, I said, "If I were you, I'd keep this information from your cousin. Deal with it yourself."

He nodded, thanked me, and counted twenty liras into my palm. I pocketed the money and bid him farewell.

Exiting the warehouse, I saw the red dot of the cigarette before noticing the man sucking on it. Amiram was sitting on a barrel, legs spread wide. Moonlight played across his face, making shadows dance on his skin.

"All done?" he asked after blowing out a jet of smoke. His tone dripped with disdain.

"Yes," I said.

"Okay, then."

I nodded and turned to go. I'd not taken five steps before his voice sounded again.

"Hey, cop."

I turned around to face him.

He held up a hand, forming a gun with thumb and forefinger. "See you around one of these days." And he pressed the thumb down, like a cocked hammer dropping, puckered his bleached lips, and made a firing sound. "See you around real soon."

12

I woke up early after a night full of bad dreams. Like the pain that used to tear Dahlia's sleep to shreds, so did my nightmares yank me into wakefulness again and again.

I felt tired, worn out, my body twice its weight. But going back to sleep was an impossibility. If I tried, I would just find myself tossing and turning in my bed.

Lowering my feet to the cool floor, I ran my hands over my scalp and face. The stubble on my cheeks needled my palms. My body was slick with sweat. Free of the blanket, my limbs began to tremble.

In my tiny bathroom, I drank cold water from the tap, then showered and shaved and ran a comb through my damp hair. I studied my reflection in the small mirror above the sink. I did not look half as tired as I felt. A good sign.

I dressed and ate breakfast. Chicory coffee with black-market sugar. Three pieces of bread I toasted in a pan and then smeared with margarine and loaded with slices of Gouda.

I'd used too much of the sugar and had sliced the Gouda too thickly. I enjoyed my meal, but my profligacy made me feel ashamed and guilty. My breakfast could have fed three men in the camps, and not just for a single meal but for a whole day.

Rinsing the dishes, I wondered what had led to my overindulgence but couldn't come up with an answer. It made me feel uneasy, as though something inside me were changing, and I did not know what it was. Once the dishes were done, I set out to begin my day. It promised to be a busy one.

I popped into Levinson Drugstore on the corner of Hamaccabi and King George and used their telephone to call Reuben Tzanani. He told me he still hadn't gotten hold of Meltzer and suggested I call him again in a couple of hours.

That left me with a decision to make. I had two places I could go, but this early in the day, I might not find the man I was looking for in the first. The second place offered no such uncertainty. All the people in it were dead.

Another call might have solved my dilemma, but I wanted no one to know where I was going, not even my client.

I started down King George, my mind still not made up. It was a beautiful morning, the sky a clear blue with just a thin smear of cloud, like a milk mustache across a child's upper lip. It was hotter than yesterday. Poor Greta. The rattling fan would see heavy use today.

I paused when I got to the corner of King George and Bograshov. Decision time. Should I turn west toward Trumpeldor Cemetery, or should I continue down King George?

The British monarch prevailed.

At the bottom of King George, I turned onto Allenby Street and walked south. I stuck my head into Greta's Café, bid Greta good morning, and told her I might come back later; I had work to do. The next corner was Balfour Street. Ohel Shem was at number 30.

Looking around, I did not see Isser Rotner's car. A bad sign.

83

But the theater must have had other entrances. Perhaps Rotner had parked near one of those.

Ohel Shem was a large building, wide and deep, with big windows and doors. I climbed the three stairs to the main entrance, passing between the tall columns that supported the second-floor balcony. Posters for upcoming shows hung on the outside walls, on either side of the lobby door. The door itself was closed, but when I pressed down the handle, it opened. The lobby was empty. A big rectangular space, it looked larger than it had the other night, when it had been packed with people. I crossed the threshold and drew the door shut.

Inside it was cooler. More posters crowded one wall. One of them was for Shoresh Theater's production of King Lear. Another was for an upcoming concert of the Philharmonic Orchestra. Beethoven and Mozart. A German and an Austrian. Not that I saw a difference between the two. Ahead of me were the stairs to the second floor, where the theater hall was.

"Hello! Is anybody here?" I called.

My voice echoed strangely, bouncing from one wall to the other before being swallowed up by the emptiness. I waited a moment in the silent lobby. The place felt deserted, but the unlocked door suggested otherwise.

"Hello!" I called again, and this time I was rewarded with a response.

It came in the form of an old woman pushing a mop in a bucket. She was small and stooped and had a weathered, heavily wrinkled face. A kerchief covered most of her hair. The little that showed was gray. She looked at me with almost no expression.

"Looking for someone?" she asked in a tired voice.

"Isser Rotner," I said. "Is he here?"

It looked like she was about to tell me no, but she half-turned and pointed toward the stairs.

"Up there," she said. Then she lowered her head, hoisted the mop out of the bucket, and began dragging it back and forth across the floor in slow, weary motions. It appeared that she'd forgotten I was there. She didn't even react when I thanked her for her help.

I crossed the lobby, climbed the stairs, and pulled open the door to the theater hall. Rows of empty wooden chairs greeted me like a gaping mouth full of way too many rotten teeth. The scent of last night's audience still lingered in the air. A mishmash of sweat, cologne, cigarettes, perfume. Nothing definite. Nothing that could be isolated. Everything mixed together into something that had no name.

The only other person in the theater was at the far end, on stage.

Isser Rotner.

His voice carried clear across the cavernous hall. Powerful and full of emotion. Not an unforgettable voice like his wife's, not even close, but certainly a strong one. He held a sheaf of papers in his right hand, and occasionally he consulted them. The text he was reading was unfamiliar. It wasn't from the play I'd seen the other night. But the style was similar. Maybe this was another Shakespeare play.

He read not only his part, but those of the rest of the cast as well. He used a different voice for the other roles, a lower, weaker one. He glided across stage as he spoke, moving his arms about, gesturing at empty space where I guessed other actors would stand. One time, he pointed at a vacant spot, and from his mouth poured a poetic accusation. Something about betrayal and death. It sent a chill up my spine.

He was so involved in his reading that he failed to notice my presence until I was within two rows of the stage. When he finally spotted me, he froze with his face contorted in such unadulterated hate and anger that I instinctively took a step back. With his face all twisted like that, I could well picture him committing murder. I could picture him stabbing a woman through the heart and leaving her corpse to grow cold in a cemetery. I had to remind myself that this hate and anger were not real, that they were directed at some character in the play he was rehearsing, not at me. He had no reason to hate me. Not yet, at least.

For a long moment, he stayed that way—his expression full of malice, his free hand balled into a tight fist, the tendons in his neck standing out. Then it was as though an eraser had been swept across the blackboard of his body. His expression smoothed out. His fingers unclenched. The tendons slackened. He had shed the skin of his character like a snake. There was something unnerving about the abruptness of the transformation.

He was still angry, though; the hardness of his stare made that clear. Probably because I had intruded upon his work. If he was the perfectionist his wife said, chances were he would not like a stranger to see him rehearse. But it was a normal sort of anger now. Sane, not murderous.

"Who are you?" he asked. "What do you think you're doing barging in here like this?"

"I didn't mean to intrude. The door was unlocked, so I just let myself in."

He didn't like that answer much. Or maybe it was my tone. It wasn't the least bit apologetic.

"Most people know enough not to enter a place where they've not been invited. Now answer my questions or get out of here."

I did not comply with his request. Instead, I stepped forward, planted both palms on the edge of the stage, and heaved myself up. I rose to my feet, turned around, and surveyed the rows of vacant seats.

I whistled softly. "So this is how it looks from this end." I grinned at him. A guileless sort of grin. "I wondered about that. I was here the other night, you know. I was sitting right there. Eighth row, just left of the middle. I watched you perform. I sure enjoyed myself immensely. You all did a great job, every single one of you. But you, Mr. Rotner, you were the best of the lot."

I flashed him another grin, friendly and nonthreatening and abundantly goofy. The sort of grin that belonged on the face of an idiot. On the way over to Ohel Shem, I had considered how best to approach him—if indeed I found him there. I decided to try to accomplish two things. Appeal to his vanity, which I judged to be considerable; and give the impression that I was not to be feared.

My reasoning was simple: I wanted his cooperation. I was not a policeman; he was not obliged to answer my questions. And if he were truly the killer and was worried I might somehow find proof of his guilt, he might stonewall me. On the other hand, if he did not view me as a threat, he might let something slip that would help me hang him.

How well this gambit would work remained to be seen.

"I'm glad to hear it," he said, his tone a mite friendlier than before. "But as you can see, I'm very busy."

I gave a quick nod. "Sure. Sure. Believe me, I don't want to get in the way of your work. But since I'm already here, I sure would appreciate a few minutes of your time. I would like to ask you some questions, if that's all right."

"You're a reporter?"

I chuckled. "No, not at all. My name is Adam Lapid, and I'm a private investigator. I'm working on a case concerning a former colleague of yours."

"Which colleague?"

"Anna Hartman."

I was looking right at him as I spoke her name. I wanted to see his immediate reaction. It was a good thing I did, because it lasted but a fraction of a second. There, and then gone.

I had caught him completely by surprise. I could tell that by his sharp intake of air and the way his jaw twitched. But there was something more. Something that couldn't be attributed to surprise. It was how his ears shifted back and up, like a hound before an attack. Or a wolf.

It took him a couple of seconds to find his voice. When he did, he sounded almost casual, but not entirely. I caught the faintest trace of what I thought was worry underlying his words. "You're talking about the murder?"

"Yes. I was hired to see if I could do a better job than the police had."

"Hired by whom?"

"I'm sorry, but I can't divulge that. It wouldn't be ethical. I'll just say it's a relative of Miss Hartman."

"Anna had no family. She came to this country from Czechoslovakia alone as a teenager. Her family stayed behind in Prague. All died."

He said this in a voice bereft of inflection. Zero emotion. Like he was relating a statistical fact and not discussing the eradication of an entire family of our people.

"Her close relatives were all killed by the Nazis, that's true," I said. "But a cousin survived and recently arrived in Israel. This cousin, upon learning of the unsolved murder of Miss Hartman, hired me to investigate it." This was what I had told Dahlia I would say. With Jews pouring into Israel in large numbers from all corners of Europe, it was a plausible story.

Rotner's jaw twitched again. He was hiding it well now, but his anger was still there, simmering just below the surface. He did not like me, or maybe just the reason I was there. His dark eyes appraised me, as though trying to weigh my worth. Or he might have been gauging the gravity of the threat I posed him.

"It seems like a fool's errand," he said, "considering the time that's passed and that the police couldn't solve the crime. Speaking of ethics, did you tell your client that?"

"I most certainly did. I told my client that the chances that I would discover the identity of the killer were next to none. I told her this would likely be a waste of money. She decided to proceed anyway." I shrugged, the grin once more plastered on my face. "Maybe I should have tried harder to convince her, but it's her money, after all. I figured she's well within her rights to give some of it to me."

"And this client is Anna's cousin?"

"That's right."

"Strange, but I don't recall Anna ever mentioning having a cousin."

"You seem to have known Miss Hartman quite well."

"We worked together for several years. Naturally, I learned a thing or two about her."

"You weren't close?"

"Not any closer than I am to the rest of the people working with me."

"You never saw each other outside the theater?"

He eyed me for a beat before answering. "What are you insinuating?"

"Nothing. Nothing at all. I'm just curious. I'm simply trying to get a sense of who Miss Hartman was, who her friends were, that sort of thing."

"Sounds to me like you're trying to rake up some muck that's not even there. If you think that I or anyone in this theater had anything to do with Anna's murder, you're insane. It's quite clear what happened."

"Oh?"

"Anna was attacked by some lunatic. Someone on the hunt for a young, pretty woman. It was bad luck. Nothing more."

"You seem very sure of that."

"That's what the police thought."

I blinked in surprise. "How do you know that?"

"From the detective in charge."

"Meltzer? You two talked about the case? When?"

"A few weeks after the murder. He explained that catching a random murderer often takes time. Between the lines, I understood that the case might never be solved."

"Why did you go see him?"

"Because I cared about Anna as a colleague, Mr. Lapid, and I wanted to make sure everything was being done to catch the animal who killed her."

Or you wanted to know what the police were up to, I thought, *whether they were taking another look at you.*

I said, "After reading the police report, I must say I agree with you. I told my client that this was probably what happened, but she said I should keep an open mind." I shrugged again. "And since she's the one paying me, I might as well try to follow her instructions."

"I think you're wasting your time. And her money."

"You're probably right, Mr. Rotner. Most likely, I'll go through the motions, ask some questions, and come to the same conclusion the police did. Still, I need to do something to justify my fee. I wouldn't feel right otherwise."

I was sending him a message. I was hinting that I wasn't going to dig too deeply, that I wasn't going to put in much of an effort. I simply wanted to do enough to be able to look at myself in the mirror and not see a thief staring back at me.

Whether he'd gotten the message or not was unclear. He was clutching the sheaf of papers—the script of the play he'd been rehearsing when I arrived—in both hands now, and I noticed his grip was so tight his fingers were crumpling the pages.

We were five feet apart. It was the closest I had ever been to him. I could smell his cologne, see the shallow lines that ran across his forehead, the tiny wrinkles at the corners of his eyes. He had a small chickenpox scar at his temple. According to his wife, he had been born in 1905 and was forty-six years old. He looked good for his age. Lean and fit, tall and straight. A man very much in his prime.

His eyes were very dark—a deep brown like old, water-soaked wood. They bored into me with a sharp intensity. I could tell that his mind was busy, but what his thoughts were, I couldn't say.

He was an actor, a good one, and now that he had recovered from the surprise I had engendered, he had regained firm control over himself. His expression was inscrutable. The little he had shown me so far might have been but the tip of an iceberg or the entirety of his emotions. There was no way to tell. But what was clear was that both my presence and my mission perturbed him to one degree or another.

If he had his way, no one would be taking a second look at Anna Hartman's murder. And this, of course, made me very suspicious.

His eyes remained fixed on my face for another long moment. Then, with a loud intake of air, he broke off his probing stare and lightly tapped his thigh with the rolled-up script. After which, for the first time, he smiled at me.

That smile filled me with awe. It was just right: warm and charming, but not overly so. The sort of amiable, easygoing smile of a person who hasn't a care in the world. The sort of smile you offer a bothersome stranger you decide to indulge out of the good-ness of your heart. The smile of someone who has nothing to hide and nothing to fear.

I had no doubt that this smile was contrived, but this was only because what I'd been told about him, and also because I had seen him that night in Café Kassit. If this had been my first encounter with him, I would have likely found his smile to be utterly genuine.

And just then it struck me that, when he was in control of himself, Rotner was more than merely a good actor. He was an excellent one. Which meant that he could tell me one lie after another, and I might fail to see through a single one of them.

Which made my job that much harder.

He was still smiling when he said, "Well, Mr. Lapid, as I said, I think you're wasting your time, but I can spare you a few minutes. Who knows? Maybe you'll find the evidence that will finally bring justice for poor Anna."

"Thank you, Mr. Rotner. I'll do my best to be brief. Can you tell me when you first met Anna Hartman?"

"It was, I believe, 1938. We were looking to hire new people, and she auditioned for us."

"She was, what, eighteen at the time?"

"Just about. She had just graduated high school."

"Do you remember the part she auditioned for?"

"It doesn't work like that. We don't hire people for a specific role. Each person who comes to audition is given the text of a scene in advance. I don't remember what scene Anna performed. We switch them from time to time."

"Her audition was good?"

"Good enough for her to be called back for another round of auditions. This time, she had to act three different roles. It's a way to make sure a person can play a range of characters. We want versatile actors."

"And I assume the second audition also went well."

"Yes. And after that, she was hired. She became one of us."

"Who made the decision to hire her?"

He frowned. "Why do you ask?"

"I was just wondering if a single person was in charge of hiring or if it was a collective decision."

"Three of us made all hiring decisions. Me, my wife, Dahlia, and—" He broke off suddenly. "But what does all this have to do with a murder that took place eight years later?"

"Probably nothing. It's just background information."

"Is this your idea of being brief? Asking me irrelevant questions?"

"I like to be thorough, Mr. Rotner."

"There's being thorough and there's wasting time. Your client may be all right with that, but I'm not. When I said I could spare you a few minutes, I meant it."

He was turning belligerent. He was willing to feign cooperation, but only up to a point. I needed to move things along.

"I appreciate your willingness to help," I said. "I'll try not to wander too much with my questions. Tell me, was there anyone who had reason to hurt Anna?"

"No one."

"What about other actors? I suppose working in a theater can get emotional. I imagine arguments are apt to turn quite heated."

"They can and do. But enough to want to commit murder? I can't see that happening."

"You'd be amazed by what drives people to murder, Mr. Rotner."

"Perhaps that's true in general, but I already told you what I believe happened to Anna."

He made a show of checking his watch. He wasn't being subtle about it. My time was almost up.

I said, "Was Anna involved with anyone at the time she died?"

"Involved? You mean with a man?"

"Yes. That's exactly what I mean."

"How should I know?" he said, but there had been a sliver of a delay before he spoke, as though he had to weigh his answer. Maybe he had been about to say that she hadn't, but had then decided it would be better to claim ignorance.

"You never saw her with anyone?"

"Look, Mr. Lapid," he said, tapping his foot impatiently, "Anna was a beautiful girl. She had lots of suitors. But I don't know of anyone serious."

"I see," I said, and decided to change the subject. "Do you have any idea what Anna was doing on the night of the murder, where she might have been going or who she planned on seeing?"

The tapping ceased. "No, I don't," he said, and I peered at his face, hoping to spot some tell that would indicate he was lying. There was nothing. No twitch, no excess blinking, and he met my gaze steadily.

"Where were you the night of the murder?"

His lips curved in amusement. "Are you actually suggesting that I'm a suspect?" His tone was lighthearted, almost playful. He was on firm ground now. He had an alibi, after all. One that had satisfied the police. If only he knew what I knew, that smug smile would be wiped from his face. I had the urge to tell him I knew the truth, but this was not the time, of course.

"I have to rule out as many people as I can," I said. "It's what you do in this sort of investigation."

"If, as you said, you read the police report, you must know the answer to that question."

"Tell it to me anyway. Pretend I don't know."

He rolled his eyes and answered slowly, as though he were humoring an idiot. "I was at home. With my wife. All that evening and night. Isn't that what the police report says?"

"It is. That's precisely what it says. But I wanted to hear it from you."

This elicited a frown. We stared at each other for a moment without speaking. The air between us seemed to grow heavier with our silence and unspoken thoughts. I sensed that he was trying to read me, just as I was trying to read him. I hoped he had about as much success as I did.

He broke the silence. "If you doubt my word, you should talk to my wife. She'd vouch for me."

"As she did at the time."

"Exactly."

You arrogant bastard. You don't have a clue.

He said, "Of course, you would be wasting your time, but you're fond of that, aren't you?"

He smiled a kindly smile, as though trying to take the sting out of his barb, but his eyes were smug and condescending. I resisted the temptation to slap that smile clear off his face. I hoped with all my heart that his wife was right about him. I would enjoy seeing him brought down and laid low.

I said, "What were you doing that day before you went home to your wife?"

"Working. We were putting on a new play the following week, and I was preparing for it."

"You worked until what time?"

"Eight, eight fifteen."

"Were you alone?"

"As a matter of fact, I was. The other actors left at six."

"Did you go straight home?"

"Yes. Any further questions?"

I couldn't think of any. "No, Mr. Rotner. I think that's everything."

"Good. Now if you don't mind..."

I knew a cue when I saw one. I turned and was about to hop down from the stage when a thought occurred to me.

"Just one more thing."

Rotner was already perusing his script. He shot me an irritated look. "What is it now?"

"I was just wondering: this new production you were preparing for, what was it?"

His lips compressed. I thought he was about to berate me for asking yet another irrelevant question. But he simply said, "Antigone. It's a Greek tragedy by Sophocles. Ever heard of Sophocles, Mr. Lapid?" The way he said it, it was obvious he believed I had not.

"It so happens that I have. Was Anna supposed to be in it?"

"Of course."

"In what role?"

"The lead. She was going to play Antigone, one of the biggest female roles in classical theater. As you can imagine, it took quite an effort to put on the play without her."

I stared at him. "You went forward with the production despite her death?"

"Yes."

"I would have thought you all would be too distraught to carry on as usual."

"The show must go on, Mr. Lapid. It's a tenet of our profession."

The way he said it, he was challenging me to pass judgment on him, even while making it clear my opinion mattered not at all.

"Who ended up playing Antigone?"

"Ofra Wexler," he said, pointedly shifting his gaze back to the script. "And now, are we finally done?"

For the moment, we finally were.

13

The cleaning lady was gone, and she had done a poor job. I could see smudges swirling along the lobby's floor. Maybe she had gone to fill her bucket with fresh water.

I exited Ohel Shem, my eyes squinting at the harsh glare of sunlight. Parked at the curb right outside the theater was a dark green Austin, at least ten years old. The trunk was open, and bending into it was a woman. She was pulling something out, and I could tell she was having a hard time of it. I started over to lend a hand, but she got her cargo out before I reached her.

It was a very large sack, and the woman couldn't get her arms to close around it. The moment she maneuvered the sack over the lip of the trunk, it slipped from her grasp and landed at her feet.

By the sound it made, I could tell whatever was in it was soft. The woman muttered something under her breath and bent to pick it up, but I said, "Let me do that."

She straightened, tucking a wayward strand of hair behind her ear. "Thank you."

I crouched, got a good grip, and heaved. The sack was much

heavier than I thought, and stuffed with something that felt like cloth. "Where to?"

She told me to follow her. We entered Ohel Shem, again not seeing the cleaning lady, and took a left through a door that opened onto a long corridor. It stretched ahead and around a corner and culminated in another door, which the woman opened with a key. It was a long walk with the heavy sack, and the muscles in my arms, shoulders, and back began burning within twenty paces. By the time we entered the room behind the door, those same muscles were screaming for mercy.

"Put it right there," she said, gesturing at an empty patch of floor next to a sewing machine and a few bolts of cloth, and I gratefully unburdened myself. "My knight in shining armor," she added with a smile.

I glanced at the dark blue slacks, scuffed shoes, and white shirt I had on. "Hardly that, I'm afraid."

She laughed, a sound like tiny bells tinkling. "You may not be dressed the part, but it's the spirit that counts. Besides, it's not as if I'm dressed like a lady, am I?"

She had that right. Her clothes were as simple as mine. Sensible flat shoes, a dove gray skirt that went past her knees, and a black short-sleeved shirt. The shirt was buttoned to her throat and tucked into the waistline of her skirt.

These were the sort of clothes most Israeli women wore. Unless it was a special occasion, in which case they would reach into the depths of their closets and retrieve the one dress, or maybe one of two, that was too fine and precious to risk tearing or staining on any regular day.

"But," she said, untying the knot that sealed the mouth of the sack, "that's easily remedied." And from the sack she drew out a very long old-fashioned burgundy dress and held it up for me to see. "In this, any woman would look like a noble lady, especially if we paired it with the right necklace. Like one of these."

She pointed at a nearby worktable topped with an open box glinting with bracelets, rings, earrings, and necklaces. At my startled gaze, she laughed again. "They're not real. They only look real. Which is why we use them."

"They're props?"

"Yes. As are the clothes you were kind enough to carry for me. And these as well." She indicated a hanging bar that ran the length of one wall. Additional articles of clothing hung on it, most of which clearly belonged to faraway lands and distant times. She located an empty hanger for the burgundy dress and then offered her hand. "Varda Navon."

"Adam Lapid," I said.

Her firm, businesslike grip confirmed my initial impression of her. She was no idle lady, but a woman who was no stranger to work. Her accent, or lack thereof, marked her as locally born, her speech and subtle humor as fiercely intelligent, her wedding band as a married woman. I wondered if her husband considered himself a lucky man, and decided he probably did.

She was of average height and had intelligent brown eyes. A womanly figure, with wide hips and large breasts. A round, mildly attractive face, with a snub nose and a fetching mouth. I could tell it was a mouth that smiled easily, as it was doing now.

"Knight or not, Adam, you're living proof that chivalry is indeed not dead. I'm lucky you were passing by when you did."

"Actually, I wasn't passing by. I had just exited the theater when I saw you struggling in your trunk."

"And you rushed to my rescue. How noble of you. But what were you doing in the theater? Are you in show business?"

"Not at all. I'm a detective."

"Oh? And why have you come here?"

"I'm investigating the murder of Anna Hartman."

That erased the cheerfulness from her face. She looked at me as though seeing me for the very first time. "You're a policeman?"

"A private investigator. I've been hired to see if the murder might finally be solved."

"Oh," she said, and then repeated herself, "Oh." There was a chair by the table, and she lowered herself into it. "So it seems you are a knight after all."

Her eyes, which a moment ago had sparkled with mirth, now glittered with sadness, belying the levity of her words.

"I'm glad you're doing this," she said. "Something tells me that if anyone can solve this case, it's you."

"You don't even know me, Mrs. Navon."

"No, but it's an impossible quest, isn't it? After all this time? And who better for an impossible quest than a knight? And please call me Varda. I've already called you by your first name, so you might as well call me by mine."

"All right, Varda. I'd like to ask a few questions about Anna, if that's all right."

"Of course. Why don't you take that stool over there?"

It was a tall, three-legged wooden stool, and I perched myself on it. I studied her for a moment. Her expression was somber, her eyes moist. Her posture was relaxed but attentive, a hand on each thigh.

I began, "How did you first learn about the murder?"

"I arrived at the theater in midmorning the day her body was discovered. Some of the actors were already here. They told me what happened. It was a huge shock."

"I can imagine. Forgive me, but I have to ask: Where were you the night of the murder?"

She answered without hesitation: "At home, with my husband."

"All night?"

"Yes. I arrived home at about six thirty and did not go out until the morning after."

"You remember the exact time after all these years? You have a good memory."

"Not all that good. But everything about that dreadful day is engraved in my mind."

"And your husband was with you the entire night?"

"Yes."

It was what she'd told Meltzer five years ago. I decided to move on.

"How long have you worked for Shoresh Theater?"

"Since 1937."

"And when did you first meet Anna?"

"The day she was hired. She came to me so I could take her measurements."

"Measurements?"

"For the outfits she would need in her work. This is what I do, Adam. I make the costumes for all our plays, and most of the set design as well." She paused for a beat. "I remember thinking she had the most wonderful figure. I just knew every dress I made her would look perfect. And they did. She said so herself."

"How did you get into dressmaking?"

"My mother was a seamstress and my father a tailor. Between the two of them, they taught me everything to know about how to work with every sort of fabric you can imagine. I still run the shop they opened twenty-five years ago. My work for Shoresh Theater is a mere sideline."

"You must be doing well," I said, "to be able to afford a car."

Color tinged her cheeks. Her eyes were downcast. "It's...it's not mine. I borrowed it, you might say." She raised her eyes and got it all out in a rush. "My husband is a mechanic, and, well, someone needs to take the repaired cars for a ride to make sure they run smoothly before their owners pick them up."

"Ah. I see."

Apparently she felt a need to explain herself further. "The

theater used to pay for a taxi any time I needed one, but these days I have to make do by myself somehow. It makes no difference to the car's owner, you understand."

I smiled. "It's all right, Varda. We all skirt the rules to get by." I wondered why Isser did not offer his costume designer the use of his car. Perhaps he felt it was beneath him. Or maybe he was just stingy. I said, "I heard rumors the theater was in trouble financially, but I didn't think it was that bad."

"Oh, it's pretty bad. Our wages were cut five percent last year and another three this year. I hope it's temporary, but who knows?"

The same question could be asked about the economy in general. It seemed no one, including those in government, knew where things were headed.

"Can the actors get by on their salaries?"

"If they tighten their belts. It's easier for the senior ones. You get a higher salary the longer you've been with the theater."

I nodded, then returned to the matter at hand: "How did you end up working for the theater?"

"One of our actresses...well, she's a former actress now. Dahlia Rotner. Have you heard of her?"

"I have," I said, keeping my expression flat. "I understand she's no longer acting."

"No. It's a terrible thing. She was injured in a car accident a few years ago, and she hasn't fully recovered. But well before that, in 1937, she came into the shop to buy a dress, and she liked what she saw, so she offered me a position with the theater. They needed someone immediately, and I leaped at the opportunity."

"You like the theater?"

"At first I did it for the extra income, but then I grew to like it. The theater is glamorous and mysterious, and I love how every night the actors turn into different people, and that I play an important role in creating an illusion for the audience. Of course, the actors get the applause, but you know what?" There was a conspiratorial smile on her lips.

"What?" I said.

She leaned toward me, and in a voice scarcely above a whisper, she said, "I'm much more important to the theater than any of the actors. I'll never say it to their faces, and they would never believe it if I did, but it's true. Without my costumes, they would look ridiculous, even if they said every line just right. I'm indispensable."

I smiled back at her. "I just bet you are."

She straightened in her chair, and her expression turned serious. "Anna and I weren't close, so I don't know all that much about her. But what I do know, what was clear just by watching her, was that she loved acting. She loved the audience, loved being looked at. It's almost as if she was nourished by all the attention."

"Was she a good actress?"

"Yes."

"As good as Dahlia Rotner?"

"Very few actresses are as good as Dahlia."

"Is that a no?"

She tilted her head an inch to the left, considering me with those clever eyes. "You never saw Dahlia perform, did you?"

I had, but not in the way Varda meant. "I know her reputation. Heard she was very good."

"Not very good. Exceptional."

"And Anna wasn't?"

"Anna was talented, but Dahlia is gifted. You understand the difference?"

I wasn't sure that I did, and said so.

"How shall I explain it?" Varda said, tapping her upper lip with a forefinger. "Some actors have a unique presence on stage. They seem bigger than they really are, and it's as though they're surrounded by energy. The audience can't take their eyes off them.

It's a special quality, very rare, and I don't think you can learn it. You can't train yourself to have it, no matter how hard you try. People that have it act on a higher plane. They soar over the merely skilled or talented. They shine on stage like a blazing fire, like the sun. Dahlia Rotner was such an actress. She was the star of the theater. She played all the leading female roles. Her accident was a terrible blow. In many ways, we haven't recovered from it."

The image of Dahlia, with her neck brace and perfect posture and indomitable dignity, rose in my mind. No wonder she had made me think of a queen. For that was precisely what she was. A queen of the stage who had been dethroned by fate and misfortune.

But who had inherited her position? The same woman who was to play Antigone had she not been killed?

I asked Varda the first of these two questions, and she confirmed it. After Dahlia was injured, it was Anna who became Shoresh Theater's leading lady. No doubt, this only aggravated Dahlia's suffering. It's one thing to be toppled from a high pedestal; it's quite another to see a woman you think so little of elevated in your place.

"So Anna was now the star of the theater?" I asked.

"Oh no," Varda said, with a note of surprise.

"Then who?" I asked, and the answer came to my lips before she had a chance to respond. "Isser Rotner?"

Varda nodded. "He was, and is, our best actor."

I took a moment to digest this. I remembered the hallway in the Rotners' apartment, how those picture-laden walls—one of the master of the house, the other of its mistress—seemed to compete for my attention and admiration.

Was this a reflection of a real-life rivalry? Had Rotner felt eclipsed by his wife's talent and position as the theater's best performer? Was he, on some level, content that now his star was allowed to shine brightest? And was this one of the reasons Dahlia now resented him? An additional reason for hiring me to bring about his downfall?

"Tell me, Varda," I said, "is Isser Rotner talented or gifted?"

Varda smiled a tiny smile. "Somewhere in between."

Dahlia would have swelled with pleasure to hear that. Even I felt a burst of satisfaction. Perhaps this was why Rotner cheated on his wife. As a form of revenge for her superior talent.

"Did Anna and Isser get along?" I asked.

"Very well. He liked her acting style. He was the one who picked Anna to take over Dahlia's roles."

"Was their relationship merely professional?"

Her eyebrows shot up in surprise. "I never saw or heard anything to suggest otherwise. Why do you ask?" She sounded completely sincere, as though this was the first time the possibility of a romantic involvement between Anna and Isser Rotner had crossed her mind.

"Just curious," I said, and quickly changed the subject. "Can you think of anyone who would want to harm Anna?"

"No, no one."

"How about one of the other actors?"

Varda looked appalled at the mere suggestion. "Why would any of them wish to kill Anna?"

"I don't know. Maybe she had a fight with someone. Maybe someone thought she was getting too many lines or too much praise from the critics."

Her tone was resolute. "I know all the actors, Adam, and I can't believe any of them would be capable of such a thing."

I was on the verge of asking her specifically about Ofra Wexler, but something tight in Varda's expression told me she would not appreciate such an inquiry. It would offend her sense of loyalty to the theater.

She said, a touch softer now, "I know it's your job to be suspicious of everyone, Adam, but I know these people. None of them is a killer."

There was no arguing with her earnestness, or her naivete. She did not know how well killers could disguise their true selves. Better than most actors could assume the identity of a character. I took a breath and got to my feet.

"All right, Varda. Thank you. I think that's everything."

14

In a drugstore on Sheinkin Street, I placed two telephone calls. The first was to Reuben Tzanani. He had good news for me.

"I got through to Meltzer," he said. "Told him what case you were working on. He's agreed to talk to you. You can meet him in Netanya today. He's free around noon."

Just in time for lunch, I thought.

"He'll be at the police station. Know where it is?"

I told him I didn't, and he read me the address. I thanked him and hung up.

The second call was to Dahlia Rotner. I reported to her that I had just met her husband.

"And?" she said. "Do you think he did it?"

"I don't know, but I can tell you he was none too happy to talk to me."

"That's because he's guilty. Just like I told you."

"Maybe," I said. "I asked him for his alibi, and he told me you'd vouch for him. He'll expect me to come by to see you. Why don't you tell him that I dropped by around noon, and that you told me the same story you fed the cops at the time?"

"It would be my pleasure," she said, clearly relishing the prospect of lying to her husband instead of for him.

I checked my watch and decided that Trumpeldor Cemetery would have to wait until I got back from Netanya. It was only about thirty kilometers north of Tel Aviv, but bus service in Israel was spotty, with timetables that were notoriously undependable. I did not want to be late for my noon appointment with Meltzer.

A half hour later, I was at the Tel Aviv Central Bus Station, and thirty-five minutes after that, I was sitting on the bus to Netanya.

A couple of rows ahead of me, two men were engaged in a muted discussion in Yiddish; while directly behind me, a solitary woman was humming a Hungarian lullaby. I recognized the tune; my mother used to sing it to me when I was little. I closed my eyes, shutting out all other sound, and my mother's voice rose from the ashes of my memories, soft and warm and comforting. Weariness crept over me, insistent and strangely sweet, like it does in childhood. I propped my head against the window and let the gentle melody lull me to sleep.

The buzz of street noise jerked me awake. The bus had stopped. We had arrived in Netanya. Glancing over my shoulder, I saw the seat behind me was empty. Turning back with a sudden, inexplicable panic, I scanned the few passengers who still hadn't disembarked, but the woman who had hummed the lullaby was not among them. I peered out the window, frantically ran my gaze over the people milling about the station, but she had gone.

Why did I seek her out? To thank her? To ask where in Hungary she had come from? Or maybe on some illogical level, her absence was tantamount to the loss of my mother.

I had no answer. Nothing that would satisfy me rationally. I didn't know whether to smile at my foolishness or worry about my state of mind.

After asking the bus driver for directions, I walked the few blocks to the police station. I asked the officer at the desk where I might find Sergeant Meltzer.

"Inspector Meltzer, you mean," he said, and asked why I wanted to see him.

I explained that Meltzer was expecting me, and he gestured down a hall to the right. "Second door from the end, left side."

Meltzer was sitting behind a metal desk, reading a paper he held in his left hand. His right was tapping the end of a pencil on the desktop.

I rapped on his open door and got his attention. I told him who I was, and he put down the pencil and paper and stood. "Hillel Meltzer," he said, and I noted he hadn't used his rank.

He assessed me with his eyes, as cops tend to do. I did the same to him. It was part of the trade, an ingrained habit. Something you learn when you first put on the uniform and never get rid of.

He was a tough-looking guy in his late forties. Not tall, but powerfully built, with wide shoulders and a deep chest. Square face, with a fleshy nose, a full mustache, and a big angular jaw. Cynical laugh lines around the eyes and mouth. Close-cropped thinning salt-and-pepper hair. Light blue eyes that appeared to be perpetually half-narrowed.

We shook hands. His was warm, fingers blunt and thick. He had quite a powerful grip, but didn't seem the type to be doing it to prove a point. His face and forearms were nicely tanned.

He didn't sit back down. "I was just about to head out to lunch. You hungry?"

I got the underlying message. I was expected to pay for the meal. It didn't surprise me. He was doing me a favor, and I was supposed to show my appreciation.

"I can eat," I said.

He plucked his cap from a wall peg and slapped it on top of his head. The uniform fit him well, maybe a bit too tight across his belly. He looked the sort of police officer criminals know not to mess with, the sort that would come down on you hard if you stepped out of line. His voice fit the part—gruff, with a scrape of gravel. We marched out of the station and onto the sun-drenched street without exchanging another word.

The silence persisted for another block. Then he said, "I gotta admit, I was quite surprised when I heard the reason you wanted to see me." He flung me a sidelong glance. "How come you're working on this case?"

"I was hired to."

He waited a beat, and when I said nothing more, a smile twitched a corner of his mouth. "Let me guess: you're not about to share the identity of your client."

"I'm under specific instructions not to."

"See, I got to wonder why that is. Your client got something to hide?"

"My client wants to see Anna Hartman's killer brought to justice. We're all on the same side here."

His short bark of a laugh let me know what he thought of that statement. We were walking west, toward the sea. The sun was at its zenith, beating down hard, making the low stone buildings shine like old ivory. I was hot all over and thirsty. My shirt clung to my spine with perspiration. Wherever Meltzer was taking me, I hoped we would get there soon.

As if reading my mind, he said, "Just a couple of minutes more." And that was as far as our conversation went until we arrived at the restaurant.

It was on the west side of Ha'atzmaut Square, not far from the beach. Half a dozen tables on the sidewalk and twice that inside. Meltzer led the way in and was greeted with a warm smile by the waiter, who gestured toward a table by the window. Meltzer's regular spot, apparently. But the inspector shook his head. "We'll take the one at the back this time, okay?"

The table was in a corner, and each of us sat with his back to a wall. Meltzer's cap ended up on a third chair. The air smelled of cooking oil, beans, and tobacco.

"Thank you for giving me your time," I said.

"I couldn't help feeling curious," Meltzer replied, and I couldn't tell by his tone whether he appreciated my involvement or not.

The waiter came to the table and asked Meltzer if he'd have the usual.

Meltzer explained: "Lentil soup, potatoes with onions, lemonade if you want it."

I said yes to everything. Half a minute later, when the waiter served us our drinks, I gulped down mine in one long, glorious swallow. Smacking my lips, I handed the glass back to the waiter and asked for another one.

Meltzer wore an amused expression. "You been hiking through the desert or something?"

"Had nothing to drink since morning," I said. "By the way, lunch is on me, all right?"

Meltzer chuckled. "You knew that before you got on the bus, I bet."

"The time of day gave it away. And I used to be a cop myself."

"Reuben told me. In Hungary, he said. Before the war."

"That's right."

"Ever think about joining the force here?"

I shook my head. "Not for a second."

The question why was in his eyes, and probably on his tongue as well, but he held it back.

The waiter returned with my glass, and this time I took a moderate sip. The cool lemonade tasted wonderful.

Meltzer said, "I understand you read the police report."

I nodded, worried that Reuben might have gotten himself in trouble for letting me see it. "You mind?"

"Not really. It's irregular, but the case has lain dormant for a while now. I don't see the harm in you reading it." He sampled his drink, set down the glass, and tapped two fingers against the side of it. "But I don't know if there's anything I can add to it."

"You ran the investigation. Your impressions and thoughts would be invaluable."

Meltzer shrugged his wide shoulders. "Not much to say. It's one of those frustrating cases where there was never the end of a thread on which to pull and unravel the whole business. No real leads, no main suspect. Just a heinous crime and one dead girl." He nailed me with those narrow blue eyes. "I don't see why you think you'll have better luck than I did. Not unless you know something I don't."

"I don't," I said.

"Uh-huh," he muttered, and then plunged into a ponderous silence, and I got the impression he was good at making suspects sweat in the interrogation room and blurt out things they shouldn't. At length he added, "I can tell you're lying, my friend, and that irritates me."

So he was perceptive as well as naturally suspicious, which meant that Dahlia's performance on behalf of her husband five years ago must have been extraordinary. Meltzer was also a good deal more than irritated. I could tell that by his clenched jaw and simmering eyes.

It was a tense moment, and it might well have proved to be the last in our conversation had the waiter not chosen it to arrive with our soup. Steam rose from our bowls, and with it the mouthwatering aromas of garlic and lentils. Sliced pieces of carrot bobbed enticingly on the brownish surface of the soup.

Neither of us reached for our spoons. Hoping to lighten the mood, I said, "Since I'm paying for this soup, you might as well have it before it goes cold." Meltzer blinked, and some of the tension drained from his face. "I don't have anything you can use," I added. "Just some rumors. Nothing substantiated. Nothing that would justify reopening the investigation. But if I get anything concrete, you'll be the first to know."

He didn't move for a while, his eyes dissecting my face. Then he let out a low grunt, grabbed his spoon, and began eating. I did the same. We did not speak again until we'd emptied our bowls and the waiter came over to clear them.

"Okay," Meltzer said, drying his lips with a napkin. "What do you want to know?"

"How well do you remember the details of the case?"

"Well enough. It's a memorable crime. The way the body was stretched out on that tombstone with a knife in her chest. Not the sort of image you're likely to forget." He paused and then added, "And I don't like failure."

Which explained his anger with me for keeping information to myself. I would have reacted similarly. Because I, too, hated the idea of a murderer getting away with his crime. And it struck me that this, more than the prospect of a free meal, was the reason he'd agreed to meet with me—to perhaps finally see justice done on this old, unsolved case of his. I was beginning to like this hardened, no-nonsense inspector.

"Maybe you can start by telling me what you think happened," I said.

"That's easy enough. I think someone accosted her as she was passing by the cemetery and forced her inside and killed her. Someone she didn't know."

"A random killing?"

"That's one possibility. Another is that it was someone who saw her act and targeted her specifically."

"A deranged fan."

"Precisely. But there's no indication who he might be."

"If he existed at all," I said. "What about a romantic involvement?"

"There was none."

"Don't you find that strange? A beautiful woman like her?"

"I do, but those are the facts. Maybe she was one of those independent types you hear about sometimes, radicals who swear off men and marriage and children."

The words were derisive, but his tone wasn't. He might have had nothing but scorn for such women, but Anna Hartman was a murder victim and he was not about to mock her.

"Did she ever voice such opinions?"

"Not to my knowledge. But her colleagues said she was a private person, not one to bare her soul."

Which might explain, at least in part, why none of them knew about her alleged affair with Isser Rotner.

"Why do you think she didn't struggle?" I said. "Or make a racket?"

"The killer had a knife. Maybe he put it to her throat, threatened to slash her if she didn't do as he said. She figured her best bet was to obey. Most women would have done the same."

"How did he know where she'd be?"

"Followed her. We managed to track her movements that night. She went to a late movie at Esther Cinema. Alone. The ticket vendor remembered her. The movie ended at midnight. Another twenty minutes back to Trumpeldor Street and then..." Meltzer slapped his hand with moderate force on the table. "The killer pounced."

"And he led her to Meir and Zina Dizengoff's grave. You think there's any significance to that?"

Meltzer drank some lemonade, regarding me over the rim of the glass. "You haven't been to the crime scene, have you?"

"Not yet," I said. "I'm going to once I get back to Tel Aviv."

"Then you'll see why he chose that spot when you do."

It was an obvious rebuke, but I allowed myself a faint smile. "I would have gone there, but I had to get here in time for lunch."

Meltzer let out a chuckle. "That you did."

"What about someone from the theater? You feel certain none of them was the killer?"

"I wasn't able to rule them all out, if that's what you're asking. Some lived alone and had no alibi. But there was no evidence that linked any of them to the crime scene. And for most of them, I could not see a motive strong enough for murder."

"Most of them? Not all of them?"

"There was the actress who got Hartman's parts after she was killed. Not that it's much of a motive, far as I'm concerned." He squinted. "Her name escapes me."

"Ofra Wexler."

"That's it. But I doubt she had anything to do with it."

"Why is that?"

Now it was his turn to bestow a faint smile upon me. "You haven't seen her either, have you?"

"Not yet."

"When you do, you'll understand."

He was enjoying this, I realized, not sharing everything with me. A form of benign retribution for my keeping information from him.

The waiter brought over the potatoes. Quartered and brownish-yellow, adorned with garlands of onion, and bathed in thick gravy. Meltzer picked up his fork, speared a hunk of potato, and deposited it in his mouth. The gravy browned the bottom edge of his mustache.

"Go ahead," he said. "It's good."

I needed no further encouragement and learned a second later that he had spoken the truth. The food was delicious.

"About Eliyahu Toledano..." I said once I'd blunted the edge of my hunger.

"I was wondering when you were going to get to him," Meltzer said around a mouthful of potato.

"The report didn't paint a complete picture."

"It told everything one needed to know. He was a useless witness."

"Tell me more about him."

"All right." Meltzer finished his lemonade. "I first heard of him three days after the murder, when a man who lived by the cemetery rang the station and asked to speak with me. His name was Kimmel. I'd interviewed him the day the body was found. Saw nothing, heard nothing, just like everyone else. But then he thought of something he hadn't mentioned when we'd first talked. Something that seemed unrelated at the time, but that on further reflection, he thought I should know.

"He'd been on his way home from visiting his ailing mother, and was passing by the cemetery at eleven that night, when he saw a man lying on the threshold of the western gate. Two empty bottles of wine lay by the man's head, and he was snoring peacefully.

"Kimmel knew the man. He was Eliyahu Toledano, a sort of neighborhood drunk, and this wasn't the first time Kimmel had seen him sleeping one off outdoors.

"It was a warm night, and Toledano was sound asleep, so Kimmel left him there and went home and forgot all about him. Until it occurred to him that Toledano might have still been there when the murder had taken place. That he might have seen or heard something. That's when he contacted the police."

Meltzer forked another potato piece into his mouth and continued.

"Toledano lived alone in an apartment on the corner of Trumpeldor and Ben Yehuda. A good-for-nothing layabout. No job, no hobbies, even. Apart from drinking, that is. His parents had left him two buildings, and he made his living off the rent.

"You should've seen him when he answered his door. Dirty clothes. Eyes all red and puffy. Unshaved. His hair sticking out. And his breath was so putrid it could have felled an ox. My guess is my banging on his door had roused him from a drunken stupor. He was groggy and hungover. It took a few minutes just to establish a normal conversation with him."

Meltzer's lips twisted in disgust at the memory.

"He confirmed that he'd fallen asleep in the street and didn't seem the least embarrassed by it. Said he hadn't heard anything strange—no scuffling sounds, no screams. Nor had he seen a woman matching Anna Hartman's description that night. It seemed like a waste of time, but then he suddenly got a bit more lucid and began telling me about a man he might have seen coming out of the main gate of the cemetery. Only he wouldn't swear to it not being a dream. And he couldn't even begin to estimate at what time this occurred." Meltzer shook his head. "Not your first choice of a witness, is it?"

He continued without waiting for my response.

"The man, Toledano said, quickly crossed Trumpeldor Street and began walking west. He didn't see Toledano, who was already lying by the western gate, already sloshed to the gills, and Toledano caught a glimpse of him as he passed under a streetlight. Not that this brief sighting proved useful. Toledano's description of the man was maddeningly vague and low on detail. Not too tall, not too short. Not rail-thin, but not fat either. Couldn't remember what he wore, only that it was dark. Couldn't say if he was carrying anything. The only thing he was sure of was that the man had a dark beard. And just to show you how unreliable his observation was, he told me he wasn't sure how long the beard was. Whether it was short and tidy or went all the way to here." Meltzer indicated the bottom of his chest and again shook his head.

"So as you can see," he said, "Toledano was a dead end. Maybe he saw someone or maybe he didn't. Maybe that person had a beard or maybe not. Not that it made much difference either way."

"Did any of Hartman's acquaintances have a beard?"

"A couple of the neighbors. None of the theater troupe."

"Actors know how to put on fake beards," I said, recalling Isser Rotner on stage as King Lear.

"That's true. But so would anyone else if he put his mind to it. I know what's going through your mind, Adam. You don't want the killer to be some stranger, with no ties to the victim. Because in that case, you haven't got a chance in hell of catching him."

"You said 'him.' You're sure it was a man?"

Meltzer looked surprised at the question. "Of course it was a man."

"A woman can stab someone just as easily."

"But a man is better able to threaten a woman into going into a cemetery in the dead of night. And a woman isn't likely to make off with the victim's underwear."

"Maybe she would, to throw the police off."

"Then why stop there? Why not rip Hartman's dress, too? And why tug her dress down to cover her groin? Why not leave her exposed, so that's the first impression we get when we find the body? Besides, you're overthinking this. It's as simple as it looks. A man did it."

He was making nothing but sense, but there was one fact that needed explaining.

"No semen was found in the victim," I said.

"True. But that could mean any number of things."

"You think the killer used a rubber?"

"It's possible, but most rapists don't. What do they care if they knock their victim up? It's her problem, not theirs. No, I think something else happened."

"Such as?"

Meltzer leaned back in his chair, drew in a breath, and enumerated the possibilities on his fingers. "One, he raped her but didn't finish. Maybe something spooked him in the middle of the act, so he killed her and got out of there fast. Two, the son of a bitch was impotent. I gotta admit, this is the option I like best. It makes me smile to think of him failing that way. And three, just before he was able to rape her, Hartman began struggling. So he stabbed her right through the heart. And once she was dead, he no longer wanted her sexually. He took her bag for whatever money was in it and her underwear as a keepsake, to remind him how thrilling it was to stalk her, threaten her, and kill her."

Neither of us spoke for a moment. Meltzer glanced at his plate. There were still some potatoes left on it, but he pushed it away. His appetite seemed to have deserted him.

"So that's it," he said. "A woman's dead, and a brutal killer is still at large. I wish it were different. I wish you the best of luck in catching him. But if I were a betting man, Adam, I'd put money that you won't."

15

I was back in Tel Aviv by three o'clock. The bus station stank of road dust and diesel fumes. The air was still and baking hot. Around me, people were flapping hats or folded-up newspapers in a feeble attempt to cool themselves.

After buying a soda from a kiosk, I consulted my notebook and settled myself on a bench to wait for the bus to ferry me uptown. As I waited, I thought over my conversation with Inspector Meltzer. Before I met him, I'd expected Meltzer to be at least partially incompetent. How else could he have been so utterly fooled by Dahlia's lies?

Now I believed differently. Meltzer had impressed me as a discerning, observant detective. I suspected that I, in his place, would have been equally hoodwinked.

Meltzer had obliquely given me two assignments. I planned to complete both by sundown.

It took twenty minutes for the bus to meander its way through the city to my chosen stop. From there it was a short walk to my destination. An apartment building in the upper section of Shalom Aleichem Street. It was, I noted, not that far from Esther

Cinema—which Anna had visited the night of the murder—and about the same distance to Trumpeldor Cemetery, where she was killed.

In five years, people can move quite a bit, so I was relieved to see the name Wexler printed in feminine script on her door. I knocked and only had to wait a little bit before the door swung open and I found myself staring at empty space. I lowered my gaze and realized in an instant why Meltzer believed that Ofra Wexler had nothing to do with the murder of Anna Hartman.

According to the police report, Anna was five eight and athletic. The woman before me was no more than five feet and petite. Even armed with a knife, I doubted Ofra Wexler would have posed such an intimidating threat as to compel the much taller Anna to enter a cemetery at night without a fight.

Still, stranger things have happened.

This was not the first time I had seen Ofra Wexler. That had been on stage two nights ago. She had played Regan, one of King Lear's manipulative, power-hungry daughters. I remembered being impressed with her performance.

She'd looked different then, in a long medieval dress and her hair looped around her head in a crown braid. Now she wore a red shirt over a modern plaid skirt, and her black hair was pulled tightly into a bun, which accentuated the sharpness of her cheekbones and gave her a severe look. Despite this, she was an attractive woman, with small symmetrical features and a pair of intense jade-colored eyes. Her arms were slim, her hands slender, her fingers dainty and tipped with medium-length nails painted a shining white. The opposite of what you'd think of as murderer's hands, but that's hardly proof of anything. She had not been in Café Kassit with the rest of the actors after the play. I wondered why.

She asked for my name and I supplied it. Then I told her the reason for my visit and watched her lips part and her eyes dilate.

It might have been surprise. But it could also have been fear. It was hard to tell for sure. When I asked if we could talk, she hesitated.

"I don't have much time. I need to get to the theater soon. We're playing tonight."

I checked my wristwatch. It was just past four. "The show starts at seven thirty, doesn't it?"

"Well, yes, but I have to get there and put on my costume and makeup. It takes time to get ready."

"I understand. I'll do my best to keep it short. I'm sure you want to help me catch Anna's killer."

"Yes. Yes, of course."

She ushered me inside. Her apartment was small and homey. Frilly white curtains at the windows. A few dozen books in a tall book cabinet. A bulky typewriter on a small desk by the window. A doily on the end table by the two-seater couch, and on it a copy of a literary magazine. Nothing new or expensive, but it all fit together nicely.

Two chairs sandwiched the small square dining table, and she pulled one up and put it to its proper use. I occupied one half of the two-seater. A pack of cigarettes lay near the edge of the table, and she extracted one and set it aflame.

She blew out a ring of smoke and watched it lose shape and dissipate. "I was just thinking of Anna, you know." But both her detached tone and her flat expression were incongruous with her words.

"Oh? What brought that about?"

"Nothing specific. From time to time she simply enters my thoughts. Not as often as she once did, but at least once a month."

Which wasn't all that much in my book. But perhaps Ofra Wexler operated under a different set of measurements.

"I understand you two were longtime friends."

She nodded and took another drag. "We first met when we

were teenagers. We went to high school together, to Gymnasia Herzliya."

"How did Anna come to study there?"

"Her parents sent her over from Czechoslovakia. She was not the only foreign student in school. Before the Second World War, lots of foreign Jewish families enrolled their children there. Gymnasia Herzliya was known throughout the Jewish world. The first high school in the Land of Israel in which all lessons were conducted in Hebrew. And it had, and has, a well-deserved reputation for excellence. I had a wonderful time there."

"And Anna?"

"Anna fit right in. She'd learned to speak Hebrew back in Prague. I recall her saying that her mother taught her. Naturally, she wasn't totally fluent when she started school, but within a couple of months, she sounded just like the rest of us. She even managed to get rid of her accent. And she was beautiful and vivacious. She became very popular."

"Where did she live?"

"On Kfar Saba Street, in Neve Tzedek. Her parents rented a room for her in Mrs. Chernick's house. She's a widow, and she would always have a student staying with her."

"Did they get along?"

Ofra made a face and tapped loose ash into an oval ashtray. "About as well as fire and water. Mrs. Chernick was stuffy, old-fashioned, and strict. Anna was the exact opposite. You would think that a fifteen-year-old girl would find it hard to live apart from her parents—I know I would have—but she relished her independence. I think that living on her own in Tel Aviv felt like a big adventure to her, like she was a young heroine in a novel."

"Or a play," I said.

Ofra nodded. "Or a play."

"Did Anna and Mrs. Chernick—what's her first name, by the way?"

Ofra frowned, then let out a small "Huh," before saying, "Funny, but I don't know. I don't think I ever knew. I imagine that Anna knew, but we just called her Mrs. Chernick."

"That's fine," I said. "Did she and Anna ever fight?"

"Oh, yes. They would have fiery quarrels. Anna would tell me about them at school the next day. Mrs. Chernick wanted things a very certain way, and Anna rebelled against her restrictions. I don't blame Anna one bit for their not getting along. Mrs. Chernick was a very unpleasant woman. She looked at you like there was something dirty about you. I visited Anna at her house just once and that was enough."

"What sort of restrictions did she impose?"

"A curfew for one. And meals were to be eaten at specific times or not at all. And Anna had to keep her room spiffy clean before she went out. Mrs. Chernick also complained if Anna wore clothes she considered to be immodest or went out with her hair loose. One flare-up they had was when Mrs. Chernick caught Anna smoking in her room. She didn't allow smoking in her house."

"How old was Anna then?"

"Fifteen, sixteen. I can see you think that's way too young for a girl to smoke."

I did, but I saw no point in confirming or denying it. "I'm surprised Mrs. Chernick didn't kick her out."

"She needed the money, I suppose. Otherwise, I doubt she would have had any boarders at all, the old shrew."

I stifled a smile. There was something sweet about the fact that Ofra still held a grudge against Mrs. Chernick over the widow's mistreatment of Anna, even though more than a decade had passed since their school years.

Of course, her perception of what had transpired between Anna and her landlady might have been colored by their friendship. I made a mental note to pay Mrs. Chernick a visit and get her side of the story. She might let me see a side of Anna that no one else would.

"Was Anna's family well-off?" I asked.

Ofra shook her head slowly. "I don't think so. Anna's father worked in a glass factory; her mother was a housewife and school-teacher. I doubt they had a lot of money."

"In that case, how could they afford to send her here and pay for her schooling and rent?"

Ofra pondered the question and then spread her hands, palms up. "No idea. But maybe I got the wrong impression. Maybe they did have money. Is that important to your investigation?"

"I don't know," I said, thinking that it probably wasn't. "I'm just gathering facts, trying to learn all I can about Anna. Did she have any siblings?"

"One brother, two years her elder. There had also been a younger sister, but she died in infancy. Her parents and brother were all killed during the war."

"Did her brother also attend Gymnasia Herzliya?"

"No."

"Any idea why Anna's parents would send her to study in Tel Aviv and not him?"

A ruminative line appeared between her thin eyebrows. "Hmmm. I must admit the question never even crossed my mind. I suppose there could be all sorts of reasons, couldn't there?"

She was right about that. Maybe Anna's brother was ill. Or maybe he had an apprenticeship of some sort in Prague. Or maybe Anna was the smarter of the two. Or maybe her brother simply refused to go. Still, it was a question without an answer, so I tucked it away in a corner of my mind for later review.

"What sort of student was she?" I asked.

Ofra waggled her hand. "So-so. Anna was bright, but she never made much of an effort with her studies. The only thing in school she was enthusiastic about was the drama club."

"The drama club? What's that?"

"A theater group of students. We used to get together, read scripts, and act out scenes. Anna and I joined together. It was a small group, and not too many students stuck around for long. It's hard work—memorizing scenes, rehearsing, and so on. And there's no test or grade at the end to validate your effort. Nothing apart from a few mediocre productions we put on, all with very low attendance. Most teenagers prefer hanging out in the sun or on the beach."

"But not Anna," I said. "And not you, either."

"No," she agreed, and a wistful expression painted itself on her face, making her look both sadder and younger. "We both loved it. Becoming different people for a time, there's magic in that. It appealed to us both."

"Who ran the club?"

"Menashe Klausner."

"Is he an actor?"

She took a final pull on her cigarette and mashed it out. "He sure wished he was, heard he tried for several theaters over the years, including ours, but never got past the auditions. He taught literature. Probably still does." From her tone I got the impression she did not like Klausner much.

"How many students were in it?"

"Ten, twelve, fifteen. The number kept changing as some students joined while others quit. Like I said, most people at that age have more exciting pastimes. And even among those who stuck it out for a while, there were only a few who were serious about it."

"Like Anna?"

"Yes. She was very passionate about the drama club, too much even."

"Why do you say that?"

"Just that she took it too seriously. Like it was a real theater, and we were already real actresses."

"So she knew early on that she wanted to be a professional actress?"

"She wanted it more than anything. And soon after graduation, Shoresh Theater was holding auditions, so we went."

"And you both got hired?"

"Yes."

"Just the two of you?"

"No, there were three of us. Anna, myself, and a boy named Haggai Geller."

"Haggai Geller?" The name was unfamiliar to me. It wasn't mentioned in the police report. "He's no longer with the theater, is he?"

"No. He was with us for only two years. He joined the British Army in 1940, I think, and went off to fight in the war."

"Did he make it back?"

"Yes. I think he works for the city. At least that's what I heard."

"Why didn't he rejoin the theater?"

"I don't know. But it wouldn't surprise me if he tried and was told to get lost. Truth is, Haggai was a mediocre actor at best. He would constantly get berated for this or that inadequacy. I'm surprised he lasted the two years."

"Did he and Anna get along?"

An unpleasant little smile slithered across her face. "Hardly. In fact, I think Anna had more to do with Haggai becoming a soldier than any desire he had to fight the Germans."

"What do you mean?"

"It was like a dreary romance novel, at least in part. He was infatuated with her. Ever since high school. But she didn't want him. It was quite pathetic to see sometimes, the way he mooned over her. Then one day he came to work and announced that he had enlisted,

127

that he was off to fight Hitler. Then he looked right at Anna and said, 'And when I get to Prague, Anna, I'll personally get your family out and bring them here.'" Ofra rolled her eyes, making it crystal clear how ridiculous she found Geller's promise to have been.

"What was Anna's reaction?"

"It was the damnedest thing. I was sure she would laugh in Haggai's face, but instead she went to him, threw her arms around his neck, pressed her body tight against his, and gave him a long, passionate kiss. We were all astounded."

"We?"

"All the actors. We were all there. We watched her kiss him in dead silence, like an audience at the most suspenseful moment of a play."

"And Geller?"

"He was as dumbstruck as the rest of us. And excited. You could tell that by his flushed cheeks, shallow breath, and, well, you can imagine what else."

"I see," I said, feeling a tingle of distaste at her flippant tone. Geller's gesture might have been juvenile, and certainly naive, but he had still gone off to fight evil. He deserved more respect.

"And the next day he shipped out," she said. "And that was the last I saw of him."

"Did he and Anna keep in touch during his absence?"

"I don't know."

"Did they meet after his return?"

"Not a clue."

"Did she ever talk of him again after he left?"

"Not when I was around. It appeared that she'd forgotten him entirely."

"Did this surprise you?"

"What surprised me was that she kissed him."

"Why did she do it?"

"I asked her that very question. She said she wanted to give him a gift before he went to war." Ofra shrugged, as if to say she found Anna's action inexplicable.

I took a moment to consider the matter myself, wondering what it meant, what it said of Anna's character, but failed to come to any conclusion.

Ofra was examining her watch. "Anything else, Mr. Lapid? I really should be getting ready."

"Just a couple of minutes more," I said, "if that's all right."

She sighed theatrically. "Go ahead."

"Can you tell me whether Anna was involved with anyone in the year before she died?"

"Not to my knowledge."

I frowned. "You don't sound sure. Wouldn't you know, you being her friend?"

"Anna and I stopped being friends long before her death."

Ah, so that was the reason she was impatient with me. Either that or she had something more sinister to hide.

"Why is that?" I asked.

"We drifted apart. It happens."

I waited, but evidently that was all she was going to say on the subject.

"Did she also stop liking you, or was it just one-sided?" I asked.

"What makes you think I stopped liking her?"

"You do, Miss Wexler. You make it quite clear."

Her eyes narrowed and she gave me a long look. The green of her eyes, peeking between her nearly touching eyelashes, darkened in hue. "You're starting to annoy me, Mr. Lapid."

I feigned contrition. "I don't mean to, Miss Wexler. But I'd still like to know why your friendship ended."

"What difference does it make? It was a long time ago, and it has nothing to do with your investigation."

"Was it because you were competing for the same parts?"

She hesitated, then shrugged, and I took it as a yes.

"Was she a good actress?" I asked.

"Yes," Ofra said, sounding as though she were offering a painful concession.

"Better than you?"

She snorted. "Not even close."

"Yet she got the bigger parts, didn't she?"

A muscle pulsed in her cheek. Her jaw clenched.

"And when Dahlia Rotner had her accident," I said, "Anna was chosen to fill her shoes and not you. That must have hurt."

Her eyes flashed as bright as a forest fire. "Fill Dahlia's shoes! That's a laugh. She wasn't fit to shine them."

"And you were?"

She closed her eyes, taking a deep breath. When she opened them again, the fire had subsided. She looked resigned and enraged at the same time. "No, I wasn't. Dahlia was a better actress than I'll ever be. But between Anna and myself, I was the better choice."

"Yet she was chosen."

"Yes."

"And that made you angry."

"Of course it did."

"Where were you the night of the murder?"

She stared at me in amazement. "Are you serious?"

"Deadly."

"I don't have to answer that question."

"No. But answer it anyway. Or do you have something to hide?"

"I was here."

"Alone?"

"You think I killed Anna? You're insane."

"You had a better motive than anyone else. And you have no alibi, do you?"

"I was in my bed. Asleep. And, yes, I was alone."

"That's quite convenient."

"It's also the truth."

"So you say."

"I. Did. Not. Kill. Her." She enunciated each word slowly and with emphasis. "I was no longer her friend, and I did not like her anymore. She thought too highly of herself and too little of me. And yes, you could say I benefited when she died. But I did not murder her." She paused, her small chest heaving, and in a voice shaking with indignation, added, "And you have no right to speak to me like that."

I studied her. Every muscle in her face was as taut as a hangman's rope. If she were acting, she was doing a fine job. God damn this case. Just about every suspect was a liar by trade. Maybe Meltzer had it right and Ofra was innocent. But she did have a strong reason to kill Anna, and she clearly more than disliked her erstwhile friend. She resented her fiercely, and such resentment can lead a person to do dreadful things.

Her size suggested it would have been difficult for her to do the deed herself, though certainly not beyond the realm of possibility. And she could have hired it out. Did she know someone who might be persuaded to take on such an assignment? And had that person decided that he would enjoy raping his victim before ending her life? I might have asked her about it, but it was clear I had pushed her as far as she would go. It was a miracle she hadn't thrown me out yet.

"I apologize, Miss Wexler," I said. "It gives me no pleasure to ask these questions, but I must." Before she could say anything, I continued, "I know it was Isser Rotner who picked Anna to take over for his wife. Do you know why he did so?"

"Because Isser likes his leading ladies to be beautiful."

Like Pnina Zelensky, I thought.

"Were he and Anna having an affair?"

She did not look shocked by the question. "Not that I know. But it wouldn't surprise me. I suspect he's having an affair with our current leading lady." She said those last two words with venomous mockery.

"Pnina Zelensky."

"Yes. So you see, Mr. Lapid, that any benefit I might have derived from Anna's death was purely temporary. As I knew it would be. I'm simply not pretty enough to remain our theater's lead actress for long."

I believed that last bit. Which made me detest Rotner even more.

"Did you, by any chance, tell Dahlia Rotner about her husband and Pnina Zelensky?" I asked, remembering how Dahlia had refused to tell me who had exposed her husband to her.

Ofra shook her head. "I haven't spoken with or seen Dahlia in years."

"You never visit her?"

"No."

"Any reason why not?"

"Because I don't wish to see her. Dahlia is an incredible actress, but she's also a horrible person. Make a tiny mistake or don't perform as well as she thinks you should, and she'll not only criticize you harshly in front of everyone, she'll encourage the others to join her. I'd prefer not to spend any time with her."

"Yet you admire her."

"Of course. She is brilliant."

It was easy to believe that as well. Ofra eyed her watch and rose to her feet. "Time's up, Mr. Lapid. I must insist that you leave now."

I stood, and she began urging me toward the door. "Just one more question," I said. "When you auditioned for the theater, there were three people who decided to hire you. Dahlia and Isser Rotner were two. Who was the third?"

She paused, and something shifted in her face, softening the lines and edges. "Eliezer Dattner. He started the theater with Dahlia and Isser."

"What happened to him?" I asked. Because he hadn't been interviewed by Meltzer.

She swallowed hard and lowered her eyes. "He's dead. He was shot by an Arab in 1939, during the Arab Revolt."

"And afterward Dahlia and Isser ran the theater together?"

"Yes." She opened the door, and I stepped out onto the landing and turned back to face her. She raised her eyes and I was startled by the hard coldness in them. "And now Isser runs it all by himself," she said, and then shut the door in my face.

16

From Ofra Wexler's apartment, it was a short walk south to Trumpeldor Street and then east to the cemetery.

Trumpeldor Cemetery had been opened in 1902, seven years before the establishment of Tel Aviv itself. Only it had a different name then, but I do not know what it was. Yosef Trumpeldor, the legendary soldier, would fall to an Arab bullet eighteen years later in Tel Hai, in the northern tip of Israel. His dying words, "Never mind, it's good to die for one's country," would immortalize him as a paragon of Zionist devotion and self-sacrifice and ensure his name would be forever spoken with reverential adoration. The street bordering the cemetery to the south would be named after him, and with it, the cemetery itself.

Initially, the cemetery served as a burial site for the Jews of Jaffa, who at the time were being ravaged by an outbreak of cholera. Those Jews would carry their dead north across the barren plains upon which Tel Aviv would soon rise and inter them here, far removed from any residence.

That soon changed as Tel Aviv expanded rapidly, sending its tendrils in every direction, so that Trumpeldor Cemetery was now enveloped by residential streets. Consequently, the cemetery itself was relatively small and saw few new burials. Nowadays, the deceased residents of Tel Aviv were mostly buried in cemeteries further afield, such as those in Nahalat Yitzhak to the east and Kiryat Shaul to the north.

The cemetery was surrounded by a stone wall, six to nine feet in height, and had three gates, all facing south along Trumpeldor Street. The western gate was locked. The main gate—the middle one—stood open. I stepped through it and onto the grounds. Then stood a moment, gazing around me.

Spread before me was a sea of headstones jutting up in irregular shapes, looking like a miniature skyline of some American city one could see in the movies. There were no people about, though the tightly arrayed graves might have easily concealed a mourner or two.

To my right, extending along the entrance path, was a communal grave of Jews who had been murdered in the Jaffa Riots of 1921. Behind that stretched two other such graves. The first of the victims of the Great Arab Revolt of 1936-1939. And the second, set against the southern wall, of those slaughtered during the Arab riots of 1929, in which local Arabs committed widespread atrocities against Jews, and in which several Jewish communities—such as those in Gaza, Jenin, and Nablus—were evacuated by the British and ceased to exist.

I stood quite still and ran my eyes over the names of the dead. All had been murdered for being Jewish. All had died as part of the terrible conflict that had raged between Jews and Arabs during the British Mandate of Palestine. One could look upon these tombstones and hope that such mass killings were a thing of the past now that we Jews had a country and an army to protect us, but I did not believe it. Our struggle for life and liberty on this tiny patch of land was far from over.

Walking on, I retraced the steps taken by Pinchas Sheftel on that fateful day five years ago, venturing to the western section of the cemetery. Here, some of the more famous residents of old Tel Aviv were buried, the men and women who had breathed life into this first modern Hebrew metropolis and imbued it with purpose and culture and meaning. The people whose names now adorned street signs throughout the city.

There was the large blocky headstone of Haim Nahman Bialik, the famous poet, and adjacent to it, the much smaller stone of his wife, Manya. Behind those towered a pinkish monolith bearing the name Ahad Ha'am, the influential Zionist intellectual and essayist. And near both lay the remains of Zionist leader Haim Arlozorov, who was shot to death on the beach of Tel Aviv in 1933 by unknown assassins.

A few steps to the north stood the mausoleum of Max Nordau, close confidant of Theodor Herzl, founder of Zionism. And a few meters north of that rested Shaul Tchernichovsky, renowned poet and pediatrician.

And in between Nordau and Tchernichovsky was the spot in which a young woman after which no street would ever be named was killed. The scene of the murder of Anna Hartman. The grave of Mayor and Mrs. Dizengoff.

The grave was far from a simple one. The couple had been accorded a grander final resting place than any other inhabitant of the cemetery.

It was also elevated from the ground, as befitted their high status. Five wide stairs climbed to a rectangular stone platform enclosed by walls on three sides. Upon the platform squatted a flat tombstone, roughly six feet long and two and a half feet wide. The tombstone itself was free of inscription. The names of the deceased and the Jewish dates of their birth and death were stamped in large letters on the rear wall, so they could be read from afar.

The sun shone directly into my eyes as I gazed at the names, and I realized that the grave itself faced east.

Was this done on purpose? To emulate the direction in which a Jew would face as he said his prayers, toward Jerusalem? Perhaps Mayor Dizengoff had wished it so.

Fronting the grave was a small open paved area, a unique luxury in the cramped and crowded cemetery. Here, I supposed, people would gather in relative comfort during memorials.

Moving slowly, as though this were still a fresh crime scene, I crossed this paved forecourt, mounted the stairs, and climbed to the platform, my eyes scanning every inch of stone around me.

Whatever I had hoped to find after all this time was gone. There was no blood. No trace of the violence committed here. No sign of the young life cut short. No sense of wrongness. There was just the dusty, featureless stone of the stairs, the platform, and the tombstone itself.

I squatted next to the tombstone and ran my hand over its surface, as though by touch I could somehow coax from the stone a detailed witness account of the tragic events of that night. The stone was smooth and warm, pleasant if one forgot that it had once borne the body of a murdered woman. Here, precisely where my palm now rested, Anna's body had lain. Here her blood had oozed from the hole in her chest. Here her life had drained out of her.

Did a part of her life, along with some of her blood, seep into the stone? Was a piece of her still here? The hair on my forearms rose with the thought. *Careful, Adam. Don't wander about. Stay focused.*

I rose to my full height, brushed dust off my hand, and descended the stairs. I made a slow circuit of the murder scene, finding more street names etched into headstones, but nothing that related to the case. Back in the open area before the Dizengoffs' grave, I took a careful look around. The headstones surrounding me ranged in style and size and grandeur. Some were simple flat stones laid at ground level, the writing on them faded. Others stood erect as obelisks, reaching up to the heavens. Some bore nothing but the names of the deceased, while others were etched with beautiful poetic inscriptions, some biblical and others that originated in the shattered heart of a mournful loved one.

Over the cemetery walls I could see the second- and third-floor apartments on surrounding streets—Pinsker, Hovevei Tsiyon, Trumpeldor, and the bottom end of Tverya Street. From those windows and balconies, one had a clear view of the cemetery. But at night, with the grounds unlit, with all these tall and irregular shapes protruding and casting weird shadows, it would be difficult to make anything out. And the murder scene itself, walled as it was on three sides, would be screened from view. Especially since it was located near the western edge of the cemetery, so that its open side—the eastern—was far from any neighbor's roving eye.

The killer had chosen the murder spot well, suggesting forethought rather than a spur-of-the-moment eruption of murderous fury. This was what Meltzer had known I'd conclude the moment I visited the crime scene.

Had the killer known Anna? Had he scouted her neighborhood and passed by the cemetery in the process? Had he wandered inside, treading between these memorials of life and death, searching for the best place to slake his depraved thirst? Had he stood where I now did and pictured in his mind how he would do it? How it would feel to bring Anna here, to this spot, where he could have his way with her?

Or had he been a stranger to her? Had he simply lain in wait for a young, attractive woman to defile, and Anna had had the misfortune of catching his eye?

The latter option was unwelcome. Because if that were the case, then my chances of catching the murderer were close to nil.

Which was why I decided to work on the assumption, at least for the time being, that Anna had known her killer.

Which made me think of Isser Rotner.

He certainly could have done it. He knew where Anna lived. He might have known of her plans for that night. Hell, he might have learned of them from her own lips.

And, of course, there was the matter of the false alibi.

But what was his motive? If he and Anna were lovers, why would he try to rape her? And why kill her?

Maybe she had broken off their affair. He was the sort of man who would not take such a rejection kindly. Or maybe she had threatened to expose his infidelity to Dahlia, and he decided to shut her up.

And then he persuaded his wife to lie on his behalf. To help him get away with the brutal slaughter of a young woman.

At that moment, I was struck by the acute wrongness of the crime that had been committed here, in this tranquil island of remembrance. A cemetery is a holy place. Which is why the defacing of headstones, or the smashing of them, enrages the soul. But little desecrates a place more than murder does.

So in a way, the killer had sinned not merely against Anna, but also against all those who slumbered here for all eternity, as well as those who were left behind to grieve over them.

All of a sudden, I felt the weight of all these stones, and the lives they commemorated, press upon me so tightly that my breath grew short and labored. Or perhaps it was the memory of other lives, and other deaths, those that were not recorded on any headstone, that was crushing me like a mountain of sorrow. All those millions who were turned to dust and ashes, or who were buried in huge mass graves without a word of prayer said for them—those whose names were lost forever.

Closing my eyes, I took a deep breath and let it out in a long, guttural sigh. For a few seconds, I felt hot and dizzy, tremulous on my feet. The mundane noises of the city grew faint and distant, as though I had been removed to another place and time.

And then, after a minute or maybe much more, the disconcerting sensation passed. My legs were steady once again. My ears resumed their normal function. My breath ran easy and unencumbered.

I opened my eyes and took another look at the murder scene. If my visit here had brought me any closer to catching the killer, I would only know this later on. For now, it seemed that there was nothing more for me to do here.

Or perhaps there was.

Scouring the earth between the closely laid headstones, I quickly found what I was looking for. With my bounty clutched in one fist, I again climbed the five stairs that led to the tombstone upon which a young actress was found dead.

And on this tombstone I laid three stones, according to Jewish custom. The first for Mayor Dizengoff; the second for his wife, Zina; and the third, smooth and small and alabaster white, for Anna Hartman.

17

It was coming up on six by the time I emerged from the main gate of the cemetery. It was still light, the sun low in the western sky, and still hot, though not as much as before.

I rubbed a dry hand over my face, getting a powerful whiff of stone dust as my palm swept over my nose. The same palm that had touched Mayor and Mrs. Dizengoff's headstone, with Anna's blood absorbed into it.

I had been to the place where Anna had died. Now I wanted to visit the place where she'd lived. It was in the northern section of Hovevei Tsiyon Street, a third-floor apartment that looked out onto the cemetery across the road. Standing at the foot of the building, I was struck by the chilling realization that every time she stepped onto her balcony, Anna had gazed upon the scene of her future violent death, without ever knowing it. This I confirmed a few minutes later, as I was invited into the apartment by the couple who now lived there, and shown onto the balcony. From there I gazed down at the forest of headstones below. As I suspected, the Dizengoffs' headstone was hidden from view by the walls of their burial plot.

The current residents had lived in the apartment for three years and had never heard of Anna. The apartment had been empty when they moved in. Nothing of Anna remained there.

I went through the building, knocking on doors, talking to whoever answered. Not everyone was home, and not all those who were had lived in the building when Anna did. One neighbor said Anna had been friendly and well mannered but claimed to know next to nothing about her. Another said she'd seen her on stage a few times, and when she'd complimented Anna on one of her performances, Anna had been gracious but did not invite further conversation. Neither of them recalled seeing Anna in the company of a man or remembered anyone visiting her apartment.

Mr. Bayefsky, an elderly neighbor with a thick Russian accent and eyes the color of storm clouds, said he had been heartbroken when Anna died.

"She was a lovely girl. Just lovely. Kind, sweet, generous. A couple of months before her death, I was hospitalized for two weeks, and I had no one to care for darling Cleo here." Cleo raised her furry head at the mention of her name, gazed at me with sleepy eyes, and lowered her head back onto her paws. She was draped over Bayefsky's lap.

"Cleo's the only family I have," Bayefsky said, "and I worried about her well-being more than I did about my own, ill though I was. None of the other neighbors agreed to care for her—each had their own inventive excuse—but Anna agreed instantly and with evident joy. She fed her, walked her, played with her, made sure she had everything she needed. And each day, she came to visit me at the hospital to tell me how Cleo was doing. I cannot tell you how much that meant to me, Mr. Lapid. I believe it played a big part in my swift recovery."

He laid a liver-spotted hand on the dog's white fur and stroked it with the tenderness of a mother's touch.

"When I came home, I offered to pay Anna for her trouble, but she adamantly refused. She said it had been her pleasure, that Cleo was great company, and said something about maybe getting a dog herself. And maybe she would have if she hadn't been killed. I wish to God you'll catch whoever did it."

I assured him I would do my best.

"You know what I think, Mr. Lapid? I think Anna jumped at the chance of having Cleo around because she was lonely. She never said as much, but that's what I intimated. Do you have a dog, Mr. Lapid?"

I told him I didn't.

"That's too bad," he said, gazing affectionately at the dog snoring lightly on his lap. "A dog's the best cure for loneliness a person could find. Much better than other people."

In the rear ground-floor apartment, I heard a much different tale. The teller was Margalit Blissberg, a twenty-five-year-old nurse with a square face, plain features, and a sturdy little body.

"I didn't like her at first," she said flatly. "Mostly because I could tell my husband was attracted to her. The man was an inveterate womanizer. Or—" she added with a sneer "—he saw himself as one. I don't know what made that idiot believe he could seduce Anna; she was much too beautiful for him."

She paused, giving me an amused look that made it clear she knew full well what this last remark said about her. "I'm comfortable with who I am, Mr. Lapid. I'll never turn heads, nor do I want to. If you ask me, too much manly attention is a curse. A beautiful woman may get a boatload of compliments, gifts, and free meals, but she also has to fend off a swarm of slobbering men with nothing but bad intentions. Not a good bargain, far as I'm concerned. All I'm after is one good man with a solid brain and a pure heart, and you don't need to look like a film star for that."

She waited for me to say something, almost challenging me to contradict her, but all I said was, "You were telling me about your husband..."

"Ex-husband," she said, showing me her ringless left hand. "Like I said, the idiot lusted after Anna. At first I blamed her for it, because there was something suggestive about her. Nothing I could put my finger on exactly, but we women can tell such things about each other. It was like she was trying to get the attention of every man in sight, and I actually thought she was trying to steal my husband from me. Which, I'm embarrassed to say, made me an even bigger idiot than he was."

"What changed your mind about her?" I asked.

"My own two eyes, that's what. I had gone out one evening for a night shift at the hospital, only when I got there, I discovered I'd gotten the days mixed up. I wasn't due until the following night. So I came back here, and when I got in the building, I heard voices drifting down the stairwell from upstairs. My husband's voice and Anna's. I padded my way up and saw my husband trying to kiss Anna by her door. But she averted her head and pushed him off her so hard he banged his back against the railing, which served him right, the bastard."

"What happened then?"

"He cursed her, called her a whore for leading him on. I stood there, dumbstruck, my hand pressed to my chest, but Anna was unruffled. She just told him to go away, back to me, and said something about not being interested in a man younger than her."

"Younger than her? You sure that's what she said?"

"I can't quote her exact words—by that point my heart was drumming so loud in my ears it's a wonder I heard anything—but it was something like that."

"Seems an odd thing to say."

"Not really. Most women wouldn't go out with a younger man."

"I mean it's an odd thing to say at that moment."

"I agree, but I don't really care what she said or what she meant. All I care about is what she did, which was to put my idiot ex-husband in his place. And for showing me in a way I couldn't deny anymore the kind of lowlife he was. She set me free. I divorced him soon after."

"You were interviewed by the police five years ago," I said. "Why didn't you tell them any of this?"

"All they asked me was whether I heard or saw anything the night Anna died. Or if I ever saw her with a man, which I didn't." She paused, and for the first time her tough veneer cracked and I glimpsed the hurt her ex-husband had caused her. "I also didn't want to talk about it at the time. I felt ashamed my husband cheated on me. Which was stupid. Now I don't care anymore."

"Where is your husband now?" I asked, thinking he likely held a grudge against Anna and might have decided to pay her back for rebuffing him.

"After the divorce, he moved to Nahariya and got remarried. As it happens, the wedding was the same night poor Anna was killed. The bastard actually sent me an invitation, can you believe that? I thought that was low even for him."

"The wedding was in Nahariya?" I asked.

"Yes. And last I heard, they still live there, still married. I feel sorry for his wife."

"You're sure it was the same night Anna died?"

"One hundred percent. I wish I could show you the invitation, but I tore it up and flushed the pieces down the toilet the day it arrived."

Which meant the husband was off the hook. He had as solid an alibi as they come. Nahariya was a few hours' drive from Tel Aviv.

Margalit Blissberg said, "My opinion of Anna changed completely that night. You might think I'd feel envious or resentful of her, but I never did. I wanted us to become friends, but that didn't happen." Her tone became softer now, when she had said her last word about her ex-husband and only had Anna to speak of. "I don't think Anna was an easy person to get close to. There was something sad about her, something you only saw if you looked hard enough to see past her beauty. I don't know what caused it, but it was there all right, deep in those pretty eyes of hers. I was terribly sorry when she died. Because she was a good person, and because she gave me the chance to build a better life. And also because I knew that when she died, it was with that sadness still inside her."

18

Emerging from the building where Anna had lived, I leaned against a tree and lit a cigarette. I expelled each lungful in a long, emptying whoosh, as though trying to get rid of all the sorrow that had invaded my chest, along with the smoke. My head throbbed and my stomach was grumbling. I'd been on the move for nearly the entire day and had eaten nothing since my lunch with Meltzer. In twenty, twenty-five minutes I could be at Greta's Café. Hot food awaited me there, as did my chessboard and the prospect of a stitch of time in which I would not have to talk or think about Anna Hartman and who might have killed her. And, of course, there was Greta herself.

I'd taken two dozen steps with that destination in mind, when it occurred to me that there was another man I might seek out first. Someone who lived very close by. Talking to him would likely prove fruitless, but as I was already in the neighborhood...

My mind made up, I hastened westward to the corner of Trumpeldor and Ben Yehuda, which was the address I had for Eliyahu Toledano.

It was a handsome three-story building, with long, narrow

balconies that curled around the building's exterior like a smile. His apartment was on the top floor.

I knocked on his door and frowned as a baby's mirthful squeal pierced through the wood. Two seconds later, the originator of said squeal was staring right at me with two huge, impossibly blue eyes.

She was too young to have opened the door herself. That had been accomplished by the woman who held her expertly with one hand.

The similarity between them was striking. A mother and daughter, no doubt. But where was the drunkard Toledano?

The baby squirmed playfully in her mother's grip, her chubby legs pumping up and down like pistons. A little pink bow was tied in her fine amber hair. She let out another joyful squeal, then stuck four fingers deep in her mouth and began sucking on them with admirable diligence.

The mother—pleasantly exhausted, as all good new mothers tend to be—gave me a smile and inquired gently as to the purpose of my visit.

"My name is Adam Lapid," I said. "Sorry to bother you, but it seems that I'm at the wrong address. I'm looking for Eliyahu Toledano. I understand he used to live here."

"He still does," she said. "Why do you think you're in the wrong place? Eliyahu's in his study. Why don't you wait in the living room and I'll go fetch him?"

The apartment did not look like the habitat of a drunk. Neat, tidy, with curtains on the windows and a few tasteful pictures on the walls. The furniture in the living room was of good quality and could not have been older than five or six years. Flowerpots bloomed on the balcony.

I was in the living room for less than a minute when I heard footsteps drawing near. I turned and saw a man approach with a held-out hand and a question in his eyes.

"My wife told me you wished to see me, Mr. Lapid?"

I shook his hand, slowly taking in his features.

"You're Eliyahu Toledano?" I asked with incredulity.

The man smiled. "Is that so hard to believe? You are in my apartment, after all."

He looked nothing like the man Meltzer had described to me. Clear-eyed, straight-backed, with recently barbered black hair and a mustache whose exact symmetry could only have been achieved by careful husbandry. His clothes were clean and pressed. His breath was fresh. The skin on his face displayed none of the slackness induced by excessive consumption of alcohol. He looked like a healthy man of twenty-five or so. This was no drunk.

"Forgive me, Mr. Toledano, but what I was told about you led me to expect a different sort of man."

"Ah," he said, and that one syllable carried with it a sea of understanding and an ocean of regret. "Perhaps you'd care to tell me why you came to see me?"

"I'd like to talk to you about the night you might have seen a murderer exit Trumpeldor Cemetery."

Toledano's face registered surprise. "Are you a policeman?"

"A private investigator. But I've read the police report and talked to the detective who investigated the case. He told me of your testimony."

Toledano glanced over his shoulder. From another room came the sound of his wife cooing to the baby, and the high-pitched, ecstatic reply of the infant.

"Let's go out on the balcony," he said.

Once there, he explained, "My wife knows about that night, but she doesn't know everything about the man I used to be." With a sigh, he leaned both hands on the stone railing, as though trying to support the weight of his past. "About how low I allowed myself to sink."

The balcony was bathed in the gentle sunlight of early

evening. The sweet scents of daisies and carnations and lilies rose from the flowerpots, wafting about us like incense.

With his head lowered, Toledano said, "After my parents died, I came apart. I was inconsolable. I found refuge in a bottle. In multiple bottles."

He turned to face me, and I saw the anguish and guilt in his eyes. "Everything they taught me, all the lessons they imparted, were scattered like dry leaves in a wind. I did nothing but drink. For two years of my life, I was a prisoner of my own weakness and self-pity. My recollection of that time is patchy, as though I was only awake for brief snatches of time. There are whole days of which I remember nothing. And then...then came that night."

"What can you tell me about it?" I asked.

"Not much. And if that policeman hadn't come calling, I'd probably remember nothing at all. Much worse, I'd probably be dead."

"Why do you say that?"

"I was drinking so much that I was barely a man anymore. I would fall asleep on park benches, on street corners. Once I awoke from a blackout to find myself on the beach with my legs soaked to my knees by encroaching waves. I was drinking myself straight into an early grave. What happened that night finally made me change course."

"In what way?"

"I was finally confronted with the consequences of my drunkenness. I cared nothing for myself in those days, but I was still my parents' son. They'd brought me up to be a good man, and here I was, a potential witness to a murderer's escape from the scene of his crime, and I had almost no recollection of it." Toledano shook his head, his brown eyes glittering with tears. "If I hadn't been so drunk, I would have remembered his face clearly."

"If you hadn't been drinking, you wouldn't have been on that sidewalk in the first place," I pointed out.

Toledano flicked me a sad, grateful smile. "I know what you're saying is true, but it doesn't change what happened. That night was like a much-needed slap in the face. I realized I could not go on the way I was. I stopped drinking, resumed living. I became a man again."

I asked, "Now that you're sober, do you remember anything more about the man you saw that night?"

Toledano screwed his eyes shut and gave a despaired shake of his head. "I thought about him a thousand—no, a million—times since then. The only thing I remember is that he had a dark beard. Everything else remains shrouded, and I can't tear through that shroud, no matter how hard I try."

"But you're sure it was no dream?"

"Yes. Of that I'm certain. He was real. I saw him."

"And you're sure he came out of the main gate?"

"It's exactly where he crossed the street. So yes, I'm sure."

"But you remember nothing about him apart from the beard?"

"Nothing." But I saw hesitation tiptoe its way across his face.

"What is it?" I asked. "Is something new coming to you?"

"Nothing specific, I'm afraid. It's just a vague sense I have about that man, about his walk."

"His walk?" A prickle of excitement darted up my back. "What about his walk?"

"I can't say for sure whether it's real or not."

"That's all right," I said. "Just tell me what it is."

Toledano sighed, dragged both hands through his hair, and said, "There was something wrong with it."

"Wrong? How?"

He threw up his hands. "I don't know. That's what I told you, it's nothing specific. It's just a feeling I have. There was something strange about his walk. Something not right."

"Did he stagger? Limp?"

"I don't know."

"Did he favor one leg over the other? Walk stiffly? Think, Goddammit!"

"I don't know!" he shouted, and then caught himself and cast a worried look into his living room. His wife stood there, still holding the baby, and on her face was a look of shock and concern.

"It's all right, Shula," Toledano called to her. "We'll be done in a minute or two."

Shula Toledano nodded and left the living room. Her husband turned back to me. "If I knew, I'd tell you. I'd tell the police. But I just don't know what about his walk was wrong, only that there was something."

"How long have you had this feeling?"

"Not long. Six weeks, two months, something like that."

"So maybe your memory is clearing up."

"Maybe. But at this rate, I'll be long gone before I remember anything useful."

I studied his face. Remorse molded every line, shaped every ridge and crease. I was angry at him, for his failure of memory, but I also felt sorry for him, sensing the burden of guilt he carried.

"How sure are you of this, Mr. Toledano? The walk, I mean. How sure are you that your memory is real?"

He examined his feet, then blew out a breath and shrugged helplessly. "As much as I can be, given my condition at the time."

I nodded, disappointed and frustrated, though I hadn't expected any better. I stared across the street at a treetop in which two birds were duetting. A love song by the sound of it.

"I'm sorry," Toledano said. "I'm so sorry. I wish I remembered more. That poor woman, I owe her so much."

I did not need to ask who "her" was.

"Without her," he went on, "I would not have met my wife. And my daughter, Hannah, would never have been born."

I looked at him. "You named your daughter Hannah?"

"Yes. After that poor woman, Anna Hartman. Hannah is the Hebrew version of Anna, you know."

I nodded, thinking how the death of one woman had saved the life of a good man, and how that good man had then brought a beautiful baby girl into this world. And I wondered how many people would never have been born if another person hadn't died. If we went back enough time, perhaps the answer is everyone.

Then I considered how, like a new shoot that grows from scorched earth, so new life can spring from tragedy, if only one decides not to mire oneself in grief. I thought about my own daughters and felt that familiar pain that is eternal as the sun and moon.

And then my mind veered in an entirely different direction, and before my eyes I saw Isser Rotner. First as King Lear, and later walking to his car on Dizengoff Street to await his lover.

His walk had been perfect. Not a single thing wrong with it.

But there was another person whose walk was definitely impaired. A person who, until now, I hadn't considered a suspect at all.

I thanked Toledano for his time and departed. My earlier desire for food had been supplanted by a more urgent need. I had one more place to be, one more person to see, before I went to Greta's Café.

And as long as she remained in character, I was certain she'd be home.

19

I could have rung her from somewhere along the way, but I chose
not to. I wanted my visit to be a total surprise. I figured she'd be
alone. Her husband was working.

Her door was locked, so I knocked, waited a bit, and knocked
again, this time harder. Then came her voice, loud and resonant,
telling me to go away. I leaned my face close to the door and called
out my name, told her I had to see her. There was quiet for a
while, then her voice again, saying it would be a minute.

It ended up close to two. I spent them in silence, staring at her
closed door, wondering if this was all an elaborate setup, if I was
simply an unwitting extra in a play written and directed by her.
Then came the click of the door being unlocked, and a second
later I stood face-to-face with her.

She looked like a grounded ship, proud and majestic, but
listing to one side. Her cane was keeping her up. She was leaning
hard on it; I could tell that by the tension in her forearm and hand.
She gripped the handle like a gun, her forefinger curled under-
neath, as though resting on a trigger, ready for firing.

Her face was tight with effort, or with the simulation of it. Who could tell with her? What was definitely real were the sweat beads on her forehead and the flush tinting her cheeks. Could she do that on command? Make herself sweat and flush? Were her powers as wide-ranging as that?

"This had better be good, Mr. Lapid," she said, eying me coolly. But I could tell she was also curious.

"Good or bad," I said, "that depends on your perspective. Either way, it's important that we talk."

I entered her apartment and waited while she shut the door. She said, "Could I borrow your arm?"

I held it out to her, and she gripped it tightly just under the elbow. And so, with slow, small steps we made our way together to the living room, like a couple entering a formal ball.

Only no one seeing us would have thought there would be any dancing in our future.

Even with the double support of my arm on one side and her cane on the other, her walk was unsteady. Her bad leg barely rose off the floor, and each time it came down again, it was like a threat that had narrowly failed to materialize—as though she had, at the very last instant, managed to keep from collapsing. And with each misshapen step, her grip on my arm intensified, fingers digging into my flesh, as though trying to transmit her pain to me, the person who had caused her to walk to the door and back again.

If this was playacting, it was the greatest performance I had ever witnessed.

Neither of us spoke on the way to the living room. I walked her to the sofa and she lowered herself to the cushion with elegant relief. Then she smoothed her well-fitting pearl-gray dress over her knees and propped her cane by her side. Only after everything was arranged did she raise her eyes to me. I remained standing and was looking intently at her face, trying to read the lie that I suspected was lurking there. But all I saw was a vain woman striving to mask the excruciating effort the simple task of walking had required of her, and doing a damn fine job of it. Or it was merely another layer of subterfuge.

"You might have called in advance, Mr. Lapid," she said. "If you had, I'd have put the kettle on."

"I wouldn't dream of putting you to the trouble."

"It's no trouble."

It would have to be, given her condition. She couldn't just load everything on a tray and carry it over from the kitchen. She would have to bring each item by itself. The pot, the cups, the saucers. Everything. A Herculean effort. If her injuries were authentic.

"I'm not here for coffee," I said.

"Then why are you here? Do share."

I stepped over to the chair I'd used on my previous visit and sat in it. I said nothing for a minute, just looked at her.

She said, "A lengthy silence at the beginning of a scene is a major faux pas, Mr. Lapid. The audience is bound to get bored and restless."

"You don't seem to be either of those things."

"Because there's something in your face that assures me you're not wasting my time. And though there's always the possibility that you've suddenly gone mad, I wager that's not it. You have something to tell me. Something related to the matter for which I hired you."

"Not tell you. Ask you."

"Ask away, then." She folded her hands in her lap.

I said, "Did you kill Anna Hartman?"

Her eyebrows jumped up, and then she burst out laughing. Her laughter was as rich as her voice, rolling and full-bodied. It was a short laugh, and when it died, she wiped her eyes with a forefinger. "Thank you, Mr. Lapid. That was quite invigorating."

"I wasn't joking," I said.

She looked at me. "No, I can tell that you weren't. So maybe you have gone mad after all."

"Answer the question."

"If I must. I did not kill that wretched woman. What on earth possessed you to think that I had?"

I hesitated, but saw no reason to keep the information to myself. "There was a witness that night who saw the killer leave Trumpeldor Cemetery, and he said there was something wrong with the killer's walk. Like a limp."

"Ah, I see. So naturally you thought of me."

"Naturally."

"You've seen me walk, Mr. Lapid. Do you really believe I'm in any shape to commit murder?"

"I've seen people do all sorts of things to avoid being suspected of murder. They lie, make up alibis; some even fake illnesses or injuries."

"You think I'm pretending to be an invalid?"

"People tell me you're a brilliant actress, Mrs. Rotner. If anyone could pull off such a ruse, it's you."

"But why would I hire you to investigate a murder that I myself committed?"

"Not for any logical reason. But people do illogical, crazy things all the time. If they didn't, the murder rate would plummet."

She squinted her eyes and rubbed her chin thoughtfully. "Today is Tuesday, isn't it?"

The question was unexpected, but the answer was easy enough. "It is."

"Good. Then Dr. Lipowsky should be in the hospital. He usually works nights on Tuesdays. Luckily for me, you've chosen today to make your outlandish accusations."

"Who's Dr. Lipowsky?"

"My personal physician. He's been treating me ever since the accident. He'll confirm that I can barely walk, let alone have the strength to commit violent murder. The telephone is over there. Call the hospital and ask to speak with him."

She recited the number, but I chose to ask the operator to connect me, just in case the number was fake as well. It wasn't. A minute later I was talking to a nurse. I identified myself, said I was calling on Mrs. Rotner's behalf, and asked to speak with Dr. Lipowsky. The nurse told me to wait on the line while she saw if he was free to take my call.

While I waited, I looked at Dahlia. She seemed completely relaxed. There was a gleam in her eye, as though she was anticipating the moment in which I'd be made to feel foolish for ever suspecting her.

Dr. Lipowsky had a Polish accent and a cultured voice. He asked me what I wanted, and I told him to wait a minute and brought the phone over to the sofa and handed it to Dahlia. They exchanged pleasantries, and then Dahlia instructed him to answer any questions I had regarding her health, both current and past.

"Mr. Lapid has my utmost confidence," she said, her tone straddling the fine line between seriousness and mockery. Then she handed the phone back to me and sat with a tiny smile on her lips while I and Dr. Lipowsky conversed about her.

The picture Dr. Lipowsky painted was grim and left no room for doubt. Dahlia was severely handicapped. Her injuries made walking a painful ordeal, one she could not sustain for long. Five years ago, at the time of Anna's murder, her condition was worse still. I did not ask him specifically, but the very idea that she would journey across town to Trumpeldor Cemetery and then viciously slaughter a healthy young woman was preposterous.

"Satisfied?" Dahlia said, once I had hung up the phone.

I returned to the chair and dropped into it. I was tired, and my hunger was back with a vengeance, biting the inside of my stomach with its invisible teeth. I knew it was more than a physical need. The collapse of my theory regarding Dahlia was getting to me. I rubbed my face with both hands hard enough so my skin felt raw.

"Don't feel bad, Mr. Lapid," she said. "I'm not displeased with you."

"That's big of you. Most people get angry when they're accused of murder."

"What I see is that you've been doing your job, just as you told me you would. You've even managed to turn up a witness. Where did he come from?"

"It's not important."

"If you say so. And he said the killer had a limp?"

"He said there was something wrong with the killer's walk. A limp is just one possibility."

"That's rather vague, isn't it?"

I shrugged, then felt the need to defend the fruits of my labor, meager though they were. "It's better than nothing. Did your husband ever have something wrong with his walk?"

She shook her head regretfully. "I'm afraid not."

"Know anyone else who has?"

"No one but myself."

I nodded, wishing like hell I'd gone to Greta's instead of here. This was shaping up to be a big waste of time, and God, was I hungry.

She said, "I'm flattered, you know."

"Flattered?"

"That you think me capable of such an incredible feat of acting, faking a handicap such as mine for five years."

"From what I understand, you have an exceptional talent."

She smiled in what looked to be genuine pleasure. "That's nice to hear." Then her expression turned bitter. "But if you think I'd have given up acting for so long, even to commit the perfect murder, you don't know me at all."

Does anyone know you? I wondered. *Or is the real you always hiding behind some role you're playing?*

"Maybe you'd have seen it as the ultimate professional challenge," I said, in another spurt of defensiveness, this one of the very reason I had come here this evening.

She thought about it and gave a tiny nod. "Maybe I would have."

I pushed myself to my feet. "I should be going."

"Mr. Lapid, I hope this matter with the limp, or whatever it was, does not cause you to think my husband is innocent of this crime."

"Mrs. Rotner, as of yet I have not reached any conclusions."

"Good. Because he's guilty. Remember that."

I assured her I would and exited the living room. I was walking quickly through the short hallway with its twin galleries of pictures when my gaze caught on a particular photo. I stopped abruptly and leaned in for a closer look. Then I lifted the photo from its nail and brought it with me back to the living room. Dahlia was exactly where I'd left her.

"Forgot something, Mr. Lapid? What's that in your hand?"

"A photograph. Perhaps you can tell me what it shows?"

She took the framed photo from me, glanced at it, and gave me a questioning look. "It's Isser, on stage."

"What's the play?"

"*The Life of Jacob Greenstadt.* Written by some forgotten Jewish playwright from the nineteenth century that virtually no one has heard of. I've no idea how Isser came to learn of the play or why he loved it so. He worked very hard on that role. He thought it would be one of his most celebrated."

"And it wasn't?"

"It flopped. Ran just four times. Isser was crestfallen." A sneer turned her face into a sinister mask. "I wasn't in it," she added significantly.

 160

"And is that a cane he's holding?"

She looked again at the picture, then back at me. Her eyes had inched wider. "Why, yes it is."

"The character had something wrong with his walk?"

"A sort of dragging shuffle. Isser trained quite hard at it. Hobbled back and forth across this living room each night in the weeks before the play."

"So he would know how to fake such a walk anytime he wanted to?"

"Indeed he would, Mr. Lapid," she said. "Indeed he would."

The cruel smile on her lips and the glint of mischief in her eyes made my skin turn cold. More than ever I wanted to be away from her, but curiosity kept me rooted to the spot.

I said, "There's one thing I wonder about."

"And what is that, Mr. Lapid?"

"If you despise your husband so much, why don't you divorce him?"

She drew herself even straighter in her seat, though she'd been so erect that I had not thought that possible. "I don't believe in divorce. It may be right for other people, but not for me. I see by your face that you don't understand."

I agreed that I didn't.

She said, "Are you married, Mr. Lapid?"

"I was."

"Are you divorced?"

"No," I said, my throat tightening.

"So she's dead?"

I nodded. It was easier than saying the word.

"In the war in Europe?"

"Yes."

"I'm sorry," she said, and she sounded completely honest, though with this queen of deception you could never know for sure. "And when you were married, could you ever conceive the possibility that one day you would declare, for all the world, that you were no longer hers and she was no longer yours?"

"No," I said truthfully.

"That's the way it is for me, too. I cannot see myself ever saying that Isser isn't mine and I am not his. That thought is unbearable. But I can see him humiliated or jailed or even dead. All that is no problem."

20

Waking early the next morning, I read for twenty minutes and smoked a couple of cigarettes at my window. Then I shaved and ate breakfast. Two pieces of rough bread smeared with soft cheese and a cup of ersatz coffee.

As I ate, I thought about Isser Rotner. His false alibi. The fear that had tormented his sleep the night of the murder. His ability to fake a limp. I did not have proof of his guilt, but I felt I was getting closer.

Still, until I had such proof, I needed to keep an open mind. There were other people who'd known Anna. One of them might be the murderer. Ofra Wexler certainly had a motive, and I refused to eliminate her from consideration, her diminutive stature and Meltzer's opinion notwithstanding.

I thumbed through the notes I had taken at the police station, listing names and addresses of various actors and actresses, plotting a route for the morning. The closest, Leon Zilberman, had lived just a stone's throw away on Rashi Street, but when I got there ten minutes later, I discovered he had moved.

My next stop was city hall, where I spent fifteen circuitous minutes trying to locate Haggai Geller. When I finally found his office, his secretary told me he was on a work-related trip and wouldn't be back in the city till the day after tomorrow at the earliest. I gave her the telephone number at Greta's Café and asked her to have her boss call me when he returned.

"What is this in reference to?" she asked.

"His time at Shoresh Theater," I said.

I had better luck on my third stop, a squat, two-story building near the corner of Yona Hanavi and Hakovshim. On one side gaped a vacant lot littered with building debris; on the other stood a stately building whose outer walls were pocked with bullet holes, which it appeared to wear proudly. The War of Independence had marked its share of buildings just as it did its share of people.

The apartment faced the street and had a small balcony with a metal railing that looked too flimsy to lean on. Two women lived there, and both were actresses.

The first, Edith Bachner, was a curvy brunette. The second, Nitza Weinraub, had hair the color of coal. Both were twenty-six.

They led me into a small living room whose walls were crammed with framed pieces of embroidery that showed a good deal of enthusiasm but little talent.

"We both love it," Edith said, seeing me staring at their creations. "Don't we love it, Nitza?"

Nitza nodded vigorously. "Edith taught me how. Now I can't get enough of it."

The two women sat side by side on the sofa, their legs crossed identically. They were the same height and build, both attired in white cotton dresses, and they had similar features—rounded smooth faces, small blunt noses, large brown eyes—so it was like looking at an orchestrated scene. They had lived together in this apartment when the murder had taken place. Two single women who worked together, lived together, and, apparently, embroidered together.

They had both played in King Lear and had sat next to each other in Café Kassit.

"How long did you work with Anna?" I asked, once I told them why I was there.

"Two years," they said, in near unison.

"We began working for the theater in 1944," Edith said.

"In the summer," Nitza contributed.

"Was she a nice person?" I asked.

"Very. Much nicer than..." Edith stopped in mid sentence, clamping her mouth shut like a child trying to catch a secret by its tail.

"Who?" I prompted.

They exchanged a glance. Then Nitza screwed up the courage to say, "Dahlia Rotner."

"Nicer in what way?"

"In every way. She would smile more often, ask us how we were doing, and wouldn't chastise us if we made a mistake during rehearsal or, God forbid, a show."

"Did Dahlia ever chastise you in front of others?" I asked, remembering that Ofra Wexler had made a similar complaint.

"That's the only way she did it," Edith said. "It wasn't to help us do better, like she pretended, but to punish us for making a mistake."

"She did it to me a few times. She made me cry." Nitza's face crumpled as the memory hit her, and Edith patted her arm. "I was glad when she got injured."

"Don't say that," Edith said.

Nitza lowered her eyes. "I know it's terrible, Edith, but I was. I don't wish that sort of injury on anyone, but at least it got her away from us."

I said, "Did it surprise you that Anna was picked to take over for her?"

"Why would it surprise us?" Edith asked.

"Someone told me Ofra Wexler would have made a better choice." I did not mention that it had been Ofra herself.

"She would like to think so, that's for sure," Edith said. "But I was glad it was Anna. Ofra isn't very nice either."

"She's full of herself," Nitza said. "Anna didn't look down at us. And she was so beautiful. Every dress looked good on her. Varda, our costume maker, is a wizard when it comes to dresses, and Anna looked dazzling every time she walked on stage."

"And she was warm," Edith said. "She wasn't stingy with praise, and if we made a mistake, she would tell us so gently, privately, in a way that didn't make us feel bad."

"Ofra is cold," Nitza said. "The only time I saw her exhibit any real emotion was when they told us Anna died. Remember how she cried, Edith?"

Edith nodded. "I felt sorry for her. I actually hugged her. Nothing like that has happened before or since. But I did see her show emotion a few times before that."

"When?" I asked.

"Whenever Anna would go on stage to the sound of applause at the end of a play. I could see the envy on Ofra's face. Could almost feel it."

"Is Ofra a good actress?"

Another glance was exchanged; then Nitza sighed. "Yes, I guess she is. But she's not fit to be the leading lady. She's not glamorous enough."

"Like Anna? Like Pnina Zelensky?"

"Exactly."

"Was Dahlia Rotner glamorous?"

"Dahlia wasn't beautiful like Anna or Pnina," Edith said, "but when she was on stage, it was difficult to look away. I watched her perform before I joined the theater. Afterward, I couldn't remember the faces of any of the other actors, just hers. And what a voice she has. The sort of voice that gives you goosebumps or makes you cry for the character she's portraying. I haven't spoken to her in five years, but I remember that voice clearly."

"I admired her, too," Nitza said, "but I didn't like her one bit."

Which seemed the usual mixture of emotion engendered by Dahlia. Did I not feel the same way?

"Did Anna talk about herself, about her life?" I asked.

The two women shook their heads. "She would ask a lot about us," Nitza said, "but I don't remember her saying all that much about herself. Strange, but I never thought about it before."

"Me neither," Edith said, and I got the impression that these two women were fully capable of talking endlessly about themselves, to the point of not noticing if someone did not share a single personal detail in return.

"She would often look sad," Edith said. "I thought it was because of what happened to her family. You know about her family?"

"Yes," I said.

"That's what it was, I think."

"What about men? Did you ever see her with one?"

"Men would approach her all the time," Nitza said. "Good-looking, nicely dressed, educated men, but she would turn them all down. I never understood why. I remember teasing her about it, but she would just laugh and shrug it off."

"You remember where you were when she died?"

"Here," Edith said, and Nitza nodded. "And then we got to the theater the next day for rehearsal and the police were there."

"I thought there'd been a break-in," Nitza said, her eyes rounded and slightly fearful as she relived that moment. "But then I saw Isser, and I knew by his face that something much worse had happened."

167

"His face?"

"It was gray, totally gray, and his eyes had this haunted look to them. I was sure something must have happened to Dahlia, but then I learned it was Anna. It, it..." Tears sprang to her eyes, and Edith patted her arm again and murmured something soothing.

"Were they fond of each other?" And when they stared at me blankly, I added, "Isser and Anna?"

"Yes, they worked beautifully together," Edith said. "Isser even became nicer."

"Nicer?"

"He used to be much more strict when Dahlia was still working."

"When she was in charge, you mean," Nitza said.

Edith shot her friend a disapproving look, as though she'd said something she shouldn't have. "Once she was gone, once Anna took over, Isser became mellower, not so quick to criticize."

"Like he'd been strict before only because he was following Dahlia's lead," Nitza said.

"Some people say the theater suffered when Dahlia stopped performing," Edith said. "But in many ways, it became a better place to work."

"But it did suffer financially, didn't it?"

They both shifted uneasily. "It's a temporary thing," Edith said with exaggerated lightheartedness. "I have faith in Isser."

"I do too," Nitza said, nodding a few times as though to convince herself.

Things must be going even worse for the theater than they appear, I thought.

I hesitated before asking my next question, but decided I could not avoid doing so. "Did either of you ever feel that Isser and Anna were more than just colleagues?"

The question had a peculiar effect on them. They both sat utterly still, wearing the same stunned expression on their faces, and then they exchanged their longest glance yet before Edith said, "No. No way. Never. Who put that idea in your head?"

The fervent way both were shaking their heads made me certain that while they might not have known for sure, they suspected it was true just the same.

And that, I decided, was as good a confirmation as I was ever likely to get.

21

I found a street bench in the shade of a cypress tree and sat smoking and thinking. I thought about the talk I'd just had with Edith and Nitza, and those I'd had with Anna's neighbors the previous evening. How none of them, even those who had made an effort to befriend her, had really known her.

Which made me wonder why. A woman who doesn't talk about herself may have something to hide. And secrets can be a reason for murder.

So I decided to change my plan and head to where I might learn more about Anna, her history, her earlier years.

The sprawling building at the northern tip of Herzl Street looked like a cross between a shrine and a medieval castle. One of the oldest buildings in Tel Aviv, and many would say the grandest, the Herzliya Hebrew Gymnasium—colloquially known as Gymnasia Herzliya—was a testament to the priorities of the city's founders. Education and the Hebrew language occupied the top of the list.

Crossing the well-maintained forecourt, with its cypresses and palm trees, and entering the building, I was enveloped by the happy, rapid-fire chatter of teenagers standing on the cusp of adulthood. Soon, these carefree boys and girls would exchange their clothes for olive-green uniforms. They would guard Israel's borders, fight its wars, and some would die defending it.

I found Menashe Klausner in an almost empty classroom, engaged in close conversation with a female student. A book lay open on her table, and he was leaning over it, pointing something out to her. She was fingering the end of one of her pigtails, moving her eyes back and forth between text and teacher. Standing in the doorway, with the clamor of the student-packed hallway behind me, I couldn't make out what they were saying.

A minute later, Klausner straightened, smiled down at his student, and patted her shoulder with a large hand. She rose, picked up her book and bag, and bid him goodbye in a sweet, girlish voice. I moved aside to let her pass and entered the classroom.

Klausner hadn't noticed me enter. He was gathering his papers from the teacher's desk and stuffing them in a leather briefcase with large metal clasps.

"Mr. Klausner?"

He raised his head and looked questioningly at me from under a pair of closely set, bushy eyebrows. "Yes. How may I help you?"

He was a big man, broad and thick-chested but soft looking, with a neck that was turning jowly and a forehead deeply creased with thought lines. His graying hair was receding in front but had recently been groomed. As had his thick mustache. I pegged his age at fifty-five. He wore black trousers and a short-sleeved white shirt with a wide collar. His clothes were neat and pressed, his shoes polished, his belt buckle gleamed. This man was no stranger to vanity.

"My name is Adam Lapid," I said. "I'd like to talk to you about a former student of yours. Anna Hartman."

His eyes went from me to the open doorway behind me and

back again. I looked over my shoulder and saw no one, but I understood his concern.

"How about I close the door?" I said in a quiet voice. "That way, none of your students will overhear our conversation."

He nodded, and I went to shut the door. By the time I came back, he'd taken the chair behind the teacher's desk. He was gazing in the direction of the nearest arched window, looking pensive.

"Why are you here?" he asked, and I realized I hadn't told him what I did for a living.

"I'm a private investigator. I'm working to find out who killed Anna."

He looked at me, blinked a few times, and sat up straight. "After all this time? Isn't it a lost cause?"

"Older crimes than this one have been solved when new information came to light."

"There's new information? What new information?"

I sat on the edge of the nearest student table. "I can't discuss that, Mr. Klausner. Not at this stage of the investigation. What I was thinking is that you'd be able to help me know more about Anna, what she was like when she studied here."

"Why is that important? She died eight years after she graduated."

"You followed the case?"

"I read about it in the newspapers. I was deeply distraught by her death."

"When was the last time you saw her?"

He frowned in concentration, pushing a pair of rectangular glasses up the bridge of his prominent nose. "Not too long after graduation, the day she was hired by Shoresh Theater."

"She came to tell you about it?"

"Yes."

"So you and her were close?"

"She was a student of mine and participated in the drama club."

"Yes, I heard about that."

"You did? From whom?"

"Another of your former students. Ofra Wexler."

"Ah," he said. "Yes. She and Anna were classmates."

"I understand they were close friends at the time."

"Yes, I suppose they were."

"You don't sound too sure about it."

"I don't?" he said, looking a bit surprised. "There's no reason why I shouldn't. Those two were practically inseparable."

"No squabbles over boys?"

Klausner cleared his throat. "I wasn't privy to those sorts of discussions, Mr. Lapid."

"How about who got the bigger parts in your productions?"

"If there was any tension between the two girls, I didn't see it."

"Who *did* get the bigger parts? Anna or Ofra?"

He gave it some thought. "Anna did. Not all the time, but mostly."

"You made that call?"

"Yes. I was the one who decided which student played which part."

Which might be the reason why Ofra didn't like him, because he'd preferred Anna to her. Could the seeds of her envy and resentment have been sown so long ago? And had they finally bloomed to a blazing hatred five years ago and driven her to murder?

"Tell me about Anna," I said.

He shifted his big bulk in his seat. "What is there to say? She was a good student and a very nice girl."

"I understand she was dedicated to acting."

He nodded. "She worked very hard at it. Did not miss a single rehearsal. That's not common, Mr. Lapid. Most students who take part in the drama club are much less reliable."

"How long have you been running this club?"

"I started it in 1926."

"Twenty-five years, then?"

"Yes," Klausner said. "Well, apart from some years I taught in Haifa. Let's see, I was there for five years, so I've headed the drama club for twenty years in total." His chest swelled with evident pride.

"What made you move to Haifa?"

"I thought a change would do me good. But Haifa doesn't hold a candle to Tel Aviv. I was happy to return here."

I wondered why it had taken him five years to move back, but saw no reason to ask.

"Twenty years," I said, "that's a long time. Why do you do it?"

"A love of the theater. Second only to my love for teaching." He smiled a slow, self-satisfied smile, liking the picture he was presenting of himself. "If not for that, I'd be an actor. But a teacher is all I really ever wanted to be."

I stifled a smile of my own, remembering what Ofra had told me about Klausner's numerous failed auditions. It was a harmless lie he'd just told me, and perhaps not even that. A vain man is capable of believing almost anything about himself, no matter how detached from reality.

It hardly mattered to me one way or the other. I was there to learn more about Anna, not him.

I said, "Was Anna a happy girl?"

"Happy? Why do you ask?"

"A girl so young, separated from her family, living all alone in a foreign city, it could lead to despondency, couldn't it?"

"I suppose so. Yes, her circumstances were certainly not ideal. But she was a positive, lively girl. And she was happy, of that I'm sure."

"Because of the drama club, you think?"

"I'm sure that played a part, yes."

"How about her studies?"

"Like I said, she was a good student. I taught her literature, and she enjoyed that. Especially when we read plays."

"Because they have to do with the theater?"

"Precisely."

"I understand she didn't get along with her landlady."

"Mrs. Chernick?"

"You know her?"

"Of her," he said with a faint smile, as though he were correcting one of his students on a fine, but crucial point. "Over the years, quite a few of my students had boarded with her. Anna never said anything about her to me, but she has a reputation, a rather unsavory one. Did you talk to her?"

"Not yet."

"I doubt she could tell you anything useful, Mr. Lapid. From what I heard, she took no interest whatsoever in the lives of her lodgers. She would know nothing about Anna, nothing you haven't learned from me or Ofra."

"You're probably right," I said, remembering what Ofra had told me about Mrs. Chernick, but knowing I'd still pay the landlady a visit. Because people who live together tend to know and notice things about each other, even if all they feel is mutual disdain. Moving on, I said, "Did Anna ever talk about her family? Her life in Prague?"

"No," he said. "At least not to me. Maybe to Ofra or another student, I don't know."

"Do you know why her family sent her here and not her older brother?"

He shook his head. "Not a clue. But how does that relate to your investigation, Mr. Lapid?"

"I don't know," I admitted, and searched my brain for another question. It didn't take me long to find one.

"Did she have a boyfriend?"

He looked about to shake his head again, but then he stopped and looked at me. "I did see her once with a young man, not here, somewhere uptown, near the beach. They were kissing rather passionately, I remember."

"In the middle of the street, in the open?"

"No, not in the open. In a doorway, a darkened doorway. And it was night."

After one of Mrs. Chernick's hated curfews, I thought.

"How did you know it was Anna if it was dark?" I asked.

"I didn't at first. Only when they disengaged and emerged onto the lighted sidewalk did I see it was her."

"And the man?"

"Never saw him before in my life. He wasn't a student here, that I can tell you."

"Can you describe him?"

He scrunched up his face, dredging up the memory. The description he gave was too generic to be useful—tall, slim, with dark hair and a fair complexion, unremarkable features—but I wrote it down in my notebook just the same.

"What about his age?"

"Young. Eighteen, perhaps. No more than twenty-one."

"And this was when?"

"1938, I don't remember the month."

Which meant that this man, if he still lived, would be between thirty-one and thirty-four years of age today.

"What did Anna say when she saw you that night?"

"She didn't," he said. "She never looked my way. She and the man simply walked off, and I never mentioned it to her."

"I see."

"I don't know what he was to her, how serious it was, or

anything at all, for that matter. I did not think it was my place to ask."

"I understand," I said, and I did. In 1938, Anna would have been seventeen. Still a schoolgirl, but old enough to marry. What business would it have been of her teacher who she was romantically involved with? Still, I wished like hell Klausner had been curious enough to ask her. And I wondered why Ofra did not know about this man. Or maybe she did and had decided not to tell me about him.

22

Kfar Saba Street was a short, straight road with very narrow sidewalks and small houses whose walls touched. It didn't take me long to find Mrs. Chernick's home.

It was a one-story structure with a flat roof and a single window facing the street. The outside had been painted a lackluster beige, but this had been done a good many years before, because plaster was flaking off the facade like dandruff.

The door was made of cheap wood and it had warped so that it no longer fitted its frame properly.

The only thing that brightened this dismal picture of neglect was a scrawny tree that grew from a small square of earth adjacent to the house's exterior. The tree was surprisingly lush, with an abundance of leaves and a scattering of lavender flowers, their petals open to the morning sun.

I knocked on the door and waited while a pair of boys on bicycles streaked by on the road behind me, both furiously ringing their bells and laughing their hearts out.

When the door was opened, its hinges squeaked and its

bottom scraped atop the floor like chalk screeching across a blackboard.

The pinched-faced woman who stood before me was short, bony, and wrinkled. Her age was hard to pinpoint. She could have been anywhere between fifty and seventy-five. Her dress was long, black, and hung a bit loose over her thin frame. Her glasses were large and thick-rimmed, and they made her dull-gray eyes look too big for her face. A wedding band adorned her gnarly ring finger, and around her wrist were two gold bracelets that looked as old as she was.

"Are you Mrs. Chernick?" I asked.

"If you're here for the room, you've wasted your time. I already have a lodger. And besides, I don't rent to men." Her voice was high and needly. The sort of voice you can't imagine ever being used to tell a joke.

"I'm not here for the room. I'm here to talk to you."

"You're with the police? It certainly took you long enough. I made the complaint two weeks ago."

"What complaint?"

"About the boys making all the racket. Laughing and hollering and ringing their bicycle bells at all hours right outside my door. Why are you here if you don't know that?"

"I'm not a policeman," I said, remembering the two boys who had bicycled by a minute ago, and thinking that Mrs. Chernick was the victim of a coordinated campaign of juvenile harassment, and that she had likely been made a target due to her stern demeanor and surly attitude. "My name is Adam Lapid. I'm a private investigator and I'd like to talk to you about Anna Hartman."

Her pencil-thin eyebrows jumped above the rim of her glasses. "Anna Hartman? What's to talk about? She's been dead six, seven years."

"Five," I corrected.

Mrs. Chernick waved a hand, her bracelets jangling. "Five, six, seven. What does it matter? I haven't seen her in much longer than that."

"I'd still like to ask you some questions. I'm investigating her death, and any information might prove useful. Can I come in?"

She informed me she was in the middle of cooking. My nose had picked up the scent. Boiled cabbage and beets and some root I could not identify. The sort of food that could leach the joy out of anyone. Perhaps it had something to do with Mrs. Chernick's disposition.

"It will only be a couple of minutes," I said.

She planted one hand on a narrow hip. "I'm sorry, but I can't spare the time."

I weighed my options. I wanted to talk to her, and I needed at least a modicum of cooperation for it to be worthwhile. The question was, how would I get it?

Then I recalled something Ofra Wexler had said. About how Mrs. Chernick would not have had any boarders at all if she didn't have need of money. That had been over a decade ago, but judging by the exterior of the house, that need had persisted.

"I'd be happy to pay you for your time," I said. "It would only be right."

She wanted me to state a number, but I chose to be vague. "That depends on the information you give me. But let's say a lira is the minimum."

And just like magic, I was invited in.

Once inside, she became self-conscious, as though aware of the bleak impression her house, and she herself, gave. She touched her graying hair—short and slightly thinning on top—and used her hand to brush the seat of a timeworn armchair before inviting me to use it.

She needn't have bothered. Her hair was as good as it was

going to get, and the living room was clean and orderly. Not that it changed the overall atmosphere.

The furnishings would have been old when Anna had first moved in here. There was an armchair, a low sofa, a dining table, and a hefty book cabinet laden with tomes with yellowing, cracked spines. The ceiling was low and the walls could have used a fresh coat of paint.

Two pictures hung on one wall. In the first, a young Mrs. Chernick in a simple wedding dress was standing beside a suited man with a weak chin and a receding hairline. Mr. Chernick, I assumed.

The second picture showed the same couple, at least ten years older. Mr. Chernick's hair had retreated further by then—as, it appeared, did his chin.

In neither of the pictures were either of them smiling.

"Can I get you anything?" she asked. "Some water perhaps?"

I realized by her wheedling tone that it was not self-consciousness that had prompted the shift in her manner, but avarice. Now that I had turned from a nuisance to a potential source of easily obtained income, I was accorded a measure of hospitality—designed to increase the payout she would receive from me.

I declined the water. She sat on the edge of the sofa, her knees touching.

I said, "In what year did Anna come to live here?"

"1935."

"How was the connection between you and her family made?"

"Through the school. I had been hosting students since the mid-twenties, shortly after my husband, God rest his soul, passed away. I received a letter from them, inquiring whether the room was available for the next school year. My then lodger was graduating, so it was."

"They paid in advance?"

"Of course. For the whole year."

"And they renewed each summer until graduation?"

"Yes. Three years in total."

"What did your services include?"

"I provided the room—" she motioned with her knobby chin to a closed door to my left "—three meals a day, and I also did her laundry. That was extra. Not every lodger I've had opted for that."

But Anna's family did even though they were supposedly of modest means.

"What did she bring with her when she arrived?"

Mrs. Chernick furrowed her brow, deepening her myriad wrinkles. "Two small suitcases, if I recall correctly."

"Matching suitcases?"

"I don't remember."

"What about her clothes? Were they new, expensive?"

"Just regular clothes. Dresses and skirts and shirts and shoes. Nothing that struck me as extravagant."

So Anna's family had come up with the money to send her to study in Tel Aviv, but had not laid out additional funds for new clothes. What this meant, if anything, was unclear to me.

"Can I see her room?"

"Sure," she said, rising to her feet. "Though you won't find anything of hers there. She hasn't lived here for fourteen years."

She opened the door and I peered inside. The room was a small square with one window equipped with worn curtains. There was a single bed with a metal headboard; a tall, narrow closet; a dresser with three drawers; and a small writing desk and an accompanying chair. There was very little open space.

I asked her if this was the same furniture that Anna had used, and she confirmed that it was, with one exception. "I changed the mattress eight years ago."

The closet door hung open, and inside I could see folded dresses and blouses and a nightgown hanging on a hanger. A woman's clothes. Not a teenager's.

"Your current lodger is not a student?"

"A recent immigrant. From Greece of all places. The last time I had a student here was before the war. With what happened to the Jews in Europe, the flow of foreign students to Gymnasia Herzliya has stopped." She gave a morose shake of her head—*for those unfortunate Jews*, I thought, but her next words proved me wrong. "It was better for me then. There were plenty of European Jewish families with money. Immigrants have very little. I had to cut my rent by thirty percent." She gave me a meaningful look, and it dawned on me that she was painting a picture of poverty and misery in an attempt to appeal to my heart so I would give her more money. I had to quell the urge to scream in her face that she was living like royalty in comparison to what I, and many others, had gone through in the camps.

Instead, I said, "These are hard days for everyone."

"True. But widows like me are especially stricken."

I told her I'd seen enough of the room, and we returned to our seats.

"How did you and Anna get along?" I asked.

"Fine. Just fine," she said after a brief hesitation, and it was obvious she was giving me the answer she thought would please me. If I wanted the truth from her, I would need to rattle her a bit.

I leaned forward sharply, pointed a finger at her, and injected a dose of menace into my voice. "You're lying to me, Mrs. Chernick. And I don't appreciate that one bit."

Seeing her stunned expression was quite enjoyable.

"You're not the first person I've talked to about Anna. I know more than you think. If you lie to me again, you'll get nothing from me. Understand?"

It took her a moment to answer, and when she did, her voice was small and meek, like that of a chastened child. "I understand."

"Good. Now, tell me the truth. Did you like Anna?"

"I did not."

"Tell me why."

"Because she was a nasty, undisciplined, immoral girl. Because she talked back to me. Because she didn't follow the rules of this house." Now she sounded more like herself, only angrier. She'd raised her voice, and the loose skin on her neck quivered as the words shot from her mouth.

"What made her immoral?"

"The way she dressed, always keeping a button open to show more of her skin than was proper. And how she walked, swinging her hips like a good girl never would. And the way she behaved around men."

"Men? You mean students from the school?"

"Them too, I imagine. But I mean older men. Married men."

"Which men?"

She made a general, all-encompassing gesture with her hand. "All sorts. The butcher, the milkman, a neighbor who used to live at the end of the street. And others as well."

"She had affairs with these men?"

"It wouldn't surprise me."

"Wouldn't surprise you? What does that mean?"

"It means that the way she would talk to them, always smiling suggestively and playing with her hair; and the way they looked back at her, like men do at loose women; and being who she was —what else could it be?"

"Did you ever see her kiss any of these men?" I asked.

She shook her head.

"Did she ever bring a man here?"

"Here? No. Never to this house. Never." She was vehement, as though the very idea was sacrilegious.

"Then you don't really know she had affairs, do you? Maybe she was merely flirtatious."

She looked at me, and a sly smile carved a crooked gap

between her wizened lips. Something glinted there, and I saw that one of her teeth had been capped in gold.

"Why are you smiling, Mrs. Chernick?" I asked, when a minute passed without her speaking.

"Because you don't know nearly as much as you think."

"So tell me," I said, doing my best to hide the spark of excitement that had lighted up somewhere behind my breastbone.

She shook her head slowly. "I don't think I should. It's sensitive, you see. It wouldn't be proper."

Which was just pretense. What she was doing was dangling a piece of forbidden information before my nose and hoping I'd bite. And I had no choice but to do just that.

I withdrew a half-lira note and held it out to her. "For you. And there's more where that came from. If you'll tell me what I wish to know."

She yanked the bill from my hand, folded it twice, and tucked it away in her dress.

"Well," she said, "I suppose it would do no harm, given that Anna and her family are all deceased. It may even do some good, since you are investigating her murder."

More pretense. She did not care one bit about Anna or her family, and unlike many of the people I'd talked to during this investigation, she did not possess the acting skills to hide it. In fact, she looked eager to share with me whatever sordid secret she hoarded.

She said, "Before Anna first arrived, I received a letter from her parents. The letter contained a set of instructions. I was asked to keep my eye on Anna, to make sure she behaved with the utmost propriety and did not develop any relationships with men."

"I take it this was not a usual request."

"I've never received such a letter before or since."

"And you agreed to do it?"

"Of course. I saw it as my duty. If I could help the girl retain her honor and dignity, it would be a source of great pride."

"But Anna made it difficult?"

"Very much so. She was headstrong and rebellious and immoral to the core. No wonder her parents shipped her here. It wasn't for the education, but to keep her out of whatever sinful activity she was involved in over there."

Over there, meaning Prague, Czechoslovakia, a capital that, three years later, would fall prey to the Nazis. And not too long after that, all of Anna's family would be killed.

"If she gave you so much trouble," I said, "why didn't you kick her out after one year? Your desire to help her?"

"Yes. Yes, that's what it was precisely."

Only it wasn't. I was sure of that. "You weren't paid extra for this additional service?"

A hint of pink tinted Mrs. Chernick's pasty cheeks. "A little. Much too little to justify all my frustration with the girl, I can tell you that."

It was not a little, I was sure. Though I was certain Mrs. Chernick found great joy in making Anna's life miserable, she would not have done so without adequate compensation.

"Do you know the details of Anna's sinful activity in Prague before she came here?"

There was that smile again. That greedy smile. I parted with another half lira.

"I tried to get it out of her," Mrs. Chernick said. "For her sake, not out of any personal curiosity. Just so I could look after her better, you understand."

"Of course," I said, impatient for her to get to the point.

"She refused to talk about it. Always answered vaguely, with a haughty smile, like she enjoyed keeping secrets from me. She was quite pretty, and she knew it. Knew that men wanted her. And she thought that made her better than me. Because she was younger and prettier and..." A spasm of mental pain cut across her face, and for a moment she looked vulnerable and forlorn, but then the old spiteful sourness resurfaced. "But she was simply sinful and wicked, nothing more. A wicked girl."

"Mrs. Chernick," I prodded gently, "you were going to tell me about what happened in Prague."

"I'm getting to it. My first clue was that the money for Anna's room and board did not come from her parents. It came from a Mr. Artur Goslar of Prague. I asked Anna if he was a relative, and she got a funny look on her face and said he was a friend of the family. This made me curious, so I asked an acquaintance of mine who had come here from Prague in the early '30s if she knew the name. She told me Artur Goslar was a leading Jewish industrialist in Czechoslovakia. A rich man."

She paused and licked her lips.

"For a time, she said, Goslar was embroiled in a scandal. The details were hazy, but the overall picture was clear. He had entangled himself with a young girl, too young for marriage even. Not that it mattered, because he was married himself. Apparently, Goslar had to grease some palms to make the incident go away."

"But this must have happened long before Anna came here," I said. "She would have been a child."

"True. The girl in question wasn't Anna. But it said something about Artur Goslar and his inclinations. And, coupled with the instructions I received from her parents, it was evident to me what had happened."

"That Goslar had an affair with Anna, and when it was discovered, he had paid to send her away. To Tel Aviv."

"Exactly."

I thought about it. It made perfect sense. It explained why Anna had been sent to study in Gymnasia Herzliya and not her brother, and also how her family could afford it. Goslar had picked up the tab. Though, apparently, he did not spring for new clothes.

Still, there was no hard evidence of this.

"Were you ever able to verify it?" I asked. "Or is this simply an educated guess?"

She looked at me as though I were a simpleton. "I told you about the letter and about how she behaved around men. What further proof do you need? In all likelihood, she seduced Artur Goslar with her indecent behavior."

She'd forgotten, it seemed, Goslar's previous involvement with a young girl. She blamed it all on Anna. She loathed her that much.

But, perhaps, the cause and effect were reversed. Perhaps Anna was not born the flirtatious, dissolute girl Mrs. Chernick had known. She might have become that way because her first experience with sex was in an illicit affair with a much older, married man. An affair that caused her family to ship her to another country. That might change a girl fundamentally, like any crime changes its victim. And a grown man, a married man, taking on a thirteen- or fourteen-year-old girl as his lover is committing a crime. At least in my book he is.

All this was supposition, but if true, it made the tragedy of Anna's death that much graver. Because long before she was robbed of her life by her killer, the girl she'd been had been taken advantage of and altered irrevocably.

Perhaps this was why she had not been dating anyone. And also why she might have chosen to have an affair with another married man. Isser Rotner.

I said, "Do you know what happened to Artur Goslar?"

Mrs. Chernick shrugged her bony shoulders. "Dead. All that money and all that crystal wouldn't have done him any good when the Germans came."

"Crystal?"

"That's what they made in his factories. Glassware, crystal. My acquaintance told me his products were very good."

Which might have been true, but I was thinking about something else. What Ofra Wexler had told me about Anna's father, that he had worked in a glass factory.

I couldn't be sure, but I imagined that Anna had come to visit her father and caught Goslar's eye. And that was how it started. Not that it made much of a difference how they met. Knowing the particulars wouldn't help me catch Anna's killer. And Artur Goslar was beyond any earthly punishment.

I reached into my pocket, took out a pair of lira notes, and held them high. Mrs. Chernick's eyes went to them like a moth to flame. I said, "Is there anything else you can tell me about Anna and her stay with you? Anything of interest that happened during those three years?"

Her eyes flicked to mine and then back to the money. She thought about it and then shook her head. "There's nothing else."

"After she graduated, she left?"

Mrs. Chernick nodded. "And I never saw or spoke to her again. Which was just fine by me. And the next time I heard of her was when they found her dead."

23

There were a few more people I needed to see, but my conversation with Mrs. Chernick was weighing on me like a necklace of stones, so I headed to Greta's Café instead.

I was hoping for a couple of hours of quiet with nothing but my chessboard and Greta's coffee for company, but that hope was dashed the second I entered the café.

"He's been waiting for you for over an hour," Greta said from her perch behind the counter. "You know him?"

The man was sitting at my regular table at the rear. He smiled when he saw me and raised a hand in greeting.

"Yes, I know him." I cursed inwardly, mourning the wreckage of my longed-for tranquility. "Get us each a cup of coffee, will you, Greta? He'll pay for them."

I crossed the room to my table. Above me the ceiling fan was behaving. Last night, after my visit with Dahlia, Greta had informed me that the fan had been repaired yet again, and that the repairman had assured her that it would operate quietly from now on.

I could only hope that her luck would prove better than mine.

"Good morning, Shmuel," I said, and went around the table to my chair without offering my hand. I sat with my back to the wall. Something the Westerns I read had taught me.

"And to you too, Adam," Birnbaum said. "I was beginning to think you weren't going to show up."

"If I'd known you were coming to see me..." I intentionally left the end of the sentence hanging.

Birnbaum's smile widened. "You'd have come sooner, of course."

"That's one possibility. Let me guess, you're here to persuade me to cast my vote for Mapai in the upcoming election."

"I would have thought that would not be necessary. A man of such high intelligence as yourself could scarcely consider voting for any other party."

"Yet so many citizens did the last time around and undoubtedly will again this time."

"I'm not worried. Mapai will win again."

"You lost in Tel Aviv," I remarked, and felt a thrill of pleasure at seeing Birnbaum grimace. The fact that Tel Aviv's mayor, Israel Rokach, was a member of the General Zionists, the party that was shaping up to be the main challenger to Mapai's hegemony, was a sore point for the ruling party and its supporters, one of which was Birnbaum.

Actually, he was more than that. *Davar*, the widely read daily where Birnbaum worked, informally served as the party newspaper of Mapai. And while Birnbaum was less fanatic in his support of the party than most of his colleagues, he was still a committed member of Mapai, a true believer in its platform and ideology, and a fervent admirer of Prime Minister Ben-Gurion.

He said, "The policies the General Zionists are advocating will drive the country into ruin, Adam."

"Some say it's heading that way right now."

"Times are hard, I'll grant you that. Which is why we need a firm and steady hand at the helm. Ben-Gurion's hand."

"People have had enough of rationing, Shmuel."

"You think I haven't? But what's the alternative? To limit the number of Jews who are allowed to make *aliyah*? To have the new immigrants starve in the *ma'abarot*?"

The *ma'abarot* were immigrant camps that dotted the length and breadth of Israel, usually in the vicinity of established towns and kibbutzim. Tens of thousands of impoverished Jewish refugees and immigrants from all over the world resided in them, often in harsh conditions. The government claimed that the *ma'abarot* were an unavoidable stopgap until the new citizens could be provided with modern housing. I hoped the government was telling the truth.

"We're a poor country," Birnbaum said. "We all need to make sacrifices until better days come. And they will come, provided we have the right leadership."

Greta brought over the coffee. Birnbaum inhaled deeply and flashed her a broad smile. "If it tastes as good as it smells, I'm in for a treat."

Greta laughed. "Can I get you two anything else?"

Birnbaum cast me a look. I shook my head. "Not right now, Greta. Thank you for the coffee."

Birnbaum blew on his cup, then brought it to his mouth. He took a small sip and smacked his lips. "I see why you come here so often."

"I don't remember ever telling you that I did. How did you know?"

"I may not be a detective, Adam, but finding out information is a good deal of what I do." He took another sip and gazed approvingly at his cup. "This is quite excellent coffee."

"Go and tell Greta; maybe she'll be flattered enough to vote for Mapai."

Birnbaum directed his clever eyes at Greta, who was once again in her usual spot, and shook his head. "Something tells me she's not the sort of woman who can be swayed by mere flattery." He looked back at me, straightening his glasses. "You have that in common."

I drank some coffee, set the cup back down, and laid both palms on the tabletop. I had grown weary of all the banter. "Why are you here, Shmuel?"

"To see what you're up to. I've been thinking about you ever since the night we met in the theater. I couldn't shake the feeling that you were there for reasons other than cultural."

"You have an overly suspicious mind, anyone ever tell you that?"

"A few people. And they were always hiding something from me."

"What could I possibly be hiding from you, Shmuel?"

"Whatever it is you're working on, of course. A case related to Shoresh Theater. And to Isser Rotner." His inflection shifted as he pronounced the name, as though he was making a suggestion rather than stating a fact. When I didn't reply, a shadow of a smile twitched at the corners of his mouth. In an oddly soft tone, like a father imparting a lesson to his son, he added, "You shouldn't have asked me about him, Adam. That made me very curious."

"You've got it all wrong, Shmuel. I was simply impressed with his performance."

"So impressed that you had to go to the theater the next day and tell him in person?"

I said nothing. Not that it was a conscious choice, for at that moment, I was struck dumb.

"But you didn't see him to compliment him on his acting," continued Birnbaum. "You had a different purpose. You wanted to question him regarding a murder that took place five years ago. The murder of Anna Hartman."

I stared at him. How could he possibly know all this? Surely not from Rotner himself.

And then a memory bubbled up to the surface of my consciousness. The memory of a kerchiefed old woman armed with a mop and bucket, followed closely by an image of the vacant lobby of Ohel Shem, its floor only partially washed.

"The old cleaning lady," I mumbled, half in disbelief.

Birnbaum gave a small nod, and I could not help but appreciate the fact that he exhibited no sign of reveling in his triumph over me. In fact, he looked somewhat sheepish. Which blunted the edge of my anger, but not entirely.

"You bastard," I said. "You told her to keep an eye out for me?"

"Yes. I had a feeling you'd be showing up at the theater sooner rather than later."

"But how did she hear my conversation with Rotner? We were alone in the theater. She didn't follow me in."

"Adam, a theater has more than a single entrance. The actors come in from backstage. And it's easy to hide in the wings and eavesdrop. You're mad at me, and that's understandable, but I have a job to do, the same as you."

Which was true enough. I could not fault Birnbaum for pursuing a story, nor for outsmarting me. I had only myself to blame for arousing his suspicion in the first place.

"What else do you know?" I asked, and nearly cringed at my worried tone.

He thought about it and decided that honesty was the best policy. "All I had time to do so far was go over newspaper reports of the murder. Other than that, I know very little."

Which was good news. The less Birnbaum knew about my investigation, the better. The shock of him knowing about my talk with Rotner began to dissipate.

But then he had to ruin it by saying, "But I plan to read the police report later today, and I may look into the matter further on my own."

My blood began to boil. I planted one elbow on the table and pointed a rigid finger between his eyes. "You stay out of this, Shmuel. You understand?"

He flinched and went a shade whiter, which made his freckles stand out like a scattering of seeds on a tablecloth. His right hand jerked toward his face, fingers gingerly touching the spot on his jaw where I'd punched him two and a half years ago, after I'd seen the picture he took of me in my hospital bed.

He cleared his throat twice and took a nervous slurp from his cup. After dabbing his lips, he said, "I have no desire to interfere with a murder investigation, Adam, but I want this story."

"There is no story. Not yet, at least."

"How close are you to catching this killer?"

"Impossible to know. It's a five-year-old cold case. I may never solve it."

"But if you do," he said, "it will be a hell of a story. And I want to be the one who writes it. I want your word that you will tell me, and only me, everything when the case is done."

I shook my head. "I can't promise that."

"Why not?"

Because I may have to do things that I would not want to appear in print, I thought.

"I just can't," I said. "But I swear that I won't talk to any reporter but yourself, and that I'll tell you everything I can as soon as I can."

Birnbaum considered my proposal and then let out a breath. "I suppose that will have to do. But tell me one thing: Why do you suspect Isser Rotner?"

"I have my reasons."

"From what I heard, he has an alibi for the night of the murder."

"That's what he claims."

195

"You think he's lying, and his wife, too?"

"Let's just say I don't consider his alibi to be solid."

"The police did, didn't they?"

"I think they were wrong."

"Think, or know?" said Birnbaum, and didn't wait for an answer he must have known would be vague. "What reason did he have to kill Anna Hartman?"

I was about to evade his question, but then I remembered how, on the night I'd run into him after King Lear, I had thought Birnbaum might prove to be a rich vein of information on the theater, in the event that my own efforts fell short. I was not yet ready to admit defeat, but since Birnbaum already knew of my investigation, there was no reason not to make use of his knowledge.

But for him to open up to me, I knew I had to give him something. A tidbit of information. A gesture of good faith.

I downed what remained of my coffee. "I have reason to believe he and Anna Hartman were lovers."

Birnbaum narrowed his eyes. "But you don't know for sure?"

"I'm pretty sure. And I know he's having an affair with another actress. Pnina Zelensky, the one who played Cordelia the other night."

"I know who she is. How do you know they're having an affair?"

"I saw them kissing in his car on Dizengoff Street after the play."

"I thought you said you were tired and going home."

"You're right, that's what I said."

"But you went to Dizengoff instead? Why?"

"Because I wanted to see Rotner up close and out of costume, and I was told he frequented one of the cafés on Dizengoff."

"I see. But there's still the question of motive. Even if he and Hartman were indeed lovers, that doesn't explain why he would kill her."

"I don't have all the answers, Shmuel, but I'm working on it."

He sat still for a moment, fingers steepled, his eyes boring into mine, and it occurred to me he might have made a pretty good interrogator.

He said, "There's something you're not telling me, Adam," and his voice was thick with unfulfilled desire. He wanted this story so bad that I almost pitied him. But then again, I did not know the full story myself.

"I don't have to tell you everything right now, Shmuel. That's not the deal we made."

"No," he agreed with evident reluctance. "Indeed it's not."

"But maybe you can help me get to the bottom of all this."

"How?"

"You told me you used to write about the theater. You know more about Shoresh Theater than I do. You can give me some background."

"I'll do you one better," he said, reached down, and pulled a battered leather briefcase onto his lap. He unclasped it and produced a folded issue of *Davar*, which he slid across the table toward me. "I thought you might wish to see this. The first newspaper report of the murder, May 29, 1946, the day after the body was discovered."

I expected the murder to be on the front page, but that space was largely taken up by reports of an attack by Jewish militants on a British ammunition dump two nights earlier, and the retaliatory steps taken by the British army against various Jewish settlements. Another front-page story related the efforts to convince Britain to allow the immediate immigration of one hundred thousand Jewish refugees to Palestine. A third announced the victory of the Communist Party in the national election in Czechoslovakia.

"It's on page two," Birnbaum said.

I turned over the page, and there, at the bottom, was a short report about the discovery of a dead woman in Trumpeldor Cemetery. The report gave her name, the cause of her death, and said the police were pursuing several leads.

Birnbaum's briefcase contained several following issues, and in them I read further reports on the police investigation.

"Anything new?" Birnbaum asked after I handed him back the final issue.

"Afraid not." Then I asked him to tell me about Shoresh Theater.

"It was founded by Dahlia and Isser Rotner and Eliezer Dattner in 1933," he said. "A smaller company than it is now. From what I gather, the bulk of the initial investment came from Dahlia."

"Where did her money come from?"

"Her father was a successful businessman and contractor. He died when she was twenty and left her a sizable inheritance, though I imagine much of it is gone."

"Gone?"

"Poured into the financial drain that is the theater. It's a tough business, with more downs than ups. Especially when you suffer the sort of *tsuris* that have afflicted Shoresh Theater over the years."

"Like Dahlia Rotner's accident?"

"That was particularly calamitous. The theater hasn't been the same since."

"You saw her on stage?"

"Many times. She's a rarity. One of those people who are born to act. Over the course of your life, if you visit the theater often and are very lucky, you might get to see one or two such people."

"How did Anna Hartman compare?"

Birnbaum gave a rueful smile. "She didn't come close. Which isn't speaking ill of the dead, because hardly anyone would compare favorably to Dahlia. Hartman was a skillful actress, and she was nice to look at, but she didn't have Dahlia's raw talent. I must admit that I was not overly impressed with her."

"And Isser Rotner?"

"You saw him act. What did you think?"

"The audience certainly approved."

"Yes, but much of it was due to the sheer power of the play itself. King Lear is one of the greatest tragedies ever written. It would take a bad actor to ruin it, and Rotner is not a bad actor. In fact, he's a rather good one, but he doesn't possess greatness, not the sort needed to carry a theater on one's shoulders. If Dahlia was a blazing light, her husband is but a mere candle flame." He grinned. "It's like Ben-Gurion and everyone else."

Disregarding his last observation, I said, "What about Eliezer Dattner? How did he enter the picture?"

"He was Isser Rotner's cousin. A few years older and a very good actor."

"Better than Rotner?"

"Oh, yes. In the beginning, Dahlia played the leading female roles; Dattner the male ones."

Which must have made Rotner burn with envy, I thought.

"Did they get along, the two cousins?" I asked.

"Who knows? They were friendly enough to start a theater together, but that was six years before Dattner died."

"I was told he was killed by an Arab."

"Yes, the damn fool ventured into Jaffa at night while the Arab Revolt was still ongoing. He was shot to death."

"What was he doing in Jaffa?"

Birnbaum shrugged. "No idea. Whatever it was, it wasn't worth it."

"Did they catch the guy who killed him?"

"No, and I sorely wished they had. It was a nasty murder. The killer stuck an anti-Jewish pamphlet in Dattner's mouth." Birnbaum shook his head. "It was a dreadful time, Adam. A frightening time. Who could have imagined that soon much worse things would befall Jews?"

I certainly didn't, which was why I didn't act in time to save my family from the catastrophe that would soon consume us. The old familiar guilt snaked its icy fingers around my heart and squeezed.

I closed my eyes and opened them. "So Rotner became the theater's leading man?"

"At least in terms of him getting the main roles."

"What do you mean?"

"In the theater, it's not always the best actor who gets the leading parts. Especially when another actor is a founder of the theater and owns a piece of it."

"Like Isser Rotner does."

"Exactly. Shoresh Theater had another actor at the time, Nahum Ornstein. He was young, tall, handsome, and had a stage presence. Not like Dahlia, mind you, but enough so a few critics, including yours truly, suggested that he might surpass Shoresh Theater's new leading man."

This was the first time I'd encountered the name Nahum Ornstein. "What happened to him?"

"He died. A stupid death, but that's what you get when you do stupid things. Apparently, Ornstein not only enjoyed drinking, but he also partook of hashish. He took a bath while intoxicated with both drug and alcohol, slipped, hit the back of his head on the edge of the tub, and drowned." Birnbaum shook his head. "And so ended a promising career on the stage."

But I wasn't thinking of Ornstein's career, but that of another man. A tingle began at the base of my neck and quickly climbed to spread over my scalp. My heart started pounding. "And Rotner was no longer overshadowed by this upstart," I murmured.

Birnbaum's mouth fell open. "What are you saying, Adam?"

"I'm just stating a fact."

"No, you're doing more than that."

"All right. Two facts. One, that Eliezer Dattner's murder propelled Rotner to the top man's position. And two, that Nahum Ornstein's death removed a potential rival, or at the very least, silenced those voices who were intimating that Ornstein was a greater talent."

"But surely you're not suggesting—"

"When did Nahum Ornstein die?" I asked.

"1940. April or May, I think."

"And Dattner?"

"July '39. I don't remember the exact day."

Which was no problem. I could find out easily enough.

"So about nine, ten months apart," I mused. "And Anna Hartman was killed six years after that. Any other members of Shoresh Theater who died a sudden death?"

"Brigitte Polisar. But if what you're looking for is a dead body to conveniently fill in the time gap between Ornstein and Hartman, you're out of luck. She died two years after Hartman did, in May '48, in one of the Egyptian air raids on Tel Aviv. Please don't tell me you think Rotner was flying one of the planes."

I ignored his sarcasm, thinking that I had one less person to interview. Brigitte Polisar had worked at Shoresh Theater at the same time Anna did.

"She was pregnant at the time," Birnbaum continued, his face grim, "and her husband, Emil, who was also an actor in the theater, shot himself a week later, right after the *shiva*. Just as soon as all his friends and relatives left him alone to suffocate in his grief."

Birnbaum took a deep breath and sighed.

"And finally there were David Azulay and Tzipi Toren," he said, "who both died during the War of Independence. Toren was an army nurse. She died in the Battle of Jerusalem. Azulay was killed in the Galilee during Operation Hiram. October '48, if memory serves."

It did. I did not take part in that operation, but I knew when it had taken place. So there were four less people to interview, not just one, because Emil Polisar, David Azulay, and Tzipi Toren had also worked with Anna, had in fact joined the theater before she did.

I sat back, letting my mind absorb this deluge of new information. "It's strange," I said after a moment. "Don't you find it strange, that seven people working for the same theater died in the space of nine years?"

"No, I don't. Because the first was killed by an Arab, the second by his own carelessness, the third by an unknown killer, the fourth in an air raid, the fifth committed suicide due to the death of his wife and baby, and the last two fell in battle. The only death shrouded in mystery is Hartman's."

"We don't know who killed Eliezer Dattner," I said.

"But we know why he was killed. And it has nothing to do with Rotner or any of the other deaths."

"There's also Nahum Ornstein. People generally don't drown in their own bathtubs."

"Generally, they don't. But it does happen every once in a while. And it's usually someone who is drugged or drunk."

He had a point. As a policeman, I had encountered a couple of such cases, and in both, an empty bottle or a vial of some narcotic was lying around.

"Still, seven in nine years."

"It's a high number," Birnbaum said, "but three of them died during the war—Azulay and Toren as soldiers and Brigitte Polisar in an air raid. And Emil Polisar's suicide can also be attributed to the war. So that leaves just three, which isn't low, but not exceedingly high either. And it's twelve years, not nine, because this is 1951 and the first of these deaths occurred in 1939."

Again, he was right. It was by no means remarkable. Still, that prickly feeling did not abate. Logic did not support it, but my gut instinct did.

"Tell me, Shmuel, did Emil Polisar pose any threat to Rotner, like Dattner and Ornstein did?"

He gave me an incredulous look. "So now you think Emil Polisar was murdered, too?"

"Just humor me, all right?"

He sighed. "Polisar was strictly a mid-rung actor, always playing secondary roles. Dependable, but nowhere near as good as Rotner."

This was not what I wanted to hear. Because if Rotner had had reason to kill Emil Polisar, I would have known I had stumbled upon the truth. Now all I had was a hunch that these deaths—some of them, at least—were connected.

"And even if he was," Birnbaum said, "what would that have to do with Anna Hartman? She was certainly no threat to Rotner."

"Not professionally."

"Not in any way you know about, or am I wrong?"

"No, you're not wrong," I answered reluctantly, and could feel myself slipping into dejection. Because I wanted my hunch to be right. Just like I wanted Rotner to be guilty of murder. And it was quite likely that this was clouding my judgment.

"I know what it's like, Adam," Birnbaum said, "to feel you're on the verge of exposing an incredible story. But what I learned is that the truth is usually simple. Chasing after wild theories will get you nowhere."

"I understand, Shmuel. But what if this is the exception? What if this time the truth is anything but simple?"

"In that case," Birnbaum said, a smile on his lips and a sparkle in his eyes, "just make sure you don't forget to tell me everything when you're through."

24

Birnbaum stuck around for ten more minutes. He used the time to try to persuade me to vote the right way, and would only leave when I threatened to cast my ballot for Menachem Begin's right-wing party Herut.

"You can't be serious," he said.

I glared at him. "Don't push me."

After he left, I went over to the telephone and placed a call to the police station in Netanya. Maybe Meltzer, unlike Birnbaum, would not find my hunch so crazy.

"You're crazy," he said after I'd told him everything. "You're talking, what, three deaths in twelve years?"

"Four, if you count Emil Polisar's alleged suicide."

"Why would you? He had every reason to kill himself."

"Yes, but—"

"God, if my pregnant wife was killed, I'm not too sure I wouldn't consider it myself."

I said nothing, because suddenly I recalled bleak days in which the desire for self-destruction had gripped me as well.

Which made me feel very foolish for doubting that Emil Polisar's death was anything but what it seemed.

"And Dattner died because he was an idiot," Meltzer said. "What was he thinking, going into Jaffa at night in the summer of '39? He was begging for trouble. And Ornstein? Sure, drowning in your own bathtub doesn't happen every day, but once in twelve years? And you think, what, that they're all victims of the same killer?"

He sounded as though he doubted more than my theory. As though he was questioning my sanity. Judging by his tone, it was quite likely he was beginning to regret ever taking the time to speak with me.

"Yeah, I guess you're right," I said, and forced out a chuckle that sounded as hollow as a lonely heart. "It was just a silly hunch, nothing more."

"Well, we all get those every once in a while." He paused, then his gruff voice came again. "You got anything new about the Hartman murder?"

I shared what Eliyahu Toledano told me, that the killer had a strange walk.

Meltzer grunted. "More useless drunken nonsense."

"Toledano's no longer a drunk. He cleaned up his life, got married, and has a baby daughter."

"Oh yeah? That's nice. Got anything else, Adam? Anything you can actually use to find this killer?"

"No. Not yet."

"Don't feel bad, Adam. Like I told you, it was a random killing. Even the best detectives would have a hard time solving such a crime."

And I was not considered among the "best detectives." Not after I told him my hunch.

"I know," I said, wishing I hadn't telephoned him in the first place. "You're right."

"Just don't lose your head, looking for links that don't exist."

I assured him I wouldn't and ended the call.

Back at my table, I lit a cigarette and sat with it burning between my fingers, staring at some indefinite spot on the front window, not registering what went on beyond it. A Sherman tank could have rolled down Allenby Street and I would not have noticed.

I was at war with myself. My logical side trying to beat my gut instinct into submission. Facts, logic, common sense, all said that Birnbaum and Meltzer were right. I was getting worked up over nothing. People die. Sometimes a lot of them die in a short time. In Europe, entire villages and towns had been erased in less than six years. Whole families—three, four generations—had been snuffed out. When you looked at it that way, seven dead actors over a twelve-year period did not seem like all that much. Especially when you discounted those who died in war.

But still...

I did not see Greta until she was standing at my table.

"Is everything all right, Adam?"

I looked up at her, saw her worried frown, and just then my cigarette finished burning itself all the way down to my skin.

I cursed, dropped the hot remnant on the table, and stuck my scorched finger between my lips. My tongue tasted ash, tobacco, and seared skin.

Greta plucked up what remained of the cigarette and laid it to rest in a glass ashtray.

"Want some ice for that?" she asked.

I shook my head.

She sat in the same chair Birnbaum had used, laid a pair of meaty forearms on the table, and clasped her solid, veiny hands.

"What's going on, Adam? The way you looked a minute ago, sitting all still, it was as though your mind was on the other side of the world."

I pulled my finger out of my mouth and examined it. A red circle marked my wet skin, like a tiny bloodshot eye.

I raked a hand through my hair and gritted my teeth in exasperation.

"It's this case," I said. "I can't seem to get a grip on it. For all the work I've done, the people I've talked to, it's like I've moved backward instead of forward. And now it's getting all complicated. Or maybe I'm the one who's making it so. I'm not sure whether I'm the right man for this job. I don't know how to proceed. Because my mind is telling me one thing and my gut another."

My hands were balled into fists. Greta reached over, laid her hands atop mine, and pushed on them gently until I unclenched my fingers and laid my palms flat on the tabletop. The heat of her palms flowed through the back of my hands and moved up my arms and shoulders before reaching my face. Some of the tension faded. Her warm wise eyes peered at me from beneath her heavy eyelids.

"Why don't you tell me about it?" she said. "Maybe another perspective is what you need."

So I did. I told her everything. Starting with the mission Dahlia had given me. Then I described the various interviews I'd conducted. My negative impression of Isser Rotner. Ofra Wexler's obvious dislike of Anna. Mrs. Chernick's unkind assessment of her former lodger. My talk with Inspector Meltzer. And Eliyahu Toledano's testimony regarding the killer's walk.

I concluded with a rundown of my talk with Birnbaum. The tingle of excitement I'd felt when I learned of the multiple fatalities among Shoresh Theater personnel. My instinctive belief that I'd uncovered a hidden connection. Followed by Birnbaum's systematic demolition of said belief.

"The phone call I just made," I said, "was to Inspector Meltzer in Netanya. I was hoping he'd have a different reaction than

Birnbaum, but he shot me down even faster." I glanced at Greta. "What do you think? Am I crazy? Seeing things that aren't there?"

She shrugged. "Maybe. But you could be onto something, Adam. And if you're right, there's a killer out there who must be stopped."

"There's no logical reason to suppose there is."

"So what? Logic isn't everything. Sometimes, your intuition knows best. Women know that better than men."

"The question is, where do I go from here? Do I ignore the other deaths and focus exclusively on Anna Hartman? Or do I start investigating multiple cases simultaneously? Because that's a tall order for a single detective."

She thought a moment, pressing her hands together, the tips of her fingers brushing her lips. "Why not combine the two? Work primarily on finding Anna Hartman's killer, but learn what you can about the other deaths without putting in too much effort, just to be on the safe side. Who knows? Maybe some detail you'll uncover will suddenly connect one case to another, leading you to the killer."

She was right. In fact, she was so right, I felt like smacking myself for not realizing it myself.

I yanked out my notebook and with excited fingers flipped to where I'd summarized Meltzer's interview with Emil Polisar five years ago. I'd remembered correctly.

The four people whose deaths were, or could possibly have been, murders, had all been with the theater when Eliezer Dattner was shot. There was Dattner himself, of course, but also Nahum Ornstein, Anna Hartman, and Emil Polisar.

If what I was dealing with was indeed a series of murders all committed by one person, then I could eliminate as suspects all the people who'd begun working for Shoresh Theater after the shooting of Eliezer Dattner in the summer of 1939. These included

Edith Bachner and Nitza Weinraub and nearly all the people I had yet to interview.

Among the few that were left, two names stood out like a pair of burning trees. Isser Rotner and Ofra Wexler. Rotner had ample motive to get rid of Eliezer Dattner and Nahum Ornstein. Perhaps he had reason to kill Anna Hartman and Emil Polisar as well.

Ofra resented her former friend's success and benefited from her death. But did she have reason to kill the others?

I did not have all the answers yet, but my blood had begun humming in my ears all the same. I had not moved backward as I'd feared. I had taken a giant leap forward. And for the first time since I'd started this case, I felt certain that I would catch this killer. I did not yet know how. I was not yet sure who. But I knew with utter, soaring elation that I would succeed.

"What is it, Adam?" Greta asked. "What were you searching for in your notebook?"

I told her, and she smiled and nodded. I smiled right back at her. Then something occurred to me that wiped away that smile like tears off a cheek.

"The problem is," I said, "that if Anna's murder is one of a bunch, it's a totally different case than if it's an isolated incident. The motive might be different, for one thing. And the killer's personality, too. A onetime killing could mean a stranger did it, or someone who simply acted out of impulse. But three or four murders, spread over years, suggest a careful, calculating, methodical murderer. Someone with an abundance of self-control, someone with a natural talent for killing."

Greta rubbed her arms. "You're starting to scare me, Adam."

"There's nothing to be scared about, Greta. If it's the latter, then this killer has no interest in you or me or anyone outside Shoresh Theater. We're totally safe."

"Unless the killer feels threatened by you. Then he might make an exception."

She had a point. I could become a target. And who knew? Perhaps I already was. I had talked to nearly all the people who'd worked at Shoresh Theater when Eliezer Dattner died. Those who were still alive. The killer might well be one of them. Dahlia certainly thought so.

"In that case, I'll be the one in danger, Greta. You have nothing to worry about."

She gave me an exasperated look. "I'm worried about *you*, Adam."

Now I felt like a moron. I said, "The killer might not even know about me. It doesn't have to be one of the people I've talked to. He could be a maniacal fan. An aspiring actor who failed to pass an audition. A supplier who had been cheated out of a payment. Someone with a reason to hate Shoresh Theater in its entirety."

I could tell by Greta's face that I had failed to ease her mind. I tried again. "He may even be dead himself, Greta, which could explain why no one working for the theater has died since 1948."

"Or he could be biding his time," Greta said. "Like he did between 1940 and '46." The time gap between Nahum Ornstein's death and Anna's murder. Six of the bloodiest years in history, but no dead Shoresh Theater actors. Strange.

Greta must have been wondering the same thing. "Why do you think he waited so long?"

"That's assuming I'm right," I said, "which is still a remote possibility."

"Remote or not, that's what your intuition is telling you. So why?"

I spread my hands. "I don't know. It's one of the reasons Birnbaum and Meltzer thought I was wrong."

"But if you're right, it has to mean something, doesn't it?"

"Yes," I said, "but I have no idea what."

25

Before I left Greta's Café, I made further use of her telephone. I called Reuben Tzanani first and asked him to find out the exact dates and places in which Eliezer Dattner, Nahum Ornstein, and Emil Polisar had died. I gave him the approximate dates of their demise and the formal causes of death.

"Only one of these is a murder," he said. "Why do you need to know all this?"

"It might have some bearing on the case I'm working on."

"You need to read our files? Because it might take some time to locate them all."

"Get them if you can, but for now the dates and places will do."

"All right, Adam. I'll probably have the information in a couple of hours. As for the files, I'll see what I can do."

I thanked him, cradled the receiver, picked it up again, and called my client.

"Hello," I said. "It's Adam Lapid. Is your husband home?"

She let out a rich, rolling laugh. "Spoken like an experienced adulterer, Mr. Lapid."

I felt my cheeks grow hot. "I'm calling on business, Mrs. Rotner."

"I was well aware of that, I assure you. To answer your question, Isser is out. What do you wish to discuss?"

There was no reason not to get straight to the point. "Do you remember the night Eliezer Dattner was shot?"

Silence reigned for half a minute. Then her exquisite voice dethroned it. "Why do you ask?"

"It would take too long to explain. Do you remember it?"

"As though it were yesterday. I was in Haifa. I heard the news when I returned the next day."

"Was your husband with you in Haifa?"

"No, he stayed in Tel Aviv. Why?"

"Do you know why Dattner went into Jaffa that night?"

Again a pause, though this time shorter. "He had a lover there. An Arab widow. We managed to keep it out of the papers. We didn't want his reputation to be tarnished."

Or that of the theater, I thought. "He would visit her often?"

"Every week or so. I told him he was taking his life into his own hands every time he went there, but he wouldn't listen. He thought that going after midnight meant he was safe, the arrogant fool."

"What about Nahum Ornstein?"

"Nahum? My my, Mr. Lapid, you certainly have been busy, haven't you? But what does Nahum, or Eliezer for that matter, have to do with Anna Hartman?"

"I'm wondering if your husband was with you when Ornstein died."

She sucked in a breath and held it. When she spoke again, her voice was throatier, thrumming with bloodthirsty exhilaration.

"Are you suggesting what I think you are, Mr. Lapid?"

"Was he or wasn't he?"

"How I wish I remembered, but I don't. It was a long time ago, and that particular night wasn't as memorable as the night Eliezer died."

"Because you were closer to him?"

"Because I was nearly killed that night as well."

"What?"

"I was in Haifa, coming out of a restaurant, when a car came to a screeching halt a few meters from where I stood. There were three men in it. Two of them stuck machine guns out of the open windows and sprayed bullets at a café. The way they were shooting, I was lucky not to get hit myself."

"But you weren't the target."

"No. It was the café. An Arab establishment. Poor Eliezer. I've always thought that he was killed as revenge for that shooting in Haifa. That's the way it was in those days. The Arabs would kill some Jews, and Lehi or the Irgun or one of the other groups would retaliate, and so on and so forth. But you think otherwise, don't you?"

What I was thinking was that she did not sound remotely upset about witnessing a shooting that likely resulted in numerous casualties. And I was also thinking that someone who knew Dattner was about to visit his lover could have easily followed him into Jaffa, shot him, and left his body there, safe in the knowledge that the death would be attributed to Jewish-Arab tensions. Leaving an anti-Jewish pamphlet in Dattner's mouth was a nice finishing touch, one that would erase any vestige of doubt the police might have had.

And Isser Rotner had no alibi for that night.

"How did your husband feel about Eliezer Dattner and Nahum Ornstein?"

"He hated them both," Dahlia responded in a gleeful sort of voice that made me cringe. "He detested Eliezer because he was the better actor and got the best parts. And he loathed Nahum for being praised by the critics. If you're searching for a motive, Mr. Lapid, you need look no further."

"You don't seem at all troubled by the notion that your husband killed these two men."

"Why would I be? I already know he killed a woman."

"There's a difference between a onetime murderer and a repeat offender."

"Yes, there is. If you manage to prove Isser is guilty of those crimes as well, Mr. Lapid, I would be extremely happy. Happy enough to give you a bonus."

"You actually want your husband to be a multiple murderer?"

"Only if you can prove it. I have no preference if you can't."

My mouth went bone dry. I wondered how Dahlia could have ever loved her husband if she hated him so much now. Or maybe she had loved him with such ferociousness that there was no middle ground anymore, no possibility for tepid emotions. Maybe his betrayal had catapulted her straight from an incandescent love to a red-hot hatred. So that now she not only believed the worst of him, she actually prayed for it.

"It might be time to reconsider your decision to stay in your apartment," I said.

"Don't worry about my safety, Mr. Lapid. I can handle Isser."

I couldn't see how that was possible, but I didn't argue. She was the sort of woman who would not be budged.

"Any other crimes you suspect my loving husband of committing?" she asked.

"Just one. Emil Polisar."

"Emil? But Emil shot himself when—" She paused and drew in another breath. "You don't say. You think Isser killed him as well?"

"I'm not sure of anything at the moment. What I want you to tell me is if you know your husband's whereabouts when Polisar died."

"No idea. But he wasn't with me. That I remember."

"Did he have reason to hate Polisar?"

"Not that I know of. Maybe he simply developed a taste for murder."

"If that's the case, are you still sure you can handle him?"

"I have no doubt."

I wanted to ask her how she could be so confident. Instead, recalling Greta's concern for my safety, I said, "Does your husband own a gun?"

"I've never seen him with one."

Which did little to bolster my sense of security. For if Isser Rotner had indeed killed Eliezer Dattner or Emil Polisar or both, he was no stranger to firearms and might have one stashed somewhere.

I scoured my mind for additional questions, but found none. I was about to bid her goodbye, when a violent cough thundered over the line, crackling like an artillery barrage from a not-too-distant front. I tore the receiver from my throbbing ear and held it at arm's length until it died down.

"Are you all right, Mrs. Rotner?"

"Quite," she said, her voice back to its usual magnificence. "One thing has just occurred to me, Mr. Lapid."

"What thing?"

"It's the unsettling realization that if Isser has managed to hide the fact that he's killed three or four people, he's a much better actor than I ever gave him credit for."

The way she said it made me think that this troubled her far more than the possibility that he was indeed a multiple murderer.

26

"It's strange," Leon Zilberman said, "what goes through your mind when you hear terrible news. The day I learned Anna was killed, the first thought that popped into my head was, Dear God, not again."

We were in the living room of his apartment on Mapu Street, where he had moved three years ago. One of his former neighbors on Rashi Street had given me the address when I'd gone looking for Zilberman there that morning.

"What do you mean, not again?"

He took a sip from his glass. It was tea, and by its whitish-brown color, he had added just a dash of milk. A lot of Israeli parents drank their tea that way, saving most of their rationed milk for their children.

Zilberman had two, a boy and a girl, five and three. Toys and doodled paper were strewn all over the living room. It gave me a twinge seeing that homey mess, knowing it had been put there by happy, laughing children.

"It wasn't the first time one of us was killed," Zilberman said.

And there it was, the opportunity I was looking for. As I'd

made my way from Greta's Café to Zilberman's apartment, I tried to figure out how to work the other deaths into the conversation. I'd decided to focus on Anna and try to slip them in somehow, but Zilberman had done it for me.

"Eliezer Dattner, you mean?"

"Yes, even though Eliezer's death was totally different from Anna's. He was shot by an Arab in Jaffa; she was knifed in the heart of Tel Aviv. But both were murders."

"And there was also Nahum Ornstein," I said.

"Nahum wasn't murdered. He drowned in his bathtub. A stupid accident."

"I understand he smoked hashish."

Zilberman nodded. "I told Nahum to lay off the stuff, but he just laughed and told me not to worry, that it didn't affect him much. And until he drowned, it looked like he was right. He never forgot a line or missed a cue."

"Seems odd then that it would cause him to drown in his own bathtub, don't you think?"

He shrugged. "You smoke that crap and drink a full bottle of wine on top of it, and you're liable to get hurt." He took another sip and made a face. "Listen to me, the man was a friend of mine and he's dead. I shouldn't be talking this way."

Zilberman was thin and loose-limbed, with a shock of wheat-colored hair. A little shorter than average, not handsome but not homely either, with a straight nose, a manly jaw, and a mouth that took up just a little too much space on his face. I recognized him from King Lear. He had played Kent.

He'd answered his door in an undershirt and khaki shorts that showed skinny legs sporting dense yellow curls. He'd asked me inside and apologized for the mess. When I'd asked him if his children were around, saying that murder isn't an appropriate topic for young ears, he said his wife had taken them shopping before a trip.

"She's taking them to the kibbutz later today to visit her parents," he'd said. "I'll be joining them in a week, after our final performance of King Lear. Not that I'm all that sure I'll be welcomed. Her parents, both staunch socialists, still haven't forgiven me for taking their daughter to Tel Aviv, where all the capitalists live. And if they knew I plan to vote for the General Zionists, they probably wouldn't let me through the kibbutz's gates." He laughed to show he was joking. Judging by the laugh lines webbing his eyes, he did that often.

Now I asked him, "Did everyone know about Ornstein's drug habit?" thinking that whoever did could have staged Ornstein's death.

"Pretty much. No one really cared. Theater people are pretty open-minded about this sort of thing."

"How about Dattner's Arab lover?"

Zilberman tilted his head a notch, regarding me with new appreciation. "You certainly know a lot about us, Mr. Lapid. No, that wasn't common knowledge. I didn't know about it until after he was killed. And neither did Ofra, of course."

"Ofra Wexler? Why do you say of course she didn't know?"

He grimaced, then shook his head and muttered to himself, "One of these days, I really should learn to keep my big mouth shut."

Leaning forward, I made my voice friendly and inviting. "Don't be hard on yourself, Mr. Zilberman. I'm a good detective. Either you tell me or I'll find out some other way. You have my word no one will know the information came from you. Okay?"

I could see him struggling with it, but eventually he sighed and said, "Ofra and Eliezer were an item. So you can imagine how she felt when he was killed and she learned he'd been sleeping with this other woman behind her back."

I kept my face blank, but inside me everything was churning. After my talks with Birnbaum and Dahlia, I had pretty much

---

settled on Isser Rotner being the killer and had practically eliminated Ofra from consideration. Because Rotner had ample reason to kill Dattner and Ornstein, while Ofra had none. But this was no longer the case. Now Ofra did have a motive to kill Dattner. A most powerful motive. Vengeance.

"Ofra was humiliated," Zilberman said. "After that, she never joined us for our after-show gatherings."

So that was why she hadn't been at Café Kassit. Even though Dattner had died twelve years ago. Sure seemed like a long time to hold on to a sense of humiliation.

"You met Ofra?" he asked.

"I talked to her."

"What was your impression of her?"

I considered lying, but then decided not to. "A little bitter, a little resentful."

He nodded. "That started after Eliezer died and she found out about the cheating. Before that she was a funny, sweet, cheerful girl."

It was hard to imagine Ofra Wexler ever being cheerful.

"What do you mean by started?" I asked.

"Huh?"

"You said she started being bitter and resentful after Eliezer Dattner died. Like it was something that happened in stages."

He drank the rest of his tea and set the empty glass on the floor. He pulled at his ear. "I guess you are a pretty good detective, aren't you?"

I waited, knowing he would spill it.

"After Eliezer was shot, Nahum and Ofra had a thing going on. It was serious, at least for her."

"But not him?"

He hesitated, probably not wanting to speak ill of the dead. "Nahum was tall, broad, handsome, had a great baritone, and he was a damn fine actor. Women liked him, and he liked them right back. Always had someone on his arm, but never for too long. Got bored easily, didn't want to settle down. He broke the hearts of a lot of women."

"Ofra's too?"

"I told him not to get involved with her. That it could harm the theater if, or when, it ended in tears. He wouldn't listen. He had a selfish streak. I was his friend, but that was something I didn't like about him. About a month before he drowned, he broke it off with her. I was there when he did it, saw Ofra run outside the theater, covering her face, crying. It was the only time I ever got angry with him."

"What happened then?"

"Nothing. I thought Ofra might quit on us, but she came to work as usual that night and acted as well as ever. But all her cheerfulness was gone. Poor Ofra, she always had terrible luck with men."

"How did she react when Nahum died?"

His expression turned grave. "I was the one who told her. She was in the women's dressing room. She just took it in, no tears, just nodded with her lips pressed tight together."

"You didn't ask her how she felt?"

"Maybe I did, I don't remember. Everything was hectic that day. We had a show that night, and I had to perform Nahum's part. I had to study all his lines, and Varda, our costume designer, had to sew me up a new suit of clothes from scratch. And poor Ofra, God only knows how she kept herself from falling apart. But the show must go on, and we performed that night, heavy heart and all."

We were both silent for a while. He looked like he was replaying that day in his head, while I was trying to corral my galloping thoughts. All my assumptions had been upended. Ofra had been jilted by Nahum Ornstein. She now had a motive to kill both him and Dattner. Isser Rotner was no longer the sole main suspect. He shared that position with Ofra. And now I had an even more difficult task ahead of me.

"She used to write poetry, you know," Zilberman said.

"Who?"

"Ofra. Some of it was pretty good, about nature and love. She even got a couple of poems published back in the day."

"But not recently?"

"Not that I know of. Come to think of it, it's been years since she showed me any of her work."

I remembered the typewriter in Ofra's apartment. Maybe she still dabbled, but I could hardly see why it mattered.

"Let's talk about Anna," I said. "Do you remember when you heard that she was dead?"

He nodded, crossing his feet at the ankles. "The morning she was found. At the theater. I remember the detective had hard, suspicious eyes. The way he looked at me made me feel uneasy, as though I had something to hide even though I didn't." He looked at me. "You have suspicious eyes as well, but not nearly as hard as that detective's. Perhaps because yours are green."

"I'm not here because I suspect you of anything, Mr. Zilberman."

He smiled faintly. "It wouldn't offend me if you did. I suppose everyone who knew Anna is considered a suspect."

"Have you ever suspected anyone?"

"Me? No, no one."

"No one among your colleagues who bore ill feelings toward Anna, exchanged harsh words with her? Hated her?"

"There's always friction in a theater. It's the nature of the work. A lot of emotion goes into portraying a different person, into becoming that person. Some actors become too invested, too involved, in their work."

"You don't?"

"I'm serious about my work, but I don't take it too much to

heart. There are actors who define themselves by what they do. They are actors first and foremost. Everything else comes after. I'm not that way. I like acting, but it's not the most important thing in my life. They are." He pointed at a framed photograph on the wall to my left. Zilberman was sitting on a wingback chair with a wide smile on his face and a girl of five on his knees. In an identical chair was a pretty plump woman holding a grinning boy of three. A beautiful family. A happy family.

"That was taken just a month ago," he said, his eyes brimming with affection.

"You have a lovely family, Mr. Zilberman."

"Thank you," he said, showing no sign of having picked up on the envy in my voice. "Acting is how I make my living, Mr. Lapid. It's not my life."

"Was it for Anna?"

"Yes, I believe it was, though we never spoke about such things. She was hardworking and ambitious, that was plain to see."

"How long did you work together?"

"Let's see, I started with the theater in 1937, and Anna came aboard the year after that, in '38. She died in '46, so eight years in total."

"Were you on good terms?"

"Not good and not bad. We hardly spoke about anything that wasn't work related. Anna wasn't an open person."

"You remember where you were the night she died?"

"Right here." He tapped the sofa. "Well, not this apartment—we lived on Rashi Street back then—but it was the same sofa bed. I was sleeping beside my very exhausted wife. She gave birth a month before Anna died."

I nodded. It was what he'd told Meltzer.

"You did not answer my earlier question," I said. "Was there anyone in the theater who argued or fought with Anna?"

"That's what I was trying to explain to you. There's an inherent competition in a theater. Actors usually want bigger roles, with more lines and a chance for acclamation. But kill for it? That's too much, even for ambitious actresses."

"Actresses, not actors?"

"In this case, it would be actresses. There are male roles and female roles. The two don't mix. But I really don't think—"

"Other actresses had to have been jealous when Anna got the main roles after Dahlia Rotner was injured."

"You know about that too? It was a scary time. For a while, I feared that the theater would close and I'd be out of work. Yes, there was talk, people whispering, wondering why Anna was chosen and not someone else."

"Like Ofra Wexler?"

"Yes, as a matter of fact."

"You think Ofra was the better choice?"

"I do."

"So why did Isser pick Anna?"

"Her looks probably. Anna was a real beauty and much taller than Ofra. That's important on stage. Both the height and the beauty." He let out a laugh. "Maybe if I were taller and more handsome, I'd be more ambitious as well."

Or you might be dead right now, I thought, *if Isser Rotner was the killer.*

I said, "Sounds like Ofra had reason to be upset, angry even."

"It wouldn't surprise me if she was, but she didn't show any sign of it. She's a consummate professional." He paused, giving me a look of soft admonishment. "Mr. Lapid, I've known Ofra for some years now. I doubt very much that she's a murderess."

Perhaps. But someone had to be guilty, and jealousy is a potent motive. And, as of right now, I knew of only one person with a clear motive to kill Eliezer Dattner, Nahum Ornstein, and Anna Hartman. That person was Ofra Wexler.

"Did she seem at all upset when Anna died?"

"Very," Zilberman said. "I remember it clearly, crying in the theater. Loud, wrenching sobs."

A nervous reaction to the presence of police? Or genuine grief over the loss of the friend she'd once had? Or maybe she'd been acting.

I took a few seconds to consider how to inject Emil Polisar into the conversation without being obvious about it.

"Were any of the other actresses upset that Anna was chosen to take over for Dahlia?" I asked. "Brigitte Polisar, for example?"

"Brigitte? I doubt it. I think she knew she wasn't made for the main roles and was happy with her lot in life."

"I understand she and her husband are also dead."

He nodded. "Brigitte died in an air attack by the wretched Egyptians, and Emil shot himself soon after." A small pause. "I think about that a lot, whether I could have stopped him."

"He showed no sign of suicidal intentions?"

"None. He was grief-stricken, of course, but what man in his position wouldn't be? But Emil was a strong person, as solid as a rock. I was shocked to the core when I heard what he did."

"Did you ever think it might not have been suicide?"

He gave me a stunned look. "No. Why would I?"

"Did he have any enemies? Anyone who benefited from his death?"

It took him a few seconds to answer, and when he did, he spoke slowly and with a touch of animosity in his voice. "No, Mr. Lapid. Emil was well-liked. No one had reason to kill him. No one got a bigger part when he died. Certainly not Ofra."

"I didn't mean to imply that, Mr. Zilberman," I lied. "It was you who said you thought Polisar wasn't the type to kill himself."

"That's what I thought, but obviously, I was wrong."

A dead end. I was hoping to find some reason for Ofra to have wanted Emil Polisar dead, but I wasn't going to get it from Zilberman. I doubted shifting my focus to Rotner would produce a better outcome.

"You know, you should be careful with such questions, Mr. Lapid," Zilberman said, his tone advisory rather than threatening. "You might upset people."

"Which people?"

He hesitated and decided to be vague. "You're casting a shadow over the entire theater when you're suggesting one of us is a murderer."

I sat without speaking, heart beating faster, as an idea began taking root in my mind.

Zilberman said, "None of us is, Mr. Lapid. You won't find Anna's killer if you think so."

He was wrong. Because one of them was a killer. Isser Rotner or Ofra Wexler. And I now knew how I was going to find out which.

27

There was a closet in my apartment on Hamaccabi Street. A two-door closet in which I'd installed a false bottom. And under the false bottom I'd stashed a box, and in the box lay a cache of currency, Israeli and foreign, and a handful of souvenirs I had collected while hunting Nazis after the Second World War.

One of these souvenirs was a folding knife. A sturdy, elegant knife with a sharp blade and a quiet spring mechanism. And near the bottom of its handle, a swastika was stamped.

I'd taken the knife from a Nazi I'd hunted down and killed. And I kept it for reasons I was not entirely sure of. Perhaps to remind myself that I had done my part to avenge my family and all the other Jews the Nazis had murdered.

Once, I'd had a Luger pistol as well, a weapon that had previously been the property of another Nazi I'd executed, but I'd been forced to give it up a few months ago.

So now all I had was the knife.

I knew a man who would be able to get me a handgun, a driver for hire for whatever criminal venture came his way. But last I heard, he was somewhere in the Negev desert, engaged in some sort of illicit activity. I had no way of reaching him.

I swore, angry with myself that I had not taken the trouble to obtain a replacement firearm. Now I would have to make do with the knife.

Pressing the small button, I watched the blade leap from its niche in the handle and lock into place. The only illumination in my room came from the naked bulb at the center of the ceiling; I'd closed all the shutters to keep out prying eyes. The blade glinted, a cold smile of deadly metal. I ran my thumb along the sharp edge, watched the skin indent, knowing that a smidgen more pressure and the skin would break and blood would well out.

It was a good weapon. A testament to German craftsmanship. It had served me well. But I still wished I had a gun.

Why had I allowed myself to remain without one? Perhaps, as with the two paintings I had hung on my walls, it was due to a subconscious desire for normalcy, an unspoken wish to return to a more ordinary life after so many years. I reprimanded myself for my foolishness.

As I sat there with the knife in my grip, I thought about the case and how it had suddenly morphed into a beast of a different nature. It had never been simple, but at least it had been clear. A regular case, with all the usual elements.

There was a crime, a victim, and a killer at large. The only unknown was the identity of the latter. Now, I was dealing with multiple possible murders and had narrowed the pool of suspects to two. But I did not know which of them was guilty, and, more important, had no discernible way to find evidence of their guilt.

Except one.

It was dangerous, some would say foolhardy, but I had taken greater chances before, and I was determined to catch this killer.

Looking back, Greta had planted the seed of the idea by saying the killer might decide to come after me, but it was Zilberman who had made it bloom with his warning that my digging around might upset people.

He had meant it innocently, but I had seen it in a different light.

I was going to flush the killer out, and there was just one way to do it. I had to make myself a target.

I could have waited until I got myself a gun. If I put my mind to it, I'd likely be able to procure one. But that might take me a few days, maybe a week, and I did not wish to wait that long. Because Greta was right. The killer might already be plotting to take me out. And one thing I knew: this killer was resourceful and smart. The more I waited, the more time the killer would have to plan my death. I wanted the killer to feel pressured, to act prematurely. I figured I had a better chance of surviving a hasty attack than a carefully planned one, even with just a knife.

When the decision was finally made, there was no hesitation. I felt confident that what I was doing was right. There was fear, yes, but the sort that comes hand in hand with determination. The sort that drives one to action instead of paralysis.

I folded the blade, tucked the knife into a pocket, returned my box of souvenirs to its hideout, and repositioned the false bottom with its covering of bedclothes and a winter blanket.

Then I drank a glass of water and went out to invite death upon myself.

28

Outside my building, I stopped to consider my destination. A choice of two, and I did not see any benefit to either one before the other. I settled on the gentlemanly course of action and went to see the lady first.

It was two o'clock when I knocked on her door. This time I had my gaze pointed in the right direction: acutely downward. When she opened her door, our eyes met instantly. She did not make an effort to hide her displeasure.

"I don't think we have anything further to discuss, Mr. Lapid," Ofra Wexler said.

"I think you're wrong about that."

"That's your opinion. Mine is the opposite, and mine is what counts."

She began closing the door, but I put a hand out to stop her.

"I have some questions, Miss Wexler, and I am going to ask them. If you close this door, I'll shout them so you'll be able to hear. You and all your neighbors. It might prove embarrassing. Or you can ask me inside, and we'll talk privately. It's your choice. Either way is fine with me."

"I'll call the police, tell them you're harassing me."

"Fine. Go ahead. But you don't have a telephone in your apartment. You'll have to go out to make the call. I'll come with you. We can talk on the way."

Her jade-colored eyes flashed. Her small pretty features tightened. She sneered. "It gives you a thrill, doesn't it, to threaten a woman?"

"Not at all," I said. "But hunting and catching a killer does. Shall we step inside? I'll keep it brief."

Her jaw worked, sharp edges of bone moving under her fine skin. Then, without a word, she turned and moved toward the living room with rapid steps. I followed, swinging the door shut.

In the living room, Ofra went straight for her cigarettes. She had one burning before she took a seat. I remained standing. I wanted to appear intimidating. I wanted to rattle her hard.

She crossed her legs, trying to appear calm, but the way she sucked on her cigarette told me she was nervous.

She wore her hair loose today. It fell straight down her back. It made her look younger, like an adolescent. Once again, I was struck by her smallness, but now I saw it as the perfect camouflage for a murderess.

No one would suspect that a woman so small could be capable of murder. And she would know this. She would cultivate this impression. As an accomplished actress, it wouldn't be difficult.

"I've learned a few things," I said, "since the last time we spoke."

"Oh?" She blew out a stream of smoke. "I don't suppose good manners are among them."

"I learned that you took Anna's death pretty hard, that you wept when you heard the news."

"Anna and I used to be close, once upon a time. The fact that we were no longer friends when she died did not mean I didn't mourn her."

"Yet you didn't shed one tear when you learned Nahum Ornstein had died, and you and he were lovers."

She paused with her cigarette en route to her lips, obviously stunned by the question. For a second there, it looked like she'd forgotten how to breathe. Then she audibly exhaled, closed her lips around her cigarette, took a pull, and pushed the smoke out of her nostrils. Only then did she speak. "Who told you that?"

"Does it matter?"

"Was it Leon Zilberman? It had to be, because he was the one who told me Nahum was dead. He had no right to tell you. It's none of your business. Nor is it relevant to Anna's death."

"Isn't it?"

Again she froze, her thin eyebrows drawing closer together. "What are you getting at, Mr. Lapid?"

"I think you know, Miss Wexler."

"I haven't a clue."

"Then I'll enlighten you in a minute. First, I'm curious to know why you cried over Anna but not over Nahum Ornstein."

"If you must know, the reason was because I'd cried myself out over him when he said he wanted nothing more to do with me."

"Shortly before he died, wasn't it?"

"A month. But you knew that already, didn't you?"

"Where were you the night he died?"

Now she looked more amused than surprised. "Is this a joke?"

"Answer the question."

Another drag. "Right here."

"Alone?"

"Completely."

"So you don't have an alibi for the night of his death."

"Why would I need one? Nahum wasn't murdered."

"Yes, he was. And you know it."

She took a final, violent pull on her cigarette, then mashed it out in quick, hard jabs. "Let me get this straight: You think I killed Nahum? Are you insane or just plain stupid?"

"You had motive. He took advantage of you. You were in love with him, but he rejected you. It must have torn your heart to shreds when he ended your relationship."

"I can't believe I'm having this conversation. Nahum drowned. He wasn't murdered."

"You knew of his hashish habit. You knew it would be easy to get the police to believe it was an accident. How did you do it?"

"Mr. Lapid," she said, in an utterly placid tone, "the list of women who had been promised things by Nahum—eternal love, marriage, what have you—only to be discarded like soiled rags once he tired of them could fill a newspaper. My motive isn't stronger than any of theirs. If you truly believe Nahum was murdered, you have plenty of other suspects. Why pick on me?"

"Because of Eliezer Dattner."

That hit her even harder than my mentioning Ornstein. Now she didn't look like she merely forgot how to breathe. She looked like her heart had stopped too.

After ten very long seconds, she said, "What about Eliezer?"

"You and he were involved, and he betrayed you. He had a lover. And he was killed."

"By an Arab."

"That's what it was made to look like. It was in Jaffa, which at the time was majority Arab, and it was during the Arab Revolt. And the anti-Jewish pamphlet stuck in Dattner's mouth sealed the deal. It left no room for an alternative interpretation."

"And you think that I—"

"I think you were enraged by his betrayal. I think you decided he had to pay. I think you lay in wait for him on one of the nights he went to visit his lover. I think you shot him dead."

She shook her head. "You're wrong. So wrong. I didn't even know he had a lover. I only found out after he died."

"That's what your colleagues believe. But I know the truth. You murdered Dattner because he cheated on you. And when Ornstein rejected you, you decided he deserved to be killed as well."

She shook her head again, this time wordlessly.

"Only it couldn't look like a murder, not after Dattner. That would have looked suspicious. So you staged the scene. You made it look like he drowned in his bathtub." I paused, looking at her, feeling sick and trying to keep down the bile burning at my throat. I knew there was a fifty-fifty chance that she wasn't guilty, that I was putting her through hell for nothing. I told myself I was doing it for the right reasons, to catch a multiple murderer, but that didn't mean I enjoyed it, or that I didn't hate myself a little for doing it. I simply forced myself to continue, to get it done, because I saw no other way.

"The first murder is the hardest," I said. "The second is easier. After that, it becomes just another way to solve your problems. When Anna got the main parts after Dahlia Rotner's accident, you were enraged. You felt that you deserved it more. Maybe if it had happened years earlier, you would have done nothing, but you were already used to killing. So you stabbed her and left her dead body in Trumpeldor Cemetery. That's what happened, isn't it?"

"No," she said in a small voice and then repeated it louder, "No."

"I can understand why you did it," I said. "All three of them. They all had it coming. Dattner and Ornstein for hurting you, and Anna for taking what was rightfully yours. Come on, admit it. Get it off your chest."

She didn't speak for a moment, just breathed in and out deeply, her eyes locked on mine. Then she turned her head and reached a slow hand for her cigarettes. Once she had one lit and had taken a puff, she was herself again. She wore the same composed, almost haughty expression that she'd worn a few moments ago. No sign of fear whatsoever.

I thought I knew what was coming, and she didn't disappoint me.

She said, "Mr. Lapid, Anna was taller than me by eight inches, and Nahum was taller still and much stronger. Do you really think I could have overcome either one of them in a fight—even, in Anna's case, with a knife?"

I let out a little breath. I was glad she said it. If she hadn't, it would have meant she'd never even thought of it, and I'd have begun doubting myself entirely.

"It's possible," I said, but even to my ears I did not sound convinced. I didn't think Ofra could have lifted Ornstein into his bathtub. But maybe she'd convinced him to go in it and then attacked?

She sneered. "You're desperate, aren't you? That's why you're here, making these wild accusations, spinning these wild theories. I don't know what you hope to gain by all this nonsense."

"Either you did it or someone did it for you."

"Ah, so now I have an accomplice. Pray tell, who might that be?"

"I don't know yet. But it would have to be someone close to you. Otherwise, he wouldn't kill for you over and over again. It's someone who likes killing. Someone with a beard."

I was watching her closely when I spoke, and I caught it. The small muscle twitching in her cheek, the flicker of fear in her eyes. It happened when I mentioned the beard. It meant something to her. She recovered quickly, turning to the ashtray, and took way too long to stub out her cigarette. When she faced me again, her features were inscrutable, her acting skills coming to the rescue.

"Who is it, Miss Wexler? Who has been killing on your behalf?"

"I," she began, but her voice cracked, and she had to clear her throat before she tried again. "I've never killed anyone, and I've never asked anyone to kill for me. I swear to God I didn't."

"Who is the man with the beard, Miss Wexler?"

"There is no man, Mr. Lapid. Only in your warped imagination."

She looked right at me. Eyes steady, no flinching. No sign she was lying. Doubt infiltrated my mind. Had I misread her? Was I being overeager, seeing things that weren't there?

"Did he kill anyone else for you besides Dattner, Ornstein, and Anna?" I said, ignoring my doubts. "Any more of your colleagues?"

She frowned at me. She blinked a few times. Then she rose from her chair and pointed to the door. "I'm through indulging your fantasies, Mr. Lapid. You need to leave."

I didn't move. "I'm going to find out the truth, Miss Wexler. I will not rest until I know everything. If you're guilty, I'll see to it that you're locked up and never breathe free air again."

Her cheeks were flaming now. With one hand she still pointed to the exit. The other was bunched into a fist.

"Get out!" she screamed. "Get out and leave me alone. If you ever bother me again, I'll...I'll—" She didn't finish her threat. She just stood there, trembling with fury.

I left. I had done it. I had rattled her good and hard. I knew that if she was the killer, plans for my death were already brewing in her brain.

29

This time, there was no sign of the old cleaning lady. The lobby's floor sparkled, so she must have finished up and gone home. I made my way up to the second floor of Ohel Shem, entered the theater hall, and found Isser Rotner where I'd left him. On stage, alone.

He held no script in his hands this time. In its place was a pen and a notebook. He moved across the stage, stopping here and there, making notes. I was five rows from the stage when I must have made a noise, because his back stiffened and he whipped his head around and saw me.

His dark eyes narrowed, and his jaw flexed. As in our previous meeting, he obviously disliked my being there. But he showed no fear. I would have to change that.

"Good morning, Mr. Rotner," I said, stopping before the stage.

He closed the notebook with a snap. "This is the second time you've interrupted me in the middle of my work, Mr. Lapid. Your rudeness is beginning to annoy me. Can't you see I'm busy?"

"What are you doing?"

He exhaled through his mouth. "If you must know, I'm working on the stage directions for an upcoming production."

"The stage directions? What's that?"

"It's where each actor will be during each scene, at every point of it."

"I had no idea you planned things to such a degree."

He smiled thinly. "You thought we just went up on stage and winged it?"

"I thought you learned your lines and rehearsed your scenes and that was it."

"Some theaters may settle for that level of preparation. But in this theater, we strive for excellence."

I levered myself up onto the stage as I had done the last time. "May I see it?"

He made a face, but his vanity won the day. He wanted to show off his efforts. He handed me the notebook. "I doubt it would mean anything to you."

I opened the notebook to the first page. Inside a large rectangular shape that represented the stage were several X marks, and next to them what I assumed were initials for either characters or actors. Arrows of varying lengths and curvatures cut across the page. At the top were a series of numbers. Acts and scenes? It looked elaborate and painstaking. The work of a man who is patient and methodical. The sort of man who can plan a murder to its finest detail.

"So," he said, "how is your investigation going?"

"Very well." I gave him back his notebook.

"Really?"

"Yes. I now know who killed Anna Hartman."

His eyebrows shot up, and it took him a couple of seconds to speak. "Well, don't keep me in suspense. Tell me who it is."

"All right," I said. "It's you."

The silence that followed had a distinct texture. It was not the empty silence of a vacant theater hall long after the audience had left. It was not the anticipatory silence before a play began. It was that unique loaded silence that followed a major turning point in a play, a moment of separation between before and after, when everything changed irrevocably.

Rotner's eyes turned to slits. His face hardened, and through the narrow space between his lips, I saw his teeth were clenched. His animosity toward me rolled off him in waves that were almost palpable, like shimmering heat rising off pavement. Good. I wanted him to hate me, and I wanted him to fear me. If he was the killer, that was the emotional combination that would cause him to strike at me.

When he spoke next, his voice was low and thick and belligerent. "You have a great deal of nerve to make such an absurd accusation."

"Yet I'm making it, all the same."

"You have no proof."

"Don't I?"

The question hung between us like a threat. It gave him pause, and for a couple of heartbeats his eyes skittered across my face, as though trying to determine if I were bluffing. I thought I saw a glimmer of fear in them before he called upon his talent and expunged it. He raised his chin, looking more amused than anything else.

"You forget something, Mr. Lapid, I was at home that entire evening and night. I know you spoke to my wife and she told you this."

"You're right, she did."

"Then why the hell are you accusing me of a murder you know I did not, and could not, commit?"

"Because I think your wife is lying, Mr. Rotner. In fact, I'm sure of it."

This appeared to stun him even more than being accused of

murder. Rotner might have wanted to believe he was a better actor than his wife, but inside he knew the truth. He recognized his wife's exceptional talent, had depended on it for his alibi. He simply could not fathom how anyone would question anything Dahlia said.

"You have no reason to doubt her," he said, sounding like he was trying to reassure himself.

"I do. I was watching her closely when she told me of your whereabouts that night. I caught a tell. You know what a tell is, Mr. Rotner?"

He didn't answer.

"A tell is an involuntary reaction when someone is lying or trying to hide something. Not everyone has a tell, and often they are hard to identify, but your wife displayed one. And I saw it." I hoped to God I was not showing a tell myself, spinning him this tale.

"I don't believe you," he said, and I realized I had failed to shake him. He trusted his wife's skills implicitly.

I made another attempt. "Believe what you want, but I know you weren't home that night. You have no alibi."

"Of course I do. The police talked to my wife. They know she spoke the truth."

"They believed her, yes, which is a testament to her acting skills, because spouses are by their nature unreliable witnesses. Maybe those acting skills have deteriorated from lack of practice over the past five years, because I was not convinced."

Again he paused, but his face did not register any inkling as to his thoughts. He was a good actor, better than most, and he longed to be the best. How it must have tormented him to be eclipsed by Eliezer Dattner and Nahum Ornstein. Enough, perhaps, to cross the ultimate line and kill them.

He said, "I did not have any reason to kill Anna."

"You were her lover," I said, and the subtle cramping of his lips confirmed it. He hadn't expected that secret to be revealed. "Don't bother denying it. I know it for a fact. What did she do? Threaten to tell your wife? Decide to end the affair? Did she have enough of you?"

He smiled contemptuously. "You're flailing, Mr. Lapid. You have nothing."

"Innocent men don't fake alibis, Mr. Rotner. And you did."

"You may believe my wife or not, that's not important. Only what the police believe is."

"The police may decide to take a closer look when I tell them about the affair."

"Tell them any lie you wish. Even if they believe you, I doubt they'll do anything about it after all this time. And if they do, my wife will tell them the same thing she did five years ago, that I was with her all that night."

"She may decide to change her story once she learns of the affair."

That made him quiet. And it achieved the dual goal I had set for this meeting. His eyes burned with rage and hate and a dash of fear. He did not want his wife to know of his infidelity. That by itself could be reason enough for him to kill me.

"Don't you dare speak with my wife about me, understand?" His voice was a low growl. "I am not some nobody you can push around."

"I know you're not. No murderer is."

"I'm no murderer."

"What did you do with Anna's bag? Why did you take her underwear?"

His Adam's apple shifted in his throat. That was his only reaction. "I did not kill Anna."

"I don't believe you. I came here to give you a chance to confess."

"You're out of your mind. I have nothing to confess to. Now I want you to leave and never come back here again. Not even if you buy a ticket to any of our shows. And if you bother my wife or spread lies about me, you'll pay dearly for it. Do I make myself clear?"

"Quite," I said, not budging. "I wouldn't want to get shot or drowned in my bathtub."

"What the hell are you talking about?"

"I'm talking about how you became the leading man of this theater. I'm talking about Eliezer Dattner and Nahum Ornstein, the two men you killed."

He stared at me, his mouth slightly ajar.

"It's a shock, isn't it," I said, "that someone else knows what you did?" I took a step closer. "I understand why you killed them. Dattner was in your way; he was the lead actor. You thought you deserved that position more, so you followed him into Jaffa one night, when he went to pay a call on his lover, and you shot him. You planned it well, down to the anti-Jewish pamphlet you shoved between his lips.

"As for Ornstein, he was getting too many glowing reviews; some of them said he was even better than you. So you went to his apartment, knocked him out somehow, and made it look like he drowned in his bathtub. You staged the scene perfectly. Like you do in that notebook of yours."

He looked down at the notebook in question, then slowly back up at me. "You think I killed Eliezer? And Nahum? You're—"

"You want to be the best," I said. "That's why you spend so many hours here, working so hard to make each performance perfect. And you're very good. Just not good enough. Not like Dattner and Ornstein. And I bet they didn't work half as hard as you. They were just born better. This must have made you mad as hell. You deserved it and they didn't. So you killed them and got what you wanted. You became the leading man. That must have felt good."

Rotner shook his head. A vein began throbbing in his temple. "I've killed no one. Absolutely no one."

"Got an alibi? Or are you planning on getting your wife to lie for you again?"

That got to him. His ears pulled back, the skin of his cheeks drew taut, the wolf in him surfacing.

"It must be killing you," I said, "how bad things are going. I know about the wage cuts. I know the theater is bleeding money. And it's all happening with you being the star. I watched you in King Lear. You're good. But apparently, you're not good enough to carry a theater on your shoulders."

"Shut up! Just shut your mouth!"

"I'm going to find proof, Mr. Rotner. And then everyone will know what you did, and why. And how, after all that, you're still a failure."

I watched it happen, the last shreds of his self-control sloughing away like dry skin. He let out a bellow of fury and came at me. One big step, a planted left foot, and then his hand was flying at my face. It was the hand clutching the pen.

I could see it coming and evaded the blow easily. His midsection was undefended, and I punched him right on the navel, not holding anything back, doing what I'd wanted to do since our first conversation. His air went out. Notebook and pen tumbled. He joined them, dropping on his ass, gasping for breath.

I crouched down beside him. I could smell his anger, a musky, vibrant scent. His face was red with rage and lack of oxygen. I'd done what I came here to do. I did not think I could make him any madder at me.

"Just one more thing," I said, noting the spittle on his lips and the twin cauldrons of hatred in his eyes. "Did you also kill Emil Polisar? Because if you did, I'll make sure you go down for that one as well."

30

I went to Greta's Café. The place was humming with customers, and Greta did not have time for me. That was all right. A dose of solitude was what I wanted. I spent the next three hours at my table, playing chess and drinking coffee, trying to think of nothing at all. But being a marked man tends to occupy the mind. I did not think the killer would act so soon, but I found myself scanning the face of each new patron and periodically touching my knife for reassurance.

Back in my building, I unlocked my door and went inside my apartment, finding it exactly as I'd left it. Feeling entirely safe for the first time since my talk with Ofra Wexler, I took my knife out of my pocket and laid it on the table. I rummaged around for my cigarettes, then realized I'd run out and forgotten to buy a new pack. Swearing under my breath, I went into the kitchen, got an apple, ran some water over it, and took a bite.

Going to the nightstand, I picked up the creased paperback with the cover showing a weather-beaten cowboy with a Winchester rifle. I thumbed open the book where I'd left a cinema stub as a marker, then sat on the bed to read. I was raising the apple for a second bite when my nose caught the smell.

It was so faint, I thought I was imagining it. Still, my body tensed up and the small hairs on the nape of my neck stood like inmates at roll call.

Then some primal instinct shouted a warning in my head, and I acted without thinking. I pitched myself forward, down to the floor, sure that I was too damn slow, sure that my next sensation would be my skin getting ripped open or my skull blown apart by a bullet.

But the only thing I felt was a whoosh of splitting air as something sliced through empty space an inch from my back. Empty space that an instant ago had been filled with my body. And then I landed hard on my stomach and chest, the book tumbling from one hand, the other somehow retaining its grip on the apple. I heard a guttural curse behind me and rolled over quickly.

Amiram Gadot was standing there, dressed all in black, a knife in his hand. The blade was stuck in the mattress, all the way to the hilt, exactly where I'd been sitting. I shot to my feet as he pried it loose.

His upper lip curled, almost as white as the teeth it revealed. His narrow face looked bony, his skin seemingly so thin the bones bleached through, like the head of a recently dead man. His bottomless eyes held a sharp, manic gleam. Something long and sleek seemed to move just under the irises, but that must have been a trick of the light. He had taken off his shoes to make his already quiet walk utterly soundless. And it had worked. I had not heard him sneaking up on me.

But he hadn't thought of removing the brilliantine from his hair. As in our last meeting, it was oiled back from his forehead, each hair in place and glinting like metal. It was that oily smell that I'd caught, and my brain had made the connection, alerting me to danger before I could even consciously name it.

The man can pop just about any lock in twenty seconds flat and not leave a mark, Meir Gadot had told me about his cousin, and he'd been right. I had not noticed a thing when I unlocked my door.

"You're faster than I thought, cop," Amiram said.

His knife had a long, bright blade. I could tell it was razor sharp even from six feet away. If I hadn't moved, that blade would have sliced me open like a fish and, judging by the way it had dug into the mattress, would have torn my heart or lung practically in two.

"I appreciate that you took off your shoes when you came in," I said with false bravado, my eyes dancing frantically around, looking for an easy-to-reach weapon and finding none. "I try to keep the place clean."

He smiled in the way hyenas smile. He looked loose and calm and confident. I felt the exact opposite. He was the one with the knife. He was lighter on his feet. And he had bloody murder in his eyes.

If I wasn't in such a bad spot, I might have laughed. Here I was, expecting an attempt on my life by either Isser Rotner or Ofra Wexler, and now, just a few hours after springing my ingenious plan, I was facing death from a totally different direction. Some lunatic I had offended on another job entirely.

I thought about yelling for help, but what good would it do? This fight would be over well before any cops showed up. And it was just as likely to cause some nosy neighbor to come see what was going on and end up dead as a result. I did not want innocent blood on my hands, just that of the guilty.

I could have rushed to the door or the table where my knife lay. But I'd never get the door open, or the knife unfolded, before Amiram would be at my back, his knife in me.

"You should have minded your own business," Amiram said, taking a small step forward, the knife pointing at my heart. "But cops always get involved in things that don't concern them."

This was payback for insulting him in front of his cousin. And for telling Meir not to share with Amiram the name of the man who was stealing from him. Which made me fear for Meir's safety.

"Where's Meir?" I asked. "Is he all right?"

Amiram narrowed his eyes, then let out a throaty laugh. "You are stupid, aren't you, cop? Like so many of you. Don't worry about Meir. Worry about me."

He took another step forward, and I backed away. That made him grin wider, showing me more teeth and a pink strip of his gums, thinning his lips to needle width. Another step, and my back touched the wall. Nowhere to retreat to. This fight would happen very soon, and only one of us would make it out of this apartment still breathing. I made my lips tremble, let all my fear show on my face, and raised my free hand before me, fingers spread, as though to ward him off. "Don't," I said in a small voice. "Please." I wanted him to think I was too scared to resist properly. I wanted him to think that when he came at me, all I'd do was cower and curl up and die.

I could tell it was working by how his expression turned gleeful and ravenous, already tasting his triumph and my death. Any second now.

I switched my gaze from his face to his feet, waiting for his move. When he tilted onto the balls of his feet to spring forward, I was ready. As he launched himself at me, knife in an underhand grip to stab upward, I snapped my wrist and hurled the apple at his face. At the same time, I threw myself toward him, the exact opposite of what he'd expected.

The apple got him high in the cheek. Not as hard as I wanted, but enough to break his stride. I came at him fast, aiming a fist at his nose. With incredible agility, he jerked his body sideways. My fist bounced against the top of his shoulder. The blow spun him around, but he kept his feet, the bastard. I swung my left fist, a wild punch, but he danced away on those light feet of his, and I knew I'd missed my opportunity. He was back in control, and now he was careful.

"You're full of surprises, aren't you?" he said, no smile on his face this time, just brutal determination. This had been fun, his expression seemed to say, but now it was time to get serious and finish the job.

We were closer to the table now, and I made a desperate lunge for my knife. Amiram slashed his blade through the air, and I felt a lick of wet fire burn along the underside of my forearm. I jumped back, clenching my teeth, the pain hot and stinging. Amiram picked up my knife, pressed the release button, looked at the blade, and chuckled.

"I bet you wish you had this with you, huh?" Then he closed the knife and dropped it to the floor and kicked it to the far corner of the room, away from me, so now I had to go through him to get it. "Go ahead," he said. "Make another grab for it."

But all I did was grip my slashed forearm with my other hand, trying to keep the blood from oozing out. It didn't work. I was dripping all over the floor, running out of blood the same way I had run out of ideas.

Then he moved, coming forward with his lips pulled back and the knife arcing upward, and I only barely managed to jerk out of the blade's path before it could rip open my belly.

He jumped at me again, feinting another low stab, but I read him right, and when he raised the knife for a downward strike, I grabbed his wrist with both hands, stopping the tip of the blade a few inches from my throat. His momentum carried us both backward, and my back smacked into a wall, knocking some of my air out. The blade moved closer before I managed to push it away again.

Up close, I could smell his sweat and breath and feel the excited heat of a predator approaching a kill wafting off him. We were pressed close together now, and with his free hand, he began jabbing at my side. The punches were not powerful, but they were well placed, and gradually they made my kidney feel as though it were being ground up. My strength was waning, my grip on Amiram's wrist slipping. He felt it too and joined both hands together to try to push the knife into me.

With one arm bleeding, I knew I could not hold him back for long. I gathered my strength and, with a deep growl, pushed the knife up and away from me. The blade scraped along the wall, then bounced over something with a dull thud, followed by the sound of ripping canvas.

Amiram jerked his hands back and forth, trying to wrench his wrist free from my grip. The knife kept colliding with something on the wall behind me, just outside my field of vision. Finally, Amiram broke loose, stumbling a few steps backward, the movement yanking the painting the knife had torn off its nail.

It bumped against my shoulder, and I instinctively caught it. The canvas was ripped to shreds, strips hanging like loose skin off the frame. I just barely had time to realize it was the inside of the frame the blade had kept colliding with, when Amiram came at me again, knife first.

With more desperation than hope, I swung what remained of the painting at his head. At the last instant, he raised an arm. The frame broke at the contact, two sides falling to the floor. Still, I could tell I'd hurt him. He fell to one knee with a grunt, a few strands of oily hair dangling over his forehead.

In my hands remained two sides of the frame, barely held together in what used to be a corner. As Amiram rose to his feet, I tore the two sides apart, dropping one and holding the other like a stake. When he sprang forward again, driven to frenzy with pain and bloodlust, I thrust the makeshift stake at his belly. I felt that split-second resistance as his skin fought against the pressure before it gave way. And then it was as though his body was sucking in the intrusion, almost welcoming it, but I knew it was me, driving it in with a bloodlust of my own, wanting to tear the insides of this evil man to pulp, to rip out his life as he had tried to rip out mine.

I watched his eyes as the stake went in. Those dark, fathomless eyes. For the first time, they did not look impenetrable. They showed shock, surprise, and panicked understanding, and then they teared up in pain.

The knife dropped from his hand. He sank to the floor, and I went down with him, still holding the stake, the blood from my torn forearm dripping onto his shirt, mingling with the blood now pumping out of the hole in his stomach.

His mouth was open, ragged breaths wheezing from his throat. It took almost a minute for him to die. I kept watching him as his eyes went blacker still and his breathing stopped and the darkness that was his life came to an end.

31

I just wanted to sit there and catch my breath, but I knew I had to hurry. Our struggle had not been overly noisy, but someone still might have heard. Someone might be coming. Besides, my forearm kept bleeding.

I pushed myself up and went in search of Amiram Gadot's shoes. When the police came, I would tell them I had come home and this man was here, intending to burglarize the place. His record would support that story, but questions would arise if he was found without shoes. That would suggest he had lain in wait for me, and I did not want to explain why he would do so.

Each step shot a lance of pain through my side that made my teeth clench, but I dared not stop or slow. There wasn't much time.

The shoes were in the bathroom. I took the opportunity to wash the blood off my hands and wrap a towel around my wound. I grabbed the shoes and stuck them on the dead man's feet.

Next, I picked up my knife and put it back in my secret box, making sure not to get any blood on the linen that covered the false bottom. I hated leaving my box there, knowing that soon the apartment would be crawling with cops, but I did not have time to take it to someone I trusted. Besides, if the cops bought my story, I did not think they would search the place. At least I hoped so.

Lack of time, and the fear that at any second someone might poke his head through the door, also precluded my going through the dead man's pockets. Whatever money he carried would probably end up divided among the very people Amiram hated most— police officers. The thought made me smile.

My eyes made a final sweep around the apartment, and I knew that it would look better if I messed it up a little. But one drop of blood in the wrong place might raise suspicion. So I left things as they were and went out to the corner, to Levinson Drugstore, where the street's only public telephone was.

It was just before closing time, and the drugstore was empty of customers. The Levinsons were behind the counter. I watched two pairs of eyes grow big at the sight of me.

Mr. Levinson was the first to speak. "Adam, what happened?"

Mrs. Levinson, always the more efficient of the two, rounded the counter and went for the telephone. "I'll ring the hospital."

"No," I said. "Call the police first. Tell them there's a dead body in my apartment."

She had the receiver in one hand, the other poised over the dial. She paused for just a second, looking at me, then gave a quick nod and began to dial. Thank God for levelheaded women.

I turned to her husband. "Can you clean and bandage this for me?"

As his wife spoke into the telephone, Mr. Levinson unwrapped the bloody towel covering my wound and pursed his lips. "This will need stitches, I think."

"Is it urgent, or can it wait until the police come and go?"

He frowned at my question, then surveyed the wound once more. "It can wait, I think, but not for long. Come into the back room. I'll bandage you up."

Which he did, with calm proficiency, first inundating the

wound with iodine, which stung like a thousand needles, then coiling a few layers of cotton dressing over the wound.

He examined his handiwork and said, "This will keep for now, but go to the hospital soon, Adam. As soon as possible, all right?"

I was back in my apartment a couple of minutes before the police arrived. Two cars screeched to a halt outside my building, four officers tumbling out and pounding up the stairs. Two remained on the landing, the other two—an inspector and a corporal—came inside, but both stopped dead in their tracks when they saw the body.

It was a sight, all right. Amiram lay on the floor, eyes open, a piece of wood sticking out of him. Seeing him made me think of Anna lying dead with a knife jammed in her chest. But that was where the resemblance ended. Where Anna's death brought with it acute sadness, Amiram's demise made me feel very little at all.

The corporal went to the body. He felt at its neck and said one word that didn't tell us anything we didn't already know, "Dead."

The inspector turned to me. I was sitting at the dining table. "What's your name?" he asked.

"Adam Lapid."

"You did this?"

"I came home and this man was here. He had a knife. He attacked me. We fought and I won."

"You live here?"

"Yes." I showed him my identification card. He nodded. Mrs. Levinson had given my name when she called. I was expected.

"You know him?" he asked, meaning the dead man.

"Never seen him before in my life."

"Then what's he doing here? Why attack you?"

"Probably came to rob the place. I walked in and surprised him."

"Looks kind of neat here for a burglary."

"I must have come in just after he did."

"Uh-huh." He squinted his eyes at me, saying nothing. It was a familiar tactic, and he didn't do it all that well. I waited. I wasn't going to be the next one to speak.

Another cop came in, this one a sergeant. He went to stand by the corporal, who was going through Amiram's pockets. The sergeant glanced at the body, then hunkered down for a closer look. "Hey, I know this guy," he said.

The inspector, who was still squint-eying me, broke off his stare and said, "What?"

"I know him. I arrested him a few years back. Amiram Gadot's his name."

The corporal, holding up Amiram's ID, nodded confirmation. "That's his name, all right."

"Arrested him for what?" the inspector called.

"Robbed a few apartments. Great with locks, if I remember right."

The inspector looked at me again, no longer squinting. "You seem awfully calm for someone who's just killed a man, Mr. Lapid."

"I was in the war," I said. "I've seen my share of bodies."

He asked me where I'd served, and I told him. He commended my unit's exploits in the war, and then the sergeant snapped his fingers and said he remembered me, too. Wasn't my picture in the paper during the war?

And just like that, the atmosphere shifted. No one suspected me of anything anymore. I was the acclaimed war hero, and the dead man was the common criminal back to his old ways. I'd done the world a favor, the corporal told me, and no one voiced any objection to that assertion.

The inspector—whose name was Bartov—asked me to tell them exactly what had happened. I did, and it was almost the whole truth. I just omitted some of the things Amiram and I had said. The entire sequence of battle was unchanged.

After I was done, the sergeant said, "You were lucky, Mr. Lapid. Damn lucky. Shame about the painting."

Only then did it enter my mind. The painting that had been destroyed in the fight. With a sinking feeling and trembling hands, I picked up the broken pieces of frame, the shredded strips of canvas. It was the painting of the woman and the two girls, the one that reminded me of my dead wife and daughters.

A strangled, hopeless, keening voice deep in my head howled, *I've lost them again.* I felt my eyes grow wet, but now was not the time for tears. The cops wouldn't understand.

Still, my face must have shown something, because Inspector Bartov asked, "You all right, Mr. Lapid?"

"Yeah," I said, struggling to control my voice. "I just really loved this painting."

Someone came with a stretcher and carted the body away. Outside my door, a few of my neighbors had congregated. The police were blocking their view of the apartment. Bartov ordered them to go home. He asked me to come to the station the next day to write up a formal statement, then offered me a ride to the hospital. A young doctor with sharp features and sure fingers prodded my pummeled flank and stated he did not believe I'd sustained any permanent internal injuries. Then he stitched up my wound, told me not to strain myself, and said my arm should be back to normal in a week or two.

32

It was after nine by the time I got home from the hospital. There was blood on my floor and it was stinking up my apartment. I threw open the windows and washed the floor till not a speck remained. Then I cleaned myself up as best I could, taking care to keep my bandages dry.

I sat on the edge of my bed and considered my day. I'd been lucky. Luckier than I deserved. If Amiram had opted to use his pistol instead of a knife, I'd be dead right now. He had wanted to kill me quietly, and that was the only reason I was still alive.

But I wasn't out of the woods yet. I still had the killer to contend with. And now, when the attack I'd invited on myself occurred, I couldn't simply defend myself. One act of self-defense was acceptable. Two in the space of a few days would raise the eyebrow of every policeman in Tel Aviv. Surviving whatever came next just became much more difficult.

I slept on my punctured mattress with my knife under my pillow. My sleep was usually beset by nightmares of Auschwitz and my family, but on days on which I struck a blow or spilled blood, I was given a reprieve. I tried not to think why this happened. I suspected the answer would not be to my liking. That night, I slept like the dead who often tormented my dreams.

In the morning, I went to Levinson Drugstore, thanked the Levinsons for their help the previous day, and assured them my arm was all right. Then I found a café on King George where no one knew me and made some calls, trying to locate Meir Gadot. I didn't find him.

I went to the police station on Yehuda Halevi Street. I sat down with Inspector Bartov, dictated and signed my statement, and was told the case was as good as closed. Only paperwork remained to be done. That and Amiram Gadot's burial.

"Scum like that," Bartov said, "they should just dump him in a pit and not waste money on a headstone."

I thought there were already too many Jews buried in unmarked graves, enough to fill the world end to end, but kept my opinion to myself.

After finishing with the inspector, I went upstairs to Reuben Tzanani's office. He leaped from his chair the second he saw me and rounded his overburdened desk.

"Adam, I just heard what happened. Are you all right? How's your arm?"

"I'm okay, Reuben. The doctor said I'll be as good as new in no time."

He peered worriedly at my face, as though distrustful of my answer and attempting to divine my true condition. I would have bet he wore the same expression whenever one of his children scraped a knee or came down with a fever.

"Sit down, sit down," he said. "I'll go get you some coffee. You want some coffee?"

I smiled. "I'm all right, Reuben. Truly. You know me, I've been hurt worse before."

He did know, of course, he had seen me on the brink of death, but this reminder did not seem to allay his concern one bit. Even when I did as he had bidden and sat down, he continued to hover about, a frown creasing his otherwise smooth forehead.

"You're making me nervous, Reuben," I said.

He threw up his hands and leaned against the desk. "I'm sorry. I know I worry too much. I'm glad that you're okay."

"That makes two of us."

"I understand it's a clear case of self-defense. You won't be charged with anything."

"That's what I was led to believe."

"I wonder what made him pick your apartment to rob."

"Probably random chance. We'll never know," I said, then changed the subject so I wouldn't have to lie to him further. "By any chance, did you get the information I asked you for?"

"The dates on which those three men died? Yes, I have it right here." He plucked a sheet of paper off his desk and handed it to me. Birnbaum's memory proved accurate. Eliezer Dattner had died on July 10, 1939; Nahum Ornstein on April 24, 1940; and Emil Polisar on May 25, 1948. I copied the dates into my notebook, one to a line, writing Anna's date of death, May 28, 1946, in its proper place between Ornstein and Polisar. I looked at the four lines I had scribbled and never felt surer that I wasn't imagining things. Meltzer was wrong. Birnbaum too. Two of the men whose names were now scrawled in my notebook, if not all three of them, had been murdered. And at that moment the killer was likely plotting how to add my name to the list of victims. But that didn't mean I should sit idly by and wait. Being prey never appealed to me. Hunter is a role that suits me much better.

"Did you manage to get any of the files?" I asked.

"Give me a minute," Reuben said, "I'll call downstairs and see if they arrived." After he hung up, he said, "Just one file so far, I'm afraid. Sit tight, I'll run down and get it."

It took him three minutes to return. When he did, he had two files tucked under his arm and a mug clutched in his other hand.

He handed me the mug with a sheepish smile. "I figured you could use some coffee, even if you're sure you're okay."

I smiled in gratitude and took a sip. The coffee was of the rationed chicory variety. To add insult to injury, it had been boiled to within an inch of its life. But someone had loaded it with sugar, probably confiscated in a police raid, and that made it halfway decent.

"I thought you said there was just one file," I said, placing the mug on an unoccupied corner of Reuben's desk.

"The other one is of your uninvited visitor. I thought you might want to take a look, see who he was."

I didn't. Amiram Gadot was of absolutely no interest to me anymore. But I thought Reuben might be taken aback if I put it as bluntly as that.

"Maybe later, Reuben," I said. "Let me see the other file first."

The file was of Eliezer Dattner's shooting. Inside were a dozen pictures and a similar number of pages, some printed and others written in either pencil or pen. All of the writing was in English, a reminder of who ruled this land in 1939. The officer in charge was probably back in Britain if the Second World War hadn't claimed him.

The report stated that Eliezer Dattner had been shot three times in the chest at very close range. One of the bullets had found his heart. That would have killed him almost instantly.

Dattner's wallet was found on the body. That bolstered my belief that the nature of the killing was other than it seemed. For if the shooter was indeed an Arab, why would he take the time to shove a political pamphlet in Dattner's mouth and not bother to rifle through the dead man's pockets for loot?

Meltzer would suggest something had scared the shooter away —an approaching vehicle, perhaps—but I was through trying to convince everyone else I was right. I would see this through alone, my way.

"Ugly fellow," I heard Reuben mutter, and I glanced up from my reading to see him in his chair, perusing Amiram's file. I didn't respond, just continued reading.

There was a picture of the pamphlet. Red Arabic letters that meant nothing to me. A translation was included. The text exhorted all Jews to leave the Holy Land of Palestine immediately, threatening those who ignored this warning with a bloodbath. All this in the name of Allah and his Prophet. The pamphlet also called upon all Arabs to rise up, to slaughter the Jews and claim all of Palestine for the Arab Nation. No one who read this pamphlet would doubt that Eliezer Dattner was shot by an Arab. The British officer in charge of the investigation certainly was of that opinion.

The investigation had been brief, almost perfunctory. There had been no witnesses—none who came forward, at least—and no evidence to point the investigators in the direction of the culprit. Reading the various reports, I got the distinct feeling that the British investigators had not exerted themselves to apprehend the killer. Dattner's death was written off as just another ethnic killing. Tragic but unavoidable, and perhaps best left alone so as not to rile up the Arab public against the British.

The perfect murder—if I was right.

"Learn anything useful?" Reuben said.

I shook my head. "Not yet. How about you?"

"This guy?" He gestured at Amiram's open file. "A career criminal. Been in and out of prison a bunch of times over the past dozen years. Never been arrested for a violent crime, though. Robbery, dealing in stolen goods, that sort of thing."

Just like Meir Gadot had told me. I wondered again if he was okay.

Reuben turned a page, and I returned my attention to the file in front of me. I began studying the crime scene photos, but nothing stood out. I had just picked up the eighth photograph when I heard Reuben mumble, "Hmmm, this is interesting."

"What is?" I said, still examining the photo.

"There's a name here I think I remember. From the other file I gave you."

"This file?" I said, meaning Dattner's.

"No, the other one, of the dead actress, the one found in Trumpeldor Cemetery."

That stopped me. I lowered the photograph and looked at Reuben. "What name?"

"This one," he said, turning the file over to me, pointing to where the name was printed. "Isn't this one of the people interviewed by Inspector Meltzer at the time?"

Indeed it was.

I sat back, gripping Amiram's file in hands that seemed to have lost sensation, my breath suddenly shorter, my mind storming with questions.

"What is it, Adam?"

"I'm not sure yet," I said. "But I think you were right. I would like to take a look at this file."

"Go right ahead. And here, take this, put it back where it belongs, okay?"

He held out a photograph across the desk. Taking it, I saw it was Amiram's mugshot, taken in January 1947. The black-and-white coloring made his eyes even more sinister than they'd been in real life.

But I didn't dwell on his eyes for long. Another aspect of his features had seized my attention. It was the trim beard darkening his cheeks and chin and neck, the tidy mustache blackening the strip of flesh between his nose and bloodless upper lip. With a sense of mounting urgency, I began flipping through the file, hunting for other pictures. I found one from an earlier arrest, in August 1939. He had a beard and mustache then, too, and presumably also on May 28, 1946, when Anna died.

But had he been imprisoned or free on that date? And what about the days on which Dattner, Ornstein, and Polisar died?

I turned over pages until I found Amiram's rap sheet. It listed all his arrests and convictions. It was a lengthy list.

He first went to jail in January 1939, serving four months for pickpocketing. It didn't take long before he was back in a cell, this time serving six months for burglary, beginning in late August 1939, meaning he was out when Dattner was shot. His next incarceration began in April 1941. So he was free when Ornstein died, as well. The charge was multiple robberies, and he got a heavy sentence—five years. He was freed in April 1946, one month before Anna met her end. Greta had wondered why the killer had not struck in six years, and I'd had no answer to give her. Until that moment. Now I knew why. The killer had been behind bars.

Amiram's next stint in prison began in February 1947. He was let out after one year, in February 1948, three months before the Egyptian air raid that claimed Brigitte Polisar's life, three months before Emil Polisar supposedly shot himself in grief.

Amiram Gadot. A man not averse to killing. A man comfortable using either a gun or a knife. A man with a beard, and, I now recalled, an exceedingly light, almost gliding walk. The sort of walk that might strike a drunken Eliyahu Toledano as strange, but do so in a way that did not leave a distinct impression on his mind.

A man who had accused me of getting involved in things that didn't concern me—which at the time I thought meant his partnership with his cousin, but now understood to mean something else entirely. A man who had tried to kill me hours after I had goaded both main murder suspects, including the one whose name was printed in Amiram's file, to make an attempt on my life.

It all fit. I had my answer. I now knew that Amiram Gadot had killed Anna Hartman, and who had told him to do so.

33

There was a knot of about a dozen people in the small dirt yard at the side of the building on Shalom Aleichem Street. Silent men and weeping women. And one distressed mother who was dragging away an eight-year-old boy by the arm while the boy was protesting loudly, digging his heels and trying desperately to pull free from her grip.

"Stop it!" the mother commanded. "Come on now. We're going inside."

"But I want to see," the boy pleaded.

"You've seen enough already. You'll have nightmares, is that what you want? Besides, show some respect. Now stop giving me trouble, or I'll tell your father about this when he gets home, and then you'll really be in for it." Even that threat did not squelch the boy's protests, but he stopped struggling physically, and his mother hauled him into the building and up the stairs. I turned my attention to the small crowd.

The people assembled formed an impenetrable curving wall, and it was only when I came closer that I was able to see what had drawn their interest. When I did, my heart gave a lurch and my breath caught in my throat.

For sprawled on the ground, arms and legs outstretched haphazardly, was Ofra Wexler. Her eyes were half open, her mouth lax, and around her crushed head was a halo of fresh blood.

As I looked at her broken body, I thought of her name in Amiram Gadot's file and recalled Leon Zilberman saying that Ofra had always had terrible luck with men. I thought now what I should have thought then, that no woman was ever described as having *always* had terrible luck with men if the men in question numbered less than three.

"What happened?" I asked one of the onlookers.

"She jumped," he said, then his gaze drifted upward, and I followed it to see curtains flapping in and out of an open window three stories up.

"When did it happen?"

He gestured toward the building. "That boy found her not ten minutes ago."

"Did anyone call the police?"

"Someone just went. Dear God, what a tragedy."

You don't know the half of it, I thought, turning away from him and hurrying into the building. I had five minutes at most to check out Ofra's apartment before the police arrived.

Her door wasn't locked. Inside, everything was as I remembered but for the sheet of paper loaded into the typewriter and the confusion of printed pages across the desk. The note in the typewriter was brief and to the point. Ofra confessed to killing Eliezer Dattner, Nahum Ornstein, and Anna Hartman—the first for betraying her, the second for breaking her heart, and the third for overtaking her professionally. She expressed remorse and stated that she wished to live no longer.

The pages scattered around the typewriter were poems, dozens of them. These poems did not deal with love or nature, as Leon Zilberman might have assumed, but with hate, resentment, and vengeance. The objects of these dark emotions were easy to determine at a glance. The three murder victims—Dattner, Ornstein, and Anna.

By their misdeeds—real or perceived—they had engendered the sort of poisonous emotional mixture that often finds an outlet in murderous fantasies and on occasion crosses the line into actual killing. In Ofra's case, it appeared, it had done both in abundance.

Skimming the poems while keeping track of the passing seconds in my head, I encountered dark, disturbing visions of revenge and retribution, of death and torment, all suffered by those who had wronged Ofra. The poems and suicide note, combined with what I had learned earlier at the police station, extinguished all doubt. The case was finished. I had found the guilty party. It was Ofra Wexler.

The sound of braking tires came from below. A number of car doors slammed in rapid succession. The police were here. It was time to go.

I left the apartment, finding no one on the landing, and shut the door softly. I descended the stairs at a leisurely pace, greeted the two policemen who entered the lobby, and exited the building as they began bounding up the stairs. Outside was another pair of officers. One was kneeling beside the body while the other was doing his very best to disperse the crowd.

Shoving my hands in my pockets, I turned left at the curb and put the scene of death behind me.

———

I made my way back to the police station, located Inspector Bartov, and fed him a redacted version of events. I told him I'd been hired to look into the five-year-old unsolved slaying of Anna Hartman. I told him I'd come to suspect that other actors of Shoresh Theater who had died over the past dozen years had, in fact, been murdered. I told him I'd suspected Ofra Wexler of being behind said murders. I told him I'd just seen Ofra's body, but kept my visit to her apartment to myself. Nor did I tell him that up until this morning, I'd had a second suspect in mind.

I would have preferred not to tell the police anything about my business, but I figured they would soon be talking to Ofra's colleagues, and that some of them might let on that a certain private detective had been asking questions about one or more of the murders mentioned in Ofra's suicide note.

As I told the inspector of my investigation and connected one dot to its companion, I watched his expression shift from ignorance through bewilderment to incredulity.

It helped when news of Ofra's death and the content of her suicide note reached his desk, and also when I showed him her name in Amiram Gadot's file. "That's why my apartment was so tidy," I said. "He wasn't there to rob the place. He was there to kill me."

Calling Netanya and getting Meltzer on the line cleared away all remnants of disbelief. But it took a while. Meltzer was not a man who admitted making a mistake easily.

But to give him credit, when he finally transitioned from skeptic to believer, he did so without rancor or bitterness. And when he thanked me for the work I'd done and apologized for doubting both me and my sanity, I could tell both the thanks and the apology were heartfelt and sincere. Any negative feelings he directed solely at himself.

"I screwed up," he said. "I should have found out Ofra Wexler had ties to this criminal."

"Don't beat yourself up. I only learned of it by accident." I told him how it was Reuben who deserved the credit, not me, and that seemed to make him feel a little better. "Besides, his record was made up entirely of nonviolent crimes," I said. "Not a record that screams murderer." *For that*, I thought, *you needed to see his eyes up close and personal.*

Bartov had me draft and sign a new statement. I kept it as brief as possible, stating most of the general facts without going into too much detail. When Bartov read it, he asked me why I'd failed to include the name of my client.

"That's confidential," I said.

His face went hard. "This is a murder case. You're not chasing after some cheating husband here. This is serious stuff."

"I know it is. I was a police detective myself, once upon a time."

That gave him pause, and we spent the next five minutes reviewing my history as a police detective in Hungary.

Still, Bartov persisted, "Not knowing who hired you, it leaves a hole in the report."

"Not one that matters. You already got the killer, and the woman for whom he killed. And they're both dead. There's not going to be a trial. No one will ever read all this paperwork, you know that."

He did, but he was the sort of cop who felt it was his absolute right to know absolutely everything.

"Listen," I said. "I'll make you a deal: you let the matter of my client's identity go and you can leave my name out of this whole thing. No need to mention my involvement at all. Take all the credit; reap all the rewards."

He eyeballed me for a moment, and I could see he wondered why I was making him this offer. But he was also tempted, and that superseded his curiosity.

"What do we do about this?" he asked, laying his palm on the statement I'd just signed.

"Misplace it somewhere," I said. "No one will care. Your superiors would much rather have the papers report that this case was solved by one of their own than by a private investigator."

We both knew this was true. The police didn't want it to look like they needed outside help solving cases, especially murders. It made them look inept and foolish. It might lead to budget cuts, which was what police higher-ups feared most.

So Bartov and I shook hands, and I watched him slide my statement under a stack of files in a desk drawer and slam it shut.

34

"Incredible," Birnbaum said with a shake of his head. "Utterly incredible."

It was early in the afternoon, a few hours after Ofra had plunged to her death.

We were seated at Café Tamar on Sheinkin Street, a stone's throw from the offices of *Davar*, where Birnbaum worked. On the table between us stood a pot of coffee and two mugs. The mugs were empty, as was the pot. We had been sitting there for nearly two hours, during which time I told Birnbaum almost everything.

"I owe you an apology," he said. "I was wrong and you were right."

"There's nothing to apologize for, Shmuel. All your objections were perfectly logical."

"What made you so sure, then?"

"I don't know. It was just a feeling."

Birnbaum regarded me with a glint of admiration. "You are a superb detective, Adam."

"Not really. If Reuben Tzanani hadn't noticed Ofra's name in

Amiram Gadot's file, and if he hadn't remembered it from Anna's, I wouldn't have made the connection."

"Is this the Reuben who saved your life in the War of Independence?"

"One and the same. You should have written about him instead of me, you know. He was the true hero."

Birnbaum nodded and offered a wistful smile. "You may be right, but no heroic tale has ever been written about someone carrying a wounded comrade off the battlefield. Our heroes either kill the enemy, sacrifice themselves for their country, or both. Still, I don't doubt that he is a remarkable man. But all things considered, it wasn't his timely assistance that solved the case, but your killing of Amiram Gadot. It was what drove Ofra to leap from her window, wasn't it?"

"I don't think it was remorse, no matter what her suicide note said. I think Amiram was supposed to come see her once he had killed me. When he didn't show, she knew something had gone wrong and worried that soon I would discover they knew each other." I smiled a wry smile. "She may have overestimated my abilities."

"Now, now," said Birnbaum, wagging a finger. "Belittling yourself is not only unbecoming, Adam; in this case, it is also unjustified. If not for your honed instincts, a woman who orchestrated three murders, and the man who committed them, would still be roaming free. You have much to be proud of."

So why didn't I feel this way? I felt satisfaction, both for having rid the world of Amiram and for bringing justice to three murder victims. But pride? No, that I didn't feel, and I wasn't exactly sure why.

Birnbaum said, "What was the nature of their relationship? Amiram and Ofra, I mean?"

"They were romantically involved. What I learned from the file is that Ofra paid bail for Amiram twice, and that she visited him in jail during his first three imprisonments."

"And other members of the theater knew about it? This Leon Zilberman, for example?"

"I believe so. That's why he made that remark about her being unlucky with men—that and her unfortunate relationships with Dattner and Ornstein."

"Why did none of her colleagues mention this to the police five years ago, after the Hartman murder?"

"I don't know. Maybe they simply didn't believe that one of their own could be responsible."

"Just goes to show that you can never really know anyone, can you?" Birnbaum said. Then he frowned. "I wonder why Amiram agreed to kill Dattner and Ornstein. They were Ofra's lovers. I can see him killing them to get them out of the way, but to do so at her request? How do you think that came about?"

"I've been wondering about that too," I said. "I think they had an intermittent relationship. If you check the dates of Amiram's incarcerations, they fit the times in which Ofra was involved with Dattner and later Ornstein. Both men hurt her badly. Amiram might have agreed to kill them in order to regain her favor, to prove his loyalty to her when other men had betrayed her. A similar thing must have happened with Anna."

Birnbaum nodded. "Love does make fools of us all." Then he smiled and his eyes twinkled with exultation. "You've given me a spectacular story, Adam. Just what I hoped for."

It wasn't a scoop, as word of Ofra's suicide, and the reason behind it, would by day's end reach the ear of every industrious reporter in Israel, but Birnbaum held the advantage. While his counterparts would spend valuable time struggling to collect all the relevant information and form the proper narrative, Birnbaum would be checking his story for misspelled words and misplaced commas. He would be the first, and in his profession that meant more than anything.

"About the story, Shmuel..."

He caught the tone of my voice and narrowed his shrewd eyes. "I have a feeling a favor is about to be asked."

"Can you keep my name out of it?"

Two years earlier, on another case, I had made a similar request. Then as now, he didn't understand me. But he neither asked for my reasoning nor did he attempt to change my mind.

What he said was: "It may prove pointless, Adam. Amiram Gadot's death is public knowledge. Other reporters might be able to put two and two together."

"Let's hope their algebra fails them," I said.

He chuckled, then held up a finger. "Even if it does, someone in the police might decide to leak the information."

"I don't think they will."

"No? Why not?"

"Because then the credit will go to me instead of them. Cops move up in rank based on their record. They'd prefer not to share the glory with a private investigator like me."

"You may be right," Birnbaum said. "Very well, I'll do my utmost to obscure your identity, though my journalistic spirit rebels against such an omission. Therefore, I would like something in return for my cooperation."

I smiled in spite of myself. "And what would that be?"

"I would like to know what you haven't told me."

"And what would that be?" I repeated, knowing full well.

"The name of your client, for one."

I shook my head. "It isn't mine to give, Shmuel."

"Surely now, with the case concluded, your client would have no cause to keep his identity a secret."

"What makes you think it's a *he*?"

He arched an eyebrow. "So it's a woman?"

"My lips are sealed, Shmuel."

He grunted. "I'll have you know you are one of the most frustrating men I have ever encountered. Very well, next question: what made you doubt Isser Rotner's alibi for the night Anna Hartman was killed?"

And there it was, the unresolved question that kept niggling at the back of my mind. Why did Rotner have his wife lie on his behalf? Where had he been and what was he doing the night Anna perished? What did he have to hide?

And why did he exhibit all that fear and dread as he slept beside his wife while Anna's body grew cold?

I said, "I can't tell you that either, Shmuel. But let's just say, I haven't changed my mind about it."

He took that in, then grinned mischievously. "I would have liked to have been there the moment you laid him out. Men of such unfounded arrogance should be brought down a peg or three at regular intervals."

"I only punch those who deserve it, Shmuel."

His fingertips brushed his jaw. "Let's agree to disagree on that score, Adam, all right?"

I nodded.

He leaned his elbows on the table. "You know he must hate you, don't you?"

"Rotner? I imagine so."

"But he has much to thank you for."

"Why do you say that?"

"Because of your tireless efforts, Shoresh Theater is about to receive a boatload of free publicity, and of the best kind there is."

"Which is?"

"Sordid, morbid, depraved, and blood soaked, of course. I predict all shows for the foreseeable future will be sold out. You, dear Adam, may have singlehandedly solved Shoresh Theater's financial woes and in so doing granted Isser Rotner the thing he wanted most—to be the leading man of a leading theater."

My guts twisted. Birnbaum was right. If there was anyone who emerged from this case better off than he had entered it, it was Isser Rotner.

And again I wondered where he had been that night. And what had made him so fearful?

35

Later that night, when I knew Shoresh Theater would be playing, albeit without its most experienced actress, I made a telephone call from a café on Ben Yehuda Street. The phone rang eleven times before it was picked up. Then came her voice, as beautiful and resonant as ever, but underlying it was a layer of dejection and despair. I thought I knew the reason.

"Good evening, Mrs. Rotner, this is Adam Lapid."

"Ah, Mr. Lapid, I was expecting your call." It did not sound like she had done so with relish.

"You've heard the news, I take it."

"Indeed I have. Three murders and a suicide. The recipe of a good tragedy."

I did not know what to say to that.

"Add a sprinkle of betrayal, a dash of humiliation, a pinch of heartbreak, and a spoonful of envy, and the dish is set. Now raise the curtain and serve it to the hungry masses. Just remember to practice your bows. For they'll be shouting your name loud enough to make the walls of the theater hall shudder."

"Who told you?" I asked.

"My dear husband, of course. The police had paid him a visit earlier today and informed him of recent developments. He pretended to be shocked and sad, but I could tell it was just a facade. In his mind, he was already making plans of exploiting this tragedy to its fullest potential. He was picturing packed theater halls, grander venues, and being bombarded with applause and cheers.

"It was a stark difference to how he had been yesterday. Upon returning home in the afternoon, he had raved and ranted about you for two hours straight. He would not tell me why he was so infuriated. I admit I took great pleasure in watching him pace back and forth like a caged animal."

I related to her my recent conversation with her husband, culminating in his errant swing at my head and my well-placed punch in his midsection.

She let out a short laugh the temperature of an ice cube. "I would have liked to have seen that. Small consolation, but better than what I have now. I must tell you, Mr. Lapid, that I am very disappointed."

"I told you when you hired me, Mrs. Rotner, that I would hunt for the killer, whoever he or she turned out to be."

"I remember. I am disappointed with the outcome, not with you."

"Aren't you glad the person responsible for the murder of three of your colleagues has finally met justice? It would not have happened without you."

She took a moment to answer, and when she did, her tone was thoughtful. "I suppose I should feel that way, but I don't. Does this shock you?"

"Not at all," I said truthfully.

"Hmmm. This does say something about what you think of me, doesn't it? I must say that I am surprised tiny Ofra had it in her. She always struck me as the sort of woman people do things to, not a woman who does things to other people."

"I suppose she was a better actress than you thought."

"So it would seem. Then again, maybe this shouldn't surprise me. I spent years being wrong about my husband, so why wouldn't I be wrong about Ofra? It makes me wonder who else I'm wrong about."

"Life isn't a play, Mrs. Rotner. We can't read everyone's thoughts or see into their heart."

"You're right, we can't." She paused to clear her throat and I feared another of her coughing fits was about to commence, but then she resumed speaking. "One thing bothers me, Mr. Lapid."

I waited, sure that I knew what it was.

"Isser's behavior that night, his tossing and turning and mumbling in his sleep. If he hadn't killed Anna, what brought about his night terrors?"

"I don't know."

"Does this bother you at all?"

"A little. But the case is over, Mrs. Rotner. The killer is dead."

"I know. I was not about to suggest you look into it. I don't suppose you'd be able to find out."

"The only way we'll ever know is if your husband decides to tell us."

"So I guess I'll have to live with not knowing."

"I guess we both will. By the way, I did not tell the police your identity. Your reputation is secure."

"I suppose that's more than nothing," she said, and that brought the conversation to a momentary standstill. The only sound was the whisper of her breathing.

After a moment, and without knowing I was about to utter the words until they spilled from my lips, I said, "I'm sorry things turned out this way, Mrs. Rotner."

A few seconds of silence passed. When she spoke, her tone

was detached, and it was as though she hadn't heard my last sentence. "You've earned yourself a bonus, I think, Mr. Lapid. Despite the outcome, you have done your job admirably."

"That's not necessary."

"I'll decide what is necessary, if you don't mind." And softer: "It is my wish, Mr. Lapid. You wouldn't want to deny me it, would you?"

"I'm not in the habit of turning down free money," I said.

This time her laughter was both warm and unabbreviated. "You may come collect your bonus whenever you wish, Mr. Lapid." She paused and now sounded more serious, even gloomy. "But not for the following week. I prefer to be as alone as possible in the next few days. You understand, don't you?"

I did. For she'd had a dream, a dream of seeing her husband in chains and on trial and humiliated, and now that dream was dead. And just like we sit *shiva* to grieve over the death of those closest to us, so do our dreams require a period of mourning.

"But don't take too long, Mr. Lapid," she said. "I wish to put this whole affair behind me."

"No, Mrs. Rotner, I assure you I won't."

36

The papers carried the story prominently over the next few days. It was one of Birnbaum's finest hours. Not only was he the one who broke the story, he also possessed a reservoir of titillating details that other reporters were ignorant of. For instance, he was the one who informed the public about Eliezer Dattner's Arab lover, and he also wrote that several dozen poems of a distinctly malevolent nature were found on Ofra Wexler's desk. Just the fodder readers' imaginations needed in order to run wild.

Most people assumed Birnbaum had a source in the police, and this was likely true, but all of the details he dished out in his column had been supplied by me.

Birnbaum was as good as his word. Not once did he mention my name, nor did he hint at my existence. It was three days before I grew confident that no other reporter would do so.

By that time, the story had sunk to the inner pages of the newspaper. Regular news reconquered the front page. The ceiling fan at Greta's Café seemed to celebrate the story's decline by resuming its rattle. This led to disgruntled murmurs among the regulars and despaired looks heavenward, or at least ceiling-ward, from Greta.

One day earlier, two days after Ofra's suicide, I arrived at the café and learned there'd been a call for me.

"A Mr. Haggai Geller," Greta said. "He asked me to tell you he'll be in his office all day and to come right over. He sounded eager to talk to you."

I didn't go. There was no reason to. Nor did I feel the need to return Geller's call. He'd soon forget about me, just as I would hopefully soon forget about him and the rest of this case.

But he didn't forget. He called again that afternoon and twice more the following day. I ignored those calls as well.

One call I didn't ignore was from Reuben. He wanted to let me know that the rest of the files I'd requested had arrived.

"I put them aside in a drawer for you," he said. "Just in case you still want to take a look."

I didn't see the point. They wouldn't tell me anything useful. Not now.

"I don't think I'll need them, Reuben. You can send them back. And thank you."

With the general election drawing ever nearer, the atmosphere at Greta's Café became decidedly more fractious. Heated arguments broke out among the patrons, whose political leanings ranged from the far left to the other extreme. On occasion, voices were raised and insults hurled, the sort that would have made my mother rush to cover the ears of whichever of my sisters happened to stand closest to her. Usually a stern word or a forbidding look from Greta was enough to pacify the unruly debaters, to remind them that, their differences notwithstanding, they had only one country and one favorite café.

On one occasion, though, a supporter of the quasi-communist party Mapam got into a squabble with a member of Maki, the

Communist Party of Israel, over which of the two parties better represented the working class. The squabble quickly devolved from an unregulated trading of insults to a rather confused free-market exchange of blows—though luckily, these were largely ineffectual.

Greta, upon seeing this, charged from behind her counter, armed with a rolling pin raised threateningly over her head—an act that brought the scuffle to an abrupt end. The two skirmishers were then ordered out of the café and given permission to return no sooner than the next morning, provided they swore to behave like civilized men.

The supporter of Mapam exited the café in a huff and turned left. Not to be outdone, the member of Maki hastened in the same direction, quickly overtaking his counterpart, but on the opposite side of the street. Both were back and on their best behavior the following day.

As Birnbaum had predicted, the murders provided Shoresh Theater with a sizable dose of free publicity. One paper featured an article that reviewed the theater's history—from the day of its founding to the recent, shocking revelations. Another dedicated a few inches to each of the victims—and this, naturally, included mention of their place of employment.

A third newspaper conducted a lengthy interview with Isser Rotner—whom the paper dubbed as "the leader of the belea-guered, mournful troupe"—in which Rotner was portrayed as a man of fortitude, resilience, and artistic vision.

The interview was a testament to Rotner's skills, as the image he conveyed was as fake as any character he had ever played. He appeared somber, wise, and grieving—all in a carefully balanced masculine manner, in which he hinted at personal emotional turmoil, but didn't let it truly show. Most of his feigned concern was for his fellow actors—"my brothers and sisters in arms," he called them—and the future of the theater. He talked of that future at length, and then, if you knew his true nature, you could see through the smokescreen. You could see his ambition, his insatiable hunger for success, and his desire to seize this moment, which fate had bestowed upon him, and make himself great in the process.

And it appeared to be working. Each evening, I would head over to Balfour Street and see the crowds milling about Ohel Shem. Every seat would be taken that night. The money would flow to the theater's depleted coffers. And Isser Rotner would be lauded.

Watching the people streaming into Ohel Shem, into Rotner's domain, I wondered for the thousandth time: If Rotner hadn't killed Anna, why did he fake his alibi? And what caused his nightmares that night?

I had no contact with Dahlia in the days following our telephone conversation. Her period of mourning was not yet over. But I found myself thinking of her often, picturing her sitting in her apartment with her broken body and shattered spirit and dashed dreams. And while I didn't pity her—knowing full well how she would detest that—I did feel a measure of sympathy for her.

It's a terrible thing, to have what you love most be taken from you. And it's even worse to see a person you despise gain it in your place.

Three days after Ofra's death, I visited the hospital to have my arm looked at. It was healing nicely, but there would be a scar. *One more for the collection*, I thought.

I chatted for a while with my doctor and then with another, and finally with a nurse who had made *aliyah* from Hungary in the 1930s. She asked if I had met any of her family during the war in Europe. Her face fell when I told her I hadn't.

Out in the hospital courtyard, I sat on a bench under the

bright summer sun and pondered all that had transpired in the Anna Hartman case. I hoped that soon I'd be able to let the case go entirely.

But there was one small bit of unfinished business. One thing left to deal with.

37

That bit of unfinished business was Meir Gadot. He had disappeared.

I had tried contacting him the day after I'd killed his cousin, with no success. I had a telephone number where I could reach him. A Bulgarian restaurant downtown he frequented just about every day. It was where I'd called to let him know I'd discovered who had been stealing his merchandise. I'd telephoned the restaurant a number of times after Ofra's suicide, but the proprietor told me Meir hadn't been by, and that he didn't know where he was.

After three days, I began to worry in earnest. As I sat on that bench outside the hospital, I pictured Meir's body floating in the Yarkon River with a bullet hole in his head, courtesy of his cousin. Or with his throat cut on a dune somewhere, being pecked at by vultures.

So after I left the hospital, I called city hall, pretending to be a police detective, and got the clerk to give me Meir's address. I went to his apartment, but no one answered his door. A neighbor told me Meir hadn't been home for a few days. "No lights on at night," he said. "And he likes to listen to music on the radio; I can hear it through the thin walls. But these past few days—nothing."

Fearing the worst, I asked the landlord to let me in Meir's apartment. He refused, saying he didn't know me.

"I think he might be dead in there," I said. "How about this? How about you go in there and check it out, okay?"

Either my tone or the prospect of finding a putrefying corpse changed his mind. He unlocked Meir's door and waited in the hall with an anxious expression while I stepped inside. Not that I needed to in order to know there was no body there. My nose told me that. Still, I went around the place, finding a half-empty drawer of socks and underwear, a vacant shelf in the closet, and a few barren hangers. It looked like Meir had made a quick getaway.

But who was he running from? Surely not his cousin. By now, he would have read about his death, or someone would have told him. I thought I knew the answer and did not like it one bit.

My next stop was the restaurant. A dim-lighted place in Jaffa, in the ground floor of a two-story building whose upper floor had a partially collapsed roof. An unrepaired casualty of the War of Independence. Inside, a dozen small wooden tables hosted about twenty people. The place smelled of cheap cigarettes, cheap food, and the sweat of people who had to work hard and make do with little. Some were nursing watered beers, while others were bent over bowls of Bulgarian stew or munching on a pastry called *banitsa*, folds of dough filled with spinach and pumpkin and cheese—but, given the times, not much of any of the three.

A waiter was attending to a table by the door. I waited while he explained to a hungry couple that, alas, the restaurant wasn't serving *almodrote* this week, and recommended an alternative. He pointed toward a table by the kitchen when I asked to speak to Mr. Moshonov, the proprietor.

Moshonov was a blocky man with an unsmiling square face, thick eyebrows, and short thinning hair the color of wet concrete.

When I told him my name and asked if Meir had made an appearance since we last spoke, he flicked his blue eyes at me and gave a quick shake of his head. "Haven't seen him for days now. Could have told you this on the phone. Didn't need to come over." Then he returned his gaze to the room.

"I understand he's a regular customer," I said.

"You could say that."

"Aren't you worried that he hasn't been around?"

"Why should I be worried? Meir's a grown man."

"I've been by his apartment. He hasn't been there for days. It looked like he packed in a hurry."

"Maybe he's taking a trip," Moshonov said, still not looking at me. "I don't keep track of my customers."

I studied his face. Either there was something he was hiding from me, or he just didn't like anyone asking questions about his patrons. Either way, I would get nothing from him.

Outside, I lit a cigarette and began walking away. I was thirty paces from the restaurant when I heard a voice at my back.

"Mister. Hey, mister."

I turned and saw a man. Thin, short, and very pale. Sandy hair, bony arms, and a bulging Adam's apple in a scrawny neck. Clothes that had been mended a good number of times and didn't fit him all that well. He shifted from one foot to the other and back again.

"I heard you're looking for Meir," he said.

I recognized him from the restaurant. He'd been sitting a table away from the proprietor. He must have overheard our conversation. I cast a quick glance over his shoulder. No one else had come out of the restaurant. We were alone in the street.

"You know where he is?" I asked.

He shifted his feet. "I know how you can find him."

I took another drag and nodded slowly as the smoke curled over my head and vanished into the night sky. "All right. How?"

A tentative, yet decidedly greedy smile tugged at one corner of his mouth, pulling it half open, like a zipper.

"I was thinking it might be worth something to you," he said.

I nodded again, then took a final pull on my cigarette, let it drop, and snuffed it out under my shoe. I took a step forward. He tensed, tried to appear tough, but I could tell he was ready to bolt at the slightest hint of trouble.

I sighed. I could threaten the information out of him, but I didn't think it would be wise. Instead, I reached into my pocket, took out my wallet, and counted out three one-lira notes, holding them up in a fan shape. At the sight of the cash, he bit on his lip and shifted his feet again.

"You want this money?" I said. "Talk. How do I find Meir?"

"Like I told you, I don't know where he's at, but every evening between seven and eight, Mr. Moshonov goes out with a package of food. I heard him tell the cook one time that it was for Meir."

"No idea where he goes?"

A shake of his narrow head.

"How long does it take him to come back?"

He thought about it. "Fifteen minutes, tops."

"Does Moshonov own a vehicle?"

"No. I don't think so."

So Meir was somewhere close by. If this pipsqueak was telling me the truth.

"What's your name?" I asked.

He drew back his chin, fearful. "What do you need my name for?"

"I don't, really. You come to this restaurant often?"

"Every once in a while."

I smiled. "Just about every day, I guess. And you're easy to describe. Which means I'd be able to find you easily enough if you're lying to me. Are you lying to me?"

He gulped, jerking his head side to side.

"You sure?"

This time his head jerked up and down.

"Good. So here, take your money."

He snatched it from my fingers and took three quick steps back before shoving the money in his pocket.

"One more thing," I said, "you'd better not tell anyone about our little chat."

"I won't. I'm not stupid."

Yes, he was. If he was smart, he would have waited until I rounded the corner before he approached me. Where we now stood, anyone exiting the restaurant could see us.

"That's good to know," I said. "Now run along."

He did, walking briskly for a few steps before breaking into a sprint. I shook my head and went to find a dark spot in which I could wait undetected for Moshonov to appear. It was just after six. If what the pipsqueak had told me was true, I had between one and two hours to wait.

38

Moshonov came out of the restaurant at seven thirty-two. He held a brown paper bag in each hand. Seeing him, I retreated deeper into the shadows in the slit of an alleyway where I stood.

Moshonov began marching in the opposite direction, whistling some lively tune. I followed at a distance, sticking to the darkest patches of sidewalk.

It took him less than five minutes to arrive at his destination, a narrow two-story building with a partially detached drainpipe that swung in the evening breeze, banging rhythmically against the outer wall. I could see a family eating at the table in the ground-floor apartment. The second-floor windows were obscured by drawn curtains. But the lights were on. Someone was home.

Moshonov climbed the stairs to the upper floor, disappearing from view when he reached the landing. I stood, hands in pockets, and watched as two shadows moved about behind the curtains. One was the shape of Moshonov. The other was Meir Gadot's height and width.

After Moshonov left, I waited fifteen minutes, just in case he'd forgotten something and returned. Then, seeing no one about, I crossed the street, climbed the steps, and put my ear to the flimsy door. Sounds of cutlery scraping on a plate, a glass being set on a table.

Gently, I depressed the handle, but the door was locked. There was no peephole. I could have busted down the door, but that would have made a racket. Instead, I knocked twice, not too loudly. The sound of eating died; there was a short silent interval, then Meir Gadot's voice, anxiously asking who it was.

Trying to sound like Moshonov, I dropped my voice a full octave and put on a pronounced Bulgarian accent. "Meir, it's me. I forgot to bring you some *almodrote*. Just made it today." Hearing myself, I winced. My impersonation was far from perfect. But apparently, the promise of a fresh Bulgarian eggplant and cheese casserole, a dish I knew Moshonov hadn't delivered, was enough to get Meir to throw caution to the wind.

As soon as the key turned in the lock and the door handle began its descent, I used my shoulder to shove the door straight into Meir's face. There was a grunt followed by a heavy thud. I charged in, closed the door and relocked it, sliding the key out of the lock and into my pocket.

Meir was sitting crookedly on the floor, hands held to his face. His eyes were huge. The splotches on his cheeks were the color of ripe tomatoes.

"Get up," I said. "Go sit on the bed."

He pushed himself up with one hand, the other still pressed to his mouth. Wordlessly, he went to the bed. It was a single, the frame wooden and very low. When Meir sat, his knees were almost as high as his rib cage.

Other than the bed, there was a dresser, a rickety nightstand, and a small table bearing dirty dishes and cutlery. An open suitcase lay at the foot of the bed, a jumble of clothes in its open maw. The air smelled of the meal Meir had just consumed, with a thick underlayer of cigarettes. The drawn curtains made the room seem smaller and gloomy, like a cell in a dungeon.

By the table was a solitary chair. I lowered myself onto it, fixed my eyes on Meir, and waited, saying nothing. He was already scared, but I wanted him to be terrified. I could tell by his eyes that I'd been right. He hadn't fled his apartment for fear of his cousin. He did it to avoid me.

After a full minute of silence, Meir spoke from behind his hands. "Adam, I—"

I cut him off. "I can't hear you properly. You sound all muffled."

He lowered his hands slowly. There was blood on his lips, on his teeth and chin, but not too much of it. Painful, no doubt, but nothing serious.

Draped over the back of the chair was a shirt. I tossed it at him and told him to wipe off the blood.

"Can I go and wash it off?" he said, not wanting to ruin the shirt.

"Later," I said. "Maybe. For now, use the shirt. Go on, don't keep me waiting. I've wasted enough time finding you." It was a little petty on my part, but I wanted him to know he would only get something from me if he cooperated.

"How did you find me?" he asked once he got most of the blood off.

"How isn't important. What's important is why you left your apartment in a hurry. I guess it has something to do with the death of your cousin. My condolences, by the way."

He stared down at the bloodied shirt in his hands. He hadn't discarded it. His tone was quiet. "I'm glad you're alive, Adam."

"No thanks to you. You knew he was coming to kill me, didn't you?"

He didn't say anything. He didn't need to. The way the splotches on his cheeks blazed was answer enough.

I leaned forward, my nose picking up the scent of his blood, the stink of his fear. "Whatever you do, don't lie to me, Meir. There's no telling how that would make me feel, what it would make me do."

Sweat sprouted on his forehead and at his temples. He shook a little, clutching the shirt tighter. He wore gray trousers, brown socks, and an undershirt that showed a lot of hair on his shoulders and chest.

I said, "What did Amiram tell you?"

"That he was going to teach you a lesson. That you had it coming."

"You knew he meant to kill me?" And when he hesitated, I added, "Remember what I said: Don't you dare lie to me."

Meir swallowed hard and nodded.

"You didn't think to warn me?"

"Amiram told me I'd better not. That he'd hurt me if I did. You gotta believe me, Adam, I tried to talk him out of it, but he wouldn't listen. He hated you because you insulted him. He wanted you dead."

"You should have come to me, goddammit."

He nodded a couple of times. His eyes welled over. Tears spilled down his cheeks. "I know, I know. But I was scared out of my mind. Amiram...he wasn't like he used to be. He'd changed in prison. There was something crazy about him now. He told me he'd slice me apart if I breathed a word of what he was planning. And he laughed when he said it. I just couldn't bring myself to disobey him."

"He hadn't changed one bit, Meir. He killed three people. Starting in 1939."

"I knew nothing about that. Nothing. I swear."

I believed him. A minute ago, I was ready to pound him. But now, seeing him all hunched up and miserable on that dingy bed in this shabby room, I mostly felt sorry for him.

"You were stupid, Meir. I told you he wasn't the sort of guy you could control. If I hadn't killed him, one of these days he would have killed you and taken over your operation, probably right after you taught him everything he needed to know."

He shook his head so hard sweat drops flew off his brow. "He told me we were going to be partners, that he would buy into the business."

"He had money? I thought he just got out of prison."

"He said he was going to get some soon. Right after he finished with you."

A planned robbery? Or did Ofra also promise him money to get rid of me?

"And you believed that? Meir, a guy as hard as Amiram will never be partners for long with someone as soft as you."

Meir shut his eyes and shuddered. He was sweating like crazy, but he also looked like he was freezing. He didn't protest, didn't claim a toughness he didn't possess. He knew I was right.

"You ever meet Ofra Wexler?" I asked.

"Sure. She and Amiram went together on and off. I just can't believe she'd do what the papers said she did. I always thought she was a good girl."

"When was the last time you saw her?"

"I don't know. Maybe eight years ago. Maybe nine."

"You're sure it was as long as that? Before 1946?"

"Yeah. Like I said, it was eight years at least. I didn't even know she and Amiram were still in touch."

I took a moment to process this, then decided it fit with what I'd read in Amiram Gadot's file. The last time Ofra's name was mentioned there was ten years ago, when she visited him in prison. Then Amiram spent five years behind bars, and shortly after his release, he killed Anna. Perhaps he and Ofra broke things off after that, so that now, in 1951, his feelings toward her were not enough to compel him to commit murder. She had to offer him money as well.

Meir had finally let go of the shirt. One end had fallen to the floor. The other still clung to one of his knees. His cheeks were red and wet and shiny, like a stained-glass window in a rainstorm.

"I'm so sorry, Adam. I know you must hate me. I deserve it. I'm just a coward. Just a stupid, worthless coward."

"Shut up," I said. "Don't talk for a minute." I just couldn't bear listening to his self-pity. Couldn't look at his pitiful face, with his glistening eyes and his nose leaking snot. I looked at my hands instead, the hands I'd planned on using to hurt Meir for letting his cousin ambush me. I just couldn't see myself using these hands to hurt the pathetic man sitting before me.

He wasn't a bad man, merely a weak one. I was angry at him, but I didn't hate him.

"Go wash your face," I said. "There's still some blood on it."

He went into the bathroom. There was no door, just a ratty curtain, and I heard him turn on the faucet and splash water on his face. He came back, wiping his hands on a small towel. Sitting back on the bed, he asked, "What now? What are you going to do with me?"

"Where's your wallet?" I asked.

"My wallet?"

"Yeah. Where is it?"

It was in the suitcase. Inside, I found fifty-three liras and change. I transferred fifty liras to my own wallet and tossed Meir's back into the suitcase. Meir didn't voice the slightest objection.

"You probably have more stashed away around here some-where," I said, "but I'll settle for fifty. A partial compensation for the cut on my arm and my painting."

"Painting?"

"The painting your cousin destroyed," I said, my anger and voice rising in tandem. "The painting of my—" I managed to stop myself before I said the words *wife and daughters*. He wouldn't understand. I took and released a long breath and made my fists unclench as a stab of pain sliced through my soul. "Never mind. Just be thankful I don't toss this place for the rest of it. I figure you'll need your money till you get settled into your new line of work."

"What new line?" he asked.

"Whatever you choose. You're done with smuggling." I paused, taking the edge off my voice. "Look, Meir, you're not cut out for this business. You're too soft. A man like you can get away with selling a little sugar on the side or a few chocolate bars out of his apartment, but you've gotten too big. You'll attract predators, like your cousin, and you won't be able to protect your operation. You'll end up dead. Take my advice: Get out of it now before you join your cousin in whatever lies beyond."

He didn't argue. He just started crying fresh tears and nodded. "Thank you, Adam. I appreciate it."

"So you're out?" I asked.

He wiped his face. "Yes. Yes, I'm out. Are we good?"

"No," I said. "But we're not bad either."

I left him there, with his split lip and lighter wallet and the chance of a fresh start. I was pretty sure he would take it, and I felt good that I'd given it to him.

39

The loss of my painting weighed on me heavily. Four days after Ofra's suicide, I went in search of the old man who'd sold it to me. Maybe I could get him to paint me a new one.

When I'd bought it, the old man had been sitting on a small stool near Masaryk Square, a slew of his paintings arrayed on the sidewalk before him. But when I got there, a little after nine in the morning, I found the sidewalk empty of both man and art. Asking around the shops in the area, I learned the old man hadn't been seen for weeks. None of the shopkeepers knew his name or where he lived or where he might have gone. One of them stated proudly that he'd told the old man to clear off. "His dirty little paintings were annoying to look at, and he took up too much of the sidewalk. It was hurting my business."

I toured the northern part of the city in search of him, my desperation mounting as the hours passed. By the time I gave up and started toward home, my feet were aching and the skin on my face and the back of my neck felt sunburned. It was almost three o'clock.

I was plodding down King George Street when I came upon a

lively gathering of men and women and children outside the three-story building that stood at number 38.

Like all Tel Avivians, I knew that building. It was Metzudat Ze'ev—Ze'ev's fortress—the headquarters of Menachem Begin's Herut party, named after Ze'ev Jabotinsky, the father of Revisionist Zionism.

A ten-year-old boy stuck a flier into my hand. It showed an unflattering caricature of David Ben-Gurion, underlined by a pithy exhortation to bring his failed leadership to an end by voting for Herut.

I folded the flier, slid it in my pocket, and continued walking— only to be stopped two seconds later by a voice calling my name.

Turning, I saw her. Varda Navon.

She was dressed as simply as in our previous encounter. White dress with black trim, brown shoes, a bag slung over one shoulder. She held a stack of fliers. More Herut propaganda.

"Hello, Adam," she said, with a small smile. "Nice to see you again."

"You too, Varda. I had no idea you were a Herutnik."

"I hope that doesn't make you think badly of me."

"Not at all, I assure you."

Her smile widened, but soon her expression became serious. "I keep thinking about our conversation, how wrong I was. I still can't believe it, you know, what Ofra did."

"By all accounts, she was a very good actress. She fooled everybody."

"Yes, she did. The papers didn't say, but I suppose it wasn't really the police who solved the case, but you."

"Unlike theater actors, I don't enjoy the spotlight," I said.

She nodded understanding. "I know it's wrong of me, but I can't help feeling a little sorry for Ofra. The way they treated her was wrong. They humiliated her. That must have torn her apart from the inside."

"You mean Eliezer Dattner and Nahum Ornstein did," I said, a little harshly. "Anna never humiliated anyone."

Varda looked taken aback by my tone. "You're right. I shouldn't have said that. I don't know what I was thinking."

Right then, a powerfully built man with hair the color and texture of iron came to stand by Varda's side. He had a peasant's face and uncompromising brown eyes. His height was around five ten.

"This is Shaul," Varda said, "my husband. Shaul, this is Adam Lapid."

We shook hands. He had a calloused palm and a grip like steel.

"Are you on our side, Mr. Lapid?" Shaul Navon asked, in a voice that matched his hair and grip.

"Your side?"

"Are you planning to vote for Herut?"

"I haven't made up my mind yet."

"Surely by now you know who is best for Israel."

Varda laid a hand on his arm. "Shaul, please."

I said, "With so many people swearing it's them, it can be a bit hard to decide who is right."

His upper lip twitched. He squared his shoulders. "Did you fight the British, Mr. Lapid?"

"No, I—"

"Neither did most of Mapai's supporters. Except for a brief time, all they did was try to appease them, while we in the Irgun fought and bled and died to kick the occupiers out of our land. When our leader, Menachem Begin, was hiding under an assumed identity to evade capture by the British police, Ben-Gurion was living out in the open, never risking a hair on his balding head. Surely, we have earned the people's trust, don't you agree?"

Varda made another attempt to quiet her husband, but he said, "In a minute, Varda. I'm interested in what Mr. Lapid has to say."

Varda seemed embarrassed by her husband's aggressive fervor, and I gave her a smile indicating that it was all right.

"I was about to say, Mr. Navon, that I only arrived in Israel in late 1947, so I did not have much of a chance to do my part against the British. But I did fight in the War of Independence."

"In what arena?"

I told him. I didn't get into the episode that earned me a medal and culminated in my picture in the paper, but it was still clear that I had risked my life for my country.

Shaul Navon was nodding his head, satisfied by my answer, but he stopped cold when I said, "And in the war, Mr. Navon, I fought alongside socialists from the kibbutzim, members of Hagannah, and former fighters of the Irgun such as yourself. I lost comrades that belonged to all three groups. That made the distinction between a Jew of one political persuasion and another a little vaguer."

His lower lip jutted out like the barrel of a gun out of a foxhole, but he had no comeback. He settled for saying, "Perhaps you'll do us the honor of attending our rally tonight, Mr. Lapid. Begin himself will be speaking."

"Perhaps I will," I said.

He gave a quick nod, murmured something about having to talk to a friend of his, and said, "Are you coming, Varda?"

"In a few minutes, Shaul," she said. "You go ahead."

He nodded again, bid me a stiff farewell, and left Varda and me alone.

She said, "I apologize, Adam. Shaul can get a bit worked up whenever politics are discussed."

"Don't worry about it, Varda," I said. "This election is making everyone a little edgy." I told her about the altercation that had taken place at Greta's Café.

She laughed a little. "It's good to know the Left isn't fighting only against us, but also among themselves. Not that it will do us much good, I fear. Mapai will probably win again and Ben Gurion will remain as prime minister."

I thought she was right, but didn't see the point of saying so. Instead, I asked her how the theater was doing.

"Oh, it's been hectic since Ofra died. A full house every night and people clamoring for more shows."

"All the publicity must have helped."

"No doubt. It's terrible, given the circumstances, but undeniable."

"I find it astounding that the actors are capable of carrying on as though nothing has happened."

"That's what actors do, Adam. They set their moods and personal lives aside each time they get on stage."

"I suppose it helps that the theater's financial troubles may soon be over."

She made a *maybe* gesture with her head. "Mostly I think it's the audience. We haven't seen such enthusiasm in years, not since Dahlia was run over."

It took a second before her words fully registered. I stared at her as a terrible feeling wormed its way into my gut. "What did you say?"

"What? When?"

"Just now. About Dahlia. I thought she was injured in a car accident."

"Well, she was."

"I mean, I thought she had been in a car that had smashed into another vehicle or into a tree or fallen into a ditch or..." I was getting breathless, and I had to stop talking in order to suck in some air, my lungs straining painfully, as though unable to fill. My legs felt rubbery, and I groped for support, found a nearby tree, and braced myself against it. "She was run over?"

Varda nodded slowly, frowning, her eyes on my face. She looked bewildered or maybe just concerned for my well-being.

"She was run over by a car?" I said, struggling with the information, needing it to be confirmed a second time.

Varda nodded again. She reached out and touched my arm. "Adam, what—"

"Was it a hit-and-run? The driver was never caught, was he?"

Varda looked at me for a long moment, then shook her head. "No, I don't think he was."

I shut my eyes as a wave of nausea hit me like a sledgehammer to the belly. It took all I had to keep my stomach from emptying out on the sidewalk. "I was wrong," I mumbled, the words barely audible over the irregular thumping of heartbeats in my ears. "So wrong."

"About what?"

"Everything," I said, answering her question though the words were meant for no one but myself.

With effort, I pushed myself off the tree, rocked a little, then found my equilibrium and began trudging away, ignoring Varda calling my name. I didn't want to talk to her. I didn't want to explain myself.

In my brain a storm was raging, thoughts bouncing around the interior of my skull like ricocheting bullets. I could feel them pinging against bone.

And flashing before my eyes was a single image. Ofra Wexler's lifeless green eyes staring up into the blue Tel Aviv sky.

40

I headed north on King George, then turned east on Dizengoff. There, from a small café, I called her apartment.

The phone rang twenty times before I gave up. Either she was not home, or she wasn't answering her phone. The former possibility was remote. What it did say, however, with near certainty, was that her husband was out.

I continued east, then cut north on Chen Boulevard. I knocked on her door, waited, and, when no one answered, tried the handle.

The door opened. The entry hallway was dark, the competing pictures of Dahlia and her husband like patches of shadow on the walls.

Before stepping inside, I called out her name. No answer, but I thought I heard a rustling sound from deeper in the apartment.

I found her in the living room, sitting like a statue of an old woman on her sofa, wearing a black long-sleeved dress that was wrong for the season. All the curtains were drawn, the room murky, the air hot and thick and stale. On the coffee table was a china teapot and a cup on a saucer. The cup was full, but no steam rose from the liquid. Untouched, it had gone cold.

"Mr. Lapid, this is unexpected. I distinctly recall telling you I did not wish to see you for a few more days."

It was Dahlia who had spoken, but if I hadn't been in the same room with her, I would have doubted her identity. Her voice was unrecognizable. It sounded stifled, small, and defeated—not like her at all.

"I remember. But I needed to see you right away."

"Money trouble?" She let out a single, raspy cough. "Can't wait a few days to get your bonus?"

"Nothing like that. May I pull the curtains?"

"If you must. But no more than one."

I chose the one that covered the largest window. I swept it aside, and sunlight splashed in. Dahlia recoiled, shielding her eyes.

Seeing her in the light was almost as big a shock as hearing her spiritless voice. She seemed to have aged a decade at least since I last saw her. The lines by her eyes had deepened, her complexion was hoary, the skin on her face looked slack, and the gray streaks in her hair had multiplied.

But it was her posture that had deteriorated the most. Gone was the erect, regal bearing. The woman before me was slump-shouldered, her upper back bowed, and she clasped the head of her cane with both hands, as though she would topple forward without it.

A ghostly smile played on her lips. "You would have made a poor actor, Mr. Lapid. You're utterly unable to mask your thoughts and emotions."

"Are you feeling well, Mrs. Rotner?"

Her mouth tightened. "Don't waste time asking questions with obvious answers. Why are you here?"

There it was. That steely imperiousness. It wasn't all gone yet. But her irises were leaden, as though there were curtains drawn along the insides of them, too.

"Why are you sitting here in the dark like this?" I asked.

"Because it suits me. I don't know why."

I did. A desire to shun all light is a symptom of depression and mourning. And I knew what Dahlia was grieving for. Only now I wasn't all that sure that grief was warranted. At least, not yet.

All of a sudden, the room felt suffocating. Hurriedly, I pushed open the window and let some air in. The buzz of the city felt like a tonic, revitalizing.

Dahlia watched me from the sofa. Curious, but detached. Yet even that faint interest made her seem more vibrant and alive.

"Why are you here, Mr. Lapid?" she asked again.

I stepped away from the window and sat in the chair facing the sofa. "I want to ask you something about your accident."

"I don't wish to discuss it."

"I understand that, but it's important."

She narrowed her eyes. "All right. What about it?"

"I need you to tell me exactly what happened."

"Why?"

I hesitated, wondering if I was making her relive a painful moment for no reason. But no. I had to ask these questions. I had to know for sure.

"Just humor me, Mrs. Rotner. Just tell me."

She drew in a breath, tapping her fingers on the horse's mane topping her cane.

"It happened just outside this building. I stepped out onto the street and began walking south. All of a sudden there was the sound of an engine revving, of wheels spinning. I managed to half turn and saw a car bearing down on me. It hit me very hard, threw me against the building. I hit the wall with my head and immediately passed out. From what I was told, I was quite a sight. A woman who saw me fainted on the spot. I came to in the hospital, bandaged and braced, awash with pain. Anything else you wish to know?"

"What happened to the driver?"

"The son of a bitch was never caught. The police found the car near an orange grove. It had been abandoned."

"What about the owner?"

"The car was stolen the morning of the accident. The owner was a lawyer by the name of Baruch Ehrlich. He was in court when the accident happened. The police said there was no way to discover the identity of the driver."

"Did you see the driver's face, Mrs. Rotner? Could you identify him?"

"I'm afraid not. It all happened very fast, Mr. Lapid."

"You said you half turned before the car struck you. Maybe you managed to catch a glimpse of his face?"

"All I know is that it was a man, and that he was dark-haired."

"How do you know that?"

"Because the driver had a beard. A dark beard."

I shut my eyes. Just like that, the awful suspicion that had gnawed at my stomach had morphed into a terrible near-certainty.

"Why are you asking me all this, Mr. Lapid?"

I opened my eyes and kneaded my hands. My palms had started to sweat, but I could not dispel the notion that the wetness was due to there being blood on my hands. Ofra Wexler's blood. There was one final question to ask. I was almost sure of the answer, but I needed confirmation from her.

"When did the accident happen? What was the date?"

"January 3, 1946. Are you going to tell me where all this is leading?"

It was what I'd expected. When I first met Dahlia, she told me that she was already back home from the hospital when Anna was killed. Given the type and extent of her injuries, she must have spent weeks, if not months, in the hospital. Amiram Gadot had been in prison between April '41 and April '46. His exact date of release was April 21, 1946. A month and one week before Anna was killed. All this had flashed through my mind when Varda told me that Dahlia had been run over.

Because in that instant, I had been struck by the realization that this had not been a random accident, but the work of the same person who had killed Anna, Eliezer Dattner, Nahum Ornstein, and, perhaps, Emil Polisar as well. Knowing that the driver was bearded only reinforced that realization.

That person could not have been Amiram Gadot because he was incarcerated at the time of Dahlia's accident. And I did not for one second entertain the notion that Ofra Wexler had been behind the wheel of that car. Not when she could have waited a few months for Amiram to be released from prison and have him do the deed for her. Ofra was innocent. Ofra was a victim. Her death was a murder disguised as a suicide.

"Well?" Dahlia said, clearly impatient.

I watched her closely as I explained it to her and saw her transform with each word. Muscles twitched and rippled in her face, drawing the skin tauter. Color suffused her cheeks. Her eyes dilated and contracted as shock and incredulity coursed through her. The curtains fell from her irises, and behind them blazed a fire. And gradually, vertebra by vertebra, her back straightened, her shoulders drew back, her body regained its majestic alignment, and she looked like a queen once more. A queen engulfed by royal fury.

Then it happened. All in a split second. Before, she had been like a fortified dam, bravely holding back the roiling waves that crashed upon her. After, it was as though the dam had given way all at once—not cracking, but splintering into a million pieces, so that all her rage erupted in a single, violent gush.

"That dirty, cheating, murderous bastard," she screamed, and, in one furious motion, she swung her cane sideways like a broadsword, sweeping the coffee table clear of teapot, cup, and saucer.

They all crashed on the floor in an explosion of china and spraying liquid. Tiny shards flew in all directions. Tea spattered my shoes, leaving dark stains shaped like teardrops on the cuffs of my trousers.

Thrown off balance by her outburst, Dahlia half-lay, half-reclined on the sofa, her body twisted, leaning sideways on her forearm, breathing hard and whimpering in pain. And, I was shocked to note, there were tears in her eyes and on her cheeks. Something told me those tears would be hot to the touch. The lady of steel, weeping molten metal.

I helped to straighten her up and gave her a napkin to dry her tears. Then I went in search of a broom and a mop. I swept the broken china into the trash can in the kitchen. I mopped the floor. All that time, she sat without uttering a sound, staring into the middle distance or the middle past—or maybe into the middle future, which was probably the worst of the three.

When I was done cleaning, I put everything away and returned to my seat.

I said, "We don't know for sure that it's him, Mrs. Rotner."

She glared at me. Her eyes had regained their power. And when she spoke, it was with her old, glorious voice. "Don't talk nonsense. Of course it's Isser. He's even more diabolical than I thought."

I thought so too, but I'd been wrong about Ofra. I couldn't allow myself to make a similar mistake again.

"If it's him, I'll make sure he pays," I said.

I was comforted to see no doubt in her eyes. She simply nodded as far as her neck brace allowed. "Good. I'm counting on you, Mr. Lapid. What is your next move?"

"I'm going to read the police files of the deaths of Nahum Ornstein and Emil Polisar. Hopefully, I'll find something there." I prayed Reuben hadn't sent the files back yet. "We have one advantage: your husband doesn't know I'm still on the case. Far as he's concerned, everyone is convinced Ofra was responsible for the murders—myself and the police included. I may be able to catch him off guard."

"Does this mean you're not going to tell the police what you discovered?"

I couldn't. Not just yet. The police were on record stating Ofra's guilt. They had an interest in maintaining that guilt, and their reputation. They wouldn't reopen the case based on nothing but my gut feeling regarding Dahlia's accident. I had no proof that the person who ran her over and the murderer were one and the same. The accident could have been nothing but what it seemed.

And there was another problem. If Amiram hadn't come to kill me at Ofra's request, why had he been in my apartment? I knew why, but the police did not.

When Inspector Bartov had been in my apartment, he had remarked upon its tidiness. I said I must have interrupted an intended burglary before it had a chance to commence. It had satisfied him at the time, but if he were invited to reconsider Amiram's presence in my apartment, he might decide to take a closer look at me—and I didn't want that.

But if I obtained incontrovertible evidence that pointed to the real murderer, Bartov and his superiors would likely wish to have as little to do with me as possible. All their efforts would be focused on presenting themselves in the best possible light in the media, as the story would likely be as big as the Ofra Wexler story had been.

I did not explain all this to Dahlia. "Not right now," I said. "Not until I have proof. As for your husband, he mustn't know I'm still on the case. You'll need to act as though nothing has changed."

She smiled a wicked smile. "You're asking me to fool Isser? It will be my pleasure."

41

Reuben had sent the files back to storage. He informed me of this when I called him a few minutes after leaving Dahlia's apartment. The unfortunate news ignited a headache.

"How come you need them again?" he asked.

"It's difficult to explain," I said, rubbing my temples. "Let's just say I have a hunch about something. Can you get the files again?"

"Sure. They wouldn't have had time to misplace them, so I'll probably have them here by tomorrow morning. I'll call storage right now. By the way, my captain had a chat with me earlier today. He said he was very impressed with how I connected Amiram Gadot to Ofra Wexler. He even hinted at a possible promotion."

Reuben sounded very proud. My headache intensified. When I had proof of who the real killer was, the prospect of Reuben's promotion would likely crumble to dust. Another thing to feel guilty about.

"You deserve it," I said. "I hope you get it."

After I hung up, I checked my watch. It was four thirty-eight. He should still be at work.

I hailed a taxi at the corner of Hanevi'im and Shmaryahu

Levin. An uncommon extravagance, but I needed to get to city hall as fast as possible.

I found Haggai Geller in his office, standing behind his desk, slipping papers into a briefcase in preparation for leaving for the day.

His look of irritation at my arrival at this unfortunate hour dissolved when I told him my name.

"Finally," he said. "You're a hard man to reach, Mr. Lapid."

I apologized for not having returned his calls and told him I was happy to meet him at last.

He put his briefcase aside, sat down in his chair, and gestured for me to sit as well. His office was small and very tidy. On his desk I saw a picture of him alongside a pretty young woman holding a pair of babies in her arms.

He did not match his wife's beauty. Haggai Geller had a plain face with unremarkable features. Short brown hair, receding a little at the temples, and brown eyes of mediocre depth and size behind a pair of round glasses. He was five nine and had the average build of a man who did not exert himself in sports nor indulge himself at the dinner table. He was beardless, both currently and in his picture. So far, I had not seen him walk.

He wore a light jacket over a white button-down shirt and dark-gray trousers. Neither the clothes nor the briefcase looked expensive. The impression he gave fitted his position perfectly—a mid-level bureaucrat with a steady, unexciting job. A far cry from his work in the theater.

He said, "I have to tell you, I was very intrigued when my secretary gave me your message. My days as an actor are long behind me."

"You quit the theater in 1940, I understand."

"Yes, that's right."

"To join the British Army and fight the Nazis."

"You're very well informed. Who told you all this?"

"Ofra Wexler."

The name of the dead often invokes silence, and this was no exception. Geller clasped his hands on his desk and his expression turned solemn. I was watching his face when I said Ofra's name because I could not eliminate him as a suspect yet, but his reaction seemed perfectly normal.

After a time, he said, "Reading the newspaper reports, what Ofra did, was the greatest shock of my life."

"You found it hard to believe?"

"Almost impossible, but I guess I didn't know her all that well."

"You were with her in high school, weren't you?"

"In Gymnasia Herzliya."

"Were you friends?"

"No, hardly that. But we were in the same class, so we saw each other nearly every day."

"And Anna Hartman, too?"

"Yes, Anna too. She and Ofra were friends. The best of friends. That's the thing I struggle with most, the idea that Ofra would have Anna killed."

"When did you last see her?"

"Ofra? Not since I went off to the war."

"I meant Anna."

"I met Anna for the final time in 1945, when I was on leave." He paused, adjusted his glasses, and clasped his hands again. "Mr. Lapid, after my secretary gave me your message, I asked around and learned you're a private investigator."

"You're not too badly informed yourself," I said.

"I assume you were involved with what happened with Ofra?"

"To a certain degree."

"Your name wasn't mentioned in any of the articles I read."

"Let's just say I prefer privacy to fame."

"Ah," he said with a wry smile. "Then you wouldn't have been right for the theater. Then again, neither was I."

"Is that why you decided to go fight with the British? By the way, when exactly did you enlist?"

"Twelfth of February, 1940. And a week later, I was in Egypt for training. You ever been there?"

I shook my head, relaxing a little in my seat. If what Geller said was true, he wasn't anywhere near Tel Aviv when Nahum Ornstein was killed, in April 1940. I would need to check it, of course, but I sensed it was the truth.

"The answer to your other question," he continued, "is a bit more complicated. I did quit the theater because I wasn't right for it—truth is, I hated it—but I chose to enlist with the British because I wanted to appear brave and heroic."

I recalled Ofra's story of how Geller had announced his enlistment. "In Anna's eyes, you mean?"

His face registered surprise and a dose of embarrassment. "Did Ofra tell you that, too?"

"Yeah, she did."

"She probably ridiculed me, didn't she?"

I shrugged.

"I deserve it. It was sort of silly." He smiled at his own youthful foolishness. "Truth is, I was in love with Anna. Had been since I met her in high school. I only became interested in the theater as a way to be close to her."

"She didn't reciprocate?"

"I never told her how I felt. Not until years later. But I think she knew all the same. I think that's why she kissed me that night. Needless to say, I didn't expect it. I carried the memory of that kiss throughout the war. In the hardest moments—of fear and homesickness and exhaustion—I would cling to it. I think it saved my life."

"You had no contact with her during the war?"

He shook his head. "I thought about writing to her many times, but I was afraid to. I didn't want to find out that she had met someone, maybe even gotten married. I wanted to make it through the war and get back to her. Ridiculous, isn't it?"

"Not at all," I said. In times of strife, like in war or in the camps, people manufacture the most outlandish reasons to survive, to carry on through another day of suffering. Geller's motivation was far from the oddest I'd encountered.

He said, "I promised Anna I would liberate Prague and save her family. It didn't turn out that way, of course. Her family was dead by the time the war was over, and I never made it to Prague. I fought in North Africa and later in Italy and served in Belgium and France for a time after the war. I met people like you there."

"People like me?"

"With numbers on their arms. The stories they told, those who were willing to talk at all, were horrible beyond imagination. Were you in Auschwitz too?"

I nodded, then retook control of the conversation before it veered into even more dangerous territory.

"You said you hated the theater. How come?" I said.

"I wasn't a very good actor, and I was reminded of this fact—excruciatingly—after nearly every performance."

"Let me guess—by Dahlia Rotner?"

"Not just her. She was the ringleader, but nearly everyone else joined in the fun."

"Including Anna?"

A needle of pain shot across his features. "Only twice. Not too long after we joined the theater. I didn't blame her. It was hard not to add your voice to the chorus of criticism. Social pressure is a powerful thing."

"Then why did she stop?"

"Because deep down Anna was a good person, and she saw how hurt some people could get when they were on the receiving end of all that criticism and mockery. And once she did, she apologized to me and any of the others she hurt, and never did it again.

But the others kept at it, and it got to the point where I couldn't stand it anymore. So I went to fight the war instead."

I felt of flash of anger at Dahlia. She might have been as exceptional as people said, but that didn't give her the right to treat others like dirt.

I said, "You told me you last met Anna in 1945."

"Yes. I was on a three-week leave, and I was a different man than the boy who'd gone to fight the war in 1940. I was braver, and I knew that life was very short indeed. So I went to see Anna, told her how I felt, and asked her to marry me."

"What did she say?"

"She smiled. That was her initial reaction. It was a strange sort of smile. Happy and sad all at once. Then she took my hands in hers, rubbed her thumbs along the back of my hands—" Geller mimicked the caress now, staring down at his own hands before lifting his gaze to meet mine "—and then she turned me down."

"She simply said no?"

"Not exactly. She told me I was courageous and kind and beautiful, and that had things been different, she would have loved being my wife, but I was too young for her."

"Too young? I thought you were the same age."

"Actually, I was born nine months before her. But when I pointed this out to her, she made it clear she was looking for someone not simply older than her, but much older." He drew a deep breath and eased it out in a long sigh. "I asked her what she meant by things that might have been different, but she refused to answer. I can say that she cried when she turned me down. And that she had never looked as beautiful as at that moment when she broke my heart."

He fell silent, and so did I. I knew what Anna had meant. I cursed that old industrialist who had taken advantage of her when she was still a child, and had marked her indelibly. I also realized that Anna's neighbor, Margalit Blissberg, had misheard what

Anna had told Margalit's husband as she rebuffed his advances. Margalit thought Anna had said she did not want a man who was younger than her, but what Anna had really said was that she didn't want a young man at all.

And judging by the tears Anna had shed as she declined Geller's proposal of marriage, she was well aware of her proclivities and hated them, but felt hopelessly trapped by them.

I was thinking of this, and descending deeper into a well of rage-tinged sorrow, when I remembered something else I'd been told during this investigation. Something that didn't fit.

"You've never seen Anna with a young man?" I asked.

Geller shook his head. "Never."

"Not even during high school?"

"No. She never went out with any of the boys, and plenty were interested."

I sat a bit straighter as a cold sharp-nailed finger began scratching a meandering path up my spine. "I was told Anna was involved with a man not older than twenty-one during her final year in high school."

"Who told you?"

"Menashe Klausner."

Geller made a face. "That old fart. Is he still at Gymnasia Herzliya?"

"I take it you don't like him all that much."

"I think he's a pompous ass, and a talentless one at that. One of the best days of my life was when I went to inform him that I was hired by Shoresh Theater. Klausner auditioned for the theater several times and always failed. From what I heard, last time he tried, Dahlia and Eliezer Dattner humiliated him, told him he was the worst actor they'd ever seen. Since he never thought I was any good, it stunned him to learn that I'd succeeded where he'd failed." Geller chuckled, but then his face went hard. "He made Anna cry that day, the bastard."

"Cry?"

"I found her on a bench as I was leaving the school. Apparently, she had gone to see Klausner just before I did. She was his favorite, so I guess she thought he would be happy for her. But that's not how it went."

"What did she say happened?" I asked.

"That Klausner railed at her, told her that Shoresh Theater was the crummiest theater in Tel Aviv, that she was too good for it, that he forbade her to work there."

"Forbade her? Who was he to forbid her anything?"

Geller shrugged. "I guess he thought that since he was the director of the drama club, he had a say in how Anna chose to pursue an acting career. I told you he was a pompous ass."

"What else did Anna say?"

"What do you think? That she wasn't going to do what he said. This was her dream, to be an actress. She wasn't going to give it up just because Klausner had a thing against Shoresh Theater."

That cold finger turned icy as it reached the nape of my neck, making all those small hairs stand on end.

"Once she told me her decision, she calmed down quickly. I walked her home to Gordon Street, and that was that."

"Gordon Street?" I said. "That's where Anna moved after graduation?"

He shook his head. "No, she lived there throughout our senior year. I remember her saying she'd moved to that apartment the previous summer. Apparently, she had to leave very soon, because she asked if I knew anyone who was looking for a tenant."

A memory popped into the forefront of my brain: Mrs. Chernick telling me it had been fourteen years since Anna had lived in her house. This was 1951. Fourteen years ago was 1937, one year before Anna graduated high school.

Later in that same conversation, I'd asked Mrs. Chernick if

Anna had left her house post-graduation, and Mrs. Chernick said she had.

That was a lie. Her earlier slip was the truth. Anna had lived on Gordon Street during her senior year. And someone had to pay her rent.

"Do you know why she had to move in a hurry?" I asked.

He didn't, but I had a pretty solid suspicion.

"Do you remember the address of the apartment on Gordon Street?"

"Not the number, but it was right on the corner of Gordon and Ben Yehuda, north side. Why are you asking all this?"

"Just trying to tie up loose ends," I said, "that's all."

He accepted my answer with a nod. Thought lines creased his forehead. "I never understood what Ofra saw in that lowlife Amiram Gadot. Even in high school he was a menace."

My mouth fell open. "Amiram Gadot went to Gymnasia Herzliya?"

"Two years ahead of us. That's where he and Ofra met."

That icy finger had now been joined by a handful of siblings, which had all climbed a few inches to grab tight hold of my scalp, making it prickle and sting.

"Was Menashe Klausner his teacher?" I asked.

"I'd say that's very likely," Geller said.

42

Music emanated from behind the door. Something dramatic, plenty of violins and cellos, ascending toward a climax. I banged on the door to be heard over the crescendo. Or maybe it was just an excuse to vent some of the fury burning inside me. But not all of it. Not even close.

The music cut off, the door opened, and I caught it when he saw me. The fleeting look of surprise and panic he tried in vain to keep out of his eyes. The look of the guilty man who thought he'd gotten away with it and now dreads being exposed.

He tried to hide it behind a smile. I could tell why he had never been hired by a theater. He wasn't much of an actor.

"Mr. Lapid," Menashe Klausner said, "to what do I owe this pleasure?"

"I got a few more questions," I said. "About Anna. Why don't we go inside?"

"I'm in the middle of something, I'm afraid."

"This won't take long. Then you can go back to your music."

He hesitated. He didn't want me in his home. He didn't want to exchange a single word with me. But there was still that sliver of hope that his fear was baseless and I knew nothing. Better, perhaps, to give me a little time and find out what I did or did not know.

"I can only spare you a few minutes."

"That's fine," I said. "After you."

He turned and walked the few steps to his living room. That was enough. In our previous meeting, I hadn't been watching his legs and hadn't seen him walk. This time I did both and noticed it straight away. His legs were bowed, and he waddled to compensate for it. An unusual gait.

"Ever wore a beard, Mr. Klausner?" I asked as he stopped in the center of his living room and turned to face me.

"What? No, just a mustache. Why?" He looked genuinely bewildered. I decided it didn't prove anything one way or the other, even if he was telling me the truth. Both a drunken Eliyahu Toledano, sighting a man across the street in the dead of night, and Dahlia Rotner, getting a split-second glimpse of the driver of the car bearing down on her, could have easily misremembered a mustache as a beard. Klausner's strange walk was a more powerful piece of evidence.

"Have you read the newspapers?" I asked.

"About Ofra, you mean?" He draped his face in an expression of sadness. "What a terrible tragedy. What a loss to the world of theater."

"I'm surprised to hear you say that, given your feelings toward Shoresh Theater."

"My feelings? What feelings?"

"Don't pretend, Mr. Klausner. You're not a good enough actor to pull it off. I know you auditioned for the theater several times and have always walked away empty-handed. I also know that during one of your auditions, you were mocked by Dahlia Rotner and Eliezer Dattner. That must have hurt, given your aspirations."

A flush pervaded his cheeks. "Where did you hear that?"

"From two former students of yours—Ofra Wexler and Haggai Geller."

"Ofra and Haggai," he pronounced their names as though they were traitors. "The first was a deranged murderess, the second an untalented little runt. Without me, both would never have amounted to anything, and this is the thanks I get—having them spread nasty rumors about me."

"I doubt very much you had anything to do with their accomplishments. Ofra was, by all accounts, a talented and skillful actress. Haggai Geller fought bravely against Germany, and, while even he would admit to being a so-so actor, he was better than you."

His large jaw clenched. "You have no idea what you're talking about."

"You don't hold negative feelings toward Shoresh Theater?"

"Not in the slightest."

"That's not what you told Anna the day she came to tell you she was going to be working there. You lost control. You shouted and raved. You told her it was the crummiest theater in Tel Aviv. You remember that?"

He didn't answer straight away. He began smoothing his mustache with thumb and forefinger over and over again, a movement designed to calm his nerves.

When he stopped, he spoke in a voice thick with emotion, driving his point home with repeated stabs of a rigid forefinger. "You know why they didn't hire me? Because they knew I was better than them, because they didn't want the competition. They knew if I stepped on that stage, their mediocrity would be laid bare."

"Then why did they hire Nahum Ornstein, who was destined for greatness? Why did they hire Anna, who due to her beauty alone might steal the spotlight? They didn't hire you because you've never been any good."

"I'm too good," he growled, his eyes flaring with a hot light. "Better than anyone they've ever seen. And they knew it. I have a special talent, a gift from God. I was meant to be on stage, but they were determined to keep me off it." Spittle dotted his lips, and he wiped it off with an angry swipe of his hand. "All those lies they told me to my face, Dahlia and Dattner, they were all meant to bring me down so that I would slink off with my tail between my legs and give up my dreams."

"Sounds like you hate them."

"Yes, all right, I admit it. I hate them—them and their lousy, stinking theater."

"So you decided to get even, to pay them back."

He frowned, eyebrows knitting close together. "What are you talking about?"

"You know," I said.

"Know what?"

I didn't answer immediately. I just stared at him, at this evil, selfish man haunted by his frustrated ambitions and depraved appetites. I wanted to hit him. Right in his arrogant face. But I needed him to confess. Because I wanted to clear Ofra's name. I owed her that much, at least.

"Mr. Klausner," I said, "Ofra didn't kill anyone, nor ordered them to be killed. You did."

He froze, his mouth falling open like a trapdoor.

I went on, "Come on, admit it. You initiated a vendetta against the people of Shoresh Theater. You killed Eliezer Dattner and Nahum Ornstein, and you ran over Dahlia Rotner in a stolen car. And you also killed Anna, though I suspect that was motivated by something other than her work for the theater."

"You're accusing me of murder? That's why you're here?"

"Your actions brought Shoresh Theater to the brink of ruin. Just a little more time, and maybe another murder or two, and the theater would have folded. Then your mission would have been complete. But then I came along and threatened to spoil your plans. So you decided to eliminate me by getting your former student Amiram Gadot to kill me."

"Amiram Gadot? I haven't seen him in years."

"When that failed, you decided to cover your tracks by framing Ofra. You pushed her out that window and typed a suicide note in which she claimed responsibility for the murders you committed. You did this because you knew she had motive for killing Eliezer Dattner, Nahum Ornstein, and Anna. But she didn't have a particular reason to kill Dahlia Rotner, so you left that out."

For a second or two, he said nothing. Then he smiled a huge smile, reminding me of those carved pumpkin heads some Hungarians put in their windows each year on St. Lucy's Day. The Devil himself could have smiled that smile.

All traces of fear had blown off Klausner's face, replaced by smug confidence. "You have a fertile imagination, Mr. Lapid, but nothing you said is true. I've never killed anyone. And I want you to leave right now."

"I never would have suspected you," I said, ignoring both his denial and his command, "if you hadn't made one mistake. You told me you saw Anna kissing a young man during her senior year. That was a lie. Anna never got involved with young men. Only with men much older than her and married as well. Like you."

"So now you're accusing me of having an affair with Anna?" he said. "What's next on your list? High treason?"

"You know, Mr. Klausner," I said, "you never asked me how I knew your address. Want me to tell you?" I didn't wait for a reply. "I paid a visit to a certain apartment building on the corner of Gordon and Ben Yehuda. Know the building I'm talking about?"

His confidence died like a snuffed flame, and the fear was back in force. He had thought I had nothing but accusations. But here was something I could prove.

"Anna lived there during her senior year," I said. "The landlord remembered her. He also remembered the *uncle* who paid the rent and visited his *niece* on an almost daily basis. That *uncle* was you. The landlord still had your address on file. He said you gave it to him so he could alert you if any man but yourself ever visited your *niece*. You said it was to protect her reputation, but it was really so that no one would steal her from you. Your jealousy, your need to dominate Anna, led me straight to your door."

I paused, but he just stood there, stunned. I said, "That's why you tried to dissuade me from talking to Mrs. Chernick. You were afraid she'd tell me Anna had moved out before her senior year. You needn't have worried. Mrs. Chernick is as corrupt as you are. I think she had already been paid for that year, and she decided to keep the money even after Anna moved out."

Right then, I heard the apartment door open, followed by the rhythmic taps of a woman's shoes approaching. Klausner heard it too, and his face went pallid. He plopped into a chair. I turned and saw a stringy woman in her fifties standing at the entrance to the living room, looking from me to Klausner.

"Menashe, what's going on?"

"Mrs. Klausner?" I asked.

"Yes, who are you?"

"My name is Adam Lapid. I'm a private investigator. Your husband didn't tell you we met about week ago, did he?"

"No, he didn't. Menashe, who is this man? What is he doing here?"

"It's nothing, Matilda," Klausner said. "Nothing you should concern yourself about. Give us a few minutes alone, okay? Go to the store or something."

Matilda Klausner didn't move. She had a narrow face with thin eyebrows and down-turned lips. She looked at me and must have read something in my eyes, because her slim shoulders sagged and her face crinkled in resignation and deep-seated anger.

"What's her name?" she asked her husband. "How old is she?"

Klausner bowed his head, hands laced between his knees.

Matilda turned to me. "Well?"

"Mrs. Klausner, I'm not here because of any woman your husband may be sleeping with. I'm—"

"Woman? I think *girl* is a better word, don't you?"

"Girl or woman. I'm here because of a woman by the name of Anna Hartman."

That gave her pause. She pursed her lips and exhaled through her nose. "What about her?"

"You know about the affair?" I asked, surprised.

She gave a curt nod. She didn't lower her head or avert her eyes. This was an old wound, and she was a proud woman.

"This wasn't the first time, was it?" I asked.

"No, it wasn't. My dear husband has a thing for young girls." She looked at Klausner as though trying to bore holes through his skull. "But she was special, isn't that right, Menashe?"

He didn't answer. His large shoulders trembled.

"You know about the apartment?" she asked.

I nodded.

"It's bad enough that your husband takes advantage of his students every once in a while. It's another thing entirely that he spends money his family desperately needs to put up a young girl in an apartment. We have two sons, Mr. Lapid, and both of them went without certain things because their father chose to throw our money away on his mistress."

She gave me a defiant look. "You're wondering why I didn't divorce him? You think I'm a weak woman?" I began shaking my head, but she was already speaking. "I did it to protect our boys and the reputation of our family. The same as I did with the girl before Anna Hartman and the one before that. But I did take steps so that it wouldn't happen again."

"The move to Haifa," I said.

She nodded, not bothering to ask how I knew. "My sister is a teacher there. She got Menashe a position in her school. She also kept an eye on him. And for five years he behaved, didn't you, darling?"

His head still hanging low, Klausner nodded dejectedly.

"After five years, he persuaded me to move back to Tel Aviv. I agreed because our boys were grown and living on their own, and because I believed he'd outgrown his inclinations. And by that time, Anna Hartman was dead, which made things easier for me."

"You moved back after Anna's murder?" I asked. This I had not expected. I was sure the five-year absence from Tel Aviv would fit more or less perfectly with the time gap between Nahum Ornstein's murder and the car attack on Dahlia.

"I wouldn't have agreed to set foot in Tel Aviv while she still lived."

This was also unexpected. I had thought Klausner had killed Anna because she worked for Shoresh Theater, or because she was involved with Isser Rotner, or because she no longer belonged to him—or a combination of the three. But here was another reason.

I looked at Klausner. He had raised his head and was staring right at me with a pair of hateful eyes.

"Mrs. Klausner," I said, "you gave your husband the perfect motive to kill Anna Hartman."

She frowned, five parallel lines engraved across her forehead. "What?" was all she said.

There was no good way to tell her, so I said it plainly. "Mrs. Klausner, I believe your husband killed Anna Hartman and many other people, too."

For the first time in minutes, Klausner spoke. "Tell him I didn't do it, Matilda. Tell him I couldn't."

She hushed him as though he were a toddler. "I don't understand, Mr. Lapid. Explain yourself."

So I did. She knew some of the story from the papers and

listened attentively as I expressed my belief that Ofra Wexler was an innocent victim, not a murderer.

When I was finished, she looked disappointed. "Mr. Lapid, I'm afraid you've got it all wrong."

"How's that?"

"Menashe didn't kill Anna Hartman. He was with me."

"You can't hide what he is any longer, Mrs. Klausner. He needs to pay for his crimes."

"You don't understand. If he were guilty, I wouldn't defend him for a second. I feel no loyalty toward him. That died a long time ago. But he was with me that night. And not just with me, but with my entire family. You see, my father passed away two days before Anna Hartman was killed. Menashe and I went to sit *shiva* at my parents' house in the Jezreel Valley. We were there all that week, including the night in question. I didn't sleep a wink all that night; I was too consumed by grief. Menashe didn't budge from our bed. He snored his lungs out till daybreak."

I surveyed her face and saw no sign of deceit. But this couldn't be true. I was sure of Klausner's guilt.

Matilda smiled a tight smile. "You don't believe me? Then you should know that my sister and her husband shared the room with us. They can vouch for Menashe as well as I can. Menashe is guilty of many crimes, but he's innocent of this one. I don't know if I can provide an alibi for him for the other murders you mentioned, but I don't believe he committed them. You see, Mr. Lapid, Menashe is a big fat coward. And he can't stand the sight of blood. He couldn't kill anyone. He's not man enough."

"Matilda," Klausner said in an angry voice. His entire face was aflame. "Enough."

She ignored him. "I'm sorry, Mr. Lapid, but you'll need to find your killer elsewhere. Do you have any other questions for my husband?"

I tried to think, but my mind was reeling. I had been sure I had the right man, but I believed Matilda. And now, my brain was struggling to free itself of my mistaken certainty.

Klausner had gotten to his feet. He pointed a shaking finger at me. "Get out!"

"Shut up, Menashe," Matilda said calmly, "and sit down. Mr. Lapid hasn't answered my question yet. Is there something you wish to ask my husband? You see, I don't hate Anna Hartman. She was a victim of my husband. If he can help you catch her killer, then he'll do so, whether he wants to or not."

"Matilda, I want him out of here," Klausner said, but he clamped his mouth shut when his wife pinned him with her gaze.

"You will sit down now and cooperate. If you do not, I'll expose you for what you are. I no longer care what people may think of me."

Klausner looked stricken. Matilda had spoken with such uncompromising iciness that it was obvious her threat was not an idle one.

"I do have some questions," I said, once my mind stopped churning and cleared.

"Go ahead," Matilda said.

"They're about your husband and Anna's relationship. Perhaps you should leave the room. You may not wish to hear the answers."

"On the contrary. I want to know everything. And I can help you. Because over the years, I've become quite good at reading my husband. Which is why I know that he has his eyes on a new girl, don't you, dear?" Klausner looked at his wife in horror. "I didn't want to admit it to myself until your visit, Mr. Lapid, but I've known for a while. I can read him. He wouldn't dare lie to you in my presence."

Matilda sat as still as a headstone as her husband told us about his affair with Anna. She didn't weep. She didn't hurl recriminations. She didn't even look at him. The only sign of her emotional state was her tightly clenched fist. It stayed balled up all the way through her husband's narration. She was an immensely strong woman, and I hoped she would finally break loose of her husband and lead a free life.

Klausner spoke with surprising candidness. It took me a minute before I realized he was proud of what he'd done. It made him feel powerful and masculine, and talking about it gave him the chance to hurt his wife even more than he'd already done.

I became sick listening to him tell with perverse delight how he had identified Anna's weakness, how her separation from her family had made her vulnerable. When he began describing in graphic detail their first sexual encounter, I told him to shut up, but Matilda raised a hand and said, "Let him talk. I want to be thoroughly disgusted with him."

So we listened. I cringed and shifted uncomfortably while Klausner expounded on his and Anna's lovemaking, comparing her glorious body to his wife's sticklike figure, Anna's passion to Matilda's frigidity. And still Matilda sat with barely a motion.

"She was the best of the lot," Klausner said. "Not only was she the most beautiful, but she was also the most inventive, adventurous, and compliant girl I had ever known. Someone trained her well."

When he grinned, I had the urge to knock each and every one of his teeth out—one with each punch.

"One of the unique things about Anna was that she liked doing it in weird places. Not just in the bedroom in the dark like some women—" a sneer at Matilda "—but in the park, on the beach, on the roof of a building. And always she would wait for me fully clothed, apart from one item. Want to guess what it was, Matilda?"

She didn't reply, and neither did I, though the answer popped in my head like the flame of a lighter.

"Her underwear," Klausner said, confirming it. "She would wait for me without underwear. First time she did it, I was stunned, and she got confused. 'Did I do something wrong?' she said. 'Does this not please you?'" He laughed. "Of course it pleased me. Of course it did. Someone sure trained her properly. She was no virgin, I can tell you that. She had experience, and she knew how to please a man."

That was when I knew that Anna had not been forced into Trumpeldor Cemetery. She had gone there for a tryst, and I knew with whom. I also knew that her killer had not stripped her of her underwear. She had taken them off herself in preparation for her lover. She must have put them in her bag, which the killer had taken with him.

Klausner began another story, but I'd had enough and no longer cared what Matilda wanted. I told Klausner to be quiet. My skin crawled as though covered by a million insects. My mouth burned with a sour, acidic taste. My knuckles itched with the desire to form fists and clobber this disgusting, perverted creature who called himself a man and a teacher.

Matilda finally stirred. Her body shook from head to toe, a single tremor followed by a long breath, as though she had come out of a trance. She turned her head to look at her husband, and I saw her eyes were utterly dry. Klausner shrank under her gaze.

"Thank you," she said in a flat voice. "I needed that." And she pulled off her wedding band and let it drop to the floor. She flexed and bent and rubbed her ring finger, as though circulation was flowing into it freely for the first time in years.

"Will you stay while I pack a bag?" she asked me.

I nodded and waited in the living room with Klausner while Matilda went into the bedroom. Klausner called after her, but she paid him no mind. He tried to follow her, but I pushed him back. When he tried again, I kicked him in the crotch and watched him curl on the floor, breathless and purple-faced.

He was still lying there when Matilda returned, clutching a small suitcase.

"Thank you again, Mr. Lapid," she said at the sight of her husband. "For myself and all of Menashe's girls."

She asked me to walk her to the bus stop. I told her to wait a minute, crouched down next to Klausner, and for the second time in as many days ended a man's career.

"Tomorrow," I said, "you'll hand in your resignation. You will not apply at any other school. You will not work with teenagers ever again. If you do, I'll come after you, and a kick in the balls will be nothing compared to what I'll do to you. Don't think you can hide from me. Don't think I'll forget about you. Every once in a while, I'll check up on you—up close or from a distance. If you ever go near young girls again, I'll hunt you down and hurt you bad. Do you understand?"

Fear wafted off him in thick waves as he stared at me with gigantic eyes. He was still holding his private parts, but then his mouth twisted and he lifted his hands, and I saw the dark stain spread from his groin down his pant leg.

I rose to my full height and backed away from him. Then I escorted Matilda down the stairs, out of the building, and into her new life.

43

I was back at square one. Back to Isser Rotner. And I didn't have a shred of evidence that would convict him in court.

But I knew without a doubt that he had been in Trumpeldor Cemetery on the night Anna died. He had arranged to meet her there. A secluded place, perfect for exciting lovemaking. And also for murder.

I went by Ohel Shem. The crowd looked bigger than ever. It was the penultimate performance of King Lear. The final one was to take place the following night at eight o'clock.

That night I slept without dreams, courtesy of the kick I'd given Menashe Klausner. I woke up very early, and time trickled past with tormenting slowness. It was ten o'clock by the time Reuben got the files back.

I hurried to the police station, bounded up the stairs to his office, and found him at his desk. Reuben handed me the files, told me he had to attend a staff meeting, and said I could use his office for the next hour.

I started with Nahum Ornstein. I read the file carefully. It didn't take very long; there wasn't a lot of material. It was deemed an accident from the get-go, so not a lot of paperwork was created. By the time I read the last page, I knew it had been a waste of time. Nothing in this file pointed to anyone, let alone Isser Rotner.

Next was Emil Polisar's file. It was only slightly thicker than Ornstein's but proved to be as disappointing. It started out well, like any normal investigation of a homicide by gunfire, but once the detective in charge learned that Polisar's pregnant wife, Brigitte, had been killed in an Egyptian air raid a week before, he came to the obvious conclusion. Suicide.

The evidence supported this. Polisar died from a single gunshot wound to the temple, and by the way the skin looked, it was clear the muzzle had either been pressed to his head or held a sliver of an inch from it. There was no sign of a struggle, and Polisar's wallet was found in his pocket. A revolver lay next to the corpse. The grip was covered with Polisar's fingerprints, and his alone.

There was no suicide note, but in this case, one was hardly required. Polisar had lost a wife and an unborn child. The reason for his suicide was clear. Case closed.

To bolster this conclusion, perhaps, a pair of stapled pages documenting the death of Brigitte Polisar had been tucked into the file. I'd set them aside when I'd begun reading about her husband's alleged suicide, sure that they contained nothing useful. But now, disappointed and frustrated and unsure of how to proceed, I picked them up, giving them a cursory glance.

So cursory, in fact, that I'd almost missed it, had carried on reading, and had to backtrack to find it again. The line on the page where another name was written. A person who had been in Brigitte Polisar's apartment when the air raid occurred. A person who had suffered but minor scratches when a segment of the roof collapsed, smashing Brigitte's skull and killing her.

I sat back, still holding the pages, feeling as though the world had tilted on its axis, settling on a new, unfamiliar angle from which everything looked and felt different than before.

My mind sprinted in a desperate attempt to make sense of this new information, to try to make it fit with everything else I'd learned since I first heard the name Anna Hartman.

It was a slippery path my mind had taken, and my thoughts kept skidding and sliding in a mess of confusion and disbelief. It couldn't be. But maybe it was.

And then I remembered something. Or, more accurately, two things—neither of which had seemed important at the time. Only now they made terrifying sense. The first I'd seen in one of the old issues of *Davar* Birnbaum had shown me. The second I'd heard from Dahlia's lips.

I picked up the phone with mounting excitement and called the offices of *Davar*. It took a few minutes before Birnbaum came on the line.

I told him what I needed.

"You have to tell me why," he said.

"Later, Shmuel."

"Patience has never been one of my virtues, Adam."

"Do this for me, Shmuel, and I'll give you the biggest story of your life."

That convinced him. I was about to hang up, but then another idea came to me. I asked Birnbaum to look up any articles mentioning the person who had been with Brigitte Polisar when she died.

"Look for anything related to Shoresh Theater," I said, "in 1938 or '39."

"I'm on it," Birnbaum said. "Call me in an hour."

It was eleven fifty-six. I decided not to stick around in Reuben's office. I was worried he'd see my face and know something big was going on, and I didn't want to answer any of his questions. I found a nearby café in which to pass the time.

While I waited, I made a telephone call, this one to the office of Baruch Ehrlich, the owner of the car used to run over Dahlia. I had just one question for him, and as I expected, his answer was yes.

Forty-five minutes later, my patience exhausted, I called Birnbaum again. He read me the front pages of the issues of *Davar* published over the three days following Nahum Ornstein's death. They confirmed my suspicions. Now I knew who had killed Anna and everyone else.

But I didn't know why. Not until Birnbaum gave me the other piece of information I'd asked him to dig up.

"Just one article," he said. "December 21, 1938. A review of a play that took place the evening prior. I wrote the review myself." He read it to me.

"Was it really as bad as that?" I asked.

"Worse, actually. I took pity on the poor soul."

Now I had my motive, too.

44

The garage was small. Two mechanics in greasy overalls were bent over an automobile with its hood up. One of them pointed toward the back when I asked if the owner was around.

I found Shaul Navon sitting behind his desk in an office the size of a ration card. He was munching on a sandwich. He smiled when he saw me, put the sandwich aside, wiped crumbs off his palms, and offered me his hand.

"Mr. Lapid, am I glad to see you."

"You are?" I said, shaking his hand, surprised by his warm reception.

"Sure. Varda told me you might be stopping by. I understand you're writing a play about the Irgun."

I am? I thought, confused. What was going on here?

"She said you'd be interested in learning more about the operations I took part in," Navon said, with evident pride.

"I am," I said, slowly recovering but still unsure of my footing, feeling like a chess piece being moved about the board by a player whose strategy I did not comprehend. "I was wondering if you were involved in three specific operations." I gave him the dates on which Dattner, Ornstein, and Anna were killed.

He began nodding as soon as he heard the first date. "Sure, I was in all three. You heard about them, huh?"

"Yeah," I said, still a little shaky from the unexpected direction this conversation had taken. "You were away from Tel Aviv during each of those operations, right?"

"That's right. The first operation took place in Haifa, the second in Jerusalem, and the last, the one in which we attacked an ammunition depot, was near Pardes Hanna. Why are you interested in those three?"

"I think they might make good scenes in the play," I said, hoping he'd fall for it, wondering what game Varda was playing.

"Ah, I understand. I'm not much of a fan of the theater, but living with Varda, I picked up a few things. What else do you want to know?"

"Actually," I said, "I was wondering if Varda was around. I went by her shop and it was closed."

"Varda closes up each day between twelve and three. Why do you need to see her?"

"I want to base a character on her. The wife of the Irgun fighter. Add a little romance, you know. The audience loves that."

"I see." He gave me a wink. "It needs a little spice to sell tickets."

"Precisely," I said. "Do you know where she is?" I'd already been to their apartment, which was one street over from the garage, but no one was home. I'd copied the addresses of the shop, apartment, and garage when I read Anna's file—which seemed like a very long time ago.

"She went to measure an outfit for one of the actors in the theater."

"Which actor?" I said, alarm bells beginning to ring.

"Leon Zilberman. You know him?"

"Yes." The bells tolled louder. "She went to his home?"

"I think so. Some last minute alteration."

"When did she go?"

"About an hour ago. You might still find her there."

A dark voice in my head told me I'd probably wouldn't, that this was part of the game, as well. I was about to head out, when my gaze landed on a framed picture hanging behind Navon's desk. It showed Shaul and Varda Navon, and between them a frail boy of three or four.

"Is that your son?" I asked, pointing at the picture.

A shadow passed over Navon's face. "That's Mickey, God rest his soul. A month before he died. A heart condition."

"I'm so sorry," I said. "When did he die? How old was he?"

"Mickey died on the first of December, 1945. He was four years old."

———

I thought about calling the police and probably would have if the garage had a telephone. As I stepped out into the street, however, I changed my mind and started running instead. If this was indeed part of some game, I needed to reach Leon Zilberman's apartment before anyone else. I dreaded what I would find there.

I caught a taxi at the corner and told the driver to step on it. I drummed my fingers on the seat, barely registering the sights of Tel Aviv streaming past my window.

When I got to Zilberman's building, I raced up the stairs to his apartment. The door was closed but unlocked. Leon Zilberman was in the living room.

He lay facedown on the floor, three stab wounds in his back, his shirt soaked with blood. He was quite clearly dead.

Draped over a chair was a suit of medieval clothes, the outfit worn by Zilberman in King Lear. On the dining table lay a piece of paper weighted down by a thimble and a roll of black sewing thread. A message was scrawled in a feminine hand.

Noble knight, meet me at the theater. V.

I sprinted down the stairs, out of the building, south to Sirkin Street, and east to Frishman. No taxis were around. Cursing in a medley of languages, I ran east, my feet pounding the pavement almost as fast as my heart pounded against my breastbone.

The day was scorching hot, and my face dripped with sweat. People jumped out of my way, giving me wary or angry looks, one or two shouting curses. A young mother pushing a baby stroller yelled at me to watch out. As I streaked past her, I heard her baby wailing, woken by his mother's yell.

I cut south to Dizengoff Square and finally caught a taxi. I threw myself into the backseat.

"Balfour Street..." I wheezed out, short of breath from my run. "Ohel Shem."

It took fifteen minutes, but it felt like fifteen hours. When the taxi stopped, I threw money at the driver, not waiting for change. Then I hurled the door open and hurtled out and up the steps and into the lobby of Ohel Shem.

There I paused, unsure of where to go. To Varda's room or up the stairs to the theater hall?

If this was a game or, better yet, a play, then there was only one place suited for the final scene.

I took the stairs three at a time and rushed into the theater hall. Then I stopped dead, rendered immobile by what I was seeing. As in my previous two visits, Isser Rotner was on stage. Only this time, he wasn't standing and he wasn't alone.

Rotner was on his knees, and behind him—one hand coiled into his hair, the other holding a long-bladed knife to his throat—was Varda Navon. A sheen of perspiration covered Rotner's face. His expression was one of pure dread. He was bleeding from one bicep. His other hand tried to stem the flow of blood.

337

"Did you get my note, Adam?" Varda called from the stage.

"Yes," I said, breaking free of my paralysis. I walked forward slowly, keeping my hands raised to show they were empty.

"It's good that you didn't dawdle. We don't have much time before the rest of the actors arrive to prepare for this evening's performance. I was worried we might have to proceed without you."

"I came here as soon as I could, Varda."

"Are you alone? Or are the police here as well?"

"I'm all by myself. I didn't think it would do any good to call the police."

"You're right, it wouldn't. That's how tragedies work. No matter what you do, no matter how hard you try, you can't escape your destiny."

I was three rows from the stage by now. "Can I come up, Varda?"

"By all means. But stay back. If you try anything, I'll slit his throat."

I climbed on the stage, keeping a distance of twelve feet between myself and Varda and her captive.

"Are you all right, Mr. Rotner?" I asked.

"Yes," he said, his voice scratchy with pain and fear. "You gotta help me. She's insane. She's—"

"Shut your mouth," Varda said, yanking on Rotner's hair. "I'm the director here, not you."

She sounded calm and collected. This wasn't a woman gripped by maniacal rage. Not a killer driven by uncontrolled urges. This was a mastermind, on the verge of seeing her long and carefully executed campaign of vengeance come to its successful end.

Her face was drawn, her eyes heavy with fatigue. She had been in control for twelve years. She had acted without cease. She had kept a mask on her face even as she spent day after day servicing the people she hated with all her might. No wonder she was exhausted.

"I met your husband," I said. "It was quite clever, telling him I was writing a play. But not as clever as how you used him and his work for the Irgun to get alibis for yourself."

She smiled. "That was ingenious, wasn't it?"

I nodded. "Your husband was engaged in an operation on each of the nights Dattner, Ornstein, and Anna were killed. As these operations took place when the British still ruled here, you and he agreed that if anyone came asking, you'd swear he was with you at home during those nights. It would give him an alibi if the British suspected him, and, as a byproduct, furnish you with one as well —for the deaths of your colleagues."

"Not my colleagues," she said, with an edge of anger. "They were actors. I am not."

"Not on stage, maybe. But you're the best actress to have ever worked in Shoresh Theater. Better even than Dahlia Rotner. Otherwise, you wouldn't have been able to fool everyone for as long as you did."

This seemed to please her, but her knife remained steady. She could slash Rotner's throat in a heartbeat.

"You knew about Eliezer Dattner's lover," I said, "so you ambushed him in Jaffa, knowing the murder would be attributed to an Arab. The pamphlet you left in his mouth made sure of that."

"You should have seen Eliezer's face when I came out of the shadows with a gun in my hand," Varda said. "It was glorious. Before that, I wasn't sure I had it in me. To kill someone, I mean. Afterward, I knew I could do it again and again. I could get them all."

"Ornstein was next. How did you do it?"

"I came to his apartment supposedly to make alterations in the outfit he wore for the play the theater was running then. I whacked him across the back of the head with a pipe, got him naked, hauled him into the bathtub, and held his head under water until he died. I made sure it would look like he had an accident due to his drug use."

"I thought it was something like that. I should have figured it out earlier. The first day we met, I carried that sack for you, remember?"

"I remember."

"It was heavy as hell. Heavier than a woman should be able to carry all the way to your room at the back of this building. But you intended to carry it yourself. You're strong enough to do it. Strong enough to lift a big man like Ornstein into a bathtub, and to throw a small woman like Ofra from her window."

"I've been carrying large bolts of cloth ever since I was a child," she said by way of explanation.

"And there was another clue," I said. "Something I missed at the time."

"Oh?"

"After Ornstein's body was discovered, Leon Zilberman took over his part. He told me you had to make him a brand-new outfit the day of the show. But at another stage of our conversation, he said Ornstein was taller than him. So why would you need to make him an outfit from scratch? Why not simply modify the existing one? Unless it could not be used for some reason, say, because it was stained with Ornstein's blood."

"He was wearing the outfit when I hit him," Varda said. "There was a little blood on the collar and back. I had to get rid of it and make a new one."

I nodded, chastising myself for not seeing it earlier.

"And Anna?" I said. "How did her murder come about?"

"I was waiting for the right opportunity," she said. "I kept my eyes and ears open. Then, one evening, I heard Anna and Isser plan a rendezvous for that very night."

"How did you hear their conversation?"

"They were on stage," she said. "They thought they were alone; everyone else had left. I stood in the wings and eavesdropped. They didn't see me."

Just like that old cleaning lady had eavesdropped on my first conversation with Rotner.

"They arranged to meet at half past midnight in Trumpeldor Cemetery," Varda said, "at the grave of Mayor Dizengoff. I didn't know why they chose that particular grave until I got there. When I saw it, I realized it resembled a bed. Sick, isn't it?"

Not as sick as you, I thought.

"So you waited there?" I said.

"Yes. I hid behind Max Nordau's mausoleum. Then Anna arrived, right on time. I waited a couple of minutes just in case someone saw her enter the cemetery. And then I stabbed her with my knife."

She said all this in a cold, flat voice, as though she were describing the carving of a chicken, the filleting of a fish, and not the slaying of a human being.

"Weren't you worried about Isser? He could have seen you."

Her smile was broad and full of satisfaction. "I made sure he was delayed."

"How?"

"I punctured one of his tires. I figured it would take him at least ten minutes to change it. I considered waiting to kill him, too, but that might have made the police take a very close look at anyone who worked for the theater, and I didn't want that. I wasn't in a hurry. I could wait for another opportunity."

Now I knew why Rotner had tossed and turned in his sleep that night. He had come to Trumpeldor Cemetery. He had seen Anna's body. The sight of her had given him nightmares.

It was also the reason he got Dahlia to lie for him. He needed an alibi because he had been there, at the scene of the crime, shortly after the murder had taken place.

"You crazy bitch," Rotner growled, and Varda retaliated by pressing the knife into his skin, drawing a slender line of blood across his throat.

"Don't be ungrateful," Varda said. "Without me, you would have kept on playing second fiddle to Eliezer, and to Dahlia, for the rest of your life."

Rotner said nothing, but his wide, rapidly blinking stare conveyed all the horror and bafflement that gripped him. He wasn't guilty of the murders. He didn't know the true cause of Dahlia's injury. But that didn't mean he was wholly innocent.

"For a while," I said, "I didn't know why the killings stopped for five years. But now I think I do. It's because of your son, isn't it?"

The corners of Varda's mouth drooped. Her throat worked, as though she were swallowing a lump of grief. "When Mickey was born, my love for him overwhelmed my hatred for all those who'd wronged me. I lost my desire for vengeance. But Mickey was sickly from the day he was born. He died when he was four years old. And when he did, the old hatred returned, more powerful than ever, and I knew I had to see this through."

"What did we ever do to you?" Rotner asked, the blood dripping from his neck staining his shirt collar.

"You don't even know," Varda said. "It meant everything to me, but nothing to you."

Rotner obviously didn't understand, so I explained it to him.

"December 20, 1938. Shoresh Theater put on a production of Twelfth Night. Dahlia was to play Viola, but she came down with a sore throat. So someone had to fill in for her."

"I studied that play," Varda said, "and how Dahlia acted, so hard that I knew not only every line, but every gesture, every expression, as well. At first Anna was supposed to play Viola, but when I showed Dahlia how well I knew the part, she decided to give me a chance."

"But it didn't turn out so well, did it?" I said.

Varda's mouth twisted as though she'd tasted something rotten. "The second I stepped on stage, everything fell to pieces. The lights, the audience, it all made me feel like I was suffocating. All the lines I had worked so hard to learn by heart fluttered away like frightened birds, leaving only a scattering of feathers. My body trembled; my stomach flip-flopped. I stumbled about as though blind; I stammered; I spoke lines that belonged to later acts. And finally, when the enormity of the catastrophe hit me, I vomited on stage, in front of hundreds of people."

"It was your first time on stage," I said. "You shouldn't have been given the main role. That was Dahlia's mistake. But it wasn't her only, nor biggest one, was it?"

Varda shook her head slightly, and I noticed that her eyes sparkled with moisture. Her pain was still fresh despite being twelve years of age.

"After I threw up, the curtain was lowered and I was pulled unceremoniously off stage. The stage was cleaned up, and the play was started anew, this time with Anna playing Viola. I sat in my small room, weeping uncontrollably, knowing my dreams had gone up in flames. And after the play ended, that's when it happened."

"Dahlia tore into you," I said.

"Her and nearly everyone else. Everyone except Haggai Geller. He was the only one who didn't feel the need to kick me when I was down. I think it was because he was often the target of such attacks. He knew how it felt. Only it had never been as vicious, as cruel, and as hurtful as what I was put through."

"I can imagine," I said. Varda's pain was so raw, so vibrant and powerful, that I couldn't help but sympathize with her.

Varda looked at me. "No, Adam, I sincerely doubt you can. Afterward, after they had flayed my spirit, Dahlia made it clear that I would never be allowed to act on stage again. She said I should be grateful that I still had my job. I could make the clothes, but I could never wear them."

"So you decided to pay them back."

"I decided to show them how well I could act. I would play the meek, humble seamstress, working in the shadow of their glamor. But every once in a while, I would emerge from that shadow, and I would bring death with me. Because if I couldn't act, then they wouldn't either."

"Which is why you let Dahlia live," I said, "after you ran her over."

Rotner gasped. Now he understood. He let out a groan and started weeping.

Varda tugged on his hair and spoke through gritted teeth. "Stop it, you faker. Don't pretend to care about her. If you did, you wouldn't have cheated on her with every woman who came along." To me, she said, "I meant to kill her, but I think I did even better. Dahlia's life was the theater. The fact that she still breathes means nothing. She is already dead. Every day is torment for her. Not because she is handicapped or suffers pain, but because she cannot act. That is a fate worse than death for her."

"That was also clever of you, how you got the car," I said.

"You know about that, too?"

I nodded. "I spoke to Baruch Ehrlich, the owner of the car. I asked him if he had been a customer of your husband's garage when Dahlia was run over, and he said he was. What did you do, make a copy of his key?"

"Yes. I don't know how to pick a lock, so that's how I did it. I had driven that car before. I felt comfortable in it. It had very good acceleration. It was perfect for the job." Her grin raised goosebumps on my arms. "Hitting Dahlia with the car, seeing her fly through the air like a rag doll, was the most exhilarating moment of my life. I dream about it sometimes, you know, and when I do, I always wake up smiling."

"Was there no chance of forgiveness?" I asked.

"Forgiveness?" Varda's chin notched upward. "Forgiveness for whom?"

"For Anna. Haggai Geller told me she apologized to you, just as she had to him, for joining in with the others."

"She did, but it was too late. The damage was done. She had to pay, too."

An ocean of melancholy swept over me, drenching me with invisible tears. Inside, I wept for Anna. All alone in the world from a young age, exploited and abused by older men, desperate to realize her acting dreams, to belong and to find a place in the world where she could be happy, even while knowing she was forever damaged.

Despite all this, she had been a good person. She had wronged others, that was true. She had slept with married men. She had taken part in Varda's humiliation. But the first act was beyond her control, stamped on her nature at a young and vulnerable age; and the second was an act she had deeply regretted and ceased doing. Yes, she had been good. But that didn't save her. Which wasn't surprising. Being good never saved anyone.

"What made you kill Ofra and frame her for the murders?" I asked.

"I knew you had made the connection between Anna and the others. I worried that it was only a matter of time before you took a closer look at me. So I decided to provide you with the killer, all wrapped up in a bow."

"How did you discover I knew about the other murders? I didn't talk about them with you."

"Leon Zilberman told me. He said you suspected Ofra. He thought you were crazy."

I closed my eyes and pressed my nails into the soft flesh of my palms, bringing forth a much-deserved pain. I had led Varda to Ofra. She was dead because of me.

Opening my eyes, I said, "Zilberman told me he always had a big mouth."

Varda half smiled. "That he did. But he won't be using it anymore."

"How did you know about the poems Ofra wrote, the ones found on her desk?"

"I didn't. I came to her apartment with a new dress for her. I knocked her out with a wrench, then typed her suicide note. The poems were stacked right there, next to the typewriter, covered by a cloth. I think she was perusing them when I arrived, had covered them up so I wouldn't see. They were perfect. They made her seem guiltier than the suicide note did."

I thought I knew why Ofra had been reading those poems. That was because of me, too. During our last conversation, when I told her about the man with the beard, she had reacted with shock and then swore to me she hadn't sent anyone to kill on her behalf. She had wanted me to believe this, because she thought the man with the beard was Amiram Gadot. That he had murdered because of her or for her, even though she hadn't asked him to. She had died with that thought in her head, with that guilt in her heart.

I had made her think of those deaths, so she had brought out her poems and read them. And there they lay, the perfect evidence of Ofra's hate, and of her guilt. Exactly what Varda needed.

"I figured no one would notice the blow from the wrench," Varda went on. "Not after Ofra dove headfirst from a third-floor window. Just like the police attributed the gash on the back of Nahum's head to him slipping in the tub and smacking his head on the edge."

She was smiling. A smile not of evil, but of unvarnished self-satisfaction. She had thought things through. She had been meticulous in her planning and careful in her execution. She had been patient and smart and determined. And she was brimming with a sense of accomplishment.

She made me shiver. She made my stomach turn. But I couldn't help but admire her just a little. I had met my share of murderers, but none had possessed her unique blend of patience, brains, and acting skills.

"And it would have worked," she continued, "if I hadn't made that slip when we met outside Metzudat Ze'ev. When I saw your reaction, when you said you were wrong about everything, I knew I had to act fast, that I couldn't hope to kill Leon and Isser and get away with it. I had to finish it." She smiled ruefully. "I knew from the day we met that you would be trouble. Remember how I told you that if anyone could solve this case, it was you?"

"I thought you meant only Anna's murder."

"From that moment on, I was busy thinking about how I would deal with you. I dreamed about it every night."

"Why didn't you just kill me?" I asked.

The question appeared to surprise her. "Because you didn't deserve to die, of course. I only punish those who deserve it. How did you figure out it was me?"

"You were with Brigitte Polisar when she died. You were in her apartment when the Egyptian Air Force bombed Tel Aviv. She supposedly died when a piece of her roof came down on her head, yet you emerged with nothing but scratches. Either you were very lucky, or you took the opportunity to kill Brigitte and make it look like she died in that air raid."

"Neither of us was hurt badly when the bombing happened," Varda said. "But part of the roof collapsed. I picked up a piece of stone and caved in Brigitte's skull. I knew no one would examine her body closely. It was perfect."

"Did you also kill her husband?"

"Emil?" Varda shook her head. "I had nothing to do with it. Brigitte was the last one I killed. Until Ofra."

"Why did you stop for so long this time?"

She bit her lip and lowered her eyes. A muscle in her jaw flexed and released. When she spoke, it was so softly, I almost missed it. "Because of the baby."

"You didn't know Brigitte was pregnant?"

Her head shot up. "Of course not. What do you take me for? I told you, I only kill those who deserve it. Do you think I'd knowingly hurt an unborn baby? That I'd deprive it of life? When I found out Brigitte was pregnant, it felt like I'd killed my own son. I had to stop after that. I couldn't go on. It was only when you showed up that I decided to start again. I knew if I didn't, I might never get the chance to complete my mission."

I could barely breathe. Ofra Wexler and Leon Zilberman would still be alive if I hadn't taken this case. Or if I had been quicker to solve it.

"Don't feel bad, Adam," Varda said, seeming to read my mind. "It's not your fault. I would have started again eventually, even if you and I had never met. The play was not yet over, you see. The final act had yet to be written. I would not have allowed this tragedy to remain unfinished."

It was odd, how she could kill with such coldness, yet display warmth toward me. If she hadn't been humiliated that night twelve years ago, Varda would probably never have hurt a fly, let alone killed anyone. Were we all just a single trauma away from becoming savage killers?

"When you killed Anna," I said, "you wore a fake beard, didn't you?"

Varda blinked in surprise. "How do you know that?"

"There was a witness. A drunk who lay just outside Trumpeldor Cemetery that night. He said he saw a man exiting the cemetery. He remembered very little about him. The only two things he was sure of was that the man had a beard and that there was something wrong with his walk."

Varda frowned. "I don't have something wrong with my walk."

"You're right, you don't. You have a perfectly normal walk—for a woman. It was only when an acquaintance of mine told me a little about the part you played in Twelfth Night that I figured it out. You played Viola. In Twelfth Night, Viola disguises herself as a man called Cesario. When I heard this, it occurred to me that a woman dressed like a man, with a man's beard, might still retain a feminine gait, and that this might strike a drunken witness as wrong, though he wouldn't be able to say precisely why." *Another thing*, I thought, *that I should have realized much earlier.*

Varda looked disappointed. "That was careless of me. I should have made sure I not only looked the part, but walked it, too. Lucky for me that witness was drunk."

"Why did you take Anna's bag?" I asked.

"To confuse the police. To make them think it was a robbery."

"What did you do with it?"

"I tossed it in the river and watched it drift off to sea."

"You didn't open it?"

"Of course not. I wasn't interested in money. I did it for justice."

Neither of us spoke for a time. It appeared that everything had been said. I now knew everything. Too late for it to do much good, but still.

"What happens now?" I asked.

"I imagine you will beg me to spare Isser's life," Varda said. "Who knows, maybe you'll convince me. I do like you quite a bit, you know."

I shook my head. Rotner let out a whimper.

Varda was surprised. "No? Why not?"

"Because he tried to have me killed. Didn't you, Mr. Rotner?"

Rotner's face was drenched in sweat and tears. His eyes were two massive red orbs of fear. His lips shook as he tried to form words. "I...No, I—"

"At first I thought it was Ofra," I said. "Then I suspected

another man. But it was neither of them. You're the only one left. And you have money to spare. Money to pay a killer."

"I don't understand," Varda said. "Isser tried to have you killed? How? Why?"

"He paid Amiram Gadot to kill me because I was a threat to him. He didn't want me to find out he had gone to Trumpeldor Cemetery in order to have sex on Mayor and Mrs. Dizengoff's grave. If that became public knowledge, it would ruin his reputation. It would destroy his career. He couldn't allow that to happen."

"Is this true?" Varda asked Rotner, and when he didn't answer, she pressed the blade into the cut on his throat.

He winced, fresh tears streaming down his cheeks. There was no sign of the wolf now. He looked like a whipped, wet, miserable junkyard dog.

"Well?" Varda said.

Instead of answering, he started speaking very rapidly, a man running out of time. "You don't have to kill me. I don't care what you did. I don't care about the others. I don't care about Dahlia. I'll make you a full partner in the theater. You and I can run it together. If you want to act, I'll let you, no problem. Just let me go and no one will need to know anything. Not about you and not about me."

"What about Adam?" Varda said. "He knows everything."

Rotner licked his lips. "You can kill him, too. Right here and now. You have the knife. I'll pay you. I'll give you anything you want. I'm sorry for what happened. I'm sorry we ridiculed you. Let me make it up to you. You could be the leading lady of the theater. You could be a star."

"It's tempting," Varda said. "But if it means letting you live, I don't want it." And with an expert, fluid movement, she ran the blade of her knife all the way across Rotner's neck and let his blood curtain down onto the stage.

I did not try to stop her. Rotner had tried to have me killed.

And since I would not have been able to prove it, it did not bother me one bit that he was dead.

He dropped on the stage at exactly the same spot where he had lain as dead King Lear when I first saw him. Now, as then, his face was turned away from me. Good. I did not want to see his eyes.

With the smell of freshly spilled blood thick in my nostrils, I looked at Varda. She still clutched the knife. Its blade dripped blood on the wooden boards of the stage.

I repeated my question from before: "What happens now, Varda?"

She gestured toward a shoulder bag lying on the stage a little behind her. "Inside, you'll find my full confession, including the killings of Leon and Isser. It's handwritten. The police will be able to verify I wrote it."

"Why not come with me to the station and tell them yourself?"

She smiled. "A tragedy only ends in one way, Adam. The hero, or heroine, must die." Then she reversed the knife, pressed the blade to her chest, and shoved it into her heart with one forceful push. She was dead before she hit the stage.

45

The story was front-page news again. And as before, Birnbaum shone brightest. He had all the information, every word of Varda's confession, and he dispensed it in a masterful fashion, crafting his columns so they read like a suspense novel.

Once again, Birnbaum and the police conspired to keep my name out of the papers. Birnbaum did it out of gratitude—I had kept my word, had given him the biggest story of his life. The police acted out of self-interest. And, as I'd predicted, the cops didn't bother to reexamine my confrontation with Amiram Gadot.

Shoresh Theater's final performance of King Lear never took place. Nor was any other show scheduled for the near or distant future. It appeared that in certain circumstances, the show doesn't go on after all.

Three mornings after the last drop of blood had spilled, I went over to visit Dahlia. This time, I found the apartment flooded with light and air, every window open, every curtain pulled. Dahlia was in high spirits, her posture as erect as in our first meeting, though she looked as ill as the last time I saw her, and her cough was stronger than ever.

I poured tea for us both, and we sipped in silence for a few minutes. When the cups were empty and back on the table, she reached into her pocket and drew out a fifty-lira banknote. I noticed she had removed her wedding ring.

"Your bonus, as promised."

I took the proffered bill and put it in my pocket.

"Thank you, Mr. Lapid. You've succeeded in the mission for which I hired you," Dahlia said.

"I thought you hired me to see your husband convicted of murder."

"That was simply a means by which to achieve my true goal, which was to see Isser humiliated and his good name destroyed, and you provided that. Now the whole of Israel knows my husband intended to engage in sexual intercourse in a cemetery, on the grave of one of the most illustrious leaders in our nation's revival. It doesn't get any more sordid than that." She laughed. "I would have liked to put it on his gravestone, but I doubt they'd let me."

"I would imagine they wouldn't," I agreed.

"Still, whenever anyone mentions his name, that is the first thing that will cross their mind."

It will also be what they'll think of Anna, I thought with a heavy heart. *But you don't care about that one bit.*

I said, "You really don't care that you were exposed as having lied to the police?"

"Not in the slightest. It was well worth it."

"What will happen with Shoresh Theater now?"

"It's closed and will remain so. Why the frown?"

"I was just thinking that it means Varda has won."

Dahlia considered it. "I suppose she has. I still can't get over the fact that she managed to hide her true nature from everyone, including me, for so long."

"You should have given her another chance. She was an excellent actress."

"Perhaps. But there's a difference between acting on stage and doing so in real life. In the former, people know you're acting. It's easier to fool them when they don't."

"Don't you regret having mocked her so harshly twelve years ago?"

"Of course I regret it. I wouldn't have done it if I knew she was insane, that it would lead her to murder." She saw my expression. "You think I'm heartless, don't you? That I enjoyed putting my fellow actors down?"

"That's what they think."

"Well, they're wrong. I did it because I love the theater, and I want it to be perfect. I found no joy in mocking anyone. I was driven by anger, not a desire to hurt others."

"But you didn't care if you did," I said.

"You can't be a theater actor with a thin skin, Mr. Lapid."

"Doesn't it bother you that you brought about the deaths of others and your own injury?"

"I told you I wouldn't have done it if I knew what would happen," she said, with a spark of irritation. Then she smiled. "Let's not talk about such things, Mr. Lapid. I don't enjoy many days of happiness. If you're intent on ruining this one, I must ask you to leave."

I ran my fingers over the fresh scar on my one forearm and then over the number tattoo on the other.

I said, "Varda was the one who told you your husband was unfaithful, wasn't she?"

Dahlia rubbed the head of her cane. "She told you this?"

"I figured it out on my own."

"She made me swear not to tell anyone. How did you know?"

"Just about everyone else I met made it a point of telling me how much they despised you, and that they haven't spoken to or seen you in years. But looking back, I should have known almost from the beginning."

"Oh?"

"It was your clothes. Every dress I saw you in fitted you perfectly. Someone had to have made them to measure. Varda made them, didn't she?"

Dahlia nodded. "She used to come here every few weeks, tell me the goings-on at the theater, measure me, and make me the best dresses I've ever owned. I actually thought she liked me."

"She only visited you in order to torment you further. That's why she told you Isser was having an affair. She knew it would hurt you. She never imagined it would make you realize he had been unfaithful before, or that it would cause you to hire someone like me to investigate Anna's murder."

Dahlia pursed her lips. "I guess she was a great actress after all. Maybe I should have given her another chance." She drew in a breath. "Well, it's too late now. Anything else you wish to discuss, Mr. Lapid?"

"Just one more thing," I said. "I know why you weren't afraid of living with your husband, even when you thought he was a murderer. You have cancer. You will be dead within three months."

She gawked at me. "How do you know this?"

"Your doctor told me."

"Dr. Lipowsky?"

"Yes. I visited the hospital a few days ago, to have my arm looked at. I met him and we had a little chat."

"He told you my condition? How dare he!" Her grip on her cane was so tight, her knuckles shone white through her skin.

"You gave him permission, remember? You told him he could tell me anything I wanted to know regarding your health, current or past."

Dahlia narrowed her eyes, then broke out laughing. The

laughter quickly devolved into a particularly nasty coughing fit that shook her entire body and made sweat pop on her forehead.

I brought her some water and she gulped it down. I returned to my chair.

"Your husband knew about your illness, didn't he?"

"Yes," she said.

"So you figured he had no reason to murder you. He could just wait a little and inherit everything. As long as he didn't know that you were the one who'd hired me, you were safe in his presence."

She smiled at me. "You see, Mr. Lapid, I knew you were the right man for the job."

46

After I left Dahlia's apartment, I spent the day wandering the streets of Tel Aviv. I was looking for the old man who had sold me the painting. I walked the length and breadth of the city, gripped by a terrible fear that the old man was dead.

I finally found him in late afternoon, sitting on a dirty street corner in the south of the city, his paintings arrayed before him like a rejected offering to some disinterested god. The old man looked tired and ancient, slumped and stooped, his lined face browned by the sun. I offered to buy him a meal, and together we sat at a rickety table in a tiny café that served hot soup and sandwiches and very little else.

The old man spooned his soup quickly into his mouth. I gathered he did not eat his fill on a regular basis. I asked him if he remembered the painting I'd bought from him.

"What painting?" he asked.

"The one with the mother and two young daughters walking together down a European street."

"I painted that one sixteen years ago. Lovely, isn't it?"

"Very. Do you remember it in detail?"

"Every brushstroke. I remember every painting I ever made."

I perked up. "Could you paint it again for me?"

"Again? Why do you need a second painting?"

"The first one was destroyed when my apartment was broken into."

The old man shook his head. "Stealing is bad enough, but destroying a work of art, that is something else entirely."

"Can you do it?" I asked. "I'd be happy to pay you double what I paid for the original."

The old man studied me, and I think he saw the anguish in my soul, because his expression turned tender. "It meant a lot to you, didn't it?"

"Yes," I said.

"I wish I could help you," he said, lifting his hands to show me fingers thick-knuckled and bent with arthritis, "but I'm unable to paint anymore. Everything I sell, I painted years ago."

I sagged in my seat, a spear of grief cutting through me.

"I can tell you about it," he offered, thinking to mitigate my disappointment. "I can tell you who the woman and girls were."

"No," I said quickly, forestalling the revelation. "Let me keep on imagining who they were. Let me have that, at least."

THE END

Thank you for reading *A Deadly Act*!

Want a free short story?

Join my newsletter and get a free copy of one of my short stories.

Go to JonathanDunsky.com/free to claim your copy.

Want to read more Adam Lapid?

The Auschwitz Detective, book 6 of the Adam Lapid series, is now available.

Please review this book!

Reviews help both readers and authors. If you enjoyed *A Deadly Act*, please leave a review on whatever website you use to buy or review books. I would greatly appreciate it.

Turn over the page for a personal message from the author.

AFTERWORD

Dear reader,

Seeing a novel take shape from the blank page to the last word is a remarkable experience. It is surpassed only by knowing your book is read by another person. So I thank you from the bottom of my heart for reading *A Deadly Act*. I hope that you enjoyed it. If you did, I'd be grateful if you'd take the time to leave a review on whatever website you use to buy or review books. Thank you. I appreciate it.

I thought you might wish to know a little about the places Adam Lapid visits in the pages of this novel. Naturally, I invent quite a bit, but some of the locations are real.

For instance, Ohel Shem is a real building on Balfour Street in Tel Aviv. It stands to this day, though the second-floor balcony and the columns that once supported it are gone. Today, it houses a children's theater. Naturally, this theater has nothing to do with anything you read in this novel.

Trumpeldor Cemetery is real, as well, and is described as accurately as whatever talent I possess allows. If you ever visit Tel Aviv, you may wish to take a guided tour of the cemetery. You may find it quite interesting.

Metzudat Ze'ev still stands at King George 38, though the building mentioned in this novel has been replaced by a high-riser. Today, Metzudat Ze'ev serves, in part, as the national head-quarters of the Likud Party. Likud was created through a merger of Herut with several other right-wing parties in 1973.

All the political parties mentioned in *A Deadly Act* did once exist. The political posters Adam saw on a bulletin board were used in the campaign leading up to the 1951 General Election in Israel.

Shoresh Theater and all the characters who worked in it are entirely the creations of my imagination.

As for the novel itself, it took me quite a long time to write. At one point I jettisoned 20,000 words and proceeded in an entirely new direction. One or two times, I wasn't sure I'd ever complete it. But little by little, word by word, the story coalesced and I realized that the end was in sight. In the final two weeks of writing, I wrote at more than double my usual pace. And when I got to the last page, I felt that I had done a good job. I hope you feel that way, too.

A Deadly Act is the fifth novel in the Adam Lapid series, which currently comprises six novels and one short story. Just in case you missed any of them, here is a list of all the entries in the series so far.

1. Ten Years Gone
2. The Dead Sister
3. The Auschwitz Violinist
4. A Debt of Death
5. A Deadly Act
6. The Auschwitz Detective
7. The Unlucky Woman (a short story)

I've also written a standalone thriller called The Payback Girl and a handful of short stories, in various genres.

I love hearing from readers, and I answer every reader email I get. If you've got any feedback, questions, or you simply want to reach out and say hello, write to me at contact@JonathanDunsky.com.

I also invite you to join my newsletter where you'll be informed of new releases and special deals. All new members get a free copy of one of my short stories. Join the club here: jonathandunsky.com/free/

I hope to meet you again soon in one of my other books and stories.

Thank you and have a great day,

Jonathan Dunsky

P.S. You can connect with me and other readers on Facebook at http://Facebook.com/JonathanDunskyBooks and also on Goodreads.

BOOK CLUB DISCUSSION QUESTIONS

1. What did you think of the opening scene? How well does it set the tone for the rest of the novel?
2. What did you think of Dahlia Rotner? How would you describe her character?
3. Did the identity of the killer surprise you? If so, who did you believe the killer was?
4. What did you make of the developing relationship between Adam Lapid and Dahlia Rotner?
5. Eliyahu Toledano stopped drinking and regained his life due to the murder of Anna Hartman. Discuss the ways in which life can grow out of death.
6. What can you say about Anna Hartman's character, considering her tragic history but also that she achieved her dream despite that history?
7. Ambition drives most of the suspects in this novel. When is ambition a force for development and achievement? And when does it become something darker and negative?
8. If you could choose one theater role you could have

seen Dahlia Rotner perform, what would it be, and why?

9. If you could visit one location described in the novel, what would it be?

10. In the end of the book, Adam finds the old painter in hopes of having him redo the painting that got destroyed in his fight with Amiram Gadot. But the old man cannot paint anymore. What deeper meaning do you find in their conversation? How does it fit with Adam's history and loss?

11. How would you describe the author's writing style?

12. Did the title of this novel fit the story? Can you suggest an alternative title?

13. Have you read other Adam Lapid novels? How did this one compare?

14. Would you recommend this novel to a friend? How would you describe it when you recommended it?

ABOUT THE AUTHOR

Jonathan Dunsky lives in Israel with his wife and two sons. He enjoys reading, writing, and goofing around with his kids. He began writing in his teens, then took a break for close to twenty years, during which he worked an assortment of jobs. He is the author of the Adam Lapid mystery series and the standalone thriller The Payback Girl.

BOOKS BY JONATHAN DUNSKY

The Adam Lapid Series

Ten Years Gone

The Dead Sister

The Auschwitz Violinist

A Debt of Death

A Deadly Act

The Auschwitz Detective

The Unlucky Woman (short story)

Standalone Novels

The Payback Girl

Made in United States
North Haven, CT
01 April 2022

17769442R00205